"Come and die," Ryan invited, beckoning to the Incarnate

J.B.'s Uzi suddenly stopped chattering, and Mildred shouted out wordlessly in anger and fear. Ryan spun on his heel in the direction of the chariot, then he was flat on his face on the ground.

His arms and legs were covered with half-frozen mud, and his thoughts stumbled and staggered, finally careening over to the brief, almost subliminal image of a nimbus of energy jumping from metal prongs.

A mahogany giant towered over him, a conical jeweled headpiece bisecting the sun and adding another six inches to his height. He wore a magnificent gem-encrusted leather harness over his muscled torso, and sunlight gleamed from the golden threads in the white fabric of his kilt.

"So," he said in a deep melodic voice, "I didn't frighten you away after all. Perhaps I'll have to try harder next time."

Then, smiling, the bronzed god kicked Ryan in the side of the head, kicked him down into a dark, spiraling hole.

**Other titles in the
Deathlands saga:**

JAMES AXLER

DEATH LANDS®

Nightmare Passage

A GOLD EAGLE BOOK FROM

WORLDWIDE®

TORONTO • NEW YORK • LONDON
AMSTERDAM • PARIS • SYDNEY • HAMBURG
STOCKHOLM • ATHENS • TOKYO • MILAN
MADRID • WARSAW • BUDAPEST • AUCKLAND

First edition January 1998

ISBN 0-373-62540-5

NIGHTMARE PASSAGE

Copyright © 1998 by Worldwide Library.

My mouth is split open by the god of the air
With that metal spear he used to split open
        the mouth of the gods.
I am the Powerful One. I shall sit beside her
Who is in the great breath of the sky!

—*The Egyptian Book of the Dead*
(Spell 23)

THE DEATHLANDS SAGA

This world is their legacy, a world born in the violent nuclear spasm of 2001 that was the bitter outcome of a struggle for global dominance.

There is no real escape from this shockscape where life always hangs in the balance, vulnerable to newly demonic nature, barbarism, lawlessness.

But they are the warrior survivalists, and they endure—in the way of the lion, the hawk and the tiger, true to nature's heart despite its ruination.

Ryan Cawdor: The privileged son of an East Coast baron. Acquainted with betrayal from a tender age, he is a master of the hard realities.

Krysty Wroth: Harmony ville's own Titian-haired beauty, a woman with the strength of tempered steel. Her premonitions and Gaia powers have been fostered by her Mother Sonja.

J. B. Dix, the Armorer: Weapons master and Ryan's close ally, he, too, honed his skills traversing the Deathlands with the legendary Trader.

Doctor Theophilus Tanner: Torn from his family and a gentler life in 1896, Doc has been thrown into a future he couldn't have imagined.

Dr. Mildred Wyeth: Her father was killed by the Ku Klux Klan, but her fate is not much lighter. Restored from predark cryogenic suspension, she brings twentieth-century healing skills to a nightmare.

Jak Lauren: A true child of the wastelands, reared on adversity, loss and danger, the albino teenager is a fierce fighter and loyal friend.

Dean Cawdor: Ryan's young son by Sharona accepts the only world he knows, and yet he is the seedling bearing the promise of tomorrow.

In a world where all was lost, they are humanity's last hope....

Prologue

The horizon had been a dreary, saffron-tinted waste for as long as he could remember. Suddenly, a dark speck crawled across the vast sea of sand.

All around was a panorama of desolation—nothing but sand stretching to the skyline in every direction, barely relieved by the gray dome rearing out of the wasteland in the near distance.

The god blinked. The crawling speck was a vehicle; that much was certain. He expanded his awareness, his mind sprouting probing, identifying tentacles. The vehicle was a Jeep Cherokee. It was more than a hundred years old, the engine reconfigured to run on methane, and the rusted bodywork was painted in a striped camouflage pattern. Its four-wheel drive carried it easily across the undulating yellow sands that rose and fell in dunes. There were precisely three men and one woman aboard.

The distant, laboring rumble of the engine rolled over the desert, and the vehicle sank from sight behind the waves of sand. At that moment, a cloud passed over the face of the sun.

The god smiled. Slowly, he climbed down from the high sand hill upon which he had been meditating for the past three days. When he reached its base, he absently adjusted the heavy collar of beaten gold encircling his neck. It was a pointless and human thing to do. One of his first actions upon awakening and leaving his tomb six months before had been to interface with the molecular structure of any article on his body so it responded instantly to conscious thought.

Holding his metauh across his left breast, the god strolled across the sandy, windswept plain in the direction of his tomb. He had waited for six months for his worshipers to arrive, and there was no hurry now, even though they would reach his tomb a few minutes before he would. They, however, wouldn't be able to open the portal.

By the time he reached the perimeter of his tomb, the vehicle was parked in front of the reinforced-stone-and-steel dome. The four people were totally engrossed in trying to figure out the workings of the massive, vanadium-alloy sec door. The god paused and looked at them. In less than a millisecond, he assimilated all that he needed from their minds.

He was pleased that English was still the primary language, though now peppered with new colloquialisms, vernacular and vulgarisms.

The four people were part of a larger group, a loosely knit conglomeration of wanderers, scavengers and self-styled salvage experts calling themselves Farers. They had come from a settlement of sorts only a day's journey away, crossing the wasteland they called the Barrens.

The god wasn't surprised by the vast changes from the world he had been born into. Even before his long sleep, the American continent was already molding itself into Deathlands.

He narrowed the focus of his probe to the individuals.

There was Danielson, the leader of this little band of survivors. He was black bearded, trim and erect, though wiry of stature. The woman beside him was Harrier, a woman who appeared brisk and no-nonsense in a neat white tunic, khaki shorts and high-laced boots. The other two men were Stockbridge and Javna, and they were identically attired in patched and stained coveralls. Javna was the oldest of the four, with thinning white hair and no teeth. Stockbridge was around Danielson's age, a muscular black man of medium height.

All four people shared similar thoughts, similar goals—they needed to survive Deathlands, and in order to do that, they had to travel, salvaging what they could from stockpiles laid down by the pre-nukecaust government. In Danielson's mind was the vivid image of a man he considered both an inspiration and a competitor in his profession. The man went by the name of the Trader, and the god glimpsed pieces of memory of vehicles called war wags. Danielson envied the Trader, but he also admired him, even though he had been cast out of the Trader's organization a short time before.

Looking into the minds of Javna and Stockbridge was like peering into the minds of small, venal rodents. Greed, anger and the resentful suspicion that they had been cheated by Danielson, Harrier and even the whole world dominated their thoughts and emotions.

The god focused on Harrier, and he realized that he was looking at her form rather than her mind. He felt a strange inner pang. It took him a moment to identify it. The pang was an emotion—remorse, seasoned with just a pinch of regret.

Harrier was a slim woman in her early twenties. She had no idea just how old she really was. Her hair was dark, and it framed her face in a silken bell. Her first name was Connie. The god realized that Connie was a diminutive of the ancient Celtic name Connaught.

The pang slowly built to a sensation of yearning, and it had been so long since the god had indulged in something so common, so *mortal* as feeling, he didn't immediately recognize the emotion.

He did, however, allow himself a certain small pride in staging a dramatic entrance. He drew breeze-driven grains of sand to him and directed them to swirl about him until he had the appearance of a miniature cyclone, a man-size dust devil.

The god moved toward the portal of his tomb, and he appreciated the expressions of dismay and surprise that crossed the faces of the people when they spied the whirling cloud of grit. When he reached an appropriate distance from the four mortals, he allowed the wind to dissipate and the sand to fall away from his body.

Danielson's mouth gaped open in shock. His leathery right hand fumbled at his hip and came up with an automatic pistol, one the god identified from the man's mind as a 9 mm Steel City War Eagle, manufactured 120 years before. The god knew the gun—the "blaster," as Danielson thought of it—contained only three projectiles. Though all four people were armed, only Javna's Taurus PT-99 carried a full 15-shot clip.

As it was, although all four people drew their blasters, they were totally unnerved by his sudden materialization. For an instant, he saw himself through their eyes.

They saw a giant, bronze-skinned man whose life hadn't been spent in savage conflict with the new nature of Deathlands, but a man whose form bespoke the intention to bend that nature to his will. That intention showed in his strong, moody face, the hard-muscled economy of his form, his heavy arms, broad shoulders and massive chest. He wore a linen loincloth, gold necklace and a royal king-cobra headdress that—the god saw from their minds—none of them recognized.

Nor did they recognize the silver, three-foot long, forked rod he held over his muscular chest as a weapon. Or perhaps they were too distracted by the shimmering crimson of his eyes.

"Good day," the god said, manipulating the pitch, timbre and vibrations of his voice to be sympathetically resonant to the inner ears of his worshipers. "Would you care to step inside, out of the sun?"

Some of the shock went out of Danielson's face, but he didn't lower his pistol. He eyed the god's six feet five inches of hard muscle and replied cautiously, "We might. You staked a claim on this here stockpile?"

The god glanced toward Connie Harrier, who stared at him with a blue-eyed intensity. He gave her his most disarming and human grin before replying, "It's not a stockpile, Mr. Danielson. It's my tomb."

Gesturing toward the heavy metal door, the god announced, "I require worshipers to help me build a dynasty. You four will do for a start."

Danielson's eyes widened, then narrowed. "How'd you know my name? You're some kind of psi-mutie."

"Yeah," Javna agreed in a voice frosty with contempt. "Got to be, with them eyes."

The god glanced briefly in the old man's direction. "Your invitation to accompany me inside is rescinded, Mr. Javna."

Javna spit out a derisive laugh and brought up his blaster, finger crooked tight around the trigger. "I'm invitin' you to die, mutie whoreson."

The god moved the metauh negligently, pointing the double prongs, positioned like an upside down V at the tip of the rod, toward the old man's bionegative weak points. Pale blue mena energy sprang up in a halo around Javna.

The dry, hot air seemed to shiver. Javna's frail body swayed, and the sway became a tremble and the tremble turned into a convulsion. His eyes remained open, but they didn't see. His toothless mouth gaped open, but no words came out. He croaked a sound of pain, terror and despair.

The old man's back arched violently, as if he had received a heavy blow between the shoulders. There was a sharp crackling sound of cartilage and bone. Spittle strings drooled from discolored gums. From the corner of each bulging eye squeezed a droplet of blood, then those eyes burst in gelid, crimson-tinged sprays. For an instant, all saw the raw, dark pits of empty sockets.

Javna coughed out a moan of horror, and the cough was followed by a torrent of blood, fountaining up from hemorrhaging internal organs. He toppled sideways, falling to the sand, arms contorting and drawing up like the gnarled branches of a leaf-less tree. He seemed to shrivel and wither like a mummy even as he fell.

Harrier, after a moment of wide-eyed shock, swung her handblaster toward the god, finger tightening around the trigger.

"Stop."

The word rolled through the air like a sudden clap of thunder. Harrier stopped, her finger frozen on the trigger. Danielson and Stockbridge stood immobile.

The god lowered the metauh and stepped toward Harrier. Her eyes stared into his defiantly, even though her limbs were paralyzed. The god looked deep, deep into her mind. What he found there pleased him. She stood there and allowed her memories, her dreams, her unrealized ambitions and most secret fantasies and passions to be riffled.

The god addressed her softly, his voice a seductive instrument stimulating her neuroenergy system. "Connaught Katherine Harrier. Connie. I need you. I intend to impose order on the remains of this world by building a dynasty that will rule for ten thousand years."

Harrier didn't respond for a long moment. "What do you need me for?"

"First, to take me to your settlement, where I will collect my followers. Then we will proceed to my royal city. It lies some distance away. And then you will bear me an heir."

Harrier's face twisted in impact to his words. "I'm sterile."

"A congenital condition, which I can rectify."

"What?" Harrier's voice was ragged, incredulous, fearful.

"Drop your weapon, Connie. It's useless against me, you know."

The woman shuddered, able to move again, and she stared in mild surprise as her blaster dropped from her hand to the sand at her feet. The god mentally nudged her toward the vanadium-alloy door. He sensed the reactions of the three people. Their emotions were a riot of conflicting questions, terrors and fears.

Harrier stopped walking, and the god was impressed with the degree of concentration she employed to break free, momentarily, of his persuasion.

"What the fuck are you?" she demanded.

The god smiled gently. "I've had many names. 'Alpha' was the first. A woman I once...knew called me 'Alfie' as an endearment. 'Hell Eyes' was more of a title than a name, and I never cared for it. Since my resurrection, I have decided to be addressed as 'Akhnaton,' an old name with a fine tradition."

Between clenched teeth, Harrier grated, "I don't care about your name. *What* are you?"

With one hand, he softly caressed the smooth, rounded line of her cheek. "I am who you have been waiting for, Connie. I am your god."

Chapter One

Sixteen Years Later

Ryan opened his eye, and Krysty was still there. The moon formed a halo around her full mane of scarlet hair, striking flame-colored highlights from the flowing tresses. Though his throat was raw from brine, he managed to ask, "How long, lover?"

Krysty leaned down, and her lips brushed his forehead. "A couple of hours. How do you feel?"

"Waterlogged." With a groaning effort, he managed to hitch himself up to his elbows. He looked around, his brain still unsteady from his near drowning and the beating he had received from the self-styled Admiral Poseidon.

Little flares of pain ignited all over his body. He lay on the gently rocking deck of the small cabin cruiser. Flinging aside the blanket, he saw that his naked body was covered with abrasions and contusions. The salt air of the sea stung his wounds, and they pulled when he moved.

Krysty handed him a cup of fresh water, and he drank gratefully, rinsing his mouth and spitting over the side. "Where's everybody else?"

She nodded toward the enclosed cabin amidships. "Down below, trying to get some rest. It was too cramped for me. What happened to Poseidon?"

Ryan sat up straighter, gritting his teeth. In a voice thick with savage satisfaction, he replied, "He sleeps with the fishes."

With Krysty's help, he managed to get to his feet. Standing at his full six feet two inches, he drew the tall, voluptuous woman against him, stroking her hair, noting that her normally brilliant green eyes were dulled by exhaustion.

"What about you?" he asked. "Are you all right?"

"I called on the power of Gaia," she answered wearily, trying to repress the catch in her voice. "Men died."

Ryan didn't ask for details. Krysty Wroth was, by definition, a mutie. She possessed the empathic ability to sense danger in the offing. Her fiery mane of red hair was the outward manifestation of this power, stirring, curling, moving as if it were a separate, sentient organism. The few others with these prescient powers were called doomseers or doomsniffers.

Krysty had been trained to hone this empathy by being in tune with the electromagnetic energies of Gaia, the Earth Mother. By tapping into these energies, the power field of the planet itself, Krysty could gain superhuman strength for a limited time. When possessed by Gaia, she entered an altered state of consciousness and turned into a raging death goddess. However, her manipulation of earth energies could only be used on occasion, as it exacted a great physical toll. Therefore, she had learned to handle her .38-caliber Smith & Wesson Model 640 revolver with devastating skill.

Ryan saw that her side arm wasn't holstered at her hip. "What happened to your blaster?"

Krysty shook her head. "I don't know. Poseidon's sec men must have confiscated it when they captured me and Jak."

"Where are my clothes?"

Krysty pulled out of his embrace and moved toward the cabin. "They should be dry by now. I'll tell everybody you're up."

Draping the blanket over his shoulders, Ryan sat on the side rail, scanning the roiling, starlit surface of the Lantic Ocean. Somewhere below swam the Dwellers, humans genetically altered to live in the depths of the sea. One of the muties, a fish-man named Mike, had rescued him from drowning when he had escaped from Poseidon's sinking submarine, the *Raleigh*.

Though Ryan Cawdor had no great love for muties, he wished the Dwellers well.

Lifting his gaze, he looked in the direction of the Kings Point naval base. Tongues of flame still licked at the night sky. He could only hope that the building containing the mat-trans unit hadn't been consumed in the conflagration. He had no inclination to cruise along the coast of North Carolina. The sea held other mutated life-forms besides the Dwellers, and they weren't as benign.

Other than that, his own blasters, the SIG-Sauer P-226 pistol and the Steyr SSG-70 rifle, were somewhere in the old military installation. He would risk another incursion into Admiral Poseidon's sick little kingdom to retrieve them.

Krysty came out of the cabin, holding his clothes and combat boots. She was followed by the other members of his group, and they clustered around him, patting his back and pumping his hand until they realized he was wincing under the affection. Mildred Wyeth shooed everyone back.

"Ryan's injuries haven't gotten in much healing time in the past two hours," she said, peeling up the lid of his single eye, his right one. She peered into it, adding, "Good. No broken veins. I was afraid you might be suffering a touch of anoxemia."

Ryan pulled away from her touch. "What's that?"

"A lack of oxygen in the blood. You damn near drowned, you know. Good thing I had Dean here to help me with the first aid. At least he learned something in that school." The stocky black woman stepped back, the ocean breeze causing the beads in her long plaited hair to click together.

Mildred Winona Wyeth was a doctor, a former specialist in cryogenic sciences. Though she was in her midthirties, she was, chronologically, well over a century old. Mildred had entered a hospital in late December of 2000 for minor surgery, but an allergic reaction to the anesthetic had necessitated her body being placed in cryonic stasis until a treatment could be found.

It never was. The world was blown apart before she was revived, and she slept, like a fly trapped in amber, for a hundred years. Ryan had found her in a shielded underground cell, her life-support system still functioning. He had brought her back to life, the cryo process miraculously healing her, into a world she could never have dreamed existed.

Other than her skills as a doctor, Mildred had also proved herself invaluable as a tenacious survivalist.

She had won a silver medal for free pistol shooting in the last-ever Olympic games. A Czech-made ZKR 551 target revolver was holstered at her waist. The weapon was chambered to take Smith & Wesson .38-caliber rounds, and she had only rarely been known to miss with one of the blaster's six shots.

"What happened to the sub?" J. B. Dix demanded.

Turning his back, trying to keep the blanket over his shoulders, Ryan stepped into his pants. "It sank."

"'Down went McGinty to the bottom of the sea,'" Doc Tanner quoted. "'Dressed in his best suit of clothes.'"

"What?" Ryan asked irritably.

"An old sea chantey. The authorship of which is attributed, I believe, to one Popeye the Sailor Man."

Ryan wasn't sure if the tall, thin, silver-haired man was joking. Dr. Theophilus Algernon Tanner was another refugee from a past time period. Unlike Mildred, who had bobbed unknowingly down the temporal stream, Doc was the only surviving subject of a cold-hearted scientific practice known in pre-dark days as time-trawling.

Since the 1940s, American military scientists, and their counterparts in other countries, had tried to reconcile Einsteinian physics with quantum mechanics. By the 1990s, the reconciliation attempts had spawned the ultra-top-secret experiment known as the Totality Concept. There were several subdivisions of the experiment, such as Overproject Whisper, Project Cerebus and Operation Chronos.

With the use of a complex matter-transfer device, or gateway, the project scientists had tried time and time again to snatch subjects from a past temporal line and trawl them to the present.

Their only success was a man trawled from 1896. Theophilus Algernon Tanner, Ph.D., scientist and scholar, was plucked from the bosom of his beloved family and deposited in a sterile subterranean chamber a century hence.

Though he learned all he could about the twentieth century, Doc never forsook the hope of returning to his wife and two children. His constant attempts to return to his own era so angered the whitecoats that they eventually used him as a trawling subject again. Rather than send him back, they opted to transfer him to a year nearly a century in the future. Like Mildred, he missed the nukecaust by less than a month.

The experiences of being trawled had unbalanced his brain to a degree. Though most of the time Doc's wit was sharp, and intelligence burned behind his blue eyes like a white-hot bar, his mind would occasionally drift back and forth across the centuries, usually to his home and family, lost in the shadows of time.

However, even with his mind befogged, he was still a deadly shot with his gold-plated commemorative J. E. B. Stuart 9-shot Le Mat blaster, which could be adjusted to fire 18-gauge shotgun shells and .44-caliber rounds. The ebony, lion's-head swordstick he had tucked under an arm concealed a razor-keen blade of the finest Toledo steel.

Everyone else in the group were the products of late-twenty-first century America, and of the hellgrounds known as Deathlands.

Sixteen-year-old Jak Lauren had all the hard, bitter experience of a man twice his age. An albino, with fearsome ruby eyes and a shock of bone white hair, he favored bladed weapons over blasters, though he normally carried a .357 Magnum Colt Python. He bore scars from dozens of near fatal encounters, the least of which curved up from the corner of his mouth and across his high-planed face.

Jak had buried two sets of families during his young life—his folks back in Louisiana and his wife and infant daughter in New Mexico. He hid the tragedies behind a taciturn mask and an eerily calm, almost detached manner.

Ryan Cawdor and John Barrymore Dix had been companions for nearly two decades, since they traveled with the legendary Trader in a pair of huge war wags. The weapons dealer had been their undisputed leader and mentor, even something of a father figure to Ryan.

J.B. had served as the Trader's armorer and gunsmith because of his knowledge and skill with weaponry. A broad-brimmed, bullet-holed fedora sat at a jaunty angle on his head, and wire-rimmed spectacles were perched on the bridge of his bony nose. His multipocketed, voluminous coat almost swallowed his short, slight frame, but it also concealed a 9 mm mini-Uzi machine pistol and a Smith & Wesson M-4000 shotgun, which fired eight rounds of razor-edged, needle-pointed fléchettes. His quiet, taciturn manner was in direct counterpoint to his ability to kill efficiently, an ability learned at the knee of the unrefuted master of the art, the Trader.

The Trader had earned a considerable fortune by uncovering hidden stockpiles of weapons and fuel and using them to barter his way through Deathlands. He had been a fearsome figure in his day, a reputation he fully lived up to and enjoyed. Not too long before, after beating a case of rad cancer, he was reunited with his former lieutenants. His long illness had changed him; he was sometimes confused, sometimes irrational, but always a dangerous man to cross. Everyone had tended to tread lightly around him, but the Trader's weathered skin had become so thin, it was anybody's guess as to what he might choose to take offense.

He had resented that Ryan was the group's leader, and that the younger man no longer showed him the deference he believed he was due. Though there was no denying that the grizzled veteran of Deathlands had gotten the group out of many a tight spot, he'd also gotten them into just as many, due to his temper and ego.

The last tight spot had been several months ago on the Western Islands. The Trader and Abe, the former main gunner of War Wag One, had apparently sacrificed themselves to save Ryan and the rest of the group from an enemy attack.

A few years before, Ryan would have searched high and low for the Trader and Abe, either to rescue them or avenge their deaths. J.B., though he rarely spoke of it, felt guilty about not doing so. But Ryan had new responsibilities, goals other than just drifting from one firefight to the next.

One of those responsibilities was embodied by his eleven-year-old son, Dean. The issue of a brief encounter between Ryan and a woman named Sharona, Dean was almost a miniature version of his father, with thick dark hair and bright blue eyes. The fierce warrior named Ryan Cawdor grew used to being called "Dad" and was totally devoted to the boy. A few months before, he had enrolled Dean in the Brody School in Colorado. He had only recently been reunited with him. While his son had received an education, Ryan had been more determined than ever to find a place in Deathlands where the boy could be raised in relative safety.

He had never truly believed he would find that safe place, but now a twinge of regret came to him, along with the memories of the beautiful valley of Ti-Ra'-Wa and his banishment from it, and he could see her own memories of the place reflected in Krysty's eyes. And yet he knew they were not of that place and didn't belong there.

The manner in which he and his companions frequently traveled was to use the gateway chambers to make mat-trans jumps. The gateways were hidden in subterranean military complexes called redoubts, which were positioned all over the continent, even in other countries.

One of the mat-trans units lay in a subterranean complex beneath the Kings Point base. Poseidon had been unable to access it, since the entrance codes to the security door had been consumed in the nuclear megacull of a century before. The self-proclaimed admiral was certain Ryan knew the correct codes, and he had been right—not that it had done him any good. His plan to destroy Shauna Watson's commune with the refitted *Raleigh* had been scuttled.

As he dressed, he told his friends about Poseidon's fate and that of his submarine's crew. Lacing up his boots, he said, "Our best chance to get out of here is to reach the gateway under the main building."

"Is it functional?" Krysty asked.

"There's no reason why it shouldn't be. I do know I don't want to spend any more time floating around out here."

"I concur," Doc said. "Though I have a bit of sailing experience, none of us are 'borned to the sea,' so to speak."

J.B. frowned, tugging at the brim of his fedora. "There may be some of Poseidon's sec men prowling around, and we're under armed."

"Poseidon chilled," Jak announced. "Second-in-command, Brosnan, chilled. Nobody alive to give sec men orders, give them pay. Won't want to fuck with us for free."

Ryan probed his twinging rib cage and grimaced. "Mebbe so. It's worth the risk. Let's move while we've still got the night."

Doc returned to the cabin and keyed the cruiser's engine to life while Dean and Jak hoisted the anchor. The motor made liquid, burbling sounds as Doc steered the craft in the direction of Kings Point. The sea itself was silent, but it was the dreadful silence that bore in it the threat of a storm.

J.B. joined Ryan in the bow, handing him the Smith & Wesson scattergun while he unlimbered the mini-Uzi. Both of them scanned the dark water ahead.

The boat cut through the sea slowly but steadily. As they drew closer to the arrangement of concrete quays and jetties extending over the water, Ryan was able to discern more details of the devastation J.B. and Mildred had visited on the installation. Smoke boiled from many of the low-roofed build-

ings in the compound and the fires cast a hellish
illumination over the entire base.

"You didn't take half measures," Ryan commented.

J.B. grinned wolfishly. "Do I ever?"

Ryan would have grinned, too, but his face hurt
too much.

Under Doc's guidance, the craft approached a
concrete jetty. Suddenly, an eighteen-foot launch
swung around the headland. It was painted a drab
military gray. The steady thud of its diesel engines
had been swallowed by the purring murmur of their
own craft.

The boat was about a hundred yards away, and
three men stood behind the steel-framed windshield.
The man handling the wheel was dark-complex-
ioned, and his companions were crew-cut, beefy
men in one-piece coveralls—the duty uniform of Poseidon's mercenaries.

Bolted to the deck behind them, Ryan spotted an
M-60 tripod-mounted machine gun. "Fireblast."

Chapter Two

The launch's engines bellowed throatily, and the craft's props chopped the water to froth. The boat lunged toward them, its prow like the snout of a gray killer whale arrowing in on helpless prey.

Even over the roar of the engines, Ryan heard short, barking sentences hurled back and forth between the three men. One of the crew-cut mercs scrambled aft, hands clawing for the machine gun, swinging around its long perforated barrel.

J.B. shouted to Doc in the pilot cowling. "Evasive! Feed her more gas!"

The sound of the cruiser's engines rose in pitch, and the craft churned forward. Synchronized with the sudden increase in speed, the tripod-mounted M-60 spit flickering spear points of flame. The blaster trembled on its fastenings. Steel-jacketed bullets sped across the rolling waves as the cartridge belt writhed like the coiling of a gleaming serpent.

Miniature waterspouts sprayed up just behind the cruiser's stern. Cursing, the man behind the heavy-caliber blaster tried to realign the barrel with the people aboard the suddenly surging cruiser. The range was too great for the scattergun, which Ryan had, to be very effective, so J.B. opened fire with his Uzi. The bone-rattling chatter of the autoblaster joined the staccato hammering of the M-60.

Sparks jumped from the metal-braced hull of the launch, and the windshield acquired a starred pattern of cracks. The pilot twisted the wheel, and the boat heeled over. The streamlined craft made a lunging port-side rush while the gunner kept up the withering machine-gun fire.

Ryan and J.B. dropped flat to the deck. Glass smashed in the pilot housing, sheet metal crumpled and fiberglass was shot away. Mildred and Krysty cried out in anger and fear as they lay beneath the stream of slugs.

Not daring to raise his head, Ryan shouted, "Dean! Krysty! Jak! Everybody all right?"

The companions answered in nervous, profanity-seasoned affirmatives.

"What about you, Doc? Are you still with us?"

"Indeed!" came the older man's angry response. "Stay low!"

The cruiser's speed increased again, cutting a liquid trough through the dark water. Ryan and J.B. raised their heads above the rail. The launch was roaring toward them again, this time approaching fast from starboard aft.

"I'm getting sick of this," J.B. grated.

"Not much we can do about it," Ryan replied grimly. "They're faster, more maneuverable and they outgun us."

"Yeah." J.B.'s reply was a sarcastic drawl. He dipped his hand inside one of his capacious pockets and came up gripping a small, apple-sized metal sphere. "One of the little goodies I picked up in the commune's armory."

Ryan recognized it immediately as a V-40 mini-gren, the smallest hand grenade manufactured before the nukecaust. "Thing is so small, you'll have to make a direct hit to do any damage."

"That's the idea."

The launch roared up parallel with the cruiser's port side, the engines roaring as though by the display of sheer speed and power, the people on board the smaller craft would be cowed into surrendering. Only a dozen or so feet separated the two boats.

J.B. rolled himself to port, took a deep breath, then rose to his knees. He unpinned the gren with his left hand, and his right arm swung up and out in a looping overhand throw. Ryan lifted himself from the deck so he could watch the arc and descent of the small object. He figured it would splash into the water just in front of the launch's bow. Instead, with unerring and uncanny accuracy, J.B. bounced the gren off the curving windshield to drop on the boat's deck.

A blast of orange flame erupted with an eardrum-slamming roar. Pieces of wood and chunks of metal rose into the air. The man behind the machine gun catapulted over the side, wreathed in a cocoon of fire.

The cruiser pulled away from the launch, leaving it to wallow in the surf. Ryan heard the screams of agony and terror from the mercs. Tongues of flame made a dazzling glow over the face of the sea.

J.B. stood and said with satisfaction, "And that is that."

Krysty and Mildred came to the bow. Krysty's high-boned face was pale, and she took Ryan's hand in hers. "Close, lover," she breathed.

Mildred hugged J.B. tightly. "Another trick out of those Captain Kangaroo pockets of yours," she said with a grin. "One day I'll have to take an inventory."

"Who's Captain Kangaroo?" Dean asked. "Another sailor, like that Popeye guy Doc mentioned?"

At the sound of his name, Doc peered out through the broken glass in the pilot housing. He reduced the speed of the cruiser, saying stiffly, "I believe my expert seamanship contributed a little something to our narrow escape."

"Congrats, Doc," Jak said dryly. "You drive good. Now drive to dry land."

Doc held the cruiser's stern straight for the concrete jetty. Turning the wheel, he ran alongside it, so close that the hull scraped the pilings. Then he reversed the engines, backed water into a smother of foaming spray. "How's that for driving?" he asked with a prideful smile.

"More like 'How's that for showing off,'" Mildred retorted darkly.

As the cruiser bobbed in the shallows, Ryan and J.B. climbed out and secured it with a hawser, snugging the craft fast. They stood watch as the rest of the companions disembarked.

"Usual red alert," Ryan said, holding the scattergun ready at waist level. "Lock and load."

Doc drew his Le Mat, Jak his .357 Colt Python, Mildred her ZKR revolver and Dean unholstered his Browning Hi-Power blaster. He brought up the rear, behind the weaponless Krysty.

Ryan took the point, since he was the most familiar with the layout. They moved alertly between the twisting columns of acrid smoke. All of them repressed coughs and sneezes and frequently wiped their stinging eyes. However, Ryan saw the devastation wasn't quite as total as he had initially figured. Only a few of the buildings in the sprawling compound were completely consumed by fire, though almost all of them were soot blackened with windows shattered by the explosive charges set by Mildred and J.B.

The vapors suddenly cleared, diminishing to a misty pall. Ryan saw the rambling, flat-roofed concrete-block building that housed the mat-trans unit beneath it. It appeared intact, and he breathed a sigh of relief. On the far side of it lay the submarine pens, where the undersea craft of the predark Navy had once been berthed.

Motioning the people behind him to stop, Ryan went to one knee, taking a slow, visual recce of the structure and the surrounding area. He considered circling the building, approaching it from a concrete slipway that ran from the rear down to the sea. However, he saw no signs of movement anywhere. He hoped the sec men on the launch were the last to have fled the base.

Standing, he gestured for his companions to come forward.

"Standard deployment," he said to them quietly. "We're going in by the front door. Triple red."

The seven people fanned out in a half circle as they moved toward the front of the building. Krysty's green eyes blazed, her hair tightly knotted at her nape.

Mildred held her ZKR 551 in a two-fisted grip, the barrel as steady as stone. Next to her, J.B. crouched to make himself a smaller target, the Uzi braced at his hip, finger on the trigger.

Doc stood sideways like an eighteenth-century

dandy practicing the *code duello,* the Le Mat at the end of his extended arm.

Dean and Jak held their blasters in both hands, barrels pointing up.

As Ryan expected, the chrome-and-glass-paneled door was unlocked. The building had been an administrative center before the nukecaust and therefore didn't possess the security measures of high-clearance areas.

As he shouldered open the door, the fluorescent tubes glowing on the ceiling showed him that the reception room and the corridor beyond were deserted. He moved in fast, shifting the barrel of the scattergun back and forth. The others came in behind him.

Stealthily, the companions crept along the corridor, but not as quietly as Ryan would have liked. Doc kept trying to stifle a smoke-induced coughing fit and was doing a poor job of it.

Most of the doors lining either side of the long hallway were open. Glancing into the first four offices, Ryan saw they were jumbled, ransacked. Evidently, Poseidon's sec men had looted everything of value from the building before leaving. A fear that their remaining blasters and other possessions had been boosted gnawed at him.

They followed the corridor along two turns, first to the left, then to the right, before it dead-ended at the set of double doors Ryan wanted. They hung open, and the big room beyond was full of desks and chairs. A bank of monitor screens was still linked to the security vid net, and they flickered with images. Ryan swept a glance over them, saw they showed essentially the same smoke-clouded pix from different perspectives and turned away.

"Hey, Dad," Dean called. "Look at this."

Turning, Ryan saw his son standing before a tall row of six gray lockers, the hasps secured by round combination locks.

Fingering a lock, Dean said, "They're not rusty. People here must have been using them."

Ryan joined him, tugged on a lock experimentally and declared, "Our blasters might be inside of them. We'll have to shoot off the locks. Mildred?"

The woman stepped forward, hefting her revolver. "Precision is my middle name. Everybody take cover."

As her friends hunkered down behind desks, Mildred dragged a table over the end of the locker row, arranging it so she would have a parallel angle of fire. Half lying across the tabletop, she brought the lock on the far end into target acquisition and squeezed the ZKR's trigger.

The room echoed with the door-slamming bang of the blaster, followed a microsecond later by the high-pitched whine of a ricochet.

Ryan rose and pulled the shattered metal away from the hasp. Hanging inside the locker was a dress uniform of one of the Kings Point enlisted men. Frustrated, he slammed the door shut and returned to his position behind a desk.

He and Mildred repeated the procedure with the next four lockers. Each one contained uniforms or personal bric-a-brac.

Aligning the sixth and last lock with the sights of her blaster, she muttered, "After burning this many rounds, I don't know if I'll feel better if our stuff is in there or not.''

The revolver cracked, the lock jumped, flew apart and Ryan checked the container's contents. He released a slow, relieved breath and removed his Steyr rifle, his eighteen-inch panga, his SIG-Sauer and Krysty's Smith & Wesson.

Sourly, Mildred said, ''It would have to be the *last* locker.''

''Depends on how you look at it,'' Dean said with a grin. ''It could have been the *first* locker. You just started on the wrong end.''

Mildred feigned a backhand slap at the boy. ''Ryan, this kid of yours is entering the smart-ass stage.''

''Then he is in the proper company,'' Doc observed sagely.

After Ryan buckled on his gun belt and slung the rifle over a shoulder, he felt about ten times better. Chambering a round into his handblaster, he said, ''Time to go down.''

He led the way across the room to an alcove barred by a wood-paneled door. Turning the knob, he stepped out onto the concrete landing of a stairway that pitched downward. Having descended the stairs a few hours earlier, Ryan again took the point.

The walls were of blue gray concrete, lit by flickering fluorescent fixtures. Arrows painted on the walls at each landing pointed down. Small air vents just beneath the low ceilings played a continuous flow of cool, recycled air.

The stairwell led to a narrow corridor, which ended a hundred feet away at a vanadium steel door recessed into the wall. It was hexagonal in shape and a bright green in color. On the floor a few feet in front it lay the bullet-blasted corpse of one of Poseidon's mercs, a bespectacled man Ryan had dubbed "Specs."

He stepped over the body and approached the portal cautiously, careful not to tread in the wide pool of drying blood spread around it. The torso of a man floated in the crimson lagoon, sightless eyes staring at the ceiling. His face was frozen in an open-mouthed rictus of agony. His body was bisected, cut neatly in half at the waist by the multi-ton door.

Krysty winced at the sight, gingerly circling the dark red puddle, not wanting to bloody the chiseled silver tips of her Western-style boots. Responding to her questioning glance, Ryan said, "Name was Jonesy. He fell down in the wrong place at the wrong time."

"And then he was beside himself," Doc muttered.

Mildred rolled her eyes. "I *knew* you'd say that."

Ryan punched in the entrance code on the keypad panel fixed to the door frame. No matter how different the layout of the many redoubts they had visited, the one constant was the numerical sequence to release the sec door's lock—3-5-2 opened the door, and 2-5-3 locked it again.

It was a sequence that had eluded Poseidon for years. He had gone mad in frustration at his inability to access the predark technical secrets that lay on the other side of the vanadium-steel door. In many ways, his obsession with those three digits had been his downfall.

A combination of hydraulics and pneumatics rumbled and squeaked, gears meshed and the sec door rose upward swiftly. As it did, it automatically tripped a photoelectric beam, and overhead lights flickered to a dim, yellowish life.

Ryan entered, stepping over the lower portion of Jonesy's body. The first time he had entered a redoubt, his mind had reeled with impossible conjectures. He had been shocked, stunned, awed. Most of the technology he had seen held no meaning for him, because there had never been anything like it in any of the stockpiles he had uncovered with the Trader.

The high-ceilinged room beyond the sec door wasn't a redoubt. It was cramped, barely twelve by fifteen. A master control console ran the length of the east wall. Liquid-crystal displays and glass-covered readouts blinked and flashed purposefully. Everything still functioned, all the circuitry still drawing on the nearly eternal power provided by nuclear engines.

The far wall was dominated by the familiar arrangement of armaglass slabs enclosing the mat-trans chamber. The semitranslucent armaglass was tinted a white yellow, the hue of old cream. For a reason he could never fathom, the original engineers of the gateways had decided that color-coding the armaglass enclosures was the simplest method of differentiating the various chambers around the globe. Ryan checked the door to the chamber, pulling up on the handle. The counterbalanced weight clicked, and the door swung outward.

The mat-trans unit, like most of the others they had seen, was a six-sided chamber. The floor consisted of an interlocking pattern of raised metal disks, and the same pattern was duplicated on the

ceiling. Though both Doc and Mildred had speculated on the fundamental operating principles behind
the units, it still seemed like magic to Ryan, Jak,
J.B., Dean and Krysty.

Ryan understood, in theory, that the mat-trans
units required a dizzying number of maddeningly
intricate electronic procedures, all occurring within
milliseconds of one another, to minimize the mar-
gins for error. The actual conversion process was
automated for this reason, sequenced by an array of
computers and microprocessors. Though he accepted at face value that the machines worked, he
had never grown accustomed to the concept that
minds that created such stupendously complicated
devices couldn't have found a way to prevent the
nukecaust.

The gateway's destination and coordinate lock
codes had long ago vanished. Though a control keypad was affixed to the chamber door, it responded
only to the LD—Last Destination—button. This key
would, if pressed within thirty minutes of a successful jump, reactivate the gateway and return them
to their original transmission point.

Ryan eased the heavy door to the chamber all the
way open, allowing the rest of his party to enter.
Once inside, everyone knew what to do, sitting on
the floor disks in their usual positions. No matter
how many times they had done it, the seconds before a gateway jump were always anxious. They seldom knew where—or into what situation—they
would materialize.

As was his habit, J.B. took off his fedora and
carefully stowed his glasses in an inner pocket of
his coat. Mildred took his hand. Doc sat beside her,

laying the ebony swordstick at his side. Jak sat cross-legged against the wall with Dean next to him.

After everyone was ready, Ryan pulled the door shut and triggered the jump mechanism. He sat next to Krysty, putting an arm around her.

The disks in the floor and ceiling exuded a glow, and a low, almost subsonic hum began, quickly rising in pitch to a whine. The noise changed, sounding like the distant howling of gale-force winds.

The glow brightened, and a mist, shot through with flashing sparks, formed below the ceiling disks and rose from the floor, thickening to a fog and swirling all about them.

Ryan closed his eye.

Chapter Three

Ryan! Help me! Ryan!

Ryan opened his eye, galvanized by the terror in Krysty's voice, her words echoing within the walls of his skull. Bounding to his feet, he reached for the door to the gateway chamber. Jerking up the handle, he shouldered it open, realizing distantly that the heavy armaglass weighed no more than a thin layer of cloth.

The door opened directly into a long, broad hall that ran away until it grew indistinct in the murky distance. He raced along the corridor, not allowing himself a moment to clear the confusion in his thoughts. The corridor walls were lined by flickering torches in metal sconces. The floor, walls and ceiling were of stone, cut into huge square blocks. The walls on either side of him were covered with brightly colored friezes, portraying olive-skinned men and women. They wore filmy robes, fantastic headpieces and many jeweled ornaments and were depicted mostly in positions of lovemaking.

The images flickered and changed whenever Ryan tried to focus his eye on them. As he ran past, it almost seemed that the women in the friezes bore Krysty's face or hair or eyes. The women smiled as their bodies were fondled by various male partners, some of them with handsome, finely chiseled features and others that looked more like dogs or reptiles.

Ryan kept running, feeling his heart thud painfully inside his chest. He dashed through a series of empty chambers, lit by a ghostly, ellusive illumination. Some of the chambers showed as black as the mouth of Hell, and he tried to avoid slowing down in these.

The long corridor abruptly ended in utter, impenetrable blackness, like a sepia sea. Ryan couldn't stop running. Smoldering in the darkness before him, he saw a pair of crimson eyes, glowing like evil stars in an empty, sunless universe.

He tried to stop, to slow down, to change direction. Instead, he hurtled forward, all control gone. The crimson radiance grew brighter, more vivid, and he saw a face. It was a man's face, undeniably human, yet with alien, hellishly glowing red eyes. Then the flesh seemed to melt away, revealing a mask of naked white bone. A grinning skull floated in the sepia sea, a skull of ivory in which sparks of livid red flame danced within the shadowed sockets.

Ryan was no stranger to fear. He lived with it daily, but it was an emotion he long ago had learned to bottle, to contain. Now it escaped and spread through him like a virus, consuming him with terror, horror and panic. He set his teeth on the scream rising from his throat.

The death's-head leered at him, and the jaws of the skull opened. A peal of hideous laughter poured from the yawning jaws.

Ryan plunged toward that gaping maw, determined not to give voice to his surge of terror.

KRYSTY OPENED HER EYES and stared in wonder at the chamber around her. Silk tapestries adorned the walls, rich rugs were on the floors and the ivory chairs, benches and divans were littered with satin cushions.

The canopy over the bed in which she lay was hung with gauzy draperies, softly stirred by an intoxicatingly sweet breeze, scented like orange blossoms.

The delicate aroma made her feel languorous and lethargic, as if she had just awakened from a deep, soul-restoring sleep. Stretching, she turned over on her side, wondering why Ryan wasn't beside her. She longed to feel his hard body pressing against hers, his hands fondling and caressing her.

At the thought, the nipples of her full breasts hardened, pushing against the thin linen covering them. She needed Ryan beside her, above her, behind her—

Krysty bolted upright in the bed, pushing herself into a sitting position, a sudden alarm casting all other thoughts aside, evaporating the sensual and lascivious sensations that had nearly consumed her. She remembered Ryan sitting beside her in the gateway chamber as the jump mechanism triggered.

She slid out of the bed and turned toward the great bronze double doors at the far end of the room. She saw no knobs or handles. She ran to it, and smote the thick metal with her clenched hands. The muffled beating of her fists echoed dimly.

Suddenly terrified, she cried, "Ryan! Help me! Ryan!"

Even as she beat and shouted, the great bronze doors swung noiselessly back on hidden hinges, revealing a heavy golden chain across the entrance. Then the chain dropped without a sound. Beyond the threshold was a long dim vista of hall. Framed at the far end was a powerful man-shape, looming gigantic in the gloom.

Krysty couldn't make out any features, then two red flickering orbs appeared, right where a normal man's eyes should be. Terror flooded through her, but she refused to scream.

As quickly as it crested, the wave of fear receded. The shadows slipped away from the figure or he stepped from them, she couldn't tell.

A man stood in the center of the hall, towering well over six feet, nearly half a head taller than Ryan. His shoulders were incredibly broad, his arms long and bronzed, his hairless chest rippling with muscles. He was stark naked, and his fully erect member seemed as bronze hard as the rest of him.

Another wave of sensations flooded through Krysty—first, a rise of fiery desire, then a possessiveness, almost fiercely maternal in the urge to protect and nurture. The man beckoned to her with his right hand, a simple gesture, but somehow very sensual. The crimson eyes blazed upon her with an unremitting, hypnotic intensity.

Krysty felt herself drifting forward, toward those corded arms spread wide in a welcoming embrace. Vaguely she was aware of her diaphanous clothing dropping from her body, floating behind her. With great effort, she tried to stop herself, but she managed only to slow her gliding approach.

She tried to say that he couldn't have her, that she belonged to another.

A twisting whisper of a laugh touched her mind,

and a voice said that she belonged to him, had always belonged to him. He had waited an eternity for her, and she would be the mother of a dynasty that would last ten thousand years.

Then she was in his arms, the sleek muscled nakedness of his body pressing against her breasts, her desire-hardened nipples digging into his chest. She felt the pressure of his erection against her lower belly, shifting even lower, seeking her warmth and wetness. She stared into the red flame of lust in his eyes. His lips touched hers.

MILDRED BENT OVER the slack forms of Ryan and Krysty, fingering the pulse beats at the base of their throats. J.B. moved closer, putting on his spectacles.

"What's wrong with them?" he asked.

"I don't know," Mildred replied tersely. "Seems like some sort of shock. Pulse rates are irregular."

Jak and Doc exchanged worried glances. "The jump was unusually smooth for me," Doc commented. "No nausea whatsoever."

"They were close to the door," Dean said anxiously. "Mebbe somebody opened it just when we jumped. Wouldn't be the first time."

"Perhaps we should minister to them in more felicitous surroundings," Doc suggested.

Jak stepped over Ryan's and Krysty's legs and opened the door to the hexagonal chamber. The armaglass was tinted a pale rust brown. "Make recce."

J.B. unlimbered his Uzi and stood at the open door in case he was needed, but Jak returned in short order. "Anteroom, control room," the albino reported. "Empty."

Dean, Mildred and J.B. grabbed Ryan's limp body by the arms and legs and half carried, half dragged the man out of the chamber. Jak and Doc had an easier time with Krysty. They carried their friends out of the small anteroom, past comp consoles and readout screens and down a short hallway that opened up into a small room. Fluorescent light strips glowed feebly from the ceiling.

As they walked down the corridor, Doc said, "Look at the murals on the walls. Hieroglyphs, too."

Jak squinted at him. "What?"

Doc looked from one wall to the other. "Ye gods. I mean that literally. Ptah, Anubis, Set, Osiris—"

"What talking about, Doc?" Jak demanded, following the older man's eye and head movements but seeing nothing but smooth, unadorned walls.

Doc started to nod toward the wall on his right, then his eyes narrowed, widened, and his mouth creaked open. He shook his head. "Perhaps the light *is* playing tricks on me."

The room was small and held only a table and a few chairs. Mildred and J.B. laid Ryan on the floor, and Krysty was gently placed on the tabletop. As her body settled, she murmured faintly, "You won't have me.... Ryan..."

Immediately, Ryan's eye snapped open, and he levered upright from the waist. He clawed at his holstered blaster. Krysty was on his blind side, and his face was a mask of agony and fear until he caught sight of her.

"What the fuck happened to me?" he grated between clenched teeth.

Dean put a comforting hand on his arm. "You were out of it for a little while, Dad. That's all."

"How's Krysty?"

"Fine," she said weakly.

Waving aside J.B.'s proffered hand, he climbed unsteadily to his feet and bent over Krysty. She, too, had returned to somewhat confused consciousness. Sitting up, she embraced Ryan.

"Gaia!" she breathed. "Never had a jump nightmare like that before."

"Me, neither," Ryan replied as she scooted off the table. "We'll talk about it later. Find out first where we are. Anybody do a recce?"

"Only to here," Jak responded.

"Nothing unusual?" Ryan inquired.

"Not unless you consider two of our friends being unable to wake up unusual," Mildred replied.

"And wall paintings being there one moment and gone in the next," Doc said.

No one asked him to clarify his comment. Their long association with Doc had accustomed them to his sometimes cryptic, often nonsensical remarks. But this time, Ryan cast him a sharp, one-eyed glance.

"All right," he said, drawing his SIG-Sauer. "Let's do this by the book. Triple red."

The group formed a wedge, with Ryan and J.B. taking the point, the others fanning out behind. The wedge was the standard formation while exploring a strange redoubt. More often than not, the installations were deserted, abandoned for a hundred years or more. Every once in a while, they came across squatters, like the crazed twins who had staked claim to a redoubt in Colorado. In that instance, Ryan and Krysty had been forced by violent circumstance to chill them.

With the toe of a boot, Ryan eased open the door on the opposite end of the room. Beyond it was a small foyer and another door. It was a disk sheathed in gleaming metal surrounded by three concentric collars of steel. Affixed on the wall beside it was a sec-code keypad. Beneath the keypad was a plastic sign bearing red lettering: Biohazard Beyond This Point! Entry Forbidden To Personnel Not Wearing Anticontaminant Clothing!

Half a dozen one-piece coveralls hung from hooks on the wall. Hoods with transparent Plexiglas face-plates were attached to them.

"Fireblast!" Ryan muttered.

As far as he knew, biological warfare hadn't played a large role in the nukecaust, since the actual active conflict had lasted less than a day.

Ryan touched one of the coveralls with the built-in baffle silencer of the SIG-Sauer. The flimsy fabric parted like an ancient cobweb, and he cursed again. He called Mildred forward. When she read the printed warning on the wall, she groaned.

"How bad could it be?" Ryan asked.

"Might not be bad at all," she replied. "Then again, all sorts of bacteria, rickettsiae, viruses and fungi spores could be floating around in there."

"Still potent, still communicable after all this time?"

"Could be," she answered. "But you, John, Jak, Dean and Krysty were born in the Deathlands. More than likely, you've developed natural resistances to infectious agents that may be fatal to me and Doc."

"Comforting notion," Doc stated.

"Dark night," J.B. muttered. "Why couldn't this place be like most of the other redoubts?"

"Odds were we'd pop up into a medical installation sooner or later," Mildred countered reasonably. "Frankly, I'm surprised we hadn't before now, since we learned that bioengineering programs were going on prior to skydark. And after."

Ryan caught the oblique reference to the perverted researches they had discovered within the Anthill complex in the Black Hills. Both she and Ryan retained vivid, sickening memories of the creatures being bred there.

"Mebbe we should try another jump," Dean suggested.

Mildred shook her head, the beads in her plaited hair clicking. "I don't think that's necessary. Just because this place may have housed biological weapons, it doesn't mean any of them got loose."

Doc shuffled his feet uncertainly. "I recall reading an account of the expedition who entered King Tut's tomb. Many of them died mysteriously, and though some believed an ancient pharaoh's curse was responsible, more enlightened minds speculated that three-thousand-year-old microbes were responsible."

"Muzzle it, Doc," Mildred snapped. "You don't have to try to scare us to death."

"That's for sure," Krysty murmured.

Ryan met her gaze for an instant, and understood it wasn't invisible germs she feared. The memory of the jump nightmare was still fresh. And mystifying. Quickly, she averted her gaze, almost as if she were embarrassed.

"Well?" he demanded. "Do we try our luck out there or back in the gateway?"

After a moment of considered silence, everyone decided, in monosyllables, to find out what lay beyond the steel portal.

Ryan's hand poised over the keypad. He paused. "Should we hold our breaths?"

Mildred chuckled. "Not unless you're trying to win a contest. If microorganisms *are* free in there, most likely they were designed to attack the human body through the skin."

"Dammit, Millie!" J.B. said impatiently. "For the last time, what do you think the odds are of us contracting some kind of manufactured disease?"

"Slim to none. I'm basing that assessment on a lack of outbreaks of incurable illnesses in most of the villes we've visited."

Ryan's hand suddenly darted to the key pad and swiftly punched in the entry code. With a rumble and hiss of pneumatics, the metal disk rolled to the left. He realized that despite Mildred's assurances he was holding his breath. An over-the-shoulder glance showed him that all of his friends were, too, Mildred included.

No one moved. Peering into the murk beyond the portal, all Ryan could see was dim light gleaming from polished metal and glass.

Doc exhaled suddenly and noisily, causing everybody to jump and glare at him. He inhaled just as noisily, then smiled and patted his chest.

"Air is fresh enough," he announced. "There is no scent of bacteria befouling the atmosphere."

Carefully, Mildred released her own pent-up

breath and replied, "There wouldn't be. Do you know what the Ebola virus smells like?"

With a snort of impatience, Ryan relaxed his lungs, breathed in air that was only a little stale and stepped over the raised lip of the entrance lock.

A wavery light blinked on overhead. He uttered a low whistle of surprise. His eye took in the heavy tables loaded with a complicated network of glass tubes, beakers and retorts, consoles with glass-covered gauges and comp terminals. The right-hand wall was completely covered by armaglass, running the entire twenty-yard length of the room. On the far wall was a twin of the disk-shaped entrance portal.

Ryan moved carefully into the room, blaster cocked and ready, barrel sweeping back and forth in short half arcs. Behind him, the others fanned out, weapons gripped in ready hands.

He didn't pause to examine anything in the strange chamber—he sidled across it. Only when he reached the metal-collared disk did he stop and look around. His friends milled around him, eyes alert and watchful.

"Want to look around in here or recce the rest of the redoubt?" he asked.

"Makes more sense to find out where we are," J.B. replied.

Another keypad was on the wall, and Ryan thumbed in the open code, the thick slab of metal rolling obediently aside. Down a short hallway, with rooms on either side, he could see the massive vanadium-steel sec door. It was down.

"Looks safe," he said.

They moved quietly down the passage. The doors

to the rooms they passed were open, and quick glances showed chambers in which to sleep, to cook, to wash.

"Smaller than most redoubts," Jak remarked.

Usually, the underground installations were multi-leveled labyrinths of corridors, dormitories and control rooms. This one was Spartan and miniaturized.

Ryan paused at the sec door, turned toward Dean and gestured to the green lever on the steel frame. "Do you want the honor, son?" he asked.

Dean smiled and moved forward as Ryan knelt at the center of the door. The others shifted position, fingers tight on triggers, blaster bores trained on the rectangle of alloy.

"Go," Ryan said.

Dean threw the lever up. Immediately came the grinding rumble of a complicated system of comp-controlled gears and chain pulleys that raised the multi-ton door off the concrete floor. Buried machinery whined faintly, and the door slid slowly upward.

As the bottom edge cleared five or six inches above the floor, Dean shifted the lever to a midpoint position. The door stopped rising.

Ryan went flat on the floor and squinted out between the vanadium and the concrete. He saw nothing but darkness, and a cool breeze played over his face. Wind-driven grains of sand danced over the threshold.

"Door leads to the outside," he declared. "You're right, Jak. Place is a lot smaller than usual. Up another six inches, son."

Dean moved the lever, and the door slid upward. This time, Ryan saw sand, silvered by moonlight.

The air was fresh, clean and very dry. In the distance, he saw nothing but a sandy sea of desolation.

"All the way up, Dean."

The massive door ascended, then stopped with a click. A swirl of air breezed into the corridor, bringing a scattering of sand. A reef of clouds crossed the face of the quarter moon, obscuring the view of their surroundings—not that there was much to see. No vegetation grew within their range of vision, not even the hardy strain of flower Krysty had named the Deathlands daisy.

"Looks like the Sahara," Mildred commented.

"Or the Gobi," Doc put in.

Both places were possibilities. The scientists of the Totality Concept had evidently been determined to link every continent with gateway units. So far, their mat-trans journeys had taken them to Russia, Britain, Japan and Amazonia. As for America, it seemed that the entire country was honeycombed with the hidden installations.

Eyeing the sky, J.B. said, "Too overcast to make an accurate sextant reading. Mebbe we should wait until dawn."

Doc hunched his shoulders in an exaggerated shudder. "I, for one, do not fancy a sleepover in an environment that may be percolating with every germ, virus and plague known to man. Or unknown to man."

"We're infected already," Mildred said crossly. "That is, if we're fated to be infected. Besides, our provisions are running low, and this looks to be the only grocery store for miles around."

Gesturing to Dean, Ryan stepped out into the corridor. The lad moved the lever, and the huge door rumbled down.

"Let's see what we've got here," Ryan said.

Chapter Four

As it turned out, there wasn't much. What they had already seen of the installation was basically all there was to it.

In a kitchen, Jak found a few sealed ration packs in a cabinet. The freeze-dried food was tasteless, but it was nutritious. Their biggest worry was water, but when they tried the faucets, the liquid that flowed out smelled and tasted fresh and untainted. Even the hot-water taps worked, so the heating system was still functional.

Though smaller by far than almost every other redoubt they had visited, the place appeared to be in better condition. When Krysty commented on its comparative cleanliness, Mildred asked wryly, "What did you expect from doctors?"

"It's not just that," Krysty replied, a faint line of worry appearing between her eyes. "It almost looks like somebody has been taking care of this place. Fairly recently, too."

A total of eighteen beds were divided between the three bunk rooms. The bathroom had five toilet stalls and three urinals. Though three shower heads projected from the tiled wall inside an enclosure, there was a six-and-a-half-foot-tall, bullet-shaped cylinder in one corner. Though everyone else was mystified by its purpose and function, Ryan was familiar with it.

"I saw one like it in the Anthill," he explained. "The freezies called it a Medisterile unit."

"What's it for?" J.B. asked.

"A bug chaser," Mildred said. "A decontamination chamber in case any of the personnel here were directly exposed to something toxic or infectious."

Ryan nodded. "Yeah, the freezies stuck me in one. Guess they thought I had cooties."

He didn't elaborate further. The memories of his experiences inside Mount Rushmore still gave him occasional nightmares. Almost every predark evil had survived there, nurtured and coaxed by the deranged, cybernetically altered refugees from the days of the nukecaust. Only Mildred had penetrated the vast installation with him and witnessed its horrors firsthand.

They searched all the rooms. One thing they expected to find, but didn't, were the skeletonized remains of the installation's personnel.

"The folks here must've jumped out a long time ago," J.B. said. "Doubt they went overland."

In an office suite, they found six partition-enclosed desks, all of them equipped with comp terminals. Two gray steel file cabinets stood in a corner. Tacked on the wall, faded and yellowed with age, was a sign reading Geneticists Do Everyone Better.

Doc read the copy aloud and added in a monotone, "Ha. Inside humor."

Mildred's dark eyes scanned the walls.

"What are you looking for?" Dean asked.

"The standard slogan of predark offices," she replied. "A sign that says You Don't Have To Be Crazy To Work Here, But It Sure Helps."

Ryan tugged on a drawer handle of one of the file cabinets. It slid open with surprising ease, though it was jammed with paper and notebooks. He pulled out one at random and read the label aloud. "Overproject Excalibur. Mission Invictus."

Both Doc and Mildred glanced toward him with interest. *"Invictus,"* Doc intoned. "Latin for 'invincible.'"

Opening the notebook, Ryan saw only columns of closely set type and mathematical formulas. Most of the words were long and difficult to pronounce, such as "adenosine triphosphate," "deoxyribonucleic acid" and "haploid karyotypal." Illegible handwritten notations were scrawled all around the columns. As he thumbed through the notebook, Ryan found a double-page spread containing the graphic of a twisting, ladderlike helix.

"DNA molecules," Mildred said. "That cinches it. This was definitely some kind of genetics lab."

Thinking about the loathsome, bioengineered blasphemies he had seen in the Anthill, Ryan slapped the notebook shut. He forced it back into the drawer and slammed it closed.

Voice thick with disgust, he asked, "Was there nothing too foul for your predark whitecoats to fuck around with?"

"Unfortunately," Mildred answered sadly, "no."

They returned to the kitchen and made a quick meal out of the contents of one of the sealed packages. It was a sort of gruelly oatmeal soup sweetened with brown sugar.

"I wish I knew if this was breakfast or dinner," J.B. commented.

Doc scowled as he spooned a bit of the food into his mouth. "What difference does it make, John Barrymore? Breakfast, brunch or lunch, these viands would still be unsatisfactory, even to the most undiscriminating of palates."

Jak pushed his bowl away. "Crap don't know if wants to be ate or drunk."

"I like it," Dean said simply.

Mildred ate only a few bites before saying, "I want to check out the laboratory facility."

J.B. swung his head toward her. "No!" He spoke with uncharacteristic vehemence. "There's no telling what kind of germs are in there, Millie."

"And there's no telling what kind of medical stores are in there," Mildred replied. "How many times have we—and others—suffered because of a lack of proper medicines? I won't pass up this chance."

J.B. opened his mouth to respond, but Ryan interjected sternly. "Enough."

All of them were weary to the point of exhaustion, their nerves frayed and frazzled. Both Dean and Doc were swallowing yawns. Krysty's head was bowed. She had yet to fully regain her strength from the toll exacted on her by calling upon Gaia.

"Let's get some rest," Ryan continued. "We'll talk about it in the morning."

"Whenever that be," Jak said wryly. "Take first watch."

Ryan shook his head. "I don't think that's necessary. This place is secure."

Mildred remained seated as the others rose and

filed from the room. J.B. paused in the doorway. "Coming to bed, Millie?"

"I caught a nap on the boat, remember. I'll stay up for a while."

J.B. angled an eyebrow at her, and she chuckled. "Don't worry. I won't go into the lab area. I do want to check over the files in the office, though."

Nodding brusquely, J.B. went out into the hall. Mildred sat for a few moments, washing the taste of her meal out of her mouth with a cup of water. She walked out into the corridor.

Although bioengineering wasn't her field, her background in cryogenics had intersected with it from time to time. Some startling advances had been made before the nukecaust, but as far as she knew, the experiments had been devoted to increasing crop yields, curing birth defects and the like. A great hue and cry had been raised, once, when a life-form had been cloned. However, she had slowly realized that genetic research and biotechnology had played a large part in the mysterious Totality Concept.

In the years before the nukecaust, she had heard many whispers about secret scientific researches conducted by the government, though most of them had been relegated to the status of paranoid rumors, spawned by crackpots fearing a New World Order.

Now, after encountering surviving pockets of pre-dark genetic experiments—the Genesis Project, Ladrow Buford's cloning farm, Mark Tomwun's mutated dolphins, the Dwellers, not to mention what she had seen in the Anthill—Mildred had developed a provisional hypothesis. She hadn't discussed it with her friends, since they would no doubt find her theories irrelevant to the simple issue of survival. As

far as they were concerned, the minds behind the
Totality Concept were long dead, consumed by the
same nuclear hell that had vaporized most of humanity. There was no way to learn the truth, and
even if they somehow managed to, the truth
wouldn't do them much good a hundred or so years
after the fact.

Though Mildred shared her friends' priority for
survival, she silently agreed that retroreasoning was
irrelevant. But one theory she didn't voice—dared
not voice—was the fear that the Totality Concept
itself was linked to the nukecaust in a mysterious
manner. She applied the iceberg principle, believing
the redoubts and the scientific wonders they contained were merely the small, visible tips of a vast,
terrifying mass hidden beneath the wreckage of the
world.

Instinctively, she knew Overproject Excalibur was
part of the iceberg hitherto hidden from her and the
rest of humankind.

Inside the office suite, she devoted twenty minutes
to methodically riffling through the contents of the
file cabinets. Most of the paperwork meant very little—requisition forms, duty rosters, personnel re-
cords. Still, a vague picture of the purpose of the
redoubt emerged. One name figured prominently in
memo headings and signatures, a Dr. Connaught
O'Brien.

Mildred frowned, turning the name over in her
mind. A faint bell of recognition chimed in the recesses of her memory.

In one drawer, she found a square leather packet.
It was imprinted with a symbol that was familiar,
but slightly different from what she had seen before.

It was a red triangle with three vertical lines enclosed within it. She and her friends had encountered a similar symbol a few months before when they'd jumped into a subterranean installation in Dulce, New Mexico. There, however, the lines had been horizontal. These resembled stylized, round-topped daggers.

The packet's flap was sealed with a tiny combination lock. Rather than waste time in a trial-and-error process to find the proper sequence, she took a penknife from a pocket and sawed through the leather. She tugged out a sheaf of papers bound in booklet form and a multimedia compact disk in a slip-sleeve. The first page of the papers bore the heading: "Overproject Excalibur. Mission Invictus. Alpha Subject Circumscription. Final report prepared by Dr. C. O'Brien."

Most of the pages of the booklet were full of technical terms, schematics and diagrams. The last half held color video-scanned images. The photographs were of two dark-haired babies, about three months old, a boy and a girl. The boy looked unusually somber. The girl, on the other hand, grinned gummily and waved pudgy hands.

Mildred wanted to smile, but she couldn't quite bring it off. The children were certainly beautiful, but their big eyes possessed no pupils, irises or whites. Their eyes were a solid bloodred.

She flipped through the photo section, noting that after a certain point, there were no more pictures of the little girl. There were, however, many of the boy child, obviously encompassing a number of years. It was as if the photographer, whoever he or she had been, had devoted inestimable hours to capturing every month of the youth's life on film.

When the pictures depicted the boy in what appeared to be his teenage years, their quality subtly changed. Mildred found a series of head-and-shoulder shots. The youth's smooth forehead was unusually high, his nose aquiline. His mouth was long, with a full underlip. His raven's-wing black hair was straight and cut short, combed back from a pronounced widow's peak. His skin was deeply tanned. Only the crimson hue of his eyes marred the classical perfection of his face.

Several photos showed the boy striking poses, wearing only white briefs. He stood with his hands on his hips, or his arms raised to show off bulging biceps and swelling pectorals. The intent seemed almost pornographic.

When Mildred saw the last photograph, she amended that—it *was* pornographic. The boy looked to be about sixteen years old. He leaned against a blank wall, hands clasped casually behind his back, one leg slightly bent at the knee. He held his head tilted at an arrogant angle, and a slight, superior smile creased his lips. He was in a high state of sexual arousal, and his erection seemed as arrogant as the position of his head.

She slapped the booklet shut, wondering what possible scientific purpose the last few photographs had served and who had taken them—or worse, who had authorized them.

Picking up the CD, Mildred went from one comp console to the other, flipping their power switches. She tried three before a monitor screen lit up and flashed to flickering life. Sitting down before it, she inserted the disk into the drive port, and the red triangle symbol appeared. Beneath it a date appeared: 1/18/08. Absently, she noted the date as being almost exactly seven years to the day after the first mushroom cloud had swallowed Washington, D.C.

A colorless male voice spoke. "Mission Invictus update. Final report. Authorized personnel only. MJ-Ultra Clearance required."

The symbol vanished from the screen, replaced an instant later by the head and shoulders of a woman. Her dark red hair was tied back, and her leaf green eyes were covered by a pair of steel-rimmed spectacles. Despite her lack of cosmetics and the impersonal, clinical expression on her face, she was very pretty. She appeared to be in her late thirties or early forties. Behind the woman, Mildred could just make out black-topped lab tables laden with glassware.

Mildred recognized her. Dr. Connaught O'Brien had enjoyed her fifteen minutes of fame in the late 1990s. A biologist and an outspoken proponent of eugenics and selective breeding, she had made the lecture-and-talk-show circuit for a few months before vanishing from the public eye.

The woman's basic thesis was that technology had changed and improved every aspect of human society, yet the human race itself was trapped in an evolutionary corral. O'Brien had maintained that human development had to catch up to technical advances.

The media had pinned the catch-all label "technogenics" as a buzzword to categorize her theories. It was one she had strenuously objected to, but the appellation stuck. As Mildred recalled, during the storm of negative publicity, O'Brien had been dismissed from her post at Johns Hopkins University, amid accusations that she was Josef Mengele in drag. Obviously, when she had vanished, it was to work for Overproject Excalibur.

In a clear voice, touched lightly by a hint of an Irish brogue, Connaught O'Brien stated, "The third revolution of human progress is well under way. It affects us so deeply that some people in high places would rather maintain an uneasy silence than see it through to its fruition. Mission Invictus is the only true success in Overproject Excalibur, and yet that success is now threatened by the same powers that insisted upon its implementation in the first place."

A line of anger creased O'Brien's brow. "You who are seeing this and hearing my words know to whom I am referring. You say I have gone too far in developing a human organism that will survive in the postholocaust world. This is not a new accusation. I will not bore you with a recitation of my own personal injuries suffered by the small-minded attitude of the mainstream scientific community in the course of my work as a geneticist.

"I agreed to work for Overproject Excalibur to be free of those constraints, of those misunderstandings. My assignment was to create a superior lifeform that exhibited the necessary adaptive traits for survival in the new world, including reproduction. Given the immutable fact that time did not permit breeding a superior race in terms of normal gestation periods and maturity cycles, I was forced to a single conclusion. Mutation."

O'Brien's voice vibrated with passion. "It wasn't just for money or to expand the fields of knowledge that I embarked on the course I followed. Certainly, money has no meaning now. It is a matter of conscience. You yourselves dictated that Mission Invictus was the only rational means to restore order and harmony to the world. I adhered to your schedules, built upon the findings of others in the field of pantropic science.''

Mildred sighed. She should have known. Before skydark, pantropy was a primarily theoretical field to bioengineer a strain of humanity that could survive and thrive in new environments. She had seen living evidence that pantropy hadn't been restricted to a set of mere hypotheses, so she wasn't surprised by O'Brien's assertion.

''The Unisex Program and the Genesis Project were deemed failures,'' O'Brien's image continued. ''Mission Invictus is not, however you may argue it. I will not explain how my biochemically synthesized gene mutations were utilized in the creation of the Alpha and Epsilon subjects. The fact that I succeeded where those others failed should provide the smallest hint of the magnitude of this miracle. The loss of Epsilon does not invalidate the miracle. No one regrets the accident more than I, but I am able to maintain my perspective while all about me, everyone has lost theirs. Now, on the dawn of a new age of human evolution, the same old primitive fear sets in again. The fear of the inferior man facing the superior man.''

Mildred leaned back in the chair, listening and watching, almost afraid of what she might learn.

Chapter Five

It wasn't that Ryan found sleep elusive—he never caught so much as a fleeting glimpse of it.

He lay with Krysty on a narrow bed in one of the bunk rooms. The others had considerately allowed him and Krysty to occupy one room, in case they wanted privacy. Presumably, J.B. and Mildred shared another of the rooms while Doc, Jak and Dean bedded down in the third.

Their consideration, as much as he appreciated it, was wasted. Both he and Krysty slept fully clothed. She murmured and stirred fitfully in her sleep. Ryan knew she was totally drained by calling upon the Earth Mother. Even after all their time together, he still didn't understand how she tapped into the electromagnetic field of the planet itself. Shortly after they had met, Krysty had offered an unsatisfactory explanation: "It's sort of like focusing, a concentrating on how I feel. I call on the Earth Mother, and she comes to me."

Afterward, the strain placed on her metabolism could sometimes result in a slumber so deep it was almost a coma. And though she continued to sleep, she was restless, moving frequently, a thread of spittle at a corner of her mouth.

As tired as he was, he was sore and itchy. Not only did his muscles ache, but the salt residue of his ocean swim had dried upon and irritated his skin. He continued trying to capture sleep, but every time he closed his eye, the image of the grinning, flame-eyed skull bobbed to the surface of his mind like a malevolent cork.

Nightmares were, more often than not, part and parcel of mat-trans jumps. He had trained himself to always expect them and to be pleasantly surprised if he didn't experience them. Still, his instincts told him he hadn't had a typical gateway nightmare. There had been no other symptoms of jump sickness, only the overwhelming wave of terror and the sense of a malign intelligence hating him.

Krysty moaned faintly. Ryan turned toward her. In a low, distant voice, she whispered, "Not your queen...not your mother..."

Ryan started up, shaken by an eerie fear. He listened and when all he could hear was Krysty's slightly labored breathing, he got out of the bed. He stared down at her in the dim light and, when he realized he was scratching at his salt-stiff hair, he cursed and turned away.

Quietly, he left the room, went out into the hallway and entered the shower room. Peeling off his clothes, he placed them on a bench near the door. He chose the farthermost tiled enclosure and turned on the faucet. A spray of water jetted from the nozzle, and he adjusted it until it was a needlelike rain. When the water was hot enough, almost at the tolerance level, he stepped beneath the flow. He used a liquid-soap dispenser affixed to the wall to work a lather all over his bruised and scarred body.

The entire room filled quickly with billowing clouds of steam. As he washed, he thought back to

the last time he and Krysty had made love. It had
been quite some time ago, in a shower room very
much like this one, and she had crept up behind
him—

He snorted out a mouthful of water. A repetition
of that night wasn't likely to happen now. Even if
he felt up to it, Krysty was in a sleep so deep that
nothing could rouse or arouse her. He contented
himself with luxuriating beneath the driving jets of
hot water, letting them soothe the muscle ache. A
hand touched his back and he jumped, whirled, biting back a surprised curse.

Krysty materialized out of the rolling vapors like
a wraith, her limbs glistening with droplets of water.
She was naked and perfect, with her narrow waist,
flaring hips, long legs, full, gem-crested breasts and
the seductive scarlet triangle at the juncture of her
rounded thighs. Her tumbles of crimson hair fell
over her damp shoulders.

Her big, slightly tilted eyes gleamed with a brilliant emerald light. The expression in them was so
intensely single-minded that Ryan was startled into
speechlessness for a long moment. He had seen passion in those eyes countless times, but always they
were misted by love. Now, the hard green glint was
unsoftened by any emotion other than a raging desire, a consuming lust.

"Again in the shower?" he asked quietly, striving
for a tone of humor he didn't feel. "Getting to be
habit, lover."

Krysty didn't reply in words. Her long-fingered
hands ran over his face, touching the cicatrix scar
on the left cheek. They trailed across his chest, one
sharp nail tracing the thin line of hair that stretched

over his flat belly to thicken darkly below it. Ryan stared into her eyes, reading nothing there but an erotic urgency. He felt his muscles tighten under her touch, and swiftly his penis engorged and thickened, rising and hardening.

Leaning forward, Krysty tongued his chest as her hands went to his erection, petting and stroking it. She slowly lowered herself to her knees, dragging her tongue down his torso, leaving a trail of heat along his skin. Her scarlet tresses wove a soft, curling web around his hard shaft, caressing and tickling.

Ryan gasped at the indescribably pleasurable sensation. He rested his hands atop her head as his hips began an involuntary back-and-forth motion. Her tongue lapped out, a slow, hot swirl over the tip of his organ. Groaning, he thrust himself forward into Krysty's avid mouth, her fingers maintaining a sliding, circling grip on the base of his cock.

When he felt the slow rise of juices, he drew in a sharp breath and her hand gripped him tightly in a firm, almost painful grasp. Drawing back, she said breathlessly, "Not yet. Not yet."

Tugging at him, Krysty guided him down until he lay flat on his back on the warm, wet tiles. Holding his erection with one hand, she straddled his thighs, lifting herself up, then slowly sitting, impaled herself. She released him as she worked his rock-hard length into her. Her hips moved back and forth. She bit her lower lip, her face a slit-eyed mask of concentration.

When he was fully embedded within her velvet, liquid heat, she voiced a keening cry and began to ride him roughly. Fingernails digging into his chest, she rocked back and forth, thrust up and down shallowly in a wild, abandoned rhythm. She gasped, whimpered, moaned and cried out.

Ryan was a little disturbed by her uninhibited sounds of passion. Because of the constant proximity of their companions, not to mention danger, neither of them was very vocal during their couplings. But Krysty grunted, yelped and moaned in an almost mindless fixation on her own pleasure.

He covered her bouncing breasts with his hands, pinching her bright pink nipples. Krysty paid no attention to the touch, her eyes wide but unseeing, clouded and glazed, her mouth open and wet.

Feeling the boiling approach of an orgasm, Ryan writhed beneath her, husking out, "Lover—"

Instantly, her wild pelvic motions ceased. With superb control, her internal muscles closed around his hard column, squeezing it like a determined fist, preventing the explosion. She whispered, "Not yet. Not yet. More to see."

When she was sure Ryan's climax had been averted, Krysty slowly lifted herself off the rod of flesh jutting up between his thighs. Her breath came in ragged pants, her full breasts rising and falling.

She went to all fours on the floor, back arched, head down and resting on her forearms, rear end curved sharply upward. Ryan rose to his knees behind her, hands grabbing her sleek, flaring hips. The sight of her beautiful buttocks fanned the flames of lust in him until he was completely unaware of anything else. He fingered the gleam of moisture shining between her legs and he leaned into her, placing the head of his member against her opening. She wriggled her backside to facilitate penetration, backing up against his cock. With one forward thrust, he glided full-length into her, the simmering heat of her snug, slippery sheath making him bite back an outcry.

Krysty groaned so loudly and deeply the tiled walls threw back the echoes. He put his hands around her waist. Her flesh felt like a bundle of charged electric cables covered with silk. She looked back over her shoulder at him as he slid a hand over her belly, through the crisp mat of hair and found the tender, responsive bud of swollen flesh nestled there. He rolled it between thumb and forefinger as he began pumping recklessly back and forth within her. Krysty twisted, moving in rhythm to his thrusts, grunting and gasping.

Suddenly, she began to speak, in a guttural, hoarse, moaning whisper. "The august god found her as she slept in the beauty of her palace. She awoke because of the savor of the god, and she laughed in the presence of his majesty...."

Ryan, lost in his own orgiastic madness, only partly heard her, and that part he didn't understand, or at the moment, care about. His steady, pounding pace didn't falter. Steam, lust and sweat blinded him. He cupped one of her dangling breasts, squeezing the desire-hardened nipple.

"He came to her straight away. He was ardent for her. He gave his heart unto her, let her see him in the form of a god after he came before her."

Krysty lifted her face from the cushion of her forearms. Between clenched teeth, she hissed, "She rejoiced in beholding his beauty. His love went through her body, then the majesty of the god did all that he desired with her. She let him rejoice over her. How great is your fame!''

Her body suddenly stiffened. Back arching, she propped herself up on her elbows. She tossed her head, whipping her long, damp tresses back and forth. She sobbed, ''You have united me with your favors! Your dew is in all my limbs!''

She convulsed and shuddered in a spasming orgasm so fierce and unrestrained that even Ryan was surprised. He felt her inner muscles rippling around and massaging his rigid cock with an amazing, insistent strength.

He knew from long experience it was useless to hold back when she exerted that extraordinary control. He trembled in a contraction, pressing his lower belly against her buttocks as he burst deep inside her, an eruption of liquid fire that seemed to last forever. He gripped her tightly by the waist to keep himself seated within her as his hips jerked back and forth in an explosion of orgasmic energy.

Gasping, Krysty sagged beneath him, collapsing facedown on the floor. Ryan fell forward, supporting himself above her by quivering arms, straining briefly against her upturned backside, unwilling to accept he had spent himself within her clutching heat. Slowly, his senses returned to him and his hips stopped moving.

Krysty's breath came out in a heavy, prolonged sigh of release, then her sigh became a sudden, sharp intake of shock. She lifted her head, looking over a bare shoulder at him, her wet hair plastered to her face, only one wide green eye visible.

''Ryan?'' Her voice was high and wild with anxiety and confusion. ''What's going on?''

It took a moment for the strangeness of the question to penetrate Ryan's postclimactic fog. She squirmed away from him and sat up quickly, raking her hair from her face, staring around in a near panic.

"How did I get here?" she demanded, fear and suspicion mingling in equal measures in her tone.

Ryan frowned. "I guess you walked."

She crossed her arms over her breasts. Haltingly, she said, "I was asleep. Last I remember was lying next to you. I was asleep."

Ryan moved toward her. She scooted away, eyeing his softening penis distrustfully. His first flash of irritation faded when he realized she was genuinely confused—and frightened. Softly, he said, "Mebbe you sleepwalked."

Krysty forced a half smile to her face. "Somnambulist sex? That's a new one for me."

Ryan chuckled, getting to his feet, extending a hand toward her. "First time for everything, lover."

For a moment, Krysty appeared reluctant to take his hand. She reached out, caught it, and Ryan pulled her up, holding her against him. He tried to kiss her, but she averted her face.

"Something's wrong," she said in a troubled whisper. "I was too exhausted to move, much less do what we just did."

Despite the heat, Ryan felt a chill tiptoe up the back of his spine. What was left of his erection vanished. "What are you saying?"

Almost stammering, she replied, "I remember doing what we did...but it was like I was somebody else...or *you* were somebody else."

Krysty pushed him away, hugging herself. Gooseflesh pimpled her arms, and she shivered. "Something controlled me, like I was a puppet, testing my...sexual responses...seeing what I could do, what I *would* do."

Ryan's belly turned a cold flip-flop. Though Krysty's Gaia-linked empathic abilities were honed to detect danger, neither he nor she could deny they had been liabilities in the past. He immediately thought back to their encounter with the plant entity in England. It had used Krysty's connection with the geo-energy of earth as a channel to temporarily take control of her. He had been forced to render her unconscious.

As if sensing his recollections, Krysty said, "No, it wasn't like when the Other possessed me. This was on a deeper, far more primal level than that."

Hesitantly, he asked, "Like the time when you were under Kaa's influence?"

She wheeled, not responding to the question and hurriedly walked out of the alcove. Ryan turned off the water and went to the bench where he had left his clothes. Krysty was dressing quickly, worming into jeans, not bothering to dry herself. Her crookedly buttoned white sleeveless blouse clung to her wet breasts.

As Ryan pulled on his pants, he said, "At least you had enough presence of mind not to walk around the redoubt buck-ass naked."

She didn't respond. Her hair was tight at the back of her neck, and her lower lip quivered.

Impatiently, Ryan said, "Talk to me, Krysty. Something must have happened to you when we made the jump."

Her eyes bored in on his face. "Why do you say that?"

"Because something happened to me, too. But it didn't make me sleep-screw or spout poetry in the middle of it."

She squinted. "I did that? Wait...I remember now. Not poetry exactly."

"No, not exactly. I didn't catch very much of it. Had to do with a god's favors and some such over-blown romantic shit."

She smiled wanly. "You're a true sentimentalist, lover. But you're right—something happened to me during the jump."

Ryan shrugged into his shirt. "Like what?"

She moved her shoulders uncomfortably. "I dreamed I was in a palace room, beautifully furnished. I was aching for my beloved to join me in bed."

"Me?"

"Yes. No." Krysty shook her head. "I don't know. Anyway, I got scared. I called for you—"

Ryan's eye widened. "I heard you."

She drew in an unsteady breath. "I ran out of the room. Then I saw...him."

"Him," Ryan echoed. "Let me guess. He had eyes burning like the fires of hell."

Her face registered her surprise. "Yes! You saw him, too?"

"Saw *it*," he said grimly. "He had a skull instead of a face."

Running a nervous hand through her hair, Krysty said, "That's not what I saw. He was a big man. He wanted me."

"Wanted you for what?"

Wearily, she answered, "I'm not really sure. Wanted me for his mate, for his queen. For his...mother."

Ryan angled an eyebrow at her. "All of those in one package? He doesn't want much, does he?"

"I can't be sure of the impressions I received." She looked fearfully around the room, as if she expected to see someone—or something—crouching in a corner. "There's only one thing I *am* sure of. Whoever he is, he knows we're here. He knows *I'm* here. He's been waiting for me a long time."

"Who?" A note of menace lurked at the back of Ryan's voice. "Who has been waiting for you?"

Krysty's eyes narrowed, and she tilted her head to one side, as if trying to listen to the murmur of unimaginably distant voices. Quietly, she said, "A god."

Chapter Six

Mildred continued to examine the material that explained Dr. O'Brien's role at the installation.

Phase One of Mission Invictus had been conducted on primates and was already a biological fait accompli before Connaught O'Brien joined the staff in early 1999. The subject animals' cells and DNA retained their structural integrity despite exposure to radiation and its concomitant free-radical damage. The only side effect of the genetic recombination had been a bizarre pigment change in the eyes when the test animals reached maturity. For a reason the scientists could only speculate upon, their eyes turned red, though their vision was apparently unimpaired.

When Overproject Excalibur resettled the twelve mission personnel—eight men and four women, including O'Brien—in the isolated redoubt, the apes had to be put down. Though deeming Phase One a success, the overseers didn't want a race of superchimps running around the installation, like something out of a bad sci-fi movie.

O'Brien found this objection amusing. "You who made that decision had, in effect, made apes of yourselves when you demanded the creation of a superhuman," she said.

According to her, Phase Two had proved more

difficult. For months, the hardships to build upon Phase One posed a puzzle to the scientists. Out of a group of thirty fertilized ova, only ten survived the first in vitro gestation period. Five were stillborn, and three others suffered from hydrocephalus, a condition in which the skull contained too much cerebrospinal fluid. These unfortunates were regretfully euthanized. Only two survived the entire neomutagenic process.

Yes, there were failures, O'Brien conceded. Abrasions, she called them. But, she explained, in any work so unprecedentedly technical that it combined all aspects of biophysics and cell-fusion techniques, no one could possibly have anticipated all the variables.

Stabilization of the basic genetic material—human beings—when exposed to the synthetic mutagen had proved to be a problem. Though it had eventually been overcome, the solution arrived after the nuclear firestorm reshaped the face of the world.

However, once the fundamental limitations of Phase Two were overcome, the Phase Three level was quickly achieved. The two surviving subjects, a male and female designated as Alpha and Epsilon, matured to the toddler stage within a month. Instead of being exultant, O'Brien accused, fear was the primary reaction.

"You are ordinary men, no matter how powerful you think you are," O'Brien said grimly. "You cannot envision my concept of a superbeing, bred to survive in the world you created. You wanted me to return to the original project of generational accelerated growth cycles. That I could not do. What you believed would require ten years or more was reduced to a mere eighteen months.''

The Alpha and Epsilon subjects showed extraordinary manual dexterity and heightened cognitive abilities almost from the moment they emerged from the incubation chambers. The infants possessed IQs so far beyond the range of standard tests as to render them meaningless. They mastered language in a matter of weeks, speaking in whole sentences, albeit grammatically incorrect.

Physically, Alpha and Epsilon were the epitomes of perfect human development. The structural properties of their bodies had been successfully modified while still in their in vitro wombs. As O'Brien put it, ''All of God's design faults in human physiology were corrected.''

Yes, the infants were perfect, despite the ruby red hue of their eyes. Some of the scientists on staff had problems relating to them because of this characteristic, referring to them half jokingly as ''children of the damned.''

As the children grew at an astonishing rate, O'Brien made a point of stopping by their nursery every night to tuck them in. Epsilon would always smile up into her face and with pudgy baby fingers toy with the strands of her long red hair, asking her questions in her high, piping, sweet voice.

Alpha, on the other hand, would gaze solemnly up into her face and never smile or reach for her. He silently studied her, examined her, inspected her. And, she suspected, judged her.

When the infants had developed to the physical age of three and half years old, but chronologically only six months out of the incubation tanks, the accident happened.

A door-lock mechanism jammed, a pressure gauge malfunctioned and a routine test in a hyperbaric chamber went horribly awry. The purpose of the experiment was to test the response time of the children as compared to normal subjects of their physical age. Epsilon was in the chamber at the time, and when O'Brien realized something was wrong, she lost all of her scientific objectivity.

The child's eyes behind the glass of the chamber were wide and sad, and Dr. Connaught O'Brien screamed frantically at the technician in charge to do something, to do *anything*. Epsilon suffocated, and O'Brien's heart broke.

The child's death was the demarcation point between what the mission had been and what it became. The atmosphere of the redoubt resembled that of people trapped aboard a slowly but inexorably sinking ship. O'Brien grew obsessively protective of Alpha. He, too, seemed changed by his sibling's death. His face took on a fixed, watchful expression.

In the months following Epsilon's suffocation, staff members began complaining of insomnia, and when they managed to sleep, of nightmares. Accidents became the rule rather than the anomalies. At first, O'Brien attributed the occurrences to stress. After all, the mat-trans unit was the only way in or out of the redoubt, and everyone was afraid to use it without Overproject Excalibur's permission, afraid of what horrific new situation they might jump into. O'Brien suspected that their fear of what was being bred within the walls of the installation was far greater than what the holocaust might have spawned outside them.

By the first anniversary of Alpha's emergence from the artificial womb, he had read voraciously of the volumes of books in the database. He absorbed the wisdom amassed over thousands of years of human history, and he began to extrapolate on that wisdom. Though O'Brien encouraged his exposure to such "survival of the fittest" proponents as Spencer and Hobbes, he wasn't much interested in their philosophies.

Alpha's area of special interest lay in ancient history, specifically the civilization of the Nile. Egypt, with its dynasties of mighty god-kings bestriding the earth, its culture, architecture and religions, obsessed him. The rebellious Eighteenth Dynasty pharaoh, Akhnaton, in particular fascinated him.

His hyperactive mind pondered the same questions that had perplexed the pharaoh thousands of years before—human history appeared to be essentially one war after another. For every golden flash of harmony, there were hundreds of blood-splattered conflicts.

Was it that man was unable to control his animal instincts and therefore his environment in order to attain a perfect society?

Alpha was certainly aware of the hellish conditions outside the shielded redoubt, but he didn't yet know who he was or what he was capable of doing. He sought an answer to that mystery by searching through the historical database. In a short time, he acquired a working knowledge of nine of the ancient written languages of the Nile Valley. In those documents, he found more than an identity; he found a means to an end. The information copied from the aeons-old papyri contained more science and less mythological esoterica than he expected.

While he studied, more of the parahuman abilities bred into him began to exhibit themselves. The modified and improved regions of his brain, specifically the hypothalamus, which regulated the complex biochemical systems of the body, continued to adjust any slight metabolic imperfections.

Alpha learned he could control all autonomous functions of his brain and body, even the manufacture and release of chemicals and hormones. He could speed or slow his heartbeat, increase and decrease the amount of adrenaline in his bloodstream.

He possessed complete control over that mysterious portion of the brain known as the limbic system, a portion that scientists had always known, in a detached, meaningless way, possessed great reserves of electromagnetic power and strength.

With this mastery of the mind, Alpha was both telepathic and empathic—and something else entirely, something quite unexpected and frightening to everyone but O'Brien.

He could—and oftentimes did—subtly influence the emotional states and thoughts of others, particularly if they were fatigued, depressed or asleep. He knew instantly if one of the mission personnel disliked him. One man, Carlson by name, made no secret of his antipathy toward the child. In a casual conversation, he referred to him as "Old Hell Eyes." The name stuck thereafter.

It didn't seem to offend Alpha—very little did—but O'Brien forbade anyone to say it, even in jest. A week after Carlson first coined "Hell Eyes," he was found dead in his bunk of a cerebral hemorrhage.

Over the subsequent year and a half, four more mysterious deaths followed. As O'Brien pointed out, they were duly recorded and reported.

By the time of the last death, Alpha had reached the physical-development stage of sixteen years old. He was already edging six feet tall. Perfectly proportioned, with the flat-muscled body of a young Hercules, he wore his hair close to the scalp, like an ebony skullcap. His features were beautiful, yet at the same time, undeniably masculine. Only his crimson eyes detracted from his beauty. They made him a freak.

It was during this stage that Alpha passed through puberty, but he didn't suffer.

Connaught O'Brien said, "At this time, another aspect of Phase Three began to assert itself. The gene-introduced life-force that determined his behavior and vitality came to the fore. The visceral desire to procreate. Obviously, with the loss of Epsilon, Alpha began to look elsewhere for a mate."

The woman paused, and a slightly abashed smile tugged at the corners of her mouth. "He showed no interest in the other female staff members, though they are younger than myself. He chose me."

O'Brien shrugged. "Yes, of course I realize he stimulated my very basic sexual urges. On another level, how can a mere mortal refuse a god? For the past three months we've been engaging in coitus regularly—oh, why be coy about it? We've been fucking. I doubt Alpha understands the concept of love. He understands only the instinct to spread his seed."

She sighed sadly. "Unfortunately, I cannot help him fulfill that instinctive desire. I'm barren—I always have been. I'm sure the increased levels of radiation leaking in through the shielding have rendered the other women here sterile, as well."

Taking a deep, determined breath, O'Brien continued. "And that is our present situation. Even though Alpha is immune to the toxins and radiation outside the installation, he will not find the mate he seeks out there, at least not for a very long time. Eighty-odd years, I estimate."

A cold, triumphant smile played over her face. "I received your transmission to abort the mission. I will not obey it. I will not accept that all my work is for nothing and that Mission Invictus, with its hopes for a sane world, is forever aborted, as well."

A flinty hardness came into her green eyes. "Mission Invictus was conceived by you as the penultimate plan to produce a superior human. I admit that I failed you on that point. I produced a god, an entity whose mutated antibodies and immune system will not succumb to the poisonous postwar environment. Whether you impotent bastards care to acknowledge it, Overproject Excalibur has been the instrument of fate in this epochal hour of humanity's bloody history."

O'Brien smiled mirthlessly as she declared, "Within seconds of transmitting this recording to you, I will deactivate the gateway. There will be no way in or out of this installation, except overland. Then, Alpha has agreed to be placed in stasis, but not in a cryonics canister.

"He will continue to grow, his development will proceed, but at a vastly reduced rate. He will slow

his metabolism to a crawl, his need for oxygen cur-
tailed to what exists within his...sarcophagus. His
heart might pump once a month. When he is ready,
he will revive on his own.

"After that, my staff and I will take a long walk
outside, our first in many years. With no way to
receive food and other provisions, staying here simply delays the inevitable. Alpha will need what remains in the stores when he awakens. Besides, I'm
curious to tour this brave new world your machi-
nations have created. Yes, Alpha altered the personnel's perceptions so they will faithfully follow me.
Cold-blooded to an extent, I cannot deny. However,
considering my audience, that is the novice speaking
to the masters of the art."

O'Brien's eyes suddenly glimmered with tears.
Her lips worked, then twisted into a contemptuous
smile. "If any of you are still alive when Alpha
emerges from this...tomb, know that you will be
instantly rendered obsolete. All of your plans,
schemes and grand dreams to control mankind under
one whip will come to nothing. You will inherit the
slag heap. Alpha will ascend to the throne of eternity
and spit upon you."

Her face smoothed itself into a clinical, impersonal mask again. "Dr. Connaught O'Brien, final
report."

WHEN THE HAND fell upon her shoulder, it required
all of Mildred's self-control to keep from screaming.
As it was, she twisted in her chair, pushing it away
from the desk on squeaking casters, whipping her
elbow backward.

J.B. grunted in pained surprise, half doubling over. "Dark night, Millie!"

Laughing in nervous relief, Mildred stood and hugged him. "I'm sorry, John, but you really shouldn't sneak up on people who are preoccupied."

Scowling, J.B. rubbed his midriff. "I wasn't sneaking," he said defensively. "It's not my fault you weren't watching your back."

He gestured to the image of Connaught O'Brien frozen on the screen. "Did she preoccupy you? Who is she?"

"A very brilliant, very disturbed woman," Mildred replied, reaching out to turn off the machine. "The mother and lover of a god."

J.B. squinted at her from behind the lenses of his spectacles. "What?"

Mildred shook her head. "I'll explain later. Where's everybody else?"

"Asleep, I guess. Except for Ryan. He's taking a shower."

"Good." She moved toward the door. "Let's go."

J.B. hung back. "To watch him take a shower?"

"To the lab. There's a story I have to confirm."

"We've had this discussion, Millie."

"We had it before I knew the back story about this place."

"Well, I don't know it."

"And I'll tell you. But checking on the details will determine how long or how short our stay here will be."

He still didn't move.

Mildred reached for his hand. "Trust me, John.

Or humor me. We can always use that Medisterile unit to decontaminate ourselves.''

J.B. took her hand, and they went through the office and out into the corridor. A dozen yards to their right, they saw Krysty walking toward them. The expression on her finely chiseled face was strangely fixed, her eyes wide but unblinking.

Gesturing to her, J.B. called in a loud whisper, ''Krysty! You all right?''

The Titian-haired woman's deliberate, measured stride didn't falter. Her eyes didn't flick toward them. Without a word or a sign of acknowledgment, she turned into the open door of the shower room.

''What's wrong with her?'' J.B. demanded. ''She sleepwalking or what?''

Mildred pulled at his sleeve. ''Ryan'll look after her. Come on.''

J.B. and Mildred walked quickly down the corridor to the disk-shaped steel portal. She tapped in the entry code, and the hatch rolled aside. Beyond it, the maze of sterile equipment glittered beneath the cold fluorescent tubes on the ceiling. The big room was broodingly silent and lifeless.

J.B. followed Mildred in, his sallow complexion worsening under the harsh, unflattering lights. He and Mildred walked down the aisle between two long trestle tables bearing large-scale fermentation tanks, a purification system and petri dishes.

A massive electron microscope stood on a separate table. In one corner, Mildred saw an oscilloscope, a fluoroscope and a stainless-steel liquid-nitrogen tank. The lid was open, revealing the honeycomb pattern of individual containers that had once held fertilized human embryos. J.B. followed her around the scientific labyrinth. She paused to examine much of the equipment, muttering beneath her breath.

Mildred stooped in front of a small refrigerator and twisted the latch. Cool air spilled out. "It still works."

Looking over her shoulder, J.B. saw dozens of small capped bottles resting on wire shelves. Mildred picked up a few, excitedly reading the labels aloud. "Penicillin, Aureomycin, Terramycin, streptomycin...tetracyclines!"

"What are all those?" J.B. asked.

Mildred stood, shutting the door of the refrigerator. "Broad-spectrum antibiotics. Before we leave this place, we're taking as many of the nonperishable ones as we can carry. I'll look around for syringes."

J.B. nodded. "Okay. And what else are we looking for?"

Mildred walked to the far, armaglass-covered wall. Peering through a pane, she saw a cylindrical hyperbaric chamber and other instruments and pieces of equipment that were unfamiliar to her. She found a door set between a pair of armaglass slabs and opened it.

"Now what?" J.B. demanded anxiously.

On the wall were six rectangular metal panels. Only two bore small, burnished plates beneath toggle switches. Mildred bent, peering at one of the plates. Aloud, she read, "Epsilon Subject, Female. Three Months. Phase Three."

She thumbed the toggle. The panel swung open on oiled pivots, and an oblong, transparent canister slid out upon a steel frame. Inside the tube, covered by a sheet of plastic, lay the skeletal remains of an infant.

"Dark night," J.B. breathed. "A baby."

"Yeah," Mildred replied sadly. "A baby born to serve a specific function in a world she never made."

She pushed the tube back, closed the panel and stepped to the next one. The ID plate read Alpha Subject, Male. 2.2 Years. Phase Three.

Flipping the toggle, the door popped open and another canister slid out. It contained nothing but air.

"This is what I was afraid of," Mildred said grimly. "He awakened."

"Who awakened?" J.B.'s tone mirrored her tension, though it was heavy with exasperation.

She pushed the canister back, slamming the panel shut. "Get everybody up. Things want us to talk about them."

Chapter Seven

Krysty and Ryan stepped out of the shower room just as J.B. and Mildred came swiftly down the corridor. Their postures telegraphed their anxiety to Ryan, and he snapped instantly to an alert mode.

"Strategy-session time," Mildred said.

"Why?"

"Get everybody together." Her dark, pretty face was set in tense lines. "I only want to tell this story once. That might be all we have time for."

It took a few minutes to rouse Dean, Jak and Doc. Yawning, they stumbled into the kitchen, knuckling sleep sand from their eyes, and took places around the table.

"I was having the most wonderful dream," Doc said wistfully. "I was at Charles Rector's restaurant on Broadway, just about to dig into a nine-course meal with Diamond Jim Brady—"

Mildred cut him off with a brusque gesture. "None of us are interested in your culinary fantasies about a nineteenth-century glutton, Doc. This is real and it's important."

Doc glared at her. "Then pray proceed, Dr. Wyeth."

The woman linked her fingers together on the tabletop. "At one time or another, I've bored all of you with my theories about the muties running rampant over the face of Deathlands.''

"Yeah," Jak said, trying to work the tangles out of his shock of white hair. "Radiation not account for different types. Muties too varied and too numerous. So?"

"So, my theories have been confirmed, at least up to a point. Though I can't be positive, I'm fairly sure Overproject Excalibur was a subdivision of the Totality Concept. The purpose of this installation was devoted not just to creating mutants, but to the birthing of the missing link, the biological bridge between predark and postdark man, a superhuman designed to thrive in the world created by the nuclear Armageddon.''

With that preamble, Mildred told her companions everything she had learned from Connaught O'Brien's recording. She soft-pedaled the hard science, placing her emphasis on the fact that the Alpha subject was more than likely alive and afoot, even after fifteen-plus years.

"It's a rad-blasted wasteland out there," Ryan argued. "Even a supermutie like Lord Kaa would have a problem surviving."

"A supermutie, maybe," Mildred responded, "but not a god."

Krysty swung her head sharply toward her. The weariness in her eyes was replaced by the bright gleam of a sudden fear. Her hair shifted, twisting and knotting. "A god?"

Mildred gazed at her keenly. "O'Brien might have been overstating his abilities a trifle, but she was a stiff-spined scientist, too. If she believed Hell Eyes could—''

"Hell Eyes?" Ryan repeated.

"A nickname for the Alpha subject, because of his red eyes."

"Gaia!" Krysty's exclamation came out in a gusty whisper. "That explains—" She bit off the rest of her words.

"Explains what?" J.B. demanded.

After exchanging a quick, furtive glance with Ryan, Krysty told her companions about the jump nightmare, saying she had suspected it was something else. Ryan related his own hallucinatory experiences.

Clearing his throat uncomfortably, Doc said, "I, too, underwent a brief waking dream. For a few minutes after making the transit, I thought I saw stone walls bearing Egyptian art."

"Lord Kaa, indeed," Mildred muttered.

All but Dean understood her oblique reference to the traumatic mind alteration they had suffered during a mat-trans jump that later resulted in their collision with the self-proclaimed mutant lord.

"That was some kind of glitch in the gateway system," Ryan said. "An accident. What me and Krysty went through was psionic, not mechanical."

"Still and all," Mildred said flatly, "Hell Eyes knows we're here, wherever he might be. With his psi-abilities, he sensed our arrival. For all we know, he might have planned it, since O'Brien claimed to have deactivated the gateway."

"Mebbe he turned it back on when he woke up," Dean suggested, "then jumped someplace else."

"Maybe," Mildred admitted. "But if we can believe O'Brien, Hell Eyes woke up at least fifteen years ago. Even if he made a few transits elsewhere, he'd return here."

"Why do you make that assertion?" Doc asked.

"O'Brien indicated that some sort of breeding instinct was bred into him. Like a salmon, he probably has the urge to return here, where he was spawned, to mate."

Krysty ducked her head.

Jak snorted derisively. "Not fish."

"No," Mildred replied. "Nor is he a human. Whatever he is, we need to distance ourselves from his sphere of influence. Let's not think that just because he's not here in front of us, he doesn't represent a threat."

Silence draped the room for a long, tense moment. Then Ryan asked, "Should I say it, or does somebody else want the honor?"

Dean cocked his head quizzically. "Say what, Dad?"

Ryan rose swiftly from the table. "Let's get the fuck out of here."

IT TOOK THE FRIENDS only a few minutes to collect their belongings and troop down the corridor to the mat-trans chamber. Dean had stowed a few of the sealed ration packs in his duffel, and Jak carried freshly filled canteens. Mildred ducked into the laboratory to retrieve the bottles of antibiotics. After a quick search, she also found a sealed package of disposable syringes. J.B. uneasily mentioned that they might want to visit the Medisterile unit before they went on their way.

"O'Brien made no reference to any infectious organisms,'' Mildred assured him. "I think we're safe. Besides, we've got the medicines, right?''

"Right,'' he replied, but his tone was dubious.

Inside the mat-trans unit, the seven people found places on the interlocking pattern of raised floor disks. Ryan stood by the door, waiting for his friends to position themselves before he pulled it shut to initiate the automatic jump mechanism.

"Ready?''

His party responded in affirmatives, and Ryan swung the door to. He quickly crossed the chamber and sat down between Dean and Krysty. He waited for the subsonic hum to begin, for the hexagonal disks to exude their familiar glow. He waited. And waited. And nothing happened.

Everyone's eyes darted back and forth, first in puzzlement, then in a growing fear. Ryan returned to the armaglass door, opened it and pulled it firmly shut. Nothing happened—no whine, no glow, no spark-shot mist.

He pushed open the door again, carefully inspecting the circuitry actuator on the lock, making certain full contact was achieved. He slammed it closed and stood silently in baffled anger.

With a sigh, Mildred pushed herself to her feet. "I think we get the idea. We can't leave this place by the gateway.''

"Thing worked before,'' J.B. grunted, moving to the door and shouldering it open. He examined the circuitry carefully, running his fingers over it. "Damned if I can find anything wrong.''

"Hell Eyes,'' Krysty said, a strange calm in her voice. "He's interfering with the machinery.''

Ryan turned toward her. Despite her tone of

placid acceptance, her eyes were green pools of dread. He felt that dread, too, and the vision of a crimson-eyed skull flashed into his mind. He fought it back.

"Hell Eyes, my ass," he rasped fiercely. "However the bastard was made, he's just another mutie."

Swinging the door wide, Ryan stamped out of the chamber. "It's probably daylight by now. Let's take a look-see outside."

He stalked through the anteroom, the control room, past the hatches and down the corridor in a fast, angry stride. Reaching the sec door before the others, he threw up the lever, his emotions making him reckless.

The door creaked and squeaked upward. Ryan fisted his SIG-Sauer, ready to trigger it at anything with legs, no matter how few or how many. A flood of brilliant sunlight all but blinded him.

Shielding his eye from the sun's assault, he stepped cautiously out of the recessed doorway. As his vision adjusted to the glare, he saw a dead land stretching away in drifting dunes of ocher and saffron. Judging by the position of the sun, he figured it was only a few hours after dawn. The air was already parched and hot.

The heat was deceptive, almost comfortable at first. Then Ryan began to sweat profusely, globes of perspiration springing to his brow and body. Within moments, he felt like a walking swamp.

His companions joined him, blinking and grimacing at the high temperature. Ryan turned around to study the exterior of the redoubt. It was a gray half dome, nearly buried on all sides by sand drifts.

"Where is this place?" Krysty asked.

J.B. took the compact sextant from the pocket of his coat. Pushing back the brim of his hat, he squinted into the eyepiece and took the necessary sighting. Then, from another pocket, he withdrew a crumpled chart and consulted it.

"Near as I can figure," he said, "we're in California, near Guadalupe, a town a good ways inland and about 150 miles north of what used to be Los Angeles."

"I thought California sank into the sea," Dean said.

"Most of it did," Ryan said. "At least, a lot of it to the south of the San Andreas Fault took a permanent dip. What was left became the Western Islands, remember?"

Dean nodded. "Yeah. Place stunk of sulfur, like rotten eggs. Place where we last saw Trader."

J.B. stowed the sextant and chart back into his coat. "If it's any consolation, we're not on one of those bastard islands. Best as I recollect, folks call this region the Barrens. Nothing and nobody around for a hundred square miles." He checked his lapel rad counter. "Midrange yellow. Tolerable."

Jak, his sensitive ruby eyes slitted against the bright blast of light, pointed to the northwest. "Something been out here. Look."

It took everyone a few seconds to discern what the teenager was pointing at. Two narrow, parallel grooves, nearly obscured by the breeze-driven sand, cut through the desert, disappearing into the distance and the heat shimmer.

"Wheels," Jak said.

"Yeah," Ryan agreed, eyeing the four-foot width

between the narrow tracks. "Wooden wheels, like a cart. Broad axle base, too."

"Not a gasoline-powered wag," J.B. observed. "No horse or mule tracks around, either."

Jak knelt, pinching a few grains of sand from one of the shallow gouges. "Week old. Mebbe ten days."

Doc said, "Then it appears the so-called Barrens are inhabited in some fashion. It also appears our only option is strike off on foot. It is a small comfort, but at least we have a semblance of a path to follow."

"Right, Doc," Ryan replied quietly. He glanced over his shoulder at the pale-faced Krysty. "That's what spooks me."

BACK INSIDE the redoubt, all of them reached the same conclusion without a protracted discussion. The supply of food was limited in the extreme, so they had no choice but to move out overland. Traveling by night was a necessity, and no one objected to staying in the climate-controlled redoubt until sundown. They used the time to catch up on missed sleep and to put together survival provisions for a boot-leather journey.

"We might be strolling into a trap," J.B. warned.

Ryan shrugged. "If the red-eyed bastard is as bright as Mildred says he is, then he'll know that we know. Traps can really only work when you're not ready for them."

"There is one possibility we have not considered," Doc said. "Alpha or Hell Eyes or whatever we care to call him might not mean us any harm."

Ryan smiled bitterly. "I considered that possibility. I don't find it very probable. Do you?"

After a moment's thought, Doc answered flatly, "No."

Ryan, even as agitated as he was, badly needed rest and he took to one of the bunks shortly after returning to the redoubt. Krysty lay down beside him. When the deep, steady rhythm of his breathing told her he was fast asleep, she got up and paced through the corridor.

She found Mildred in the laboratory, searching the medical stores. She looked up from deciphering a label on a bottle of tablets. "Krysty. What's wrong?"

The red-haired woman sat on a stool, propping her elbows on a table. Her tresses curled, straightened and curled again. "Am I that easy to read?"

Mildred smiled. "That unstable coiffure of yours is. Tell me about it."

Inhaling an unsteady breath, Krysty said, "You mentioned Lord Kaa earlier...his influence over us. Particularly me."

"Jak, too, remember."

"Something like it is happening again." Krysty's voice, low pitched, quavered. "I didn't tell you everything about my jump nightmare. Or what happened later between me and Ryan."

Krysty bluntly told Mildred of her vision of the red-eyed man, her feelings during it and of how her sexual desires had been aroused to a fever pitch while she slept the sleep of the utterly exhausted.

Mildred's eyebrows rose. "And you don't remember making love to Ryan?"

Smiling crookedly, Krysty answered, "It was like

I was in a trance, performing for someone. My capacity for passion, my inhibitions were being stimulated, tested. I think I passed.''

"As I recall, Lord Kaa invoked your mating instinct and your loyalty. How close are the two incidents?"

"Superficially similar. But with Kaa, it was the result of his psionic powers and the mat-trans mindmeld. After a jump, whatever spell he had over me was broken. In this case, the emotional resonances are much more sensual, more primitive. Lust, possessiveness and even maternal feelings are all mixed-up inside of me.''

Squeezing her eyes shut, then opening them again, Mildred groaned. "Sweet Christ. I should've guessed.''

"Guessed what?"

Mildred sighed. "Connaught O'Brien was both mother and lover to Alpha. Physically, you resemble her. Red hair, green eyes, though you're considerably younger.''

"I don't get you."

"Rudimentary psychology," Mildred replied. "The first protosexual feelings a male child experiences are often directed toward his mother. O'Brien played that role for Alpha, and later he influenced her to become his lover—though I doubt he had to go much out of his way to entice her. He's a god with very human failings, an Oedipus complex for one. I think he's transferred it to you. If the situation wasn't so serious, it'd be almost comical.''

"I don't see much humor in it. I'm afraid to go to sleep, afraid he'll try to make me perform again."

"I don't blame you. But if it's any consolation, I

imagine you can put up psychic shields against his influence. Besides, he's probably learned what he wanted to learn. Next time, though—''

Mildred realized what she was saying and didn't complete her thought. Krysty picked up the thread. ''Next time, though, it may be in the flesh.''

Smiling encouragingly, Mildred said, ''You were too strong for Kaa.''

''Barely. Alpha's influence operates on a different level entirely. Lust, love, protectiveness. I may not be able to withstand all of that.''

Mildred touched Krysty's hand, which felt cold and clammy. ''We'll all help you, when and if the time comes.''

Krysty's intense emerald gaze fixed on Mildred's dark eyes. ''That's the problem, isn't it? When and if the time comes, I might not want you to.''

Chapter Eight

The flat western horizon slowly swallowed the sun, painting the sky a lurid red and splashing the desert with purple pastels.

Ryan, Krysty, Dean, Jak, J.B., Doc and Mildred moved out of the redoubt. The silver-haired man used the ferrule of his ebony swordstick to punch in the three-digit code on the keypad. The massive slab of vanadium steel slowly squealed down, the bottom edge joining the floor with a dull boom.

The redoubt had been stripped of everything useful that could be carried. Besides the dozen jugs of water distributed among the seven friends, they also packed bed linens to serve double duty as tents and makeshift burnooses, if need be.

Ryan followed the wheel trace cutting across the desert floor, and the others followed him. He didn't speak. Once again, he and his friends were embarking on another nightmare passage, another long march into the unknown, into the domain of another megalomaniac.

He accepted that Deathlands seemed to breed them, and he had collided with a lot of them in his time. The names were legion, and it was difficult to keep track of them all. Hell Eyes, whoever he was, was just the latest entry in a long line. Ryan had once toyed with the notion that he and his companions had been dispatched by some all-powerful force to scour the rad-blasted shockscape and impose some kind of order on chaos, a last gasp of freedom against tyranny.

The concept had both amused and repulsed him. He was too pragmatic to truly believe he and his people were pawns in a war between Light and Darkness. Yet, not even he could deny that he and his group seemed to lead exceptionally charmed lives. Still, he knew their string of good fortune couldn't last forever. He had made too many enemies among too many powerful barons, brought too much hell in his wake.

One day, if the baronies managed to put aside their territorial squabbles and unite, he and people like him would be hunted down like criminals. Poseidon had hinted that such overtures to unification were already under way in some places.

Ryan swallowed a weary sigh. The lush valley of Ti-Ra'-Wa seemed farther away than ever.

In the short span of time between the setting of the sun and rise of the moon, the desert became shrouded in more than dark. It was pitch-black, and J.B. unlimbered a small flashlight so they wouldn't lose the trail.

Mildred stumbled over an irregularity in the ground and would have fallen if Dean hadn't caught her. She smiled wryly and said, "I thought desert nights were supposed to be clear."

Dean wiped at the sheen of perspiration on his face. "Yeah, well, they're supposed to be cool, too. This one is almost as hot as the day."

By the time a half moon had risen, providing enough illumination so J.B. could turn off the flashlight, they had trudged over three miles. Krysty, snatching a backward glance, could see no hint of the half dome of the redoubt rearing out of the sands.

Though the sandy soil was hard packed, they occasionally crossed areas where it was loose and their feet bogged down in it. Fortunately, except for a few shallow dunes and drifts, the terrain was board flat.

After three hours, Ryan called a halt so they could rest and drink. They sat down and passed around a jug of water, drinking sparingly.

"Was this place so desolate before the nuke-caust?" Krysty asked, handing the container to Doc.

"Pretty near," Mildred answered. "Believe it or not, this area was popular with Hollywood movie-makers."

"Why?" Jak inquired.

"It could double for anyplace—the Old West, alien planets, even countries in the Mideast."

Doc gulped down his ration of water and made an exaggerated show of examining their surroundings and finding them wanting. "I see very little that would stimulate the imagination or hold much in the way of entertainment value."

Ryan, who had been silent since calling the halt, suddenly chuckled.

"What's so funny, Dad?" Dean asked.

The one-eyed man gestured to the vast sweep of sand all around them. "A couple of days ago, we were surrounded by more water than I ever wanted to see. I remember saying to myself that if I ever got back to dry land, the only body of water I'd ever go near again would be a bathtub. Now this."

J.B. drawled, "Well, if we wanted to turn south, we'd come to the Cific by and by. According to my old chart, it's about eighty or so miles away. Mebbe closer now.''

Ryan shook his head. "This is just like Trader used to say…'Be careful what you wish for, 'cause you'll be bastard sorry when you finally get it.'''

"A version of that bromide was popular in my time," Mildred remarked. "We used to call clichés like that 'bumper-sticker philosophy.'''

Jak frowned at her. "What that?"

"Before skydark, almost everybody in America owned cars. Companies used to manufacture little adhesive signs with the silly slogans of the day printed on them, and people would stick them on the bumpers of their cars. Things like Keep On Truckin, or Beam Me Up, Scotty, There's No Sign Of Intelligent Life On This Planet—"

Seeing the perplexed expressions on the faces of her friends, Mildred added, "I guess you had to be there."

"I remember seeing one," Dean piped up. "Back in a Newyork salvage yard. It said Honk If You're Horny."

J.B. frowned. "Don't recollect Trader saying anything like that."

Doc brayed out a laugh. "I submit that was a good thing. He was already unpopular enough."

Ryan got to his feet. "Time to move. No matter where we're headed, we need to find some kind of shelter before the sun rises."

The march resumed. Eventually, the temperature dropped just enough to make the air comfortably cool. As the hours wore on, the endless ocean of sand began to sprout sparse signs of life. Sagebrush, cactus and ocotilla shrubs grew from the desert floor in thin silhouettes of shadow.

At one point, they spotted a peculiar humped hillock a dozen yards to their right. Ryan and Jak noted how the wheel tracks veered sharply away from it, then resumed their northwesterly direction. They followed the slight detour without question.

J.B. continued to eye the long bump in the flat expanse. Lowly, he asked, "You remember that giant sand spider back in White Sands?"

"Too damn well," Ryan answered.

All of them increased the length and speed of their stride for the next eighth of a mile. They managed to maintain the sprightly pace for another hour. After rising from a midnight rest break, the seven companions moved slower. Dean noticed Doc was lagging behind, and he dropped back to offer him an arm.

Doc waved him away, but acknowledged the boy's concern with an appreciative smile. "No need, young gentleman. I'm merely conserving my strength in case it is needed for running."

"Not much to run from—or to—around here, Doc."

"That's one of the truly invigorating elements about following your father—the situation could change at any moment."

Dean laughed, his deep blue eyes flashing in merriment. "I really missed all of you when I was in school. I didn't miss all the running, though."

The smile fled Doc's lips. "Our portion, I fear. The lot of the survivor, to run from one broken dream to another."

Ryan called back over his shoulder. "Pick up the pace back there."

"See what I mean?" Doc asked.

For the next couple of hours, nobody talked much. Silence lay upon the arid vista of emptiness with a crushing hand. Then, from far off, came a sound, a faint, moaning wail. Jak jogged forward to join Ryan. He sniffed the air. Ryan glanced at the albino teenager, feeling worry grow within him.

"Storm coming," Jak said. He pointed northward. "That way."

Ryan sighed, his worst fear realized. "How long?"

"Hour, mebbe. More, mebbe. Less, mebbe."

Ryan ground his teeth. He had been caught in desert storms before. The lingering effects of sky-dark still made the weather not only unpredictable, but vicious. Some peculiar geothermals in Deathlands attracted such bizarre weather as 250-mile-per-hour dust storms. Regardless, he knew that when a storm wind howled across the desert, the only thing to do was to keep moving. If you didn't, you were dead and buried in minutes.

He announced a halt and directed his companions to drape themselves in the bed linens and told them to use belts and straps to keep themselves connected to one another.

"We'll lose the trail when the wind hits," Krysty said.

J.B. nodded tersely. "Yeah. But so far, it's been heading northwest. We'll just keep on moving in that direction."

After everyone was attired in the makeshift robes, they got under way. This time, Doc kept up with

the others. Inside of the hour, the distant moan built
to a dry, shrieking wail that filled the whole sky.
They saw the first tiny dust whirls, lifting and dancing across the terrain.

They moved in an erratic, jerking pattern, gath-
ering strength from one another. The swirls merged,
then the wind screamed, rising in pitch. Without
warning, the storm struck them broadside, blinding
the sky with dust, tearing at everything in its path
with a clawing fury. Ryan covered his lower face
with a scrap of sheet and turned toward Krysty,
making sure she held on to her end of the belt in
his hand. She was only a few feet away, but almost
obscured by the veil of mingled sand and dust.

The wind roared around them, setting their sheets
to flapping like the wings of giant, ungainly birds.
At the top of his voice, Ryan roared, "Keep moving!" He doubted if anyone heard him.

The storm slapped at them, pushed them as they
staggered and stumbled. Wind-driven grains of sand
scoured the exposed part of their bodies like a fiery
lash. Blinded, half-deafened and half-suffocated,
they fought their way onward, struggling to gain a
foot, then a yard. No sight of anything was possible
in the swirling, howling inferno. The sand underfoot
rolled like water, and it was all Ryan could do to
maintain his balance. The ache of his bruises, which
had faded somewhat over the past few hours, returned with a vengeance. His muscles throbbed, and
he was afraid if he so much as paused, they would
seize altogether.

They kept walking as if through a nightmare.
Ryan focused on a single necessity: to survive, they
had to keep moving. So they plodded onward, linked

together, ears filled with the shriek of the wind, eyes slitted but seeing nothing but a never ending curtain of grit. His feet dragged, and he kept himself from falling only by a savage effort of will.

Ryan's head began to flash visions of the snow-capped mountains and clear, rushing streams of Ti-Ra'-Wa. Krysty lurched into his back, and he reached behind him to give her hand a reassuring squeeze.

His body lost all feeling, numb to every sensation except putting one foot in front of the other. One minute, he was sure the wind was dropping; the next, it seemed to increase his ferocity.

After an eternity, he fancied the storm was crying his name. He paid no attention, shambling and reeling forward. A heavy weight dragged against the belt wrapped around his wrist, yanking him backward. He turned blindly to help Krysty up from where he was sure she had fallen. Then he realized it wasn't the wind calling his name, but Krysty.

He pawed the sheet from his face and gingerly inhaled a deep breath. The air was clear and tranquil. The wind had dropped, and the air around him was no longer clogged with dust and sand.

"It's over," Krysty said hoarsely.

Squinting through his stinging eye, Ryan made a quick head count. All six of his people were there, swaying on weary legs.

"What do you know?" he croaked. His tongue felt like a strip of shriveled, ancient leather. "We didn't die."

Doc coughed rackingly and sank to the ground. "I am gratified you made that observation. Up until this moment, I was not sure."

All of them followed Doc's example, dropping in their tracks. They quenched their thirsts and rinsed out their gritty mouths with water. J.B. fumbled in his coat pocket and brought out his compass.

"We didn't stray too far off course," he announced. "What now?"

Ryan eyed the position of the moon. "Only a couple of hours until daybreak. We rest for half an hour, then start moving again."

Dean scrubbed sand from his hair. "Do we have to, Dad? I'm beat."

"If we stay here, we roast by midday."

Everyone was too tired and thirsty to talk during the half hour. When it elapsed, the seven companions slowly climbed to their feet.

Krysty pressed herself briefly against Ryan, lips brushing his, but it was a painful kiss, for their lips were dry and raw from the terrible chafing of the wind.

"We'll get through this, lover," she whispered. "Been through worse."

"Yeah," he replied, cupping her cheek in one hand. "Shining times await."

Wind-drifted sand glimmered in long ripples, as if a sea had been suddenly frozen and turned to powder. The moon grew red and menacing as it sank. Before they had covered two miles, the first glintings of dawn peeped over the horizon. Within four miles, the sun topped the edge of the world and drove away the cool of the night. Inside of six miles, the air was heavy with radiating waves of sheer, hellish heat. The desert hardpan seemed to soak it up and reflect it back. There was no shelter in sight from the rising inferno.

Jak and Krysty were fair-skinned and suffered the worst. They bundled themselves in the linens, leaving only their eyes uncovered. They quickly soaked the sheets through with perspiration.

"Omnia sol temperat, purus et subtilis," Doc muttered.

"That's Latin," Dean said. "What's it mean?"

"'The sun, pure and clear, tempers everything.'"

They slogged on through the sand. Cacti of twisted, distorted shapes grew nearby, but no trees, not even a decent-sized bush. The terrain inclined slightly, and Ryan, his mind clouded by fatigue, was only dimly aware of climbing. His feet slipped on a lip of sand, and he went rolling down a smooth slope.

Struggling to his hands and knees, Ryan looked up and thought he spotted their salvation. Beneath a shading hand, he squinted through the haze of the skyline at a collection of structures. They looked far away, blurred by the heat shimmer. Distance in the desert couldn't be measured by the eye alone, but he was certain the buildings were closer than they appeared. Or they could be mirages, fabricated by his brain slowly boiling away in the pressure cooker of his skull. Even so, the sight of the structures galvanized him, raised him quickly to his feet.

Looking back behind him as his companions topped the low dune, he called, "Jak! Do your eyes still work?"

"Halfway," came the albino's dour response. "Why?"

Ryan gestured. "What do you see out there?"

Jak cupped both hands around his eyes, protecting them from the dazzle. He stared. At length, he declared, "Shade."

Chapter Nine

The settlement, if it could be called that, looked like the rough sketch of a shanty town someone intended to build one day.

Two dozen shelters made of splintering wooden siding and rotted canvas formed a horseshoe shape around a spacious central area. At the apex of the horseshoe, several of the ramshackle structures converged, leaning into one another. The suggestion of a stockade fence was barely identifiable in the drifts. Nothing stirred in and around the structures except wind-driven swirls of sand.

On the far side of the settlement, down a short embankment, a thin stream of water trickled, curving around the farthermost outbuilding. A line of gray peaks could just be made out on the distant horizon—mountains or clouds. If they were mountains, it could only be the foothills of the Sierra Madre range. Or it could be a new range, birthed by the Russian earthshaker bombs that had resculpted much of the West Coast.

The seven companions cautiously approached the perimeter of the settlement, not that one was clearly defined. A square wooden sign hung crookedly on a tall post. The words painted on it were nearly indecipherable due to long exposure to the harsh elements, but Mildred was able to read it.

"Fort Fubar," she said. "Members Of Kiwanis And Rotary Clubs. Population Who Gives A Shit."

Her teeth flashed in a grin. "Whoever lived here had a sense of humor, at least."

"Fubar?" Dean repeated. "What kind of word is that?"

"Old acronym, dating back to World War II," she answered. "Fucked Up Beyond All Repair."

Everyone was too hot and tired to expend much energy on laughing. The sun was higher, and the heat increased with every passing minute. Under other circumstances, one or two of their party would enter the potential killzone for a recce. There was no time for that now. Sunstroke was a very real possibility, particularly for Jak.

Drawing his SIG-Sauer, Ryan cycled a round into the chamber. He was dismayed by the gritty, grating sound made by the slide mechanism. All of their blasters needed to be stripped and cleaned of sand before they were one hundred percent reliable again.

"Lock and load," he said lowly. "Move in fast and quiet."

The seven people fanned out in a V formation, Ryan taking the point of the wedge. They crept into the perimeter of the settlement, alert for any movement or sound. All they heard was the eerie hum of the wind, singing through the grains of sand.

The stillness was uncanny. Ryan repressed a shiver, despite the blazing heat, feeling the hairs on his arms and neck stir uneasily. It seemed to him that a silent host of invisible watchers regarded them curiously.

Glancing over at Krysty, he mouthed, "Anything?"

Her sun-reddened face was troubled, her green eyes darting back and forth. Although her head was swathed in a linen fold, Ryan saw the shifting motions of her hair beneath it.

"Yes," she whispered. "Not danger to us, exactly. Fear. Curiosity. Someone lives here."

He peered at the ground for some sign and saw nothing. "Search the houses. Stay on triple red."

They spread out over the settlement, peering into shacks, checking outbuildings, no matter how small or ramshackle. Quite a few people had lived here at one time, but they had disappeared. All the structures were empty. The population of Fort Fubar was simply gone, all their tools and belongings and cooking utensils left where they had last been used, as if the people had only stepped away for a second and intended to return in the next second. Moreover, it appeared as if the people had vanished a long time ago, and any clues to their whereabouts had been erased by the merciless passage of years. Several of the huts and squats were strewed with rubbish, as though a single someone had lived in them until they were so full of trash he or she was forced to move on.

One of the buildings was larger than the others, which wasn't saying much. Its long-ago construction crew had tried to make it two-storied and called it quits after propping up a sagging loft-type contrivance with crudely hewed square beams. Ryan pushed aside the square of canvas hanging in front of the doorway and made a quick visual circuit of the interior.

It had been designed as a storage facility. Crates, boxes and dirty cloth bundles were stacked to the ceiling. The loft was weighted down with cartons and junk of all sorts. Ryan stepped in, his nose leading his eye to a covered galvanized bucket in a corner. He didn't have to lift the lid to check its contents. The stale air was redolent with the acrid odor of urine and excrement. On a makeshift table, he found a fat candle in a saucer. The melted wax collected at its base was fairly soft. An opened can of tuna lay on the ground. The little remaining in it didn't smell ripe.

Ryan back-stepped out of the building and gestured for the others to join him. When they were clustered around him, he whispered, ''Somebody's living in here. J.B., you, Krysty and Jak come with me.''

They entered the building, and Ryan approached the loft. A ladder made of hammered-together two-by-fours stretched from the ground to a dark opening. Motioning for the others to remain where they stood, Ryan put his foot on the first rung. The old, dry-rotted wood broke beneath his weight with a crack that sounded unnaturally loud. That sound was instantly followed by another—a terrible masculine scream of utter wordless fury erupting from above.

A dark, ragged shape plummeted from the opening in the underside of the loft, all flailing limbs and screaming sound. The scream ended abruptly as if a volume-control knob had been turned down. The sound replacing it was a shrieked, ''Get on out of here, you hairy sons of whores!''

He was a wiry, craggy man, incredibly grimed and browned. His mouth worked in a snag-toothed snarl beneath bewhiskered lips. A foot-long sharpened shard of metal was gripped in his right hand, with strips of cloth wrapped around the handle.

Though shock and surprise had rooted everyone to the ground, the man was moving. He made a clumsy, stabbing motion, but Ryan was faster, blocking the thrust with his left forearm and knocking the knife from the man's hand with a slashing swipe of his blaster.

Jak and Krysty lunged forward, pistols questing for a clear target, even as the two men grappled. Ryan didn't use his fists on the man, and he resisted the instinct to shoot him dead. He seized the man by the frayed collar of his ragged coverall and pivoted deftly. The man flipped over Ryan's outthrust hip and slammed full-length to the floor. A cloud of dust mushroomed up around his body. He lay groaning and gasping, trying to regain the wind the impact with the ground had driven out of him.

Ryan kneeled beside him, quickly joined by J.B., Krysty and Jak. "Who else is with you?" he snapped, prodding the deeply rutted forehead with the bore of the SIG-Sauer.

The man had no breath to answer, but he shook his head vigorously, flinging fine particles of dust from his salt-and-pepper hair.

"Get the others inside," Ryan said to Krysty. "The place isn't much, but at least it's out of the sun."

By the time Mildred, Dean and Doc had entered the storage building, the man had regained enough air to talk. His gray eyes passed over everyone, then fastened on Ryan. His gaze became fierce, and he reached up, one hand closing tightly over Ryan's forearm. His mouth worked. "Cawdor? You come to take me back?"

Ryan stared at the man for a numb, silent second.

The gray eyes shifted to J.B. "Dix? Is Trader with you?"

Ryan and J.B. exchanged blank glances. "Who are you?" the one-eyed man demanded.

Leathery, bristled lips peeled back over rotten stumps of teeth. "Don't recognize me. Been a long time. A long time, yeah."

"What's your name?" J.B. asked.

"Danielson. Gunner. War Wag One."

The name was only vaguely familiar to Ryan. He dredged his memory for a face to put to it. J.B. made the connection before he did.

"Dark night!" he exclaimed. "Danielson!" He turned toward Ryan. "Remember? Trader gave him the boot for holding out on some stuff from a stockpile we found around Detroit."

Danielson husked out a raspy laugh. "Yeah. Old field telephones. Weren't worth a crap to anybody. Obsolete before the nuke, even. Trader threw me out, anyhow."

Ryan strained at his memory and came up with nothing, but he accepted J.B.'s words at face value. Trader had only a few rules, but he strictly enforced them. If Danielson had been kicked out of the organization for violating one of them, he was only one of dozens over a period of many years.

"How long ago was that?" Ryan asked.

"Long time, like I said. Seventeen, eighteen, mebbe nineteen years. I'm no clock-watcher. What are you doing here in the Barrens?"

"We might ask you the same thing," J.B. retorted.

Danielson grunted. "Can I sit up?"

Ryan trained the blaster on him. "Do it slow."

Groaning, the man hitched himself up on his elbows, then onto his backside. He looked past J.B. and Ryan to the rest of the group.

"Don't see Trader," he said. "Where is the hard-assed son of a bitch?"

Ryan ignored the question, asking one of his own. "You live alone here?"

Danielson nodded. "Yep. Last citizen of Fort Fubar. The only Farer town in the Barrens, if that means anything."

"Don't," Jak grated.

Farers were a loosely knit but far-flung conglomeration of nomads who traveled Deathlands trading goods, tech and even themselves to villes. However, Farer territory was usually confined to the Midwest.

"You're a long way from your stomping grounds," J.B. said. "Where's everybody else?"

Danielson sucked in shuddery breath. "Taken."

"Taken where?" Krysty asked.

"The First Kingdom."

"Talk sense," Ryan growled.

"The city of Aten." Danielson's tone was matter-of-fact. "I lived there, too. For a long time. I was a trusted member of Pharaoh's court. But after Connie died, things changed. I wanted out. I came back here."

J.B. gave Mildred a baffled look. "You have any idea of what he's rambling on about?"

"Yes," she said tersely. "Let him talk."

"I escaped Pharaoh's power, you see." Danielson

tugged open the front of his coverall. Hanging from his weathered neck by a loop of rawhide was an amulet the size of a man's hand. Made of a dull, nonreflective metal, it was shaped like a cross with the traverse arms squared and the top rounded.

"An ankh," Doc spoke up.

"Yeah," Danielson replied. "Keeps Pharaoh's mind out of mine. Not that he noticed he couldn't get in there anymore. Guess even a god-king's heart can break. They left me alone out here. Lately, though, the Incarnates started nosing around, like they were hunting for something. Or somebody."

"You, mebbe?" J.B. asked.

Jak suddenly stiffened. "Hear noise."

The others waited tensely, expectantly, as the teenager turned his head to the right and to the left, like a hound casting for a scent.

"Not sure what it is," he stated. "Coming closer."

Ryan arose and went to the doorway. Pushing aside the hanging, he looked up and down the sand-swept avenue between the shacks. The dry air vibrated with a low-pitched hum, like a distant swarm of bees, undercut by a steady mechanical clicking. The others peered through the cracks and chinks in the wall boards.

Two shapes hove into view from the far end of Fort Fubar. Ryan stared, screwed up his eye and stared some more. Almost unconsciously, he muttered, "What the hell."

A pair of two-wheeled vehicles rolled from the direction of the desert, but they didn't resemble in configuration or form other wags he had ever seen. Boxlike wooden chassis were overlaid with intricately worked borders of brass, copper and bronze. The vehicles were two yards long, shaped roughly like upside down, elongated U's. They sat on low-slung platforms atop heavy axles, positioned between two very large spoked wheels. The wheels were of some dark wood and rimmed with metal. No power source was visible, though sunlight flashed dazzlingly from a reflective surface at the rear of the platforms. They looked like carts, but they obviously had some artificial source of power.

"By the Three Kennedys," Doc muttered, gazing over Ryan's shoulder. "Horseless chariots."

Ryan realized Doc's description was fairly accurate. He had seen pix in books of those ancient modes of wheeled transportation. The absence of harnessed horses or other beasts of burden had confused him.

As the chariots hummed and clicked closer, Ryan saw that each one carried three man-figures and none of the six looked human at first, or even second glance. Muties, was his first thought. A moment later, he was forced to reassess his snap judgment.

"Gaia!" Krysty breathed in a trembling tone. "What are those things?"

Each of the six men in the chariots was similar in build and clothing. They were naked except for loosely woven white linen kilts. Glittering collars of beaten gold rested on their broad shoulders and enclosed the bases of their necks. All of them were dark skinned, deeply tanned by long exposure to the merciless desert sun. In height and breadth, they looked enormous, with heavily muscled arms and legs. Each one held a long, slender silver rod, tipped by V shaped prongs.

Only their heads differentiated them from one another. The men wore jeweled helmetlike headpieces, which were secured snugly beneath their jaws by an interlocking arrangement of leather straps.

One man wore the stylized image of a dog's head, with pricked up ears and a canine snout. Another headpiece resembled the horned skull of a bull, another a ram and yet another a scaled, blunt-nosed serpent. A beaked face represented a hawk; another helmet looked like the head of a crane or a stork.

In a voice hushed with awe, Doc whispered, "The major deities of ancient Egypt—Anubis, Serapis, Khnum, Set, Horus and Thoth."

"Stupes in costume," Jak growled.

Quietly, Danielson said, "They are the Incarnates."

"What are they doing here?" Krysty asked fearfully.

Danielson smiled a sad, almost pitying smile. "Looking for you, I imagine."

Chapter Ten

The chariots rolled and clicked to simultaneous halts in the center of the compound. The humming noise ceased abruptly. As the big, helmeted men disembarked, Ryan noticed how they carefully stepped over or around some object at the rear of the vehicles. Their gait was an arrogant, self-confident swagger. High-strapped sandals encased their feet and muscular calves.

"Osorkon!" Jackal-headed Anubis roared. "Where are you, you demented old prick?"

"Who's Osorkon?" Dean asked.

"Me," Danielson answered. "My Aten name."

Danielson shuffled toward the doorway, but Mildred restrained him with a hand. "What do you mean they're looking for us?" she demanded.

"They probably seen your tracks," the man replied calmly.

"And if you're asked about us, you'll simply point us out to them?" Doc inquired.

Danielson blinked owlishly, as if the question contained a hidden meaning. "Sure. They're the Incarnates. You don't lie to them."

"Osorkon!" Anubis bellowed peevishly.

"What do they want us for?" Dean asked.

"To bring you to Pharaoh." Seeing several sets of eyes glare at him suspiciously, he added, "They probably have need of you in the work gangs. You won't be hurt...'less you take the notion into your heads to resist.''

"Funny thing," Ryan said grimly, stripping off the sheet. "That's exactly the notion I've taken into my head.''

Jak hefted his Colt Python. "Take out. Not armed, except for frog giggers.''

Danielson's face paled under its layer of grime. "Not armed? Boy, they've got metauh rods! They'll drop you like fried flounders!''

"Osorkon! Get out here or we'll burn this shit-heap down!'' The deep voice throbbed with an unmistakable note of menace.

Grimacing, Ryan made a move to fling aside the door flap. J.B. stepped forward. "Hold a sec. I got an idea.''

"I am delighted that somebody does," Doc muttered.

ANUBIS, SERAPIS, SET, Thoth, Khnum and Horus all turned at the rustle of coarse cloth. From beneath their helmets, they stared imperiously at the two men shuffling out of the storage shanty. They ignored the ragged figure of Danielson and focused their attention on the slightly built, sallow-faced man timidly edging out into the hot blast of sunlight. His thin, mousy hair was uncombed, his clothes shabby, and he gaped goggle-eyed from behind the lenses of round, steel-framed spectacles. In the kingdom of the nondescript, this little gnome was the heir apparent to the throne.

Anubis pointed to him with the metauh rod. "Who's this feeb, Osorkon?''

Ducking his head respectfully, Danielson said, "He arrived here from across the Barrens, O mighty incarnation of the guardian of the underworld."

Hawk-headed Horus demanded shrilly, "What's your name, feeb?"

"Name's Dix," J.B. replied meekly. "Lost my way from a trading party. Wandered for days. Ended up here."

"Who else was with you, Dix?" ram-horned Khnum growled.

J.B. shook his head dolefully. "Couple more. They died in the desert."

"We found the tracks of at least five people," Thoth declared, the long, curving bird beak casting a goateelike shadow on the human chin beneath it. "Maybe more."

"Don't know nothin' about that. Mebbe you miscalculated. Terrible fierce storm last night. Mebbe messed up the ground."

"We know all about the storm, pissant," Set hissed. "Osorkon, was there a red-haired woman with him?"

Danielson fidgeted for a hot, silent moment, shifting his weight from one foot to the other.

"Answer us, you old fool," Serapis ordered. "Who else was with him?"

Before the old man opened his mouth to answer, a deep, flat voice announced, "Me."

The Incarnates pivoted on their heels. A big, scarfaced man with a black patch over his left eye stepped from a narrow alley between two shacks. The autoblaster in his fist was as rock steady as his voice.

"And me," another voice said. A slender figure

emerged from behind another shack, his body swathed in white linen folds. Intense ruby red eyes stared out from an unnaturally pale face. The satin finish of the six-inch-long barrel of his revolver reflected the sun in dancing pinpoints.

"Me, too," another voice added, this one with a husky yet undeniably feminine lilt to it. A sturdily built dark-skinned woman sidled into view, a long-barreled pistol held in a two-fisted grip.

"And last—and perhaps the least, though that is purely subjective—is my humble self." A skinny, silver-haired scarecrow of a man stepped into the street, the hollow bores of his double-barreled blaster fixed on them like hollow, dead eyes.

J.B. made a casual move as if to adjust his clothing, and an Uzi connected to his neck by a lanyard appeared in his right hand.

The Incarnates were surrounded, outflanked by unwavering blaster barrels. They stared in disbelief, in something more than disbelief. They were shocked into speechless immobility.

J.B. indulged in a low, laconic chuckle of self-congratulation. His hurriedly concocted plan to divert the helmeted men while his friends went out the back of the storage building and took up positions around them had been accomplished very smoothly. Knowing that Krysty's Smith & Wesson and Dean's Browning Hi-Power were trained on the so-called Incarnates from inside the building made him feel even better.

"This isn't necessary," Horus squawked. "We mean you no harm."

"Right," Jak said, his single word heavy with irony.

"You're sec men," Ryan stated. "Sec men for Hell Eyes."

All six of the Incarnates visibly flinched at the last two words.

"Heresy," Khnum bleated. "We are the servants in the city of truth, sworn to serve the First Kingdom and the glorious dynasty of Akhnaton."

"A glorious dynasty," Horus interjected, "you are invited to play a part in its destiny."

"Not a very significant part, of course," Anubis said, "but it's far better than being left out of it altogether."

Ryan wasn't sure if the dog-headed man was serious or trying to defuse the situation with sarcasm. Nor did he much care at the moment. "Take off those helmets," he said sharply. "Drop your giggers."

The Incarnates didn't move. Anubis said, very matter-of-factly, "That we will not do. You will put up your arms and come with us. You will not be harmed. My word of honor on it."

The arrogant, self-confident tone sent prickles of anger rushing through Ryan. "Do what I say, or I'll chill you where you stand. My word of honor on it."

The V of the slim rod in Khnum's hand shifted slightly. Ryan blinked as a puff of wind tossed a pinch of grit into his face. In the tiny tick of time before and after the blink, Ryan's eye registered a flash of light, like an errant reflection of the sun.

The shock of the blow, which wasn't just a physical impact, picked him up, flung him back and bowled him over. He fell as limp and cold as a corpse to the sandy ground.

Before his body had fully settled, the air shivered with a scream of rage from Krysty, followed a shaved fraction of an instant later by the ear-knocking report of her handblaster.

The .38-caliber round fanned cool air on the right side of J.B.'s face as it drove from the doorway behind him and struck Khnum in the center of his bare back. The ram-headed man flailed forward, as if he had just received a kick, a small, blue-rimmed hole sprouting in the hollow of his spine. The bullet exited just above his pelvis in a splattering welter of scarlet liquid ribbons and blue-pink intestinal tissue.

The metauh shafts in the hands of the Incarnates flicked back and forth, spitting little white flares of light. Doc twisted his lean body in a painful contortion as a thread of miniature lightning passed very close by him. He squeezed the trigger of his Le Mat, and a clump of deadly 18-gauge grapeshot ripped into the flat-muscled abdomen of Set. His lower torso flew apart in a greasy explosion of blood and bowels. The snake-headed man went over backward, bent double, voicing a very unreptilian howl of agony. The silver rod spun from his hand.

J.B. depressed the trigger of his Uzi, but nothing happened. He instantly realized that sand had worked its way into the blaster, fouling the trigger and firing pin. The double prongs of a metauh rod swept toward him. What saved him from ending up like Ryan was a wild jostle from Danielson, who waved his arms and shrieked, "No! Stop this!"

At the same second, Krysty and Dean bolted from the doorway of the building, pushing Danielson out of their path. Light flashed, but the energy bolt cleaved nothing but air.

J.B. tucked and rolled across the ground, snatching up Set's fallen rod. He raised it hastily, surprised by its light weight. He sighted down it, framing Anubis between the V tip. As with the Uzi, nothing happened.

Serapis began a charging run toward the nearest chariot, yelling wordlessly in panic. Jak, Mildred, Krysty and Dean all fired at him more or less simultaneously, the combined gunshots making an extended thunderclap of noise. Four rounds of different grains and calibers struck Serapis in the chest, in the ribs, in the hip and the side of his helmeted head. The horn on the right side sheared away as he staggered and jerked from the multiple impacts. He twisted this way and that before crashing headlong to the ground.

The pair of bird-headed Incarnates, Horus and Thoth, screeched and swept their rods in left-to-right arcs. Krysty and Dean lunged in opposite directions, each squeezing off a shot as they did so, and missing with both.

A nimbus of wavery blue sprang from Danielson's chest. He husked out a loud ''Ah!'' before careening backward, fetching up against the splintery wall of the storage building and sliding down it to the ground.

Sighting down the barrel of her ZKR target revolver, Mildred triggered a shot at Thoth. A splash of blood bloomed on the back of his right hand, and the silver shaft dropped from suddenly nerve-dead fingers.

The crane-head pivoted toward her, the human

mouth beneath the long beak opening to utter a shriek of pain and anger. Krysty shot him through the heart. Arms flung wide like a pair of featherless wings, he lifted up on his toes and fell face first to the sand, a banner of blood trailing from the hole in his left pectoral. The long beak of his helmet dug into the ground, propping up his head and neck at a grotesque angle. Immediately after, five blaster barrels trained on Horus.

"Enough!" Anubis's maddened yell rolled and echoed through the air. "No more or he dies!"

The jackal-headed man stood over Ryan's prostrate form, one sandaled foot on his chest, the prongs of his rod touching the hollow of his throat, as if he were planting a victory flag.

The five fingers tensed on five triggers, the blaster bores dropping slightly. The broad shoulders of Horus sagged briefly in relief, then straightened. He gestured with his silver rod. "Drop your weapons, or my brother will send this heretic into the care of the *ushabti*."

The jeweled hawk eyes turned toward Krysty. "You—red-haired woman. You are the guest of Pharaoh and will be treated as such."

No one moved. The scene in the blood-spattered, corpse-littered street froze like a three-dimensional diorama. The steady, unremitting blaze of the sun added to the dreamy, unreal quality of the tableau.

"Did you not understand?" Anubis snarled, digging the prongs into Ryan's neck.

"I understand perfectly," Ryan said. Then he shot the jackal-headed man three times between the legs.

Anubis howled, releasing his metauh rod so he

could clasp at the tatters of his testicle sac. Blood from the bullet-severed femoral artery squirted out in a long stream between his clutching fingers.

While the arid air still vibrated with the sound of the triggered rounds and Anubis's agonized scream, Jak, Krysty, Dean and Mildred all fired in perfect synchronization at Horus. The hawk head flew away in fragments, the bullets tearing through neck ligaments, cartilage and cervical vertebrae. The human face dissolved in a wet, red blur. By the time he fell sideways, there was nothing identifiable remaining of either the hawk or human head.

Ryan struggled to rise, but he only shambled to one knee. His face was covered with sweat, his lungs felt shriveled and he labored for breath. Although his vision was shot through with swimming gray spots, he saw the death convulsions of Anubis. Blood gushed from the wounds in his groin as he lay on his side, cutting a crimson runnel through the sand beneath him. As he watched, the jackal-headed man's struggles to cling to life ceased, and he jerked in postmortem spasms.

Then the medley of his friends' voices filled his ears, and hands pulled him to his feet. Krysty fought back sobs, clinging to him. Ryan's face was pale and drawn, glistening with perspiration.

"I'm all right," he said, stroking her hair with trembling fingers. He reached out for Dean, who took and placed his hand on his shoulder for support.

They led Ryan to a wedge of shadow and lowered him into a sitting position. Jak offered him a jug of water, and he drank from it long and gratefully. J.B.

scowled at the metauh rod in his hands, revolving it between them.

"What kind of crazy bastard weapons are these?" he demanded. "No trigger, no power source. I couldn't get it to work."

"That's because you don't have the training."

They stared in surprise as Danielson approached them, stepping over the eviscerated body of Set. He looked down at the corpse and said, "You chilled them all. Jesus."

"That's what happens when you bring frog giggers to gunfights," J.B. responded.

Mildred said to Danielson, "I saw you take a direct hit with one of those things. You're not hurt?"

Danielson fingered his ankh amulet. "This absorbed and redirected the nerve-traumatizing effect of the mena energy." He looked keenly at Ryan. "Cawdor, I always knew you for a nervy bastard, even when you were just a sprout. Your nerves must be made of steel cable."

"What do you mean?" Ryan asked.

"I mean you should be lying there chilled—or at the very least, comatose and paralyzed."

"I didn't miss that last by much," the one-eyed man replied. "It was like having a live wire connected to a suction pump jammed up my ass. All my strength felt like it was sucked away."

Danielson nodded sagely. "The discordant-resonance effect. Your bioenergy harmonies were disrupted. You were stronger than the Incarnates figured. And very lucky."

Ryan passed a shaking hand over his sweat-pebbled forehead. "Oh, yeah," he said sardonically. "That's exactly how I feel."

Krysty swung her head toward the ragged man, green eyes blazing with a fury. "You've got a story to tell us, old man."

"Yeah," J.B. said stiffly. "Like how did these overdressed stupes know about Krysty?"

Danielson shook his head. "I can't answer that question, but I'll give up what I know. First, we'd better get the bodies out of sight. There's some damn big buzzards with damn big appetites around here."

Chapter Eleven

Krysty and Ryan accompanied Danielson into the storage shed while J.B., Dean and Jak dragged the corpses of the Incarnates into an outbuilding at the far end of Fort Fubar. The bodies were placed in shallow graves and covered in shrouds of canvas. On close examination, the helmets proved to be constructed of cunningly crafted wood, inlaid with colored ceramic tiles. The craftsmanship was of a very high order, bordering on the artistic.

Mildred and Doc sifted handfuls of sand over the puddles of gore on the ground and policed the area, picking up metauh rods and spent shell casings.

J.B. gave the horseless chariots a quick inspection, feeling a grudging admiration for the design which was both ornate and functionally elegant. The conveyances were steered by a simple guide bar, the speed controlled by a joystick lever projecting from a very simple gearbox. It took him a minute to figure out the vehicles' motive power—a stacked array of concave mirrored squares occupied an open box at the rear end of the chassis platform. The angle of the mirrors was controlled by a small crank winch.

J.B. knew that some predark industrialists and environmentalists had experimented with ways to convert the sun's energy to electricity with solar cells. The little reflective squares were semiconductor chips and provided power to drive the vehicles. Despite himself, he was impressed with the technology. Still, he couldn't even hazard a guess at the operation of the metauh rods.

Dean pulled sentry duty in the street while the adults returned to the storage building. Krysty spread out one of the sheets, and while J.B. and Ryan fieldstripped their blasters, meticulously oiling and cleaning their moving parts, they posed questions to Danielson.

"You built Fort Fubar?" Mildred asked.

Danielson nodded. "Yeah, about eighteen years ago. After Trader gave me the heave-ho, I hooked up with some Farers. Rather than scrape around in a barony, I convinced them to come out here with me."

"Why?" J.B. demanded. "There's nothing out here but sand and sun."

A sly, almost abashed smile played over Danielson's whiskered face. "I'd made copies of some of Marsh Folsom's maps, y'see."

Everyone understood. Marsh Folsom had been the Trader's partner and the primary reason why he had been so successful in ferreting out predark stockpiles. Folsom had a collection of old military maps that at best specifically pinpointed stockpile locations and at worst provided clues to areas of possibility.

"So you thought there was a stockpile out here in the Barrens," Ryan said.

"Yeah," Danielson replied. "If not a stockpile, then some sort of installation I could use to build a power base. I figured I wouldn't have any competition out here."

It was the old Deathlands dream of empire, of carving out a substantial piece of territory and building a personal fiefdom to extort tribute from the surrounding areas.

"By the time we got out here and built this place," Danielson continued, "there was about fifty adults, ten, twelve teenagers and some kids. A couple of babies. I organized us like the way Trader had done. Connie Harrier was my woman and my second-in-command. My first lieutenant was Mel Stockbridge. And after him was old Javna."

Danielson's eyes seemed to cloud over as he looked into the past, his voice growing hushed with the weight of memories. "After we got the fort built, we spent a few months searching the Barrens, looking for the place on the map. By that time, our food was running low. We had to find it, or we'd starve. Then one day we found the place. The redoubt. And we found him. Or he found us. Don't know which is which no more."

"Found who?" Krysty asked. Although her voice was crisp, her eyes were narrowed.

"Akhnaton, our pharaoh. Our god." Danielson laughed bitterly. "He'd been waiting in his tomb for his people, you see. We strolled up and we became his people. Just as simple as that."

"And you just let him take over?" Ryan asked.

"Didn't have much choice. Javna tried to throw down on him, and he chilled the old fart as easy as swatting a fly. He took Connie into his tomb and did something to her insides so she could bear him children."

"Did Connie have red hair and green eyes, by chance?" Mildred asked.

"No, her hair was dark. Blue eyes. I think. Hard to remember now." Danielson's voice sank to a slur, his eyes going vague as he looked back over the years to a time that still caused him anguish.

He spoke of Akhnaton arriving in Fort Fubar with ration packs from the redoubt, which he distributed among the strongest of the Farers and the healthiest children. No one resisted him. Rather, they worshiped him almost immediately, their former loyalty to Danielson evaporating like a drop of water in the desert at high noon.

Later, when the chosen Farers had regained their strength, Akhnaton led them farther into the Barrens, to excavate his royal city, the city of Aten.

"Hold it," Mildred snapped. "*Excavated?* You mean there was a city already out there?"

Danielson nodded. "Oh, yeah. Buried in the sand, but most of it was still intact, even all the statues—"

"Wait," Mildred interrupted again. "You expect us to believe the city of Aten was out there in the desert, waiting for him?"

Impatiently, Danielson retorted, "That's what I said, isn't it? Anyhow, once the sand was all cleared away, Pharaoh set about making the city livable, repairing it, fixing it up, establishing our society. He knew ways to irrigate the plains and grow crops, he designed the chariots and the metauh rods. He shared all the ancient arts of the people of the Nile with us."

A slight smile tugged at the corners of the old man's lips. "It was a happy time, productive and busy. He named me and Stockbridge as high counselors. He took Connie to wife in a ceremony that lasted a week."

Doc eyed him keenly. "And you did not resent having your woman stolen from you?"

Danielson's face screwed up in contemplation. "I've thought about that off and on for the last sixteen years. I sure as hell should have been jealous. I remember feeling jealous for a little while, then it went away...it was like I couldn't feel jealous, no matter how hard I tried."

He exposed his discolored, broken teeth in a lascivious grin. "What the hell, though. I had three wives and three kids myself. Kind of hard to be too jealous with that kind of diversion."

"How many women for Pharaoh?" Jak inquired. "A hundred?"

"Not hardly. He stuck with Connie. He truly seemed to love that woman. When their daughter, Nefron, was born, the celebration lasted two weeks. For a long time after that, we dwelt in peace in the city. Oh, there were a few medleys with some nomads and Roamers who stumbled into our territory. The ones that we didn't chill joined up with us, absorbed by our society. Yeah, for years we dwelt at peace in Aten, doing damn little but eating, drinking, making love and making babies. It was kind of like paradise."

"Even a paradise has its price," Doc challenged. "What were you expected to give Pharaoh in return for this bucolic existence?"

Danielson shrugged. "The usual. Unswerving, unquestioning obedience and loyalty."

"In other words," Ryan said softly, grimly, "your free will."

Danielson's gray eyes flashed in anger. "What would you have done, Cawdor? First of all, Pharaoh has a power, and I've had a long time to study on it, on how it works."

Pharaoh's power was subtle, Danielson explained, an amplified application of will and emotion. The strength of his mind-energy required only a focal point to guide it, a vibration it followed like a torch flame in the wind. If your mind was naked and un-guarded, you were immediately under Pharaoh's in-fluence. Even if you were prepared, the influence was so persistent that resistance was eventually eroded away.

"You're thinking that all of us in Aten are weak-brained fools," Danielson said. "You're thinking we let Pharaoh turn me and my people into zombies. That's sort of right and sort of wrong. He gave back as much as he took. He provided us not only with emotional sustenance but material sustenance. No suffering, no poverty, no going hungry, no night-crawling coldhearts slitting your throat for your shoes. Who wouldn't go along with that? You'd go along with it, too, if you'd been us."

Danielson's voice grew soft with a touch of mockery beneath it. "You know why you'd go along with it, Cawdor? Because you're afraid to die, just like the rest of us zombies. I never believed in any god but myself and a blaster, but I believed in him. And even if Pharaoh is a mutie, spawned in a test tube and not heaven, who gives a shit?"

"What about Connie Harrier?" Krysty asked. "You said he loved her. Did she love him back, or was she just under his influence?"

"Doesn't matter. Like I said, when you're in the presence of Pharaoh, you end up loving him even-tually."

Taking a deep breath, Danielson continued, "After a few years, Pharaoh decided his dynasty needed a son. To make sure of it, he took Connie back to his tomb—the redoubt—to do something to her. Don't know what, exactly."

"Genetic preselection, probably," Mildred said. "Prenatal manipulation to determine the sex of the offspring."

"Yeah, whatever. Connie died." Danielson's tone thickened with anger and grief. "She died, and something died inside of Pharaoh, too."

Pharaoh brought his wife's body back to Aten. The period of mourning went on for months, went on so long that the atmosphere of brooding and grief became the norm. Pharaoh locked himself away in his palace, shutting out his daughter, Nefron, his counselors and even the needs of his own people.

Danielson wasn't sure how long Pharaoh's self-imposed exile lasted, but he was certain that well over two years elapsed. Then came the day when Pharaoh emerged. He made several announcements, issued a number of decrees.

The old man uttered a short, sneery laugh. "He claimed that Connie had never been meant to be his mate, that he had been deceived by her. Henceforth, he wouldn't recognize their union, and he wouldn't recognize Nefron as a legitimate heir to his kingdom."

Furthermore, he knew his true queen, his true consort, lay out in the world somewhere and in order to prepare himself and his kingdom for her arrival, a pyramid in her honor would be erected. Its power would act like a beacon to draw her into his arms.

The population was divided—slaves to build the

pyramid and slaves to serve the increasingly erratic whims of Pharaoh. There was much dissatisfaction. The bitterness became a quarrel and then open rebellion. From the rebellion two factions emerged—Pharaoh and his inner circle of advisers to which he, Danielson and Stockbridge belonged, as well as the newly formed security force called the Incarnates. The other faction was led by supporters of Nefron, at that point a young woman of fourteen.

"The rebellion turned from words into a week of bloodshed, murder and assassination attempts," Danielson stated. "At the end of that week, the revolution was crushed—ruthlessly. Over twenty people sympathetic to Nefron died, including one of my wives and two of my children."

Danielson shuddered and his eyes were wet. He dried them with a frayed sleeve. "Despite that, I was still in Pharaoh's favor, since my only son was killed while trying to assassinate me. But I had begun to doubt."

He touched the ankh amulet. "I had this made by one of our craftsmen who knew it blocked Pharaoh's power. Most of the rebels had worn them, acting on Nefron's advice. When construction on the pyramid began, I decided I had had my fill of Aten. About a year ago I came back here, to Fort Fubar, where it all began."

He glanced over at Krysty. "I don't know why the Incarnates should be looking for you, young woman. Unless Pharaoh thinks you're his true, predestined consort. If that's the case, my advice to all of you is to put as much distance between yourselves and Aten as you can before another search party is sent out."

"How long will that be?" J.B. asked.

"Dawn tomorrow, at the earliest. "The chariots can't travel very far at night."

"How far to city?" Jak inquired.

"Thirty miles or so. About an hour by chariot."

"How many people are there?" Ryan demanded.

"Three hundred and fifty or so, counting the kids."

J.B. extended a metauh rod. "Tell us about this."

Danielson scowled. "What part of me advising you to run didn't you understand, Dix? You got no time for this—"

"Tell us." Ryan bit out the words.

The old man ran a hand through his hair. "They operate on some kind of ancient principle about channeling the *sekhem*—the 'life-force.' You got to be trained in how to use them. My amulet keeps my body helix from being warped."

"How?" Mildred asked.

With a forefinger, Danielson traced a line along his arms, head and chest. "The shape of the amulet is a closed double-helix energy pattern. It protects my bioaural field from the resonating mena energies. Get it?"

"No," Jak growled.

Danielson ignored him. "That's why Pharaoh is building a pyramid—to increase the power of his bioaural field, to saturate him and his queen completely with the *sekhem,* so they'll be immortal."

Krysty looked at him skeptically. "Pharaoh told you that?"

"Not exactly," Danielson admitted. "Stockbridge said it. He said once the pyramid was built, the capstone put in place, it would draw power from the energy field of the planet, even other planets. Anybody standing inside the pyramid would be made immortal.''

"The old pyramid-power theory," Doc interjected. "In my day it was called electromotivism. A pseudoscience.''

"By *my* day," Mildred said, "the theory had gained some respectability. With the translations of ancient Egyptian texts and codices, reputable scientists performed experiments and came up with empirical evidence that the old Egyptians had a kind of energy-transference technology.''

Ryan had completed reassembling his SIG-Sauer. He tested the action, then slid a clip into the butt. "We've got plenty of ammo. J.B., you have any other surprises you rat-holed from the commune?''

The Armorer shook his head. "Sorry. That gren I used on Poseidon's sec men was my last surprise.''

Ryan turned his attention to the Steyr. "We've gotten by with just our blasters on many an occasion. Guess they'll have to do this time.''

"'Do'?" Danielson echoed. "Do for what?''

"We're going to the city.''

"What are you, a jolt-brain?" Danielson exploded incredulously. "Boost them chariots and get back to where you came from!''

"We came from the redoubt. It's a door that opens only one way, at present. Your pharaoh saw to that. And there's a good reason why this region is called the Barrens, right?''

"Right," Danielson admitted.

"There's nothing out here, no settlements, no villes, not even a pesthole outpost. Only Fort Fubar. And Aten. Right?''

Danielson nodded.

"Besides, Hell Eyes is expecting us." Ryan showed his teeth in a humorless grin. "Far be it from me to disappoint him."

"You'll be walking into a trap," Danielson muttered.

Doc laughed. "We never let that stop us before."

"Yeah," Jak grunted. "People try trap us, we chill."

"See?" Doc said. "A marvelously simple approach to the vagaries of life."

Danielson sighed, shaking his head. "You're all crazy."

J.B. reached out and tapped the amulet hanging from the old man's throat. "Look who's talking."

DEAN WAS BORED with standing watch. He had patrolled up and down the sandy, heat-baked perimeter of Fort Fubar several times, squinting out into the wasteland in all directions. He saw nothing that interested him.

Returning to the square, he looked over one of the chariots. Ryan stepped out of the storage building as Dean examined the simple controls.

"Think you could drive one of these things, son?"

"Could I, Dad? That'd be a real hot pipe!"

"Good." Ryan's face held no particular expression. "The rest of us will be moving on at dawn. We'll leave one of these wags. You'll stay here."

Dean gaped, stricken, at his father. "Move on? Where?"

Tersely, Ryan gave the boy an overview of Danielson's story about Pharaoh Akhnaton and the city of Aten.

"Wait for us here four days," Ryan concluded. "Then take this wag back to the redoubt and try the gateway."

"Why don't all of us do that?"

"I'm taking a calculated risk. It's possible that once we arrive in the city, whatever power is being directed to deactivate the gateway controls will end and be directed toward us. But there's no guarantee any of us will make it back."

"Why can't I share the risk?" Dean asked.

"I won't have you deliberately strolling into a tiger trap with us."

"I'll follow you," Dean said defiantly.

"No!" Ryan's tone was ragged, harsh, brooking no discussion. "You'll do what I say."

Dean turned away, ashamed of the tears suddenly stinging his eyes and the thickness growing in his chest.

In a softer tone, Ryan said, "Listen to me, son. If we're not back in four days, then more than likely we won't be coming back. At least not for quite a while."

"We've only been back together a few weeks," Dean muttered. "Not fair to leave me behind."

"No, it isn't fair," Ryan agreed. "But dragging you into a trap isn't fair, either. Do you understand?"

"No," Dean whispered. "I'm not a kid anymore. I can make my own decisions."

"Not this time. You'll stay here until we come back...or until we don't. Now, get out of the heat and grab some grub."

Dean didn't look at him as he turned and marched toward the storage building. He passed Krysty as she came out, and he evaded her patting hand as if she were contaminated. She had a metauh rod angled over a shoulder like a fishing pole. "Guess you told him."

Ryan nodded. "Think all of us can squeeze into one of these wags?"

Krysty eyed it. "Tight fit, but we'll manage. Better than walking."

She paused and added quietly, "You sure this is the right idea, lover?"

"Hell, I'm not sure of anything!" Ryan snarled out the words. "But this Hell Eyes bastard wants you, and he's interfering with us and he sent sec men after us. I'm sick and fed the fuck up with deranged sons of bitches dogging us, no matter where we go."

"Well," Krysty observed sagely, "we're making it awfully easy for this particular deranged son of a bitch."

"Why delay the inevitable? There's no place to run, and this fort is about as defensible as a strawberry patch. And even if it wasn't, combining Danielson's food supplies with ours still doesn't give us the provisions to hold out against a siege. But I'm open to suggestions."

Krysty didn't offer any. She looked away, nodding, lightly biting her lower lip. She swished the metauh rod in clockwise and counterclockwise swirls. Extending the V prongs toward the chariot, a thread of light, like a static-electricity discharge, popped toward the metal-rimmed wheels.

Surprised, Ryan asked, "You know how to operate that thing?"

Krysty smiled wanly. "Bioelectric-energy manipulation, the same principles of drawing on natural electromagnetic currents taught to me by my mother. Like Danielson said, it's all in knowing how to channel and focus them."

She glanced into Ryan's face, and the smile fled her lips. "You're wondering if I should stay behind with Dean."

"Something like that."

"Hell Eyes will just come for me, you know. You said it—we'd only delay the inevitable."

"But to give you up—"

"No choice," she said grimly. "I'm just as sick of running as you are. He got into my head and played with me, like I was a sex puppet. Whether he's a pharaoh, god or mutant, and whether he wants me to bear his children or warm his bed, I'll provide him with a surprise that will give him nightmares for the rest of his life."

A smile twisted the corner of Ryan's mouth. "Pretty tough talk for a sex puppet."

Krysty leaned the metauh rod against the side of the chariot and came into his arms. She trembled slightly. Lowly, she intoned, "It is. And I mean every word of it."

Chapter Twelve

Gray dawn stole over Fort Fubar when Ryan, Krysty, Mildred, Doc, J.B. and Jak trooped out to the chariot. Dean stood by the door and watched them pass wordlessly, not responding to Jak ruffling his hair or the kisses bestowed by Mildred and Krysty.

Before he joined the others aboard the vehicle, Ryan said grimly to Danielson, "I expect you to treat my son with hospitality. You don't have to feed or baby-sit him. The food we've left should be enough so you won't have to share your own larder."

Danielson spread his hands wide, palms outward. "Cawdor, I don't mind the company. Long as he behaves himself, we'll get along fine."

Ryan favored him with a steely, slit-eyed glare. "It's not his behavior I'm worried about."

It took a second for the implications of Ryan's words to penetrate Danielson's comprehension. "Don't be vulgar, Cawdor. I had three kids of my own, remember? 'Sides, Trader gave me the boot for putting things in my pants, not for taking things out."

Ryan nodded shortly, glancing at Dean. The boy refused to meet his gaze. The big man turned away, paused, then heeled around, unslinging the Steyr from his shoulder. He walked over to his son, thrusting the rifle into his hands.

"I leave this in your care. You may need it for hunting game."

Dean ran his fingers lightly over the wood-grain stock and slid the strap over his shoulder, letting the long blaster hang down his back. "Okay."

Ryan began to move away again, then turned quickly, catching his son's slim form in a crushing embrace. He pressed his cheek against the top of the boy's head.

"We'll be back," he whispered fiercely.

Dean only nodded, struggling to keep the tears bottled up.

Ryan pushed him away and climbed into the chariot, sitting at the edge of the chassis platform, beside the solar-cell array. J.B. engaged the drive, and with a purring hum and only the slightest of lurches, the vehicle rolled forward. Hands on the guide bar, J.B. steered it around in a wide half circle and out into the open desert. Ryan kept watching Dean, even after his figure was swallowed by the distance and dimness.

Though Krysty sat beside him, she didn't speak to him. She didn't need her empathic abilities to know what her one-eyed warrior was feeling.

The afternoon before, J.B. had experimented driving the chariot, testing its limits and capabilities. The battery charged by solar energy retained sufficient energy to keep them on their way, provided he kept the wag's speed at a moderate level. After a few minutes of scanning the desert floor with his flashlight, he found the tracks cut into the sand the day before by the Incarnates. The two sets of parallel grooves curved ahead. The wind hadn't had the time to do more than blur the edges of the individual tracks.

He notched up the rate of speed only slightly. Without the solar rays to recharge it, the storage battery would drain fast in the darkness.

Time and sand rolled on, and their ears grew accustomed to the clickings and hummings of the chariot and soon forgot them. Around and beyond, the desert flowed out unbroken and featureless. The sand was soft, and the wheels of the overburdened chariot sank into the deep drifts, struggling to turn themselves free. Even if J.B. wanted to speed up, the Barrens wouldn't have allowed him.

A rust red sun rose, splashing the sky with variegated scraps of color. By the time it was a finger's width above the horizon, Ryan figured they had traveled about twenty miles. The desert gradually ebbed, funneling into a broad roadbed made of crushed, grit-encrusted gravel. J.B. steered the chariot down its middle and shifted to a higher speed. The drone and mechanical clickings rose in pitch, and a cloud of dust floated behind the wag.

The road widened, and within five miles tall palm trees began to line it on either side. J.B. guided the chariot toward one on the right, reaching out to slap the bark as they passed by.

"What'd you do that for?" Mildred asked.

J.B. shrugged. "Wanted to see if it was real or not. It sure felt like it."

The road twisted between two heaped hillocks of sand. Vegetation sprouted from them, scraggly leaves moving slightly in the breeze. When the road straightened again, in the midst of the desolation beyond them lay a city.

J.B. decreased the chariot's speed until it crawled to a droning halt. Swallowing hard, he husked out, "Dark night."

He engaged the brake, and everyone climbed out, staring from beneath shading hands. The city was about a quarter of a mile away, and it was alive with movement. The high outer walls loomed, white and massive, above the sands. The road wound past a collection of squat, low-roofed buildings and through an open gate. The stone archway above it bore bas-relief profile carvings of archers in racing chariots. Four gigantic statues of seated men wearing elaborate headdresses flanked the gate.

Beyond it, people moved to and fro through an open plaza large enough to contain a small army. Around its edges fluttered the brightly colored canopies of merchants. Straight ahead, a very wide avenue ran past the plaza, guarded on either side by four great sculpted figures, representations of animals half-reclining on tall, rectangular pedestals. At the end of the avenue appeared to be a large building of some sort, backed up against the far wall. It was too distant to distinguish details.

A chain of rocky hills rose behind the city, curving across the horizon like the fossilized vertebrae of some prehistoric monster. Green pastureland rolled to the south and they could make out several flocks of either cattle or sheep or both.

Above the west wall a vast, pyramidal structure shouldered the blue sky. It was composed of countless fitted blocks of stone, the top flat and irregular, like a row of broken teeth. The early-morning light played along the white facade of the monstrous monolith. Ryan tried to estimate its size by using the city walls as a reference point. He could only hazard a feeble guess—a forty-story building rising angularly from a thirteen-acre base was the best he could come up with.

He realized the pyramid was of such staggering proportions as to make its true distance from the city difficult to gauge. He also realized he was so stupefied by what his eye was seeing that he was in a mild state of shock. Danielson's words of Aten and the pyramid hadn't prepared his mind to grasp it all.

Doc was the first to find his tongue. "By the Three Kennedys, this isn't Deathlands. This isn't even our time!"

Not removing his gaze from the city, J.B. shook his head doggedly. "My readings were true. We're exactly where I said we were."

"How can this be?" Krysty's voice was hushed with awe. "I saw pix of places like this in books. There hasn't been a city like that in thousands of years...and never in America."

Mildred suddenly uttered a screechy little laugh and slapped her forehead, startling them so much she broke the mesmeric spell the vision of the city had woven. They turned toward her questioningly.

"Not thousands of years, folks," she claimed with a relieved chuckle. "More like close to 180."

"Talk sense," Jak snapped.

"Remember when I said this area had been popular with filmmakers?" She gestured to the city walls. "The holy city of Aten is a movie set, built by Cecil B. DeMille back in the 1920s for the first, silent version of *The Ten Commandments*."

J.B. eyed her skeptically. "Come on, Millie. How could a movie set have survived for so long in such good shape, weathering the nukecaust and sky-dark?"

"I remember reading about this place," Mildred replied. "Unlike later movie sets, which were made of plaster and papier-mâché and plastic, old DeMille built this thing to last—out of concrete, plaster and limestone. When the filming was over, he figured it was cheaper to bury the whole shebang rather than dismantle it and cart it back to Hollywood. The site was lost for over sixty years. It was relocated back in the early 1990s with ground-penetration radar. Best as I remember it, plans were under way for a full excavation. Guess those plans were put on hold until Hell Eyes came along."

"A movie set," Ryan said slowly. "If it was buried, there's no reason why it couldn't have come through all the geological changes since skydark fairly intact. How did Hell Eyes know about it?"

Mildred shrugged. "The redoubt had an extensive database. The story about finding the site was fairly well-known, so he probably came across a reference to it while he was file-browsing."

"Do we ride or walk from here?" Krysty asked.

Jak shook his head. "Expecting us anyhow. Make easy on selves. Ride."

Doc shook his head in disbelief at the teenager's placid audacity. "Whatever we choose as a conveyance—the horseless chariot or our feet—let us proceed with all due caution."

Ryan hitched his gun belt and climbed back into the chariot. "Let's travel in style. If Pharaoh is going to chop our heads off, he might as well do it before the real heat of the day begins."

Once everyone was back in the vehicle, J.B. let it creep forward along the tree-lined road. Ryan kept consulting Krysty's hair, but it hadn't stirred, so she wasn't detecting any immediate danger.

They rolled past the outlying buildings, then toward the four identical statues of seated men, sculptures Doc identified as replicas of far larger pieces in Egypt's Abu Simbel Valley.

There were sentries on the walls, and though they watched their steady approach, none of them raised an alarm or hailed them with a challenge.

As they drew closer to the open gate, Doc fidgeted with the lion's head of his swordstick and murmured, "Interesting how necessity forces mature human beings to do things against their better judgment."

Mildred overheard him and cast a sidewise glance at Krysty. Under her breath, she muttered, "And maybe against their wills."

With no fanfare and just as little notice, the chariot entered the city of Aten.

The marketplace wasn't particularly busy so early in the morning. The merchants hawked fruit, vegetables, woven linens, pottery and wooden kitchen utensils. There were wines and spices and even hand-loomed rugs.

The merchants wore simple tunics, and their hair was cut and styled in a strange fashion, some of them sporting completely shaved pates except for a long braid and others with long, plaited hair. They were similar in their well-fed physiques and eyes that didn't once look in the direction of the rolling chariot.

The women were all black haired, their eyes outlined by equally black mascara. They walked with sensuous, graceful strides, their diaphanous ankle-length robes slit to the thigh. Some wore few ornaments, and others were so weighted down with bracelets, rings and necklaces they seemed like ambulatory bangles.

Other people thronged the plaza, all lean and dark. In fact, everyone they saw had swarthy skin and jet black hair. In all of the marketplace there was no sound; no voices spoke, shouted or laughed. There was only a serene silence from the citizens of Aten, and that in itself was a bit frightening.

A fountain bubbled and sparkled in the center of the plaza, surrounded by stone decorated with hiero-glyphics. Nearly naked children drank from it, and women filled earthenware jugs. Like everyone else, they ignored the six people as they rode past.

J.B. drove the chariot out of the plaza and along a boulevard by the bestial statues Ryan had glimpsed earlier. They were sphinxes, anthropomorphic creatures with the bodies of lions and the heads of noble-looking men. A great, rambling, multiter-raced building loomed at the far end of the boulevard. It looked as if its walls were faced with marble and the fluted columns inlaid with gold. Ryan studied the broad steps leading up to a massive door of beaten bronze. He knew, without knowing how he knew, that Hell Eyes waited and watched from behind that heavy portal.

Aten was beautiful and exceptionally clean. All of the companions had difficulty believing that it was nothing more than a huge play set, constructed for predark entertainment purposes. Regardless of its origin, Aten possessed a heart and a soul, beating with a pulse of life, very strong and sensual.

J.B. found a side lane that paralleled the boulevard of sphinxes and he turned the chariot down it. Braking to a slow halt, he said, "This is too weird. We don't belong here, certainly not in one of their wags. Nobody's paying any attention to us. Like we're invisible...or ghosts."

"I'm not going to complain," Mildred said.

"They're playing some kind of game with us," Ryan stated. "Pretending we're not here."

Doc quirked an eyebrow. "What would be its point?"

"To disorient us," the one-eyed man answered. "Confuse us, throw us off balance. Make us doubt."

Doc pursed his lips contemplatively. "If that is so, the cooperation on the part of Aten's citizens is truly extraordinary—and an unsettling example of Pharaoh's hold over them."

Ryan looked toward the top of the terraced building, pondering the tactical wisdom of simply banging on the bronze door and demanding an audience. He quickly dismissed the idea. Without an ace-on-the-line to play, such a brazen confrontation had too many possible outcomes—all of them gloomy.

Krysty suddenly stiffened, her long tresses lifting as if riding a wind. She raised her fists to her temples, and her lips worked. "J.B.!" she shrilled. "Get us out of here!"

The Armorer's reflexes were lightning swift. The chariot lunged forward with a whine. He steered it down another side lane that ran at right angles along one wall. He followed it until they emerged back at the marketplace, at its inner end. Only now it was a marketplace without merchants and shoppers. It was completely deserted.

"Now what?" J.B. growled, looking this way and that. He saw the gate, and the heavy barricade of painted wood spanning its length.

"*Now* they're paying attention to us," Doc said grimly.

From behind them came the quick scuff and scutter of many running feet. Men wearing the heads of animals efficiently fanned out in a ring around the chariot, sunlight glinting from the pronged shafts gripped in their dusky hands. The companions saw duplicates of the helmets worn by the Incarnates in Fort Fubar, but new ones, as well—a hippopotamus, a crocodile, a donkey, even an insect.

Between clenched teeth, J.B. warned, "Hang on."

He manipulated the chariot's controls, and it spun on one wheel in a complete circle, revolving as if on an axis. As it rotated, the Uzi fairly leaped into his hand, and flame and noise lipped from the short barrel. He played the stream of 9 mm rounds over the encircling Incarnates like water from a high-pressure hose.

The first half-dozen bullets sewed bloody little dots across the broad chests of three Incarnates, smashing them backward into screaming, tangle-footed sprawls.

In the same instant as the Uzi began its deadly stutter, Ryan and Jak leaped from the pirouetting chariot, rolling with the momentum, hitting the flag-stoned ground with their blasters out and working.

Light flared from the tip of a metauh rod just as Ryan went into a sideways lunge. He felt a pins-and-needles tingle on the top of his left shoulder. He didn't know from which Incarnate the energy bolt had come, so he shot the nearest, a triburst that drilled Anubis's twin in the midsection. The triple impacts swatted him double, slapping him off his feet.

Jak's Colt Python boomed, and the heavy .357-caliber slug broke a crocodile head and the human skull supporting it. Blood gushed down the Incarnate's face as he flailed over backward, arms windmilling.

A metauh rod swept toward him, and the albino's steel-spring legs propelled him into a one-handed cartwheel. As his feet spun over his head, the Colt belched flame and thunder again, the recoil only slightly affecting his balance as he landed lithely in a crouch.

The bug-headed Incarnate shrieked, slapping at his right shoulder as the bullet bit a chunk of meat and muscle out of it amid a spray of blood.

Ryan kept moving, never still for a microsecond, ducking and weaving, dodging the flashing crackiles of energy. The metauh rods flailed at him like whips, and the helmeted men wielding them cursed in frustrated anger.

His eye caught a flicker a motion from behind him, and a double-pronged tip stabbed toward the barrel of his blaster. Just as it touched the steel, wreathing it in a momentary shower of sparks, Ryan opened his hand. Before the SIG-Sauer hit the ground, he snatched the eighteen-inch panga from its sheath.

The long, razor-edged blade, a flash of silver in the sun, slashed in a flat horizontal arc, his whole body powering the stroke. The shock of impact shivered up his right arm into his shoulder socket, and a head encased in a bird-beaked helmet tumbled like an awkward ball to the flagstones.

As the blood-spouting trunk of the Incarnate toppled forward, Ryan whirled to face a hippopotamus-headed man who gaped at him in open-mouthed horror.

"Come and die," Ryan invited, beckoning to him with the crimson-streaked knife.

J.B.'s Uzi suddenly stopped chattering, and Mildred shouted out wordlessly in fear and anger. Ryan spun on his heel in the direction of the chariot, then he was flat on his face in the dust, wondering aloofly what he was doing there.

His arms and legs were filled with half-frozen mud, and his thoughts stumbled and staggered, finally succumbing to the brief, almost subliminal image of a nimbus of energy jumping from metal prongs.

Something hard and unyielding insinuated itself between Ryan's ribs and the ground. He felt no pain, only a steady pressure. He realized a foot was lifting him, turning him, rolling him onto his back.

A mahogany giant towered over him, a conical jeweled headpiece bisecting the sun and adding another six inches to his height. The hard beauty of his face had none of the softness of youth left in it. He wore a magnificent, gem-encrusted leather harness over his muscular torso. Sunlight gleamed from the golden threads worked into the white fabric of his short kilt.

The giant's eyes, under straight black brows, were like drops of hot blood.

"So," he said in a deep, melodic voice, "I didn't frighten you away, after all. Perhaps I'll have to try harder next time."

The sound of his voice touched off sweet vibrations somewhere deep inside of Ryan. He was hungry to hear more of it.

Then, smiling, the bronzed giant kicked him in the head, kicked him down into a spiraling black hole.

Chapter Thirteen

Ryan opened his eye and at first saw nothing. He felt a surge of panic, wondering if he had been struck blind, but when he shifted his head, he caught a yellow glimmer of dim light. He stirred feebly, and the motion sent a hot bore of pain drilling through his chest to his back. Sweat broke out on his forehead. His mouth was dirt dry, he felt feverish and nausea was a clawed beast trying to tear its way out of his stomach.

Gritting his teeth, he lay quietly for a long time, listening to the slow, steady thud of his heart. Then, by degrees, he turned his head and again caught the glow of light, and by it, he squinted at his surroundings. He was in a tiny, bare-walled chamber, hardly large enough to accommodate the narrow, very hard cot he was lying on. It was made of woven reeds that exuded a musty vegetable odor. Craning his neck, he saw that one wall of the room was covered by a latticework of wooden bars, the crosspieces bound with rawhide thongs. The door was hinged on the outside and secured by a crude padlock and hasp. He smiled humorlessly. Not a room—a cell. The floor and walls were of old stone. A bucket occupied one corner.

The light peeking in between the bars was provided by a guttering torch jammed in a wall sconce

in the corridor beyond. With a trembling hand, he
fingered the tacky patch of drying blood on the right
side of his head. Sharp pain drove through his head
at the touch, and he couldn't repress a curse.

From the corridor beyond, he heard Doc's anxious
voice. "Ryan, good fellow, are you awake? John
Barrymore, can you see if he is awake?"

"Ryan? Are you all right in there?" J.B. asked.

"No," he managed to say, dismayed by how
weak and hoarse he sounded. "But I can manage."

Slowly, he levered himself to a sitting position
and, after enduring a wave of vertigo, he realized he
was naked.

"Krysty," he called. "You okay, lover?"

His only response was the faint echo of his question. Doc coughed uncomfortably. "I regret to say
she is not among us. Nor is young master Lauren."

Ryan groaned. "Where are they?"

"No idea," Mildred said. "All of us in the chariot
were knocked on our collective asses by those metauh weapons. We came to a few minutes ago. You
must have been hit harder than the rest of us, or you
were still weak from the shot you took yesterday."

Ryan forced himself to his feet. His arms and legs
felt rubbery, and his heart beat with great, erratic
poundings in his chest. Slowly, painfully, he managed to stumble over to and use the barred door as
support. "Or Hell Eyes kicked me in the head, as
an added little bonus for not being scared away."

Gazing through the bars, he saw Doc, J.B. and
Mildred all in identical cells and all naked. Doc,
always tall and skeletally lean, looked pathetically
vulnerable. His rib cage protruded from beneath his
pale skin, and his hipbones jutted out as sharply as

his ribs. His stomach was concave. He kept both hands clasped discreetly over his groin.

J.B. looked a bit ludicrous, too, wearing nothing but his sallow skin and spectacles. He gripped the wooden bars tightly, his knuckles white.

Mildred stood with one arm crooked over her breasts and her hand spread at the juncture of her thighs.

The four cells formed the transverse bar of a T. J.B.'s cell faced the juncture corridor. Ryan leaned his forehead against the bars, swallowing painfully. His throat felt like it was lined with sandpaper. "Was Krysty in the chariot with you?"

"Yes," Doc answered dolefully. "It is safe to assume she and Jak were separated from us for some reason."

Ryan inhaled slowly. Strength was returning to his limbs, the fierce pain in his chest fading to only a persistent ache. "Any idea where we are?"

"No," J.B. said. "Came to in here, as naked as a newborn babe."

"We could be in ancient Egypt for all we know," Doc commented. "Buried in a hidden chamber in the pyramid of Giza."

"Don't go jolt-brained on us," J.B. ordered.

"I have no intention of doing so," Doc retorted irritably. "However, you may have noticed how the citizens of Aten appeared to be of Egyptian origin...all dark haired and dark skinned. Not an Anglo-Saxon in the bunch. The odds of Pharaoh finding only that physical type in the Barrens are so astronomical that they are not even worth discussing."

Mildred chuckled lowly. "You're forgetting where we are."

"I believe that was my topic, Dr. Wyeth."

"We're in a movie set, Doc. In some remnant of California, not Egypt, ancient or otherwise. And if it's a movie set, it's basically an illusion. And therefore, the so-called Egyptians we saw are probably the product of hair and skin dyes, to maintain the illusion for Pharaoh's benefit."

Doc uttered a "Hmph" of interest. "Pray proceed."

Mildred started to gesture, as was her habit when talking, then kept her hands where they were. "I got a good look at the citizens of Aten. Regardless of their coloring, their body and facial structures are not the Egyptian norm. I saw a few blue eyes in the mix, too."

"So," Ryan said, "this is just some big play-acting set for Hell Eyes. Is that what you're saying?"

Mildred shook her head. "Not exactly. He's gone to a great deal of trouble to evoke the look of the Eighteenth Dynasty, so it's more than just a fantasy land to him. We've got to take it seriously because he takes it seriously."

J.B. suddenly hissed, *"Shh!"*

Sandaled feet slapped against the floor down the corridor. A moment later, two tall men walked into the cell-block area. They were dusky skinned with completely shaved heads. Gold earrings glinted in the flickering torchlight. Both were dressed identically in simple linen tunics. One of them carried a long metal key attached to a strap looped around his right wrist. They glanced impersonally into each cell and stopped in front of the lock to Mildred's door.

At the clink of metal on metal, J.B. demanded, "What are you doing?"

The pair ignored him.

"Listen," Ryan said to the man without the key, "how long are we supposed to stay here?"

There was no answer.

"Why don't you tell your pharaoh that we came here to see him?"

"He knows that," the man grunted.

"I want to talk to him," Ryan stated.

Again, there was no reply.

The turnkey removed the lock and swung the barred door wide. Mildred backed up against the wall, a snarl twisting her lips, assuming a defensive stance, all thoughts of modesty vanishing. "Whatever you assholes are selling, I'm not in the market."

"This is no time for insolence," the turnkey rumbled coldly.

He stepped in, reaching out for her. Mildred struck at him with her clenched fist. The turnkey, with the skill of long practice, twisted away from the punch and caught her wrist. He wrenched her arm up between her shoulder blades.

Crying out, Mildred back-kicked him, her heel connecting with his right kneecap. The man made no sound. He merely increased the pressure of the hammerlock and forced her to her knees. The turnkey's companion cuffed her brutally on the side of the head with an open hand. Stars swirled before her eyes, and her head snapped back with a tendon-twinging force.

Shouting in wordless fury, J.B. reached between

the bars, clawing for the turnkeys. They ignored him, pulling Mildred to her feet, both of her arms pinioned behind her in a grip she remembered was called the "police come-along."

She allowed herself to be manhandled out of the cell. She made no further resistance, but rage smoldered in her dark eyes. J.B. swatted for the nearer man, but his fingers fell inches short of a target.

"Calm down, shorty," said the turnkey. "We aren't going to hurt her unless she forces the issue."

"Where are the rest of our people?" Ryan asked. "The red-haired woman and the albino kid?"

They offered no response, marching Mildred between them down the corridor and out of sight. J.B. slumped against the bars, hanging his head like a sick dog.

"Don't become despondent, John Barrymore," Doc said soothingly. "I believe we can take their words at face value. They will not harm her."

J.B. nodded miserably. "I don't suppose they left you your swordstick?"

Doc sighed. "Alas, no."

"I thought mebbe since they let me keep my glasses—"

"An obvious physical infirmity," Doc said. "As is Ryan's vision. When I was stripped, I surmise they found no reason I should need a walking stick."

Ryan listened to the exchange without really hearing it. His knees were wobbling, so he eased down on the edge of the cot. He and his friends at one time or another had been cast into the role of cap-

tives, but repetition didn't make the part any easier
to play or endure.

He held on to the ragged scrap of hope that Krysty
and Jak had eluded capture, but he could not imagine how. He forcibly steered his imagination away
from the vision of Krysty in the hands—or arms—
of Hell Eyes.

He reconstructed his last conscious memory before awakening in the cell. He began rebuilding the
image of the bronze giant towering over him, but all
he could really call to mind was a pair of red, blazing eyes. Those eyes swam through his brain—solid
red, not like Jak's crimson-hued irises.

And the deep, throaty voice had held a note of
triumph, of patronizing amusement. Ryan remembered something else about the voice, a vibration
that had set up throbbing ululations in his ears.

Then the red-eyed giant had kicked him.

Ryan touched the welt on the side of his head. It
still hurt. He tried to make himself angry about it,
promising to give as good as he got at his first opportunity, but he found that he couldn't.

And that scared him.

THE TWO MEN ESCORTED Mildred through a door
standing opposite the one leading to the cell block.
Crossing a corridor, they entered a broad chamber
whose walls were veiled by heavy tapestries, embroidered with scenes of dark-skinned people involved in all sorts of activities, most of them lascivious.

The men released Mildred and backed out of the
room, shutting a wooden door inlaid with ivory and

chased with gold leaf. She heard the unmistakable click of a lock.

She stood for a moment, rubbing feeling back into her wrists, studying the chamber. It wasn't very spacious, but it was nicely appointed with a low, highly varnished table, a couple of chairs and a curtained alcove. A square of light shone through an open window high in one wall, so high that she couldn't reach it even by standing on one of the chairs. She wondered why the quality of the light seemed suffused, then guessed that the window faced east and it was late afternoon, with the sun shining on the other side of the building, whatever it was, wherever it was.

Padding over to the alcove, Mildred tugged the curtain aside. She saw a sunken tub surrounded by a white stone rim and a short ceramic cylinder projecting from the floor. A pull cord dangled from a water tank attached to the wall above it. Realizing with relief that it was a toilet, she quickly used it. She had refused to squat over the bucket in her cell and had already begun to wonder how long she could control the building pressure in her bladder.

When she was done, she pulled the cord, and a gush of water swirled and flushed the contents of the toilet away. It began to fill again almost immediately. Mildred knew ancient Egyptians had possessed indoor plumbing, but she was impressed nevertheless. Even the tub had cunningly crafted faucet spouts and knobs.

As she considered drawing a bath, she heard the door lock turn. Peering around the curtain, she saw a woman enter, holding several folded articles of clothing in her arms.

Tall, slim and lithe, moving with the soundless grace of a panther, the woman returned Mildred's stare with impersonal, black-outlined eyes. Her features were haughty and imperious, yet sensual, with a touch of ruthlessness about the full lips. She was dressed simply in a brief frock that left her arms and legs bare, the material so gauzy that her small breasts and black pubic triangle were only slightly blurred, not obscured. Jewels glittered and winked on her slim throat and slender wrists.

"Who are you?" Mildred asked, still standing behind the curtain.

The woman gazed at her speculatively, inclined her head toward the door and listened intently. Then she moved swiftly to the alcove. "What is your name?" the woman whispered.

"Wyeth. Mildred Winona Wyeth," the doctor replied, whispering herself.

"You must bathe and get dressed. Mimses awaits you."

"Who?"

"The high counselor of Aten. He's heard about you. He wants to see you immediately."

Mildred narrowed her eyes. "Let him wait. I asked who *you* are, remember?"

"A friend."

Mildred smiled wryly. "That's great. I can use one in this place. Does my friend have a name?"

In a voice pitched so low it was barely audible, the woman answered, "I am Nefron. You must trust me."

"Nefron? Pharaoh's rebellious daughter?" Mildred eyed the woman closely and saw that though her manner was mature, the skillful application of cosmetics made her appear older than she really was.

Nefron arched a delicate eyebrow. "I had nothing to do with the uprising. I was used as a rallying point during my father's self-imposed exile. I accepted Pharaoh's decision."

"Even when he disowned you?"

"Who told you that?" Suspicion colored Nefron's tone.

Sensing she was treading on uncertain ground, Mildred replied, "It doesn't matter. Besides, you're just a kid."

"I am sixteen. That is quite old in this kingdom. Old enough to do what must be done. Now, do what I say."

"Why should I?" Mildred's voice rose slightly. "Where are my other friends? Are they alive?"

Nefron hushed her, eyes wide with urgent apprehension. "You must be quiet. If the guards think you're giving me a difficult time, they'll come in and bathe you themselves. I don't think you'd like that, would you?"

"Not particularly. But answer my questions."

Nefron sighed. "The red-haired woman is alive, held here in another part of the palace."

"And the men? What will happen to them?"

"What are their names?"

"Ryan Cawdor, Theophilus Algernon Tanner—he answers to 'Doc'—and John Barrymore Dix."

"They will be well treated. At least for a while."

"And Jak—the young one?"

"He was not captured."

A thrill of hope leaped through Mildred. "Do you know where he is?"

Nefron shook her head and pushed Mildred gently toward the tub. Turning on the faucet, she waited until the gush and gurgle of water was loud before whispering into her ear, "I do not know where he is at present. That ignorance is of my choice and for his own safety...as well as mine and yours. When the time is appropriate, I will find out. And so will you. Now, we must stop wasting time."

Mildred hesitated, locking eyes with Nefron. They were dark, even darker than her own, but she saw a glint of red swirling in those sepia depths. Shuddering inwardly, Mildred stepped into the tub. In spite of her fear, anger and anxiety, she was happy for the opportunity to wash away two days' worth of dried sweat and grit in the warm, rose-scented water. Using a small pitcher and a cake of soap, Nefron wet her head and shampooed her beaded hair.

Mildred allowed it, not even complaining when lather dripped into her eyes. For whatever reason, Nefron was trying to be kind to her, and she decided it would be foolish to question her about her relationship with her father. If Pharaoh had reduced the girl's status to that of a bath attendant, there was no point in interrogating her about what had to have been a humiliating reversal of fortune.

"It will take too much time to remove the beads and comb out all your braids," the girl said. "Mimses will just have to get used to a different hairstyle for women."

"Why am I supposed to meet this Mimses?" Mildred asked, sponging water over her limbs.

"As I said, when he heard a black woman had been captured, he ordered you to be brought before him. He is very important, very powerful. Second only to my father in his influence over Aten. When you go before him, you must curb your tongue and not anger him."

"Why?"

"Pharaoh has left the decision of what to do with you and your friends in Mimses's hands. Unfortunately, since you killed so many Incarnates, he's tempted to torture all of you to death."

"Even Krysty, the red-haired woman?"

Nefron shook her head. "No. Her fate has already been decided. By Pharaoh."

"Why am I not surprised?" Mildred muttered.

Nefron used the pitcher to rinse the soap suds from Mildred's hair. As she poured the water, she leaned in close, her lips almost brushing Mildred's earlobe. "One last thing, Mildred Winona Wyeth. When you're in with Mimses, do not think of anything I have told you. Send your thoughts in another direction."

Knuckling water from her eyes, Mildred asked, "Why don't you just ask me to think about elephants?"

"What?" Nefron's eyes were puzzled.

"When you tell someone not to think of something, invariably the first thing they think about is what they're *not* supposed to think about."

She paused and added, "Is Mimses a psychic or a telepath or something along those lines?"

"Not exactly. But he to whom Mimses is answerable—"

A sharp, impatient rapping came from the door. A voice rumbled, "The counselor awaits the outland woman."

Mildred quickly rose from the tub, water cascading down her body. Nefron handed her the garments, and she dressed in them quickly. When she had put them on, Mildred looked down at herself and growled, "Somebody has got to be kidding."

Instead of a frock or a skirt, she wore a broad strip of purple cloth fastened to a leather belt girding her hips. Another strip at the back fell to her upper thighs. Circular cups made of thin, gilt-edged leather barely covered her breasts, exposing a good amount of cleavage. High strapped sandals completed the costume. She shook her head in disgust, the beads in her hair clicking. "Who does he think I am, Scheherazade the dancing girl? I'm not really built for this outfit."

Nefron smiled for the first time. "That's for sure. Here." She touched a red pencil to Mildred's full lips, rouging them quickly. "No time to make up your eyes with kohl, but your eyelashes are long enough as it is. Besides, you've got good bone structure. You're very pretty for a woman so old."

"Thanks," Mildred said dryly, pressing her lips together. It had been a long time since she had worn any cosmetics. "Did Mimses pick out this ensemble?"

"Yes, but consider yourself lucky. Usually the women he calls for aren't allowed to wear anything at all."

The door opened and one of the shaved-headed guards beckoned to them. "Come on."

Mildred obediently crossed the chamber, feeling like a contestant in a Miss Belly Dancing contest. Before stepping through the door, she cast a glance over her shoulder. Nefron stared after her, her eyes burning with a strange, indecipherable light.

Chapter Fourteen

The two men marched on either side of Mildred, this time not laying a hand on her. At the end of the corridor, they ascended a winding staircase that led directly to a great, high-ceilinged hall. Her eyes darted around the vast room in wonder. She had seen splendor on this scale before, but only in movies, costume epics of the type DeMille had favored.

The hall attested to the wealth and power of its owner, not just by its size but by the richness of the furnishings. Lotus-topped pillars upheld the high ceiling, and smoldering bronze braziers filled the air with a spicy, aromatic scent that was at first unpleasant, then somehow soothing.

The polished surfaces of the walls bore a confusing jumble of pictographs and symbols and colors—bright reds, vivid greens, deep cyans, brilliant yellows. Plush chairs, divans and settees were scattered about, seemingly in a random pattern, but laid out and arranged so the eye followed the furniture to the open terrace at the far wall.

Late-afternoon sunlight shafted down a heavyset black man reclining on a cushion-piled dais. His gray-sprinkled hair was blunt cut and very short. He wore a linen tunic that exposed arms and legs that had once been firm with muscle but were now sagging with flab. His deeply lined face had a sensual, lupine quality about it. His eyes were almost hidden by puffy bags of flesh. A supple-bodied girl barely into her teens kneeled behind him, massaging his neck and shoulders. Her fingers moved deftly and expertly. When Mildred drew closer, she saw that his youthful masseuse was stark naked except for hieroglyphic designs painted on her arms, legs and budding breasts.

A pair of huge men, one wearing the head of a jackal and the other the head of a bull, stood on opposite ends of the terrace. Both gripped metauh staves in their fists.

Mildred's two-man escort suddenly halted, turned smartly on their heels and strode back to the door. Mildred stopped, almost wishing they hadn't left her.

The black man gestured to her. "Get over here, woman. You've kept me waiting long enough."

Mildred hesitantly edged onto the terrace, then to the base of the cushion-heaped dais. She locked her gaze on his face, dark eye to dark eye. His strength shone nakedly in his eyes, but it was an ugly strength, devoted only to fulfilling his own wants and whims. His eyes bored into hers as though they were trying to gauge her own strength. Remembering Nefron's warning, she sent her thoughts skittering in different directions, tumbling over one another. For a woman with such a disciplined mind, she found it difficult to allow chaos to fill her thoughts, but she managed. She knew the man expected her to turn away, unable to bear that gaze. She met his expectations, casting her glance down.

"Gen-you-wine brown sugar," the man drawled. "Real color by birth, not by a fucking bottle."

Although Mildred was pleased that her guess regarding the uniform skin and hair color of Aten's citizens had been correct, she said nothing.

The man grinned, showing off large, discolored teeth. "What's your name, brown sugar?"

"Mildred." She didn't offer her full name, acting on the impulse to provide him with as little information as possible.

The man nodded. "I'm Mimses. Not my real name, of course, but it'll do."

"What *is* your real name?" Mildred asked.

His eyes narrowed for a moment. "Stockbridge. Mean anything to you?"

"No."

"Thought not. I was a nothing as Stockbridge. A goddamn Farer. Not worth a rat's fart in a hurricane. Mimses is a different story altogether."

Mildred said nothing, standing and waiting silently.

"You're a pretty woman, you know that?" Mimses stated. "Kind of stocky, but I like that. Built for strength and breeding."

Mildred didn't respond. She remained silent, fear beginning to grow within her.

"Lovely and a real brown," Mimses continued. His right hand stole beneath the hem of his tunic and moved slowly, back and forth, fondling himself. "Yeah, a real lovely brown."

Her rising fear was suddenly outstripped by a rush of anger. "Stop it, you goddamn pervert."

Mimses stared at her in surprise for a long moment, then threw back his head and laughed. He withdrew his hand and pushed himself to his feet. "I haven't gotten going yet, Mildred."

Staring at the man as if she were a disinterested observer, Mildred vaguely realized she was disassociating. She noted a brief metallic gleam beneath his tunic. She watched him step off the platform, smile at her, then draw back his right hand. It swung around in a swift arc to connect with her face.

The open-handed slap was stinging, shocking. She stumbled back a pace, rage flaring bright and hot within her. Mildred knew the psychology behind Mimses's display—it wasn't about sex at all, but about control and power. She had only two options at the moment. For the sake of her pride, she could plant her foot where Mimses's hand had been a few moments before, but she would probably die—or end up wishing she had. He would probably enjoy her physical assault so he could indulge his sadistic impulses in either torturing or killing her.

Or she could feign humility and fear.

Mildred brought her hand up to her face. "Please...I'll do what you want." She forced a few tears to her eyes, wetting her lashes and spilling down her cheeks.

Mimses beamed at her. "Of course you will, brown sugar." The grin twisted into a fierce glower. "You better not give me any more of this 'pervert' bullshit, or I'll rip your bowels out and make you feed them to the work gangs. I decide what's perverted around here and what's not. Understand me?"

Mildred nodded meekly. "Yes, sir."

Mimses smirked, as if pleased to be called sir without having expressly ordered it. "Where did you and your friends come from? Where'd you get your blasters?"

"They're not really my friends," Mildred said. "They had weapons when I joined up with them about a month ago. They kind of just forced me to fall in with them. You know how it is with scavengers, living off the land."

She managed to squeeze out a few more tears. "We came across the Barrens. We almost died, all of us."

Mimses regarded her silently for a long moment, then he pounded his right fist hard into Mildred's bare midriff. She folded over his arm, lungs emptying of air with an agonized *woof*. She was only dimly aware of falling to the cold, slick floor. Mimses nudged her with a foot while she gasped and gagged.

"You're fucking lying to me, brown sugar," he said in a low croon. "You were in Fort Fubar and killed my Incarnates to get their chariot. Do you have any idea how hard it is to train new recruits?"

The man's voice grew shrill with outrage. "You and your scavenger friends chilled the cream of the cream. It took three years to train them, and you left them to lie like so much vulture's meat! Worse, you did it in front of the citizens. You've handed me a real—what's the old term?—public-relations nightmare."

Mimses stopped prodding her. He kicked her hard on her left thigh. She had no breath to cry out. Snarling, he continued, "You were in Pharaoh's tomb, too. I ought to toss you into the Incarnates' barracks so they can have a little fun with you, and if there's anything left of your lovely hide, I'll strip it off an inch at a time...make myself a new pair of sandals with it."

Raising his voice, Mimses called to the pair of guards. "Get her out of here. Take her to the women's quarters, but keep her isolated. I'll talk to that old bag of bones after supper."

She heard footsteps, then felt hands close around her upper arms and heave her up to her feet. The two men hustled her away from the terrace and out of the hall. By the time they went through the doorway, she was able to breathe more or less normally again, though her stomach muscles screamed with pain.

Mildred was escorted into a corridor that led off to the left from Mimses's hall. The passageway wasn't very broad, but it was long. She noted an absence of guards prowling the corridors. She could only presume that Pharaoh was so confident in his power, he saw no reason for security forces other than the Incarnates.

The men turned Mildred right at an intersection and stopped before a door bound with strips of brass. One of the men hammered on it with a fist. A small wicket in the door slid open, and a dusky face peered out with bland eyes.

"Open up, Grandmother," the guard said. "Mimses wants this woman looked after, but locked away from the rest of your bitches."

The wicket snapped shut, and an instant later the door swung wide. From within came an echo of laughter and scraps of feminine voices. Mildred didn't move. The place smelled like a trap. The very air reeked of danger and worse.

One of her escorts planted a hand between her shoulder blades and propelled her over the threshold. The door slammed shut immediately behind her.

Mildred whirled, and just managed to bite back a cry of revulsion.

A woman stood beside the door, her incredibly obese body covered with a linen caftan that covered her from neck to ankle. Only her arms were bare, two shapeless masses of flesh ending in blunt-fingered hands. Her features had long ago blurred into a sagging mass. Her hair was thin and white and hung about her shoulders like a tattered shroud.

Her eyes were a bright sky blue, and her voice, when she spoke, was surprisingly mild and sugary. "We haven't had a new arrival in a long time. Everybody here calls me Grandmother. What are you called?"

"Mildred."

Grandmother smiled. "Well, Mildred, if you do as I say, we'll get along fine. Come with me."

In a shambling, lumbering gait, she led the way through a series of doorless, box-shaped chambers. Torches burned here and there along the walls, and by their flickering, smoky glare, Mildred saw rows upon rows of narrow cots and many, many women, most of them so young they were still girls. They were engaged in all manner of activities—sewing, sweeping, chatting, scrubbing the floors or stretched out on the cots sleeping the sleep of the utterly exhausted.

She saw very little modesty among the sea of girls—most of the women walked, worked and talked in the nude. Mildred wasn't surprised, inasmuch as the standard articles of women's clothing were so scanty or diaphanous they might as well not wear anything at all. Aten was a patriarchy in every sense of the word, a sexist pig's fantasy world come to life. The whole atmosphere was charged with an anything-goes kind of erotic energy, wicked yet disturbingly arousing at the same time.

Mildred understood she was in the dormitory for the female servant class of the city, not the handmaidens of ranking citizens such as Mimses, but the drudges, the cooks, the scullery maids. Their situation probably wasn't as extreme as slavery, but it wasn't very many notches above that state, either.

Mildred followed the jiggling bulk of Grandmother down an aisle formed by two parallel lines of large wooden tubs. A few women soaked in them, while others sponged an oily brown substance over their bodies.

Grandmother wheezed, "At least you won't need a treatment before you're sent out to perform your duties."

"What is that stuff?" Mildred asked. "Some kind of vegetable-derived stain?"

Grandmother shot her a steely glare over one sloping shoulder. "It is the color of Aten, the people of Pharaoh. That is all you need to know."

Mildred couldn't help herself. With a derisive chuckle, she argued, "Granny, you don't have the color of Aten. Is that why you're down here, as the serving-girl wardess?"

"A good guess," Grandmother responded. "We serve Pharaoh when and where we can. You'll come to appreciate that."

Mildred eyed the woman surreptitiously, gauging her age and combining it with her slovenly appearance. "You're one of the original crew of Fort Fubar, aren't you?"

Reprovingly, Grandmother said, "We don't speak

of that blasphemous half acre of hell, child. It's forbidden.''

Mildred started to say something else, then shut her mouth.

Grandmother stopped before a low, open doorway. It was hardly tall enough for Mildred to step through without stooping, and that made it very low indeed. Gesturing with one hand, Grandmother announced, ''Here's your room, child. It's all yours, you don't have to share it with anyone else—at least until I'm told otherwise.''

It was very dark inside the cell, but Mildred took a determined breath, bent her head and walked in. The door shut behind her, and a locking bar rattled and clanked. A small, barred grille at eye level on the door allowed a feeble sort of light to filter through.

The cell was about eight feet wide and twelve long. There was no cot or pallet to sleep on, but it did have a toilet and tank in one corner. She sat down on the hard stone floor and rubbed her eyes.

Mildred had visited a lot of strange places, been in many a bizarre situation since Ryan Cawdor had revived her from cryogenic stasis, but this place and this situation was so strange, so utterly bizarre, she wondered if she were still in the throes of a jump nightmare.

A murmur of lilting voices reached her through the door grille. Though she couldn't know for sure, she doubted the women's dormitory was part of the original movie-set blueprints, despite DeMille's legendary reputation as a strict taskmaster.

Sixteen years was more than enough time to build additions and tinker with the original specs. But the building materials had to come from somewhere, especially the stone used in the pyramids.

The walls threw back her heavy sigh. She wondered about Jak, about Krysty and what Mimses would do when Doc started to quote Dante or Lewis Carroll. If he spoke the truth about his origins, and Mildred's, then their lives were probably forfeit. She feared for him. She feared for them all.

She couldn't work off her stress by pacing the cell, so eventually she lay on the floor, pillowing her head on her arms. In spite of her anxiety, she fell asleep.

She was jarred awake, almost immediately it seemed, by the rattle of the door's locking bar. She sat up, blinking, stiff and aching from sleeping on the hard floor. The door swung open, and a slim girl in a white frock came in, carrying a wicker tray containing a bowl of some kind of soup, a wooden spoon, a thick slice of darkish bread and a jug of water.

The girl knelt, carefully placing the tray on the floor in front of Mildred. Like all the rest, she had black hair and a dusky-hued complexion. However, her eyes were pale, perhaps gray or a light blue. A touch of pink lipstick brightened her mouth.

Stifling a yawn, Mildred asked, "What time is it?"

"The dawn bell has just been rung. Here is breakfast."

The girl cast a swift glance behind her and said softly, "My name is Kela. Nefron sent me to bring you word of the one called Jak."

Chapter Fifteen

Jak Lauren couldn't read, write or cipher very well, but he excelled at calculating the odds.

He came out of his handspring in time to see J.B., Mildred, Krysty and Doc writhing under the combined energy assaults of four metauh staves. He watched as they slumped unconscious, J.B. tumbling limply out of the chariot, his beloved fedora falling to the dust.

Though shouting, running pandemonium ruled the plaza, Jak was able to focus on several sights more or less simultaneously, all of them occurring within heartbeats of one another.

Ryan spun in the direction of the chariot at the precise instant a giant of a man, like a bronze statue given life and mobility, stalked out of the press of the milling Incarnates. The V prongs of the silver rod in his hand thrust toward the one-eyed man's back. A shout of warning rose in Jak's throat, but before it left his lips, Ryan crashed heavily to the ground, to lie motionless on his face.

Three animal-helmeted men turned savage eyes on him, and Jak saw three more racing to flank him. Ryan had long ago impressed on him the importance of counting bullets in a firefight, and he knew he had only four rounds for six rapidly moving targets.

Jak pivoted on his heel, put his head back and

started to run. He heard a deep voice shout, "Take him alive!"

"Easy to say, stupe," Jak whispered.

A raging chorus of orders and counterorders erupted behind him. He raced across the plaza, feeling as if his feet scarcely touched the ground. He ran down the narrow side lane that J.B. had followed, then up a narrow alley hardly wide enough to accommodate his slight frame. The much larger Incarnates would find it difficult and painful to negotiate.

Emerging into a broad street, he spotted a stone stair leading to the roof of a building. He loped up the steps, taking three at a time. Though he was the smallest in stature of his companions, except for Dean, he was the fleetest of foot and arguably had the deepest reservoir of stamina.

Running at full sprint across the flat surface of the roof, he took an alleyway yawning before him in a single leap. He misjudged the distance of the adjacent building, came down too low, fumbled his one-handed grip on the edge, scraped skin from his wrist and pulled himself onto the other side. He dashed across the top of the building and jumped over another alley, down a few feet to a tiled rooftop.

Only then did he pause to look back and catch his breath. Though the early-morning sun wasn't even at midpoint in the sky, the blazing heat and the exertion had already drenched him in sweat. His shock of white hair was a soaking mass, and salty, stinging trickles slid into his eyes. He considered removing his camouflage clothing, not only because of its weight but because there was nothing in sight to use as decent cover. At any rate, his white skin and ruby eyes couldn't be disguised.

He listened intently, but he heard very little aside from a distant shout. He had lost his pursuers. Swinging over the edge of the roof, he dropped down into the street below, landing lightly in a crouch. He moved along the street warily, trying to stay close to the sparse shadows.

The street funneled into a lane, then narrowed to an alley. The short, squat buildings hemming it had recessed doorways and windows covered with wooden shutters. It was fairly shady there, not yet exposed to the direct blast of the sun.

As Jak walked, he encountered no one, not even a dog. He crept along the alley, holstering his blaster and unsheathing one of his flat, leaf-bladed throwing knives. If he ran into trouble, he didn't want to pin-point his position by firing the Colt. A blade was just as quick, just as deadly and it was silent.

Jak had no plan except to evade capture. Escaping the city and leaving his friends behind never entered his mind.

A voice suddenly wafted to him on the air, a female voice lifted in a lilting song. A very small space, fifteen inches wide, between two of the build-ings was the only bolt-hole available. As thin as he was, it was a struggle to cram himself in sideways, pushing himself back from the alley. He waited, staring out with slitted eyes, his thumb resting on the razor-keen edge of his knife.

A nearly naked girl strode down the alley, her slender body draped in the filmiest of coverings. Her heavy black hair was as shiny as a raven's wing and rested on her shoulders. Impudent breasts swayed beneath the thin material. She carried a water jug in one hand and she sang as she walked.

"The evening river's calm and still
The evening flowers drink their fill
The north wind comes to cool the night
And put the river's waves to flight."

Jak stared, entranced by the girl's grace, sensual beauty and sweet voice.

Lingering grief over the deaths of his wife, Christina, and their infant daughter had frozen the softer emotions in him, particularly toward members of the opposite sex. That ice had thawed a bit during a brief sojourn in Japan a few months earlier, when he had been deeply attracted to a young geisha. But Issie had apparently perished in an earthquake, and the ice had slowly formed again.

The singing girl with her glossy black hair, soft pink lips and petite figure reminded him strongly of Issie.

She passed out of sight, still singing.

"The ripples wash the moon away,
And will not let the starlight stay."

The sound of a door slamming cut off the song, and silence fell over the alley again. Jak released a slow, pent-up breath of mingled relief and regret. He worked his way back out of the opening. Because of the scrape of his clothing on the walls, he didn't hear the faint scrabbling of feet until he poked his head out.

A hand closed over his long hair in an agonizingly

tight grip, and a tremendous, muscle-wrenching jerk catapulted him out into the alleyway. Through the tears of pain that sprang to his eyes, he caught a fragmented glimpse of a scowling bull's head.

Jak kicked himself off the ground, flowing into the momentum of the heave. He slashed backward and blindly with his knife, feeling the tip drag through flesh.

The hand tangled in his hair opened, he heard a grunt and Jak flung himself into a forward somer-sault. He came out of it on one knee, blade held between thumb and index finger, arm cocked for a throw.

He stared into the double prongs of a metauh rod, the V only inches away from his face. He didn't hesitate—his leg muscles propelled him in a side-ways lunge to the left, his body angled parallel with the ground. His arm and wrist snapped out and down in perfect coordination of eye and hand. He wasn't able to see if or where the knife struck because his optic nerves were suddenly overwhelmed by a flare of light.

Jak hit the ground with all the grace of a piece of cordwood. His entire left side was numb, the only sensation a dull, prickly creeping under the flesh. His heart thudded slowly, lurching in his chest. Breathing took such a deliberate, conscious effort than he didn't bother with it for what seemed like a long time.

His vision cleared fast, though, and he saw the Incarnate staring with foolish eyes at the knife hilt vibrating in his breast. A red line of blood shone on his ribs where Jak had nicked him.

Slowly, the bull-helmeted man dropped to his

knees, the metauh rod falling to the street dust. He gazed beseechingly toward Jak and in an aspirated whisper, said, ''I am the incarnation of Serapis. Tell me this is not happening to Serapis.''

Then he fell forward on his face, expiring very quickly and quietly for such a big man.

Jak tried to speak, found he couldn't.

He sucked in a noisy, rattling gasp and clawed himself forward by the strength of his right arm. His head pounded, like sharp hammers were beating on the inside of his skull.

He fought, wrestled and cursed his way to his knees, then to his feet. The buildings tilted and spun all around him. He staggered, fell to hands and knees, forced himself erect again, face glistening with sweat. His left leg shook violently in a tremor, and he dragged it behind him like a sack of flour, the toe of his boot gouging a furrow in the sand.

''Stupe,'' he husked out. ''Triple stupe.''

He fixed his eyes on the nearest doorway, six yards or six thousand miles away. He stumbled, reeled and fell into it, leaning his entire weight against the door.

With fingers that felt like cucumbers, he unbuttoned his shirt. Outlined in blue and red against the bone whiteness of his skin, a spiderweb pattern of broken blood vessels and ruptured capillaries extended from his left shoulder across his chest.

The door suddenly opened behind him, pulled from the inside, and he lost what remained of his balance, very nearly falling flat on his back. The hands clutching his arm and holding him more or less upright were small, brown and strong.

A gray-eyed, pink-lipped, black-haired girl held

him tightly, and it took him a dazed moment to recognize her. She was the girl with the water jug and the sweet song. She had reminded him of somebody, but he couldn't recall who.

His hands made an automatic slap for his knives or his blaster. The girl restrained him easily. Though she was about his height, she was astonishingly strong—or he was exceptionally weak.

"No," she said tersely. "I will not harm you. I want to be your friend."

She tugged him away from the door so she could shut and latch it. He stood swaying in the gloom. "Who you?" he managed to mumble.

"My name is Kela. What is your name?"

Everything seemed to stop inside him. It was as if he had been operating on a giant mainspring, and it had suddenly gone slack. Darkness, cold and excruciating pain swarmed over him at once.

He thought he croaked "Jak" before diving headlong into a deep, black well.

"ARE YOU SURE he still sleeps?"

Jak felt like he was floating.

"Yes. I gave him the right dosage."

Jak could feel the jostling vibration of a moving vehicle, hear the creak and squeak of wheels. He also heard the voices of two women, speaking in hushed tones. They whispered over him in silky blackness.

He felt a warm breath caress his right ear. "Jak," a melodic voice rustled, "can you hear me?"

He tried to answer, but he couldn't find or feel his tongue. He couldn't seem to feel his eyes, either. He could move neither his arms nor legs, nor did he care to do so. He was very warm, he was very comfortable, he felt no pain and he was in a good place. He was satisfied with it. He had no inclination to leave.

"Very good," the voice said. "Very good. Sleep, then."

And a woman laughed softly.

BARON TOURMENT and the General had turned the West Lowellton Holiday Inn into a casino, and they asked Jak to be the croupier at the craps table. He agreed before he realized all the dice were carved from the bones of his father, Christina and his darling Jenny. He was ashamed that he had forgotten the baron had murdered his father and the General was responsible for chilling his wife and child.

So Jak turned and ran through the old hotel, seeking out the humid comfort of his beloved bayou. He couldn't find the door. He wandered through dark tunnels toward a dim, distant light, only to find himself walking deeper and deeper into the black. At last he emerged into a tomb. Cobwebs hung in the corners and they fluttered toward his face. He tasted the dust of centuries on his tongue and he entered another door, scared and sweating.

He found himself sitting in a little amphitheater, looking down at a small central stage. Two naked girls danced to music only they could hear, their beautiful bodies twirling and pirouetting, tossing their heavy black hair and laughing in delight. They touched each other as they danced and laughed, fingers playfully darting here and there, and they kept stealing shy glances toward him, as if seeking his approval.

Jak applauded, feeling an admiration, a lust and almost a love for the girls who danced with such wild abandon for his pleasure. He watched, slowly aware of trickles of sweat flowing down his face from his hairline. He lifted his hand to mop away the moisture, and one of the girls stopped dancing and pointed at him with a long finger. She announced, "You are awake."

A DAMP CLOTH LAY across Jak's forehead. The pungent smell of herbs entered his nostrils and seemed to push back the nausea boiling in his stomach, and with each whiff, strength seemed to return to his limbs.

A hand cradled the back of his head, the rim of a cup pressed against his lips and a soft woman's voice said, "Drink this."

Unhesitatingly, Jak swallowed the liquid. It was warm and tasted strongly of copper, like mustard greens mixed with honey. He coughed, and the cup was removed. Carefully, he opened his eyes and saw a girl's face leaning over him. She was the same gray-eyed young woman who had pulled him into the house. He tried to rise.

She pressed a hand gently against his shoulder, pushing him back against the soft cushions beneath his body. She was as pretty as he remembered, and her full, pink lips smiled at him. Memory slowly seeped back to him.

"Kela?" he croaked, noticing that she kept her hand on his shoulder.

The smile widened. "Yes, my name is Kela. Your name is Jak. You are among friends."

Jak stared at her lovely face as she spoke. The

bare-walled room was lit by tapers, and the play of
light and shadow did interesting things to her features.

"My friends. Where?"

A different voice answered, "They are in the cus-
tody of Pharaoh."

Kela glanced up and to her left, and another
woman stepped into Jak's field of vision. She was
very tall and slim, with a touch of arrogance
stamped on her stirringly beautiful face. Her mouth
was agreeably, coquettishly shaped, and her almost
imperceptibly slanted eyes contained a dark, mocking curiosity.

Whereas Kela was lovely in an innocent, almost
childlike way, this woman's beauty was regal,
sculpted perfection. With a faint, drowsy shock of
recognition, he realized he had seen the woman before. He couldn't immediately recall, but he had an
impression that she had danced for him.

"I am Nefron," the woman continued. "I will
help you and all of your people if you will but trust
me."

Kela stood to allow Nefron to move to Jak's bed-
side. His eyes ran over their forms. Both women
wore thin, loosely woven tunics that seemed like
cobwebs, barely a concession to clothing. He felt
himself responding to the proximity of the two near
naked females. He hoped they didn't notice. He
glanced down at himself, making sure he still wore
his pants. He did, but he felt a distinct pressure
building in his groin.

"You have been brought to a safe house," Kela
said. "No one will find you here. You have been

unconscious all day and for the better part of the night.''

Jak started to speak, then thought better of it. He felt awkward, even a little foolish. It wasn't like him to start having erotic reactions in unsecured circumstances. He wondered briefly what had been in the drink.

"You must stay here and regain your strength," Kela said.

"Feel fine now," he grunted.

As he pushed himself up to his elbows, his head swam and his surroundings spun. Still, he forced himself to sit up on the edge of the pallet. "My things. Where?"

Nefron pointed to his camouflage vest draped over a footstool. "There. Your weapons, even your knives, are safe."

Jak started to stand, but a wave of dizziness crashed over him. He felt himself falling, but Nefron and Kela caught him by the arms and steadied him. As they lowered him back onto the pallet, Nefron said, "Do not be an idiot. You are still very weak."

Jak swiped shaking hands over his eyes. "Know that now. Thanks."

"What is your full name?" Kela asked.

"Jak Lauren."

"Listen to me, Jak Lauren." Nefron knelt beside the cot, one hand on his leg. "Life is very complex here in the kingdom. It will soon become even more complex. You must stay here, out of sight, until certain plans are laid and come to fruition. I or Kela will keep you advised as to the progression."

"Progression?" Jak looked into her eyes and once again felt a physical stirring, despite his weakness. Nefron's eyes were like dark flames, burning in his imagination, stimulating it with an almost erotic energy.

"I have a plan to get you and your friends safely out of here. But you must trust me. It all has to come together perfectly. All of you must go, or none of you will go. Do you understand?"

As she spoke, her fingers slowly crept up his thigh, and the exquisite tension strained against his crotch. He stared hard at her, then glanced away, toward Kela. She stood with her hands clasped primly behind her back and avoided his gaze.

"Do you understand?" Nefron asked in a husky whisper.

Jak nodded. "Yeah."

Nefron got to her feet, gesturing toward Kela. "I will not be able to visit you very often. Kela will attend to your needs and carry messages—to me and from me."

"Want to see friends," Jak declared stubbornly.

"That is not possible, Jak Lauren," Nefron snapped. "However, it is possible to get messages to them. That will have to suffice."

Then she turned and strode away, into a darkened foyer. A door clicked open, then shut. Jak leaned back on the pallet, realizing his breathing was slightly labored, but not simply because of his debilitated physical condition. Nefron had exerted a strange influence over him, and he didn't know how or why.

He looked over at Kela. "Who Nefron?"

She shrugged. "She is my princess. I do her bidding. She holds the key."

Jak remembered Danielson's story of Pharaoh and

how he had disowned his daughter, stripping her of the right to assume the throne. He wanted to ask what Kela had meant about Nefron holding the key. Instead, he found himself more concerned with his erection. It hadn't abated with the departure of Nefron. Grunting, he shifted position, to ease the pressure.

"Are you in pain?" Kela asked.

He shot her a quick, abashed glance and said dryly, "Not exactly."

Stone-faced, she inquired, "In discomfort, then?"

"Little, yes."

She moved toward him. "Nefron charged me with attending to your comfort."

Kela's hands went to his belt, unbuckling it so swiftly and deftly he had no opportunity to say anything. When her fingers undid the snap-catch on his pants, Jak decided there was no point in saying anything. Instead, he reached for her.

Chapter Sixteen

Krysty opened her eyes and stared in wonder at the chamber around her. Silk tapestries adorned the walls, rich rugs were on the floors and the ivory chairs, benches and divans were littered with satin cushions.

The canopy over the bed in which she lay was hung with gauzy draperies, softly stirred by an intoxicatingly sweet breeze, scented like orange blossoms.

The delicate aroma made her feel languorous and lethargic, as if she had just awakened from a deep, soul-restoring sleep. Stretching, she turned over on her side, wondering why Ryan wasn't beside her. She longed to feel his hard body pressing against hers, his hands fondling and caressing her. Krysty bolted upright in the bed, pushing herself into a sitting position. Memories returned to her in a flooding rush—the redoubt, the trek, the fight and finally the capture. She looked around wildly. The chamber was identical to the one in her jump dream, and for a split second her careening thoughts turned to the possibility that she was still hallucinating. She looked toward the great bronze double doors at the far end of the room. As in her dream, she saw no knobs or handles.

Climbing out of the bed, she saw she was naked.

Snatching up the brightly colored bedspread and draping it around her, she saw that the chamber walls were made of huge, white-faced stone blocks, perhaps limestone. The ceiling was exceptionally high. Light shafted it through slotlike skylights, filtered by the colored panes of glass. The air was heavy with the familiar scent of orange blossoms. The stone floor was covered by large woven mats. There were wall hangings with designs that complemented those of the bedspread. The furniture was of varnished wood, of an extremely advanced level of craftsmanship.

She walked cautiously to the massive double doors, a feeling of primitive fear and an unreasoning panic in the pit of her stomach. She fought to control it, employing a breathing exercise taught to her by her mother.

Krysty closed her eyes, inhaling and exhaling deeply and regularly. The terror ebbed a bit, but when she opened her eyes again, the double doors were still there. She heard nothing on the other side of them and started to turn away. Then the locking mechanism clicked and slid aside.

Krysty dropped into a combat stance, clenching her right fist, stiffening her left wrist, locking the fingers in a half-curled position against the palm so as to deliver a leopard's-paw strike.

One of the doors opened just enough to admit a young woman. She wore a short linen tunic, and her shining black hair framed a startlingly beautiful face. Her eyes were lined with dark pencil. She carried a covered tray of food in her hands.

Appearing not to notice Krysty's fighting posture,

she smiled wanly and walked past her to place the tray on a low table. "How are you feeling?"

Krysty answered the question with two of her own. "Who are you? Where am I?"

"One question at a time," the woman responded. "To answer your second question first, you are in Aten, in the guest chamber of Pharaoh's palace. As for your first, I have been sent to see to your wants. My name is Nefron."

Krysty tried to keep the surprise she felt from registering on her face. She remembered what Danielson had said about the girl, but it didn't seem the appropriate time to bring the matter up. "Where are my friends?" she demanded.

"They are here, separated from you but safe. If you wish them to remain so, you must listen carefully and trust that I will tell you the truth."

She gestured to the tray. "Sit and eat. I'm sure you're very hungry. You have been resting for nearly six hours. I will tell you what I can."

Krysty realized she was famished, so she selected an assortment of fruit and sweetmeats from the plates.

"How are you called?" Nefron asked.

"Krysty Wroth," she mumbled around a mouthful of fig.

"Krysty Wroth, you are the guest of Akhnaton. He foresaw your arrival here."

The red-haired woman stopped chewing for a moment. "How?"

"He has the ability to sense thoughts, especially thoughts charged with emotions. He can direct the thoughts he senses to run in channels of his own choosing. When you and your friends came into the range of his influence, he sensed your *ka,* your soul, immediately.''

Krysty felt her hair stir and shift. ''Can he read minds, then?''

''He can sense, in a general fashion, the substance of your mind, so you must be very careful what you think and what you allow yourself to feel when you come before him. Do you understand?''

Krysty shrugged. ''To an extent. What I don't understand is why I've been isolated from the rest of my party.''

Nefron smiled a wry, mocking smile. ''Pharaoh has singled you out, as I'm sure you guessed.''

''Singled me out why? To add to his harem?''

Nefron shook her head. ''Pharaoh does not have a harem. He leaves such indulgences to his counselors, like Mimses. No, I imagine Pharaoh has a greater destiny for you in mind.''

Krysty didn't reply. She was thinking of her own psionic abilities, the power to sense and semi-interact with strong emotional states—or conversely, be influenced by them if they were too strong. Images of the inhuman Other and the crazed Kaa flitted unbidden into her mind.

Nefron's words only confirmed what Mildred had postulated, and confirmed Krysty's own fears. She was familiar enough with telepathy to know that human brains and the energy they exuded could—under the right kind of sympathetic stimuli—act like mirrors and respond in unconscious ways.

If Hell Eyes or Akhnaton or whatever he chose to call himself wielded this stimuli, she was particularly vulnerable.

''Nefron, I've got to get out of here now. I don't

know if I can screen him out, if he's as powerful as he seems to be.''

"I know, Krysty Wroth. However, take solace in the knowledge that I am trying to help you and your friends. You must have patience and trust in me.''

Krysty gazed into Nefron's dark eyes, seeking out indications of deceit, trying to sense treachery. She saw and sensed nothing at all. She had no choice but to take the young woman at her word. "All right," she declared resignedly. "I don't have many options.''

Nefron's black eyes flashed at her tone. "We are all in this together, Krysty. Bound to each other. You must use all your strength to resist Pharaoh's desires. He will bend your body and mind to his purposes and leave you an empty husk, as he left my mother.''

Krysty's bare arms tingled with gooseflesh, as though she stood in the path of a wintry wind. Nefron didn't try to blunt the anger, the bitterness, the hatred in her voice. Rather than react to it, she asked, "Where is Ryan?''

"The one-eyed man?''

"Yes. I must talk to him.''

Nefron shook her head sorrowfully. "That is not possible. I can perhaps relay a message from you to him.''

"When? How?''

"When the opportunity arises. How is my own affair. Now it is time to get ready for your meeting with Pharaoh.''

Nefron showed Krysty a door, hidden behind a decorative wall panel. Behind it was a lavishly appointed dressing room with a bathing area. The tub was more like a small pool, sunken into the floor, about six feet in diameter. It was rimmed with ceramic tiles a gorgeous shade of turquoise, and the fixtures appeared to be solid silver.

Nefron showed Krysty how to control the flow of water and where all the soaps, perfumes and lotions were stored. She withdrew into the bedchamber while Krysty dropped her covering and walked down the three steps into the foaming bath. She settled down in a cradlelike seat at the far corner of the tub and washed herself, even shampooing her long hair. Despite herself, she felt tension ebb from her limbs and mind. A part of her marveled that she was able to relax under the circumstances.

In her wanderings with her friends across the length and breadth of Deathlands, she had learned to snatch every moment of happiness and comfort that came her way. She tried to live as if every day was her last. On many occasions, it had very nearly been. She had lived a hard life, filled with danger and death, but she fought to keep her heart and her soul untouched and uncorrupted by it.

She thought of Ti-Ra'-Wa and how happy she and Ryan had been there. Floating on those thoughts, buoyed by the scented water, Krysty almost drifted off to sleep. Her hair straightened languidly as she remembered the few short days she had spent in the valley with Ryan.

Slowly, the image of Ryan dissolved, the eye patch and scar melting away. The figure who took his place was still tall and dark haired and her lover, but his eyes glowed crimson.

Krysty sat up with a start, unable to repress a cry of surprise. Though the water was still warm, she felt very cold. She stood, climbed out of the tub, toweled herself off and dried her hair.

A soft knock came from the door, and Nefron entered with a garment folded over her arm. "I forgot to leave this before."

She flicked her eyes up and down Krysty's naked form, and appreciation and envy glinted in them. "You are so beautiful already, Krysty, but we need to make you more presentable for Pharaoh."

"How do you do that stuff on your eyes?" Krysty asked.

Nefron pointed to a mirrored dressing table. "It's called kohl, that black pencil there. Shall I show you how?"

Krysty nodded, ignoring the faraway voice shouting a dim warning in her head. She allowed Nefron to skillfully apply the cosmetics to her face, and within minutes she looked very different. With her eyelids outlined in black, her large green eyes seemed huge, with an innocent yet aristocratic expression in them. Nefron painted her lips a deep red and used a blush to accentuate her high cheekbones.

She allowed the girl to swab her with a perfume that smelled like the sweetest of garden flowers, then she put on the dress Nefron had brought. It was a high-waisted white gown that plunged at the neck almost to her navel. The right side was slit to above the thigh, but at least the material wasn't the semitransparent gauze worn by Nefron. She put on bracelets and rings, and Nefron slid a collar of beaten gold around her slender neck.

"Pharaoh will be pleased," the girl said with something like sarcasm buried deep in her tone.

Krysty shot Nefron a stricken look of guilt. "I

wasn't thinking about dressing for him.... I don't want—''

Squeezing her eyes shut, Krysty rubbed her forehead with her fingers. ''What's wrong with me? Why should I dress up like a gaudy slut for a man who's keeping me a prisoner? This isn't me.''

Nefron put a hand on her shoulder, saying earnestly, ''For the time being, it must be. Krysty, if you can make Pharaoh believe you are who he *wants* you to be, he will treat you and your friends kindly.''

She chuckled dryly. ''Who does he want me to be?''

''That you will learn. I cannot prepare you for it.''

Krysty shook her head, her scarlet tresses coiling. ''This is a charade. It's like I forgot that or something—''

''We need time to make our plans for your escape. You can buy us that time.''

Taking a deep, calming breath, Krysty said, ''This could get out of control. I know what's happening. I'm already responding to the bastard's psychic cues.''

''You must be strong, now that you are aware of them.''

''All right, Nefron. I just want to get this over with. I want Pharaoh to let us leave.''

Nefron nodded. ''As do we all. Now, he is ready for you.''

Krysty balled her fists, her nails biting into her palms. ''That's what I was afraid you were going to say.''

NEFRON LED Krysty into a very broad corridor. High up in the vaulted ceiling, skylights like the ones in the bedchamber let in colored sunlight. Two balustraded galleries ran along each side of the corridor, one above the other.

They turned into an open door, and Nefron announced simply, "Pharaoh Akhnaton."

Krysty hadn't been sure of what to expect, but the chamber into which she was escorted was almost Spartan in its furnishings. It certainly wasn't a throne room or royal living quarters. It was more like a study or a library. Shelves laden with books and bound volumes of magazines covered two walls. A worktable held the tools and materials of a sculptor—clay, stone, chisels and delicate picks.

A huge predark map of the United States hung on the far wall. Krysty noted that large sections of it had been altered by red ink, no doubt to make it conform to the geophysical changes since the nukecaust.

The man seated at an ornately carved desk was a stranger, yet when he stood, she knew with a sick, sinking sensation in her stomach that she had seen him before. He looked to be in his midthirties, his black hair was short cropped and his shoulders almost impossibly broad. He wore only a brown, gilt-edged vest and a white linen kilt, which showed off his deeply tanned, muscled arms and legs. However, it was the deep red hue of his big eyes that captured Krysty's attention.

He stared at her silently for a long moment, then stepped toward her. It wasn't until he was next to her that she realized just how tall he was. At one inch shy of six feet, she was hardly petite, but he truly towered over her, not just in height but in breadth.

In a low voice, he said, "I must have the name to which you presently answer."

Disregarding the odd phrase he had used, she said, "Krysty."

He bowed his head, as if ashamed. "Krysty, please forgive the manner in which we meet again, but the circumstances dictated it to be the only way."

His voice seemed to echo and vibrate around her skull. Instead of feeling fear or anger, she felt flustered.

"How should I address you?" she asked, tilting her head back, trying to meet his gaze.

A smile creased his lips. "You may call me Akhnaton. There's no need for the two of us to stand on formalities. I feel I know you intimately."

She felt her cheeks burning with a blush of embarrassment or a flush of anger. She wasn't sure which. Rather than saying anything, she walked around him to a chair facing the desk and sat in it. Akhnaton chuckled and returned to his seat behind the desk.

"What did you mean about meeting me again?" she demanded, deliberately trying to sound abrupt.

Akhnaton drummed his fingers on the desktop. "Are you telling me you don't remember? Ah, well, that's unimportant. All that matters is you are here now, when the monument nears completion. Would you like something to drink?"

"That would be very nice," Krysty said, more to have something to say than to quench her thirst.

Akhnaton closed his eyes for the briefest of moments. When he opened them, Nefron came through the door. "You wish something, Pharaoh?"

"Dandelion wine. The batch from three summers ago."

Nefron ducked her head. "By your command." Though her tone was subservient, anger glinted in the dark depths of her eyes.

The woman quickly went to a cabinet across the room and removed a corked earthenware bottle and two goblets. She brought them to Akhnaton's desk, allowing the Pharaoh to remove the cork with a negligent twist of thumb and forefinger. Nefron filled the goblets, handed one to Krysty, then lingered by her chair.

"You may go," Akhnaton intoned.

Nefron bowed her head again and left the room. She steadfastly avoided making eye contact with Krysty.

Akhnaton sipped the wine and cast Krysty a questioning look. She tasted it, found it sweet with just a hint of a bitter aftertaste, but more than palatable overall.

Akhnaton placed the goblet on the desk, and his eyes gazed directly into hers. "Now that the wine has cleansed our palates of falsehoods, let us speak truthfully and plainly, shall we?"

Krysty met that crimson stare and felt a distinct shock somewhere in the back of her mind. "Yes," she heard herself saying, "we shall."

"I knew our individual roads of destiny would converge at this time."

"Destiny?" She crooked an ironic eyebrow at him. "I'm not sure if I understand you."

He gestured with both hands. "My monument

could not be completed without your presence, but I continued to build it, knowing you would arrive before the capstone ceremony. And you have.''

''A strange coincidence, I can't deny that.''

''Coincidence?'' Akhnaton spluttered with laughter. ''Krysty, I have searched for you for many years.''

''Why?''

''Because you are my fated queen—now, as always. We have always been together. When I, as Amenhotep, took the name of Akhnaton, I took you to wife.''

Krysty stared at him incredulously. ''When was this?''

''At the height of the glorious Eighteenth Dynasty...over three thousand years ago, give or take a decade or two. Your name was Nefertiti. You know that, don't you? You have the same psychic memory as I, stretching back over the long track and tide of time. You and I have been reborn many, many times, and always we have been together.''

Krysty wasn't frightened by the man's words, or by the obvious sincerity that charged them with emotion. She accepted, if not necessarily believed, the doctrine of reincarnation and was intrigued. But all she said was, ''I belong to another.''

Akhnaton waved aside her statement as if he were brushing off a bothersome gnat. ''As did I. Merely way stops on the road of fate, temporary patches on the wounds of loneliness. Always I knew my *ka* mate was coming. It was hard to be patient, but I was. I waited. And here you are, at last.''

Krysty inhaled deeply, noting how Akhnaton's eyes suddenly flickered toward her half-revealed bosom. "You said we would speak the truth to each other."

He nodded. "So I did."

"Then let us do so, without dragging souls, destiny and past lives into the mix. I was in the redoubt where you were born—or created. There was another like you, a female. She died. I found out about you, about O'Brien, about Harrier."

Akhnaton's face remained an immobile bronze mask, impassive and unreadable.

"Somehow, when my friends and I jumped into the redoubt, you got into our heads—Ryan, Doc and most of all, me. You were testing us from here, finding out who was the most psi-sensitive, and you locked in on me. Your abilities are like mine, operating on an empathic level rather than telepathic. You made me—" she searched for a tactful word, then chose the first one that popped into her mind "—perform for you. Later, when we tried to leave, you kept the mat-trans chamber from working. Psychokinesis?"

"Yes. After many years of practice, I possess a small degree of it."

Krysty didn't delve further. She supposed that since distance meant nothing to psi-powers, as long as Akhnaton retained a clear picture of the redoubt, he could mentally reach out and interact with it. "Have I spoken the truth?"

"You have. Your perception of it, at least."

"Then speak of your perception. Why have you done all of this?"

"I believe I explained that."

Krysty smiled coldly. "You explained nothing. I possess a limited precognitive gift, but for you to have known well in advance that one day I would appear in your redoubt is too thin for me to consider the truth.''

Akhnaton let a sigh of weariness escape his lips. Slowly, he rose from the desk and paced over to his worktable. A closed cabinet hung on the wall above it. He opened the door panel, saying softly, reverently, ''Look at this, Krysty. Look.''

Inside the cabinet rested a life-size painted bust of a woman. Her face was smoothly contoured, the cheekbones high, the nose straight and finely chiseled, the chin round and firm. The mouth was straight with a full lower lip. The slender column of the throat was long and graceful. Above a high, smooth forehead rested a cylindrical, flat-topped headpiece, concealing all the hair. But beneath curved brows, the wide, slightly tilted eyes were a brilliant green.

Krysty felt as if she were looking into a mirror rather than inspecting a piece of statuary. Her heartbeat sped up, and her red tresses slid and curled.

Akhnaton fingered the chin of the bust lovingly. ''This is an exact copy of a bust found in a workshop in Akhnaton's royal palace. The original was over three thousand years old. Historians agreed that it is probably the only true likeness of Akhnaton's queen, Nefertiti.''

Krysty's tongue seemed to cleave to the roof of her mouth. She drained the last of the dandelion wine as Akhnaton closed the cabinet door and regarded her quietly.

She shook her head. ''What do you expect me to say?''

''That you will at least contemplate the possibility

that your spirit, your *ka* and mine were meant to meet again, that we are fated to rule as god and goddess over this blighted planet.''

''I can't contemplate anything,'' she replied sharply. ''Not when I'm so concerned about my friends.''

''They mean much to you?''

''Yes. Especially Ryan.''

''The one-eyed man.''

''Yes.''

A hint of a grim smile touched Akhnaton's lips. ''He is a true warrior, that one. The *ka* of the leopard lives within him. However, Aten has no need of leopards or warriors. There may be no place for him or your friends.''

She fixed an unblinking, emerald gaze on his face. Flatly, determinedly, she stated, ''If there is no place for them, there is no place for me.''

Akhnaton returned her gaze for a long, speculative moment, then returned to his chair behind the desk. ''My high counselor, Mimses, took responsibility for containing your people. I will speak to him, though he is very angry over the losses you caused him.''

''Losses?''

''The Incarnates.''

Thinking of the sheep-headed man she had back shot in Fort Fubar, Krysty elected to say nothing.

As he had a few minutes before, Akhnaton closed his eyes, and a moment later Nefron came into the study. He said to her, ''Fetch Mimses. Bring him here immediately.''

The girl ducked her head and left the room.

''Was that telepathy just now?'' Krysty asked.

Akhnaton looked at her uncomprehendingly for a moment. "You mean with Nefron?"

"Yes. You closed your eyes and she—"

"There are certain minds I can touch, minds with which I can establish psychic links. Not very many, because the other mind must possess a certain degree of psionic abilities, as well. Nefron is one. You, obviously, are another."

Krysty didn't like the direction of the conversation, but to abruptly change the very subject she had raised would arouse the man's suspicious. She kept wondering, too, why neither Nefron nor Akhnaton had mentioned their familial connection.

Choosing her words carefully, she said, "And you can't influence psi-null minds unless they're unwary or unguarded."

"Or asleep," he replied pointedly. And he smiled a very genuine, almost boyish smile.

An overweight black man entered the chamber, head at a deferential posture. A blue robelike cloak draped his body. "You wished to see me, Pharaoh?"

He gave Krysty a quick appraising glance. She found his deeply creased face and small, flesh-bagged eyes repulsive.

Akhnaton asked him several questions about Krysty's friends.

Reluctantly, he answered, "I interviewed a woman named Mildred. She lied to me about herself and the others."

"She was afraid," Krysty interjected.

Mimses ignored her. "I intend to question the others."

"No need," Akhnaton said. "Where is this Mildred now?"

"In the hall of women, in isolation."

"Release her and the rest of the newcomers. Send Iwat to begin their education."

Mimses scowled and extended a pair of fingers. "Lord Pharaoh, two matters must be addressed. First, one of their group is still at large. An Incarnate was found in Baltic Alley. He had been stabbed to death."

"Continue the search for him. My order to take him alive still stands."

"The second matter is of murder and reparation. Eight of my Incarnates have been slaughtered. Six are missing, and I presume them dead."

"There will be reparation," Akhnaton said firmly. He gestured toward the door.

Mimses bowed, gave Krysty a grudging nod and stalked out of the study.

"What did you mean by education?" Krysty asked.

"If your friends are to remain among us, they must learn our customs, our beliefs, our ways."

"I don't suppose," Krysty ventured, "that simply letting us return to the redoubt and jump out of here is an option."

"No. It is not. The people who come among us learn to live by our ways or they don't live at all."

"When may I see my friends, then?" she asked.

"Soon," he replied promptly.

Akhnaton stood and walked toward her, extending a hand. After a hesitant moment, she took it and allowed him to gently pull her to her feet.

"You must absorb what you have learned," he

said kindly. "Nefron will take you back to your quarters. We will speak again tomorrow."

Then, swiftly, unexpectedly, he pulled her against him. He bent his head and whispered into her ear, "He came to her straight away. He was ardent for her. He gave his heart unto her, let her see him in the form of a god after he came before her."

His voice rolled and vibrated through her head, like the echoes of a gong. As swiftly as he had embraced her, he released her, guiding her out into the corridor. Nefron stood there, her mouth set in a tight, grim line.

A dew of sweat had gathered at Krysty's temples, and she realized she was moist elsewhere. Looking down at herself, she was shamed and a little shocked to see her nipples, hard and hot, poking against the thin fabric covering her breasts.

"Let us go," Nefron said stiffly.

Krysty tried to engage her in conversation on the walk back to her chambers, but she refused to speak until they were behind closed doors. Krysty said faintly, "He's not what I expected."

"Krysty, be on your guard. His power is working on you too quickly. If you are seduced before—"

Whirling on her angrily, Krysty said between clenched teeth, "I've done what you told me to do. Nobody—not Pharaoh, baron or god—will seduce me. You wanted me to buy you some time by playing nice. Did I or didn't I?"

Nefron's face twisted momentarily in anger, then she shook her head, exhaling sharply. "I apologize. I spoke out of turn. But you must always keep in mind the power he can bring to bear. It's not a simple matter of Pharaoh wanting to have his way…he *always* has his way.''

She forced a bitter smile to her lips and patted Krysty's arm. ''Just remember to guard your thoughts…and your dreams.''

Chapter Seventeen

Ryan, Doc and J.B. had spent a relatively miserable night in their cells. Relatively, because they could easily recall worse nights spent in far worse places. Still, they were a long way from being comfortable.

The bald turnkeys gave them food at one point—something resembling cold oatmeal—and water, but they steadfastly refused to answer questions or to even respond to the insults J.B. hurled at them. He addressed them as Baldy One and Baldy Two, but they ignored him. Only Doc was able to sleep. He snored so loudly that J.B. and Ryan were unable to hold a conversation, not that Ryan felt much like talking.

As the hours dragged on, his strength slowly returned to him, the pain fading. And with it faded the emotional memory of the red-eyed giant's voice. When he felt a tiny ember of anger glow within him, he happily fanned it to a full flame of fury, but he kept it banked, under control.

With the anger came a sick fear, stealing over him like a virus. He feared not for himself but for the people he had led into a trap. He feared most for Krysty. More than once, she had fallen into the hands of coldhearts who wanted to possess her or violate her. This time was different in a way he couldn't quite identify. This time, he was genuinely worried about the strength of her resolve, since his own had cracked in the presence of Pharaoh, even if only for a short time.

He replayed Danielson's words in his mind: *When you're in the presence of Pharaoh, you end up loving him eventually.*

He touched the blood-crusted welt on the side of his head and thought of the man who had inflicted it. "No love lost here," he whispered. "Bastard has to pay."

A sound floated down the corridor, a woman's faraway voice and a man's gruff response. It was followed a moment later by a burst of bawdy laughter from Baldys One and Two. Doc awoke with a snorting start and pulled himself to his feet by the barred door.

A young woman came hurrying into the cell blocks, carrying a basket full of dark loaves of bread. As one, Doc, J.B. and Ryan stepped back from the bars, unconsciously covering themselves. She swept her gray gaze over the men, then rested it on Ryan. She stepped forward, thrusting a long loaf between the bars.

"My name is Kela," she said in a brisk, nononsense whisper. "I bring you word of your missing friends."

They listened quietly as she told them of the whereabouts of Jak, Mildred and Krysty. Anticipating more questions from Ryan, she added, "She is all right. She is a guest in the palace, under the personal protection of Pharaoh."

Ryan stepped back to the bars, forgetting his nudity in his anger. Gripping the bars, he snarled, "What the hell do you mean?"

The corners of Kela's pink lips twitched. "She is your woman, isn't she? You have no need to worry, yet. Krysty is prepared for his probes."

"What?" The word exploded from his lips.

The woman tapped her forehead. "Psychic probes, Ryan Cawdor. Yes, I know your name." She glanced over at J.B. and Doc. "I know all of your names and I and others intend to help you."

Doc cleared his throat. "Why are you befriending us at such great personal risk?"

Kela made a dismissive gesture with one hand. "That is a long story. But keep in mind that forces are at work to free you. In the meantime, you are scheduled to be released from your cells shortly. That should give you some comfort. But you must not try to leave the city, and you must cooperate with everyone who deals with you. If you do not, every one of you will be killed."

With a swirl of her hair, she turned and left the cell block.

Doc looked after her, commenting wryly, "Now, who in this den of holiness would care about heretics such as ourselves?"

J.B. tore off a mouthful of the coarse-grained bread. "Think we should believe her?"

Ryan sighed and sat on the cot. "Wait and see. That's all we can do. At least we know Jak and Krysty are alive. That's something."

Within the hour, the turnkeys strode in, tossing folded squares of linen into the cells. "Put these on," one ordered. "You're moving to new accommodations."

It took them a couple of minutes to figure out the proper way to wear the kilts. When Doc pointed out they were like oversize diapers, they adjusted them accordingly.

After they were dressed, the cell doors were unlocked and they walked out under the scrutiny of the turnkeys. They appeared unarmed. J.B. shot Ryan an up-from-under questioning glance, but the one-eyed man shook his head. Starting a fight in such closed quarters wouldn't gain them anything.

They followed Baldy One down the corridor while Baldy Two dogged their heels. They walked out into the cold sunlight of dawn, marching across a walled-in compound. Interest temporarily displaced Ryan's other concerns. In the center of the yard was an array of very large, open-topped, wheeled metal cubes, resting on a double-railed track. Men wearing apronlike garments fed fires beneath the cubes, and other men stood over them, using long-handled paddles to stir the contents. An odd smell, like lime combined with acid, bit into his nostrils. The men wielding the paddles wore strips of cloth over nose and mouth, and coughed frequently.

A line of men formed a bucket brigade, passing containers full of rock chips to other men, who dumped their contents into the metal cubes. To the accompaniment of a rhythmic chant containing no words Ryan recognized, several other laborers poured the contents of sacks into the gooey, putty-like mix.

Another group of men used mallets to pulverize cactus lobes laid out on big squares of muslin, pounding them to pulp.

The entire operation was very organized, very efficient, like an assembly line.

The three outlanders were herded into a building on the far side of the compound. The room the guards guided them to contained furniture. It was simple, but much appreciated by Doc, who flopped down in a thickly upholstered chair with a sigh. A dark, polished table stood in the middle of the room, and beside the table stood a dark, polished man, though Ryan had to look hard at him to make certain he was a man.

"You may go, but remain outside," he said to the guards. They obediently left the room. Smiling nervously all around, he announced in lilting tones, "My name is Iwat. I am to be your instructor in the customs of Aten. I serve as scribe and scholar in the court of Pharaoh. You will listen to me and you will learn."

Ryan wasn't sure if the man had a slight speech impediment or had just adopted an affected manner of speaking. As it was, he was almost too precious for words, too precious to stomach.

Iwat was a plushy man in his midtwenties, soft faced with limpid, liquid brown eyes. He wore a green-and-white ankle-length mantle cinched at the waist by a gold-tasseled cord. The toes poking out from beneath the hem of his mantle were painted a shocking pink. An opal the size of a robin's egg hung from one fleshy earlobe. His short black hair was a mass of tight curls.

"Let's get on with it, then," J.B. said gruffly.

"We shall, when the other member of your party arrives."

As if on cue, a scantily clad black woman stepped through the door. Everyone stared at her in nonplussed silence for a heartbeat, then J.B. rushed to her, exclaiming, "Mildred? Dark night! Mildred!"

J.B. and Mildred embraced and kissed passionately, then the Armorer held her at arm's length and looked her up and down. "Where'd you get that rig?"

She laughed shortly. "Costume of the day."

"My, Dr. Wyeth," Doc said in a laconic drawl, "don't you look as professional and as medical as can be. I'd let you freeze me anytime."

"Look who's talking, Dr. Tanner." Though her voice was sharp, her mouth was smiling. "Past time for your diapers to be changed, isn't it?"

Iwat waved beringed hands. "Please, people, please. We must begin so you can be assigned to your individual duties."

"What do you mean by that?" Ryan asked darkly.

Iwat pursed his lips in disapproval. "Listen and learn."

He began to speak, telling them that, among other things, Akhnaton had been reborn into the world, to be the pharaoh of the world. "I only tell you what mystics knew ages ago—that the savior of humanity was coming, Akhnaton, to whom all the peoples of the world will one day bow their necks."

Akhnaton's powers derived from Osiris, Iwat said, and with the god's help, he was building an empire, a dynasty that would last ten thousand years and all who took part in forging it would share in the benefits.

Iwat's eyes glowed with a fanatical fervor as he spoke of Akhnaton, and he spoke sincerely of his worship of the god-king. His pride in Aten was evident in his tedious descriptions of all it had to offer and the glories it would offer in the future.

"It will be once again as it was in the before-times. Our people will spread out from Aten, bringing the word of Akhnaton into the wastelands. We will reshape this world and make certain that the evil that sprouted in it never grows again. Pharaoh will unite all the different peoples and tribes. All will join us, and the old divisions of race, nationalism and sexual preference that nearly destroyed the world will be forgotten."

Mildred, Doc, J.B. and Ryan had restrained themselves from commenting during the long dissertation, but now they had heard enough.

"Hell Eyes is going to conquer the world with the force of his personality?" Ryan asked sarcastically.

Iwat blinked at him in shock. "Do not use that term. It is forbidden and carries with it ghastly penalties."

Doc nodded agreeably. "As you wish. However, the question still stands."

Iwat smiled serenely. "The force of his personality, you ask. Yes, you might say that...and the *sekhem* energy that will be his to command once the pyramid is completed."

"Those sticks the Incarnates used," J.B. said uneasily. "That's an example of the whatchamacallit energy?"

Chuckling patronizingly, Iwat replied, "The 'sticks' channel mena energy, which is the opposite of the *sekhem.* The mena effects are debilitating, not fatal. We seldom use lethal weapons."

"That's real decent of you," Ryan commented.

"Pharaoh is benevolent by nature. He wishes only to pass on the blessings of his kingdom to all of his subjects. When new subjects like you and your friends come among us, we show you the many benefits to be gained from living as a citizen of Aten."

"Such as?" Mildred inquired.

"Security, lack of want, shelter, education and a purpose in life. We remold people like you into the ideal Aten form. You are educated and corrected."

"Corrected?" Ryan growled. "Brainwashed?"

Iwat's face registered sincere displeasure. "Of course not! By correcting, I mean that all the unproductive habits and attitudes are tweaked and rechanneled into productivity. In Aten, all people know they are part of something larger, something better than they are. They work toward a common goal. Willingly."

Ryan thought of the pyramid and the many laborers needed to construct it, but he didn't raise the issue.

Iwat continued. "You will come to see how working together for the glory of Aten is superior to wandering across Deathlands. Once you have your audience with Akhnaton and receive your Aten name, and so on—"

"When do we meet your Pharaoh?" Ryan asked.

"What's an 'Aten name'?" J.B. demanded.

"What do you mean by 'so on'?" Mildred inquired.

Iwat shook his head and held up his hands in a gesture of appeasement. "You will meet Akhnaton at a time of his choosing. Your Aten name comes with the makeover, so you will live among us in the ideal form."

The three men and one woman simply stared at him.

Iwat touched his hair and rubbed his hands. "The color of your hair and skin must be changed. By dye and by stain."

Doc laughed. "The very thought of these gray locks of mine dyed black and done up in the Egyptian style makes me incontinent."

"No need to worry, old one," Iwat replied. "Your advanced age excuses you from that part of the makeover." He glanced toward Mildred. "And there is little point in subjecting you to it."

"Thanks," she said dryly.

Ryan kept his eye on Iwat, not finding the prospect of having their skin and hair altered the least bit amusing. Though Kela had urged patience, allowing his fate and that of his friends to rest in the hands of others wasn't something he could lightly accept.

Iwat gestured to J.B. and Ryan. "You will follow me." He minced his way into an adjacent room.

Ryan, J.B., Doc and Mildred all exchanged dubious glances, then J.B. and Ryan walked into a small room holding only two wooden tubs. They brimmed with a dark liquid. Ceramic jugs and big sponges lay on the floor.

"Climb in," Swat said.

Ryan regarded the tub's contents suspiciously. "What is that shit?"

Iwat sighed in exasperation. "As I thought I explained, it will convey upon you the color of Aten."

Mildred called out, "Don't worry, guys, it's just some kind of vegetable dye. The stain isn't permanent."

J.B. took off his spectacles, placing them carefully on a wall shelf, stripped off the kilt and stepped into a tub. He sat with the liquid sloshing around him and grimaced.

After another moment of hesitation, Ryan followed suit, making sure his back was to Iwat when he removed his loin covering.

Only J.B.'s hair needed darkening, though both he and Ryan were forced to endure soaking for an hour in the tubs of oily brown liquid, with a tittering Iwat sponging their backs, necks and faces with it.

After Iwat announced enough time had passed, they stepped out of the tubs and into calf-length apronlike garments, identical to the ones worn by the men in the compound.

When they returned to the room, Doc and Mildred couldn't help but laugh. J.B. was the most changed and bore the brunt of the hilarity.

"Speaking strictly as a man who never wore a skirt in his life, John Barrymore, I must say that you strike a very fetching picture."

Ryan sat down glumly, looking at his deep brown hands. He felt like he was trapped within a jolt addict's delirium, dressed and stained as he was. He couldn't help but wonder if Kela was playing a cruel game with them.

Iwat beamed at them proudly, as if they were his creations. He clapped his hands sharply, and Baldy One and Baldy Two stepped in immediately. To Mildred, the scholar announced, "You are assigned a food-preparation station in the palace."

Mildred's eyes flashed. "I'm a doctor, not a hash slinger."

"You have nothing to say about it," Iwat retorted. He nodded toward Baldy One. "Escort her there."

The shaved-headed man grasped her by her upper arm, and Mildred jerked angrily away. Baldy One grabbed her again, so roughly she cried out in pain. J.B. instantly stood toe-to-toe with the much larger man, glaring up into his face.

"Take your bastard hand off her, or I swear I'll feed you your balls." He spoke in a ferocious whisper, packing every word with a deadly conviction.

Baldy One glanced quizzically toward Iwat, who stared back with wide, disconcerted eyes.

"Tell him to do it," Ryan advised. "Or you'll have a hell of a mess to clean up in here." The last was directed toward Baldy Two, who looked as if he were considering the wisdom of pouncing on J.B.

"It is against the rules," Iwat stammered. "I cannot allow this insolence—"

"Yeah," Baldy One rumbled. "Don't start a fight you can't win, One-eye."

Draping a comradely arm over Iwat's shoulders, Ryan said, smiling, "Allow it just this once." He bent his arm sharply, hooking Iwat's soft neck in the crook of his elbow. "This may be a fight we can't win, but you'll die first. Get me?"

Iwat's respiration became fast and harsh. "Release her!"

Baldy One slowly removed his hand. J.B. and Mildred embraced, kissed then she turned to the door, the guard falling into step behind her.

Ryan took his arm from Iwat, who rubbed his throat, coughed delicately and said to Doc, "You are assigned to transportation maintenance."

Doc nodded brusquely, then shook hands with

both J.B. and Ryan. "Gentlemen." He departed with a quiet dignity, despite Baldy One nearly treading on his heels.

"Now us," Ryan said.

A jittery smile tugged at the corners of Iwat's mouth, but his eyes were fearful. "You will join a pyramid work detail, shift two. The men's barracks are through there." He gestured toward a short hallway. "Shall I go with you to make sure you're properly settled?"

"No, thanks," J.B. told him. "You've done enough for us already."

They walked through a series of small chambers and stopped before a door. A young aproned man with a sheathed dagger at his hip stood beside it. He swung it open upon their approach and gestured grandly for them to enter.

J.B. and Ryan stepped into a long, low-ceilinged hall, so long that its far end seemed to run away in the distance. A dull clamor of male voices filled the dim interior, and the air was redolent with the stink of old sweat and urine. When their eyes adjusted to the murk, they saw a dormitory, a barracks with pallets laid out in facing rows on the stone floor. Many of the pallets were occupied, many more weren't.

The two men moved down the wide aisle between the pallets. "Do we just grab a rack at random and sack out?" J.B. queried.

Ryan shook his head. "There's got to be an overseer or boss around here someplace."

A fat, repellent figure shambled toward them from the dark end of the aisle. He wasn't very tall, but he was two men wide. A huge paunch swelled out over the top of his breechclout. His head was shaved except for a wispy strand of hair on the left side of his head. His flabby pectorals gleamed with a combination of oil and sweat. His rank, unwashed odor was very nearly overpowering.

Touching the butt of a wooden truncheon hanging from his broad belt, he brayed, "You newcomers?"

Ryan nodded. "Yeah."

The man grinned, revealing black gums from which every other tooth seemed to be missing. "I'm Shukeli, sort of the warden around here. You're on the noon-to-sundown shift, block-moving detail. You've got a couple of hours yet. Follow me."

Shukeli lumbered back in the direction from which he had come. J.B. and Ryan followed him for what seemed like a very long time. Finally, the man stopped in an area so shrouded in shadow it was only a few gray degrees above pitch-black.

Pointing to a pair of frayed pallets on the floor, Shukeli said, "There you go. This is as good a place as any."

Ryan glanced around. "It appears we have this good place all to ourselves."

Shukeli chuckled. "It's private, all right. Nice and quiet back here."

"And dark," J.B. commented.

"And dark," Shukeli echoed agreeably. "Sometimes men need the dark, need it private." His voice dropped to a conspiratorial whisper as he ran his fingertips up Ryan's right biceps. "I know you know what I mean."

"Sure," Ryan said, and hit him as hard as he could in the middle of his swag belly.

The stomachs of some fat men are deceptively solid. Shukeli's wasn't—it was all flab and at the moment of impact, Ryan's fist sank into it like a finger jabbed into dough.

Shukeli doubled up, gagging, clutching at his middle. A string of saliva drooled from his lower lip. He didn't fall, and Ryan didn't act on his impulse to jack a knee into his face. As the man fought to get breath into his lungs, Ryan reached out and ran a finger under his double chins, up to his ear. He pinched the lobe savagely, twisting at the same time.

Shukeli made mewling noises. Ryan leaned down and whispered into his ear, "I know you know what I mean, you stupe bastard. We're not interested in your blue-boy pastimes. Keep that in mind and we'll get along fine for the short time we're here. You don't keep that in mind and you die. Understand?"

Shukeli's "Yes" was a faint burble.

Ryan released him. "Good. Let us know when it's time for our shift."

The warden tried to straighten, but opted to remain in a slightly stooped posture as he shambled away on unsteady legs.

Looking after him, J.B. said sourly, "We're not winning any popularity contests in the holy city of Aten."

"Good," Ryan replied flatly. "I'd be a hell of a lot more worried if we were."

Chapter Eighteen

Ryan had never really devoted too much thought to how ancient peoples had constructed massive megalithic structures. Even the magnificent step pyramid he and his friends had seen still standing in the jungles of Amazonia several months before had failed to rouse his curiosity.

He retained a memory from a picture book he had read as a child, an illustration depicting half-naked slaves working like oxen, yoked to huge stones and dragging them up earthen ramps while overseers lashed their straining backs with whips.

When he and J.B. followed the workers out of the barracks at the afternoon period of labor, he received a distinct surprise. Near the end of the long line of aproned men, they marched out of the walled compound and into open ground. They looked up the great pyramid, a man-made mountain gleaming white and awesome in the noonday sun.

Both he and the Armorer gaped at the most massive and finely engineered structure they had ever seen. It was almost too awesome to comprehend, and Ryan had to consciously resist the impulse to pinch himself. As it was, he stared so long and so hard without blinking in the blaze of sunlight that his eye began to sting and water. He and the column of workers were a hundred yards from the pyramid's base, yet the immensity of it completely filled his field of vision.

J.B. muttered, "It's got to be four hundred feet tall, and about seven hundred feet square at its widest point. God only knows how many millions of blocks are there."

A rangy, middle-aged man standing behind him said blandly, "Actually, once the capstone is put in place, it'll be 481 feet tall. It's 756 square. There are probably about two million blocks. It's designed to be an exact duplicate of the Great Pyramid of Cheops at Giza."

The man paused, smiled and added, "For an uneducated guess, you didn't do too badly. You've got a good eye. Mebbe you should be working with the royal architects."

Without looking at the man, J.B. asked, "How long have you been working on it? Ten years at least."

"No, just a little over two."

Tearing his eyes away from the monument, he stared distrustfully at the man who had supplied the information. "Bullshit. I don't know old Egypt from old eggs, but I know it took at least a generation to build the original pyramid."

"Longer, probably," the man replied. "But Pharaoh expanded on the original construction techniques."

"How do you know so much?" Ryan challenged.

The man shrugged. "I've been working at the site since it was staked out. My name is Fasa."

"Is that your real name or your Aten name?" J.B. asked.

Fasa seemed to experience momentary difficulty

in understanding the question. "Since I live in Aten, I guess Fasa is my real name."

He didn't ask their names, and neither J.B. nor Ryan provided them.

When they drew closer to the enormous megalith, Ryan and J.B. saw the double-railed track extending out of the compound and stretching upward, supported by a complex and very solid looking framework of beams and cross braces. The angle of the track's incline was gentle and gradual, eventually leading up to the very apex of the pyramid.

The metal cubes rolled along on their casterlike wheels, drawn by a heavy winch-and-pulley device attached to a pair of scaffolds on the side of the structure, one above the track, one below it. Men operated the winches by turning long crank handles.

It required ten minutes to climb to the top of the pyramid, scaling a stair sunk into the stone-block facade. By the time they reached it, they were perspiring heavily and panting. At that height, the sun seemed only an arm's length away.

A brisk-looking overseer bustled up to Ryan and J.B. "You're the newcomers. Get to work removing the blocks from the molds."

Ryan glanced at J.B., who shrugged, and both turned to obey.

To their surprise, the labor wasn't quite as backbreaking or as dangerous as they supposed. A fresh wind played over the top of the pyramid, which helped to offset a little of the debilitating heat.

Through close observation and by asking a few questions, they came to understand not only the basic engineering theory but the construction techniques and materials.

The building blocks for the pyramid weren't slavishly quarried and hauled; they were cast on the spot. The key of the process involved the aluminum and silicon that made up common clays. When alkali, a common substance in the desert, was added in the right proportion, the aluminum bonded tightly to both the oxygen and silicon in the clay.

Pharaoh had developed a powder containing silicon and aluminum that, when added to an alkali-saturated liquid, formed a molecular glue. Limestone and granite were stirred into the mixture and poured into a mold. The acidic sap from cactus dissolved the larger pieces of limestone. Exposed to a low heat for a few hours, the puttylike substance became stone.

According to Fasa, who seemed to take pleasure in acting as a mentor for the newcomers, ancient Egyptian stonemasons understood mineral chemistry enough to transform stone into a plastic, moldable compound.

"After all," he said, "the Egyptians knew enough food chemistry to make wine, beer and vinegar. And their embalming techniques are proof they understood body chemistry, too."

Ryan and J.B.'s assigned task was to roll the metal-walled molds containing the dried casing blocks and put them into proper position. The sides of the cubes were equipped with small hinges. Once the block was in place, the mold was easily removed, joining the block with the others so precisely that there was barely a hairbreadth in between.

Fasa explained that the center of the pyramid was hollow, comprising a Grand Gallery and several chambers honeycombed with crawl-spaces and air shafts.

Something else they learned over the course of that hot, sweaty afternoon was how little the laborers resented their servitude. Building the monument to Pharaoh, their god-king, left them with no other responsibilities than obeying orders, and they were essentially content with that.

"What happens when the pyramid is completed?" Ryan asked Fasa at one point.

"There will be a great ceremony and celebration. Pharaoh will drink in the *sekhem* energy drawn down from Osiris by the pyramid."

"I mean, what will you and the others do? Don't you want to be free?"

Fasa thought it over, frowned and shook his head. "I wouldn't like that. Who would take care of me? How would I get food? I like to eat. Don't you?"

Ryan considered the query rhetorical, so he didn't bother with a response.

The sun didn't begin its decline until well after seven o'clock—at least, J.B. estimated that was the time, since their chrons had been confiscated with the rest of their belongings.

Overseers shouted back and forth across the pyramid, and like automatons, the laborers stopped working and lined up at the stair. As before, they marched down, two men across. In some ways, the descent was more difficult than the ascent, because the shadows had thickened. One misstep could result in a bone-breaking fall.

Deep twilight darkened the sky when Ryan and J.B. set their sandaled feet on solid ground again. They heaved audible and simultaneous sighs of relief and marched back into the walled compound, toward the dormitory.

Shukeli stood by the door and when he saw them, he beckoned for them to step out of formation. The fat man snapped to J.B., ''Not you, just One-eye here.''

J.B. hesitated, but when Ryan nodded to him, he stepped back into line and was swept out of sight by the column of marching men.

Ryan regarded Shukeli solemnly. ''Payback plan or what?''

A flush of anger colored Shukeli's chins and sagging jowls. ''Someone wants to see you. Come with me.''

He turned and walked along the side of the barracks, not bothering to check if Ryan was following him or not. Ryan caught up with him before he turned the corner, senses on full alert, muscles tensing and tightening.

Rather than the ambush he expected, he saw a large pavilion erected in an open lot. Banners fluttered from poles driven into the ground near the entrance.

''In there,'' Shukeli growled. ''The royal architect's office.''

''Why does the royal architect want to see me?''

Shukeli lifted a sloping shoulder in a shrug, as if the matter were of little importance or interest to him. ''How do I know? I was told to fetch you. I fetched you. Do what you want from here on out.''

With a surprising quickness for one so bulky, Shukeli turned smartly on his toes and stalked away in the direction they had come.

Ryan studied the pavilion suspiciously, seeing no

sign of movement in or around it. A single light burned from within. He strode purposefully forward, thrusting aside the door flap.

A brass lamp suspended from a support pole cast the interior with a wavery yellow illumination. Directly beneath the lamp, seated at a paper-covered table was the hard, bronze figure of Akhnaton. He looked up as Ryan entered, and even at a distance, his crimson eyes shone like baleful flames.

He wore a simple brown leather belted jerkin that bore a disk worked in gold thread upon the breast. His head was bare, and he was completely alone.

Ryan cursed his split second of hesitation, then he crossed the dozen feet separating him from the giant man of bronze. "You're the royal architect?"

"Among my other functions," Akhnaton replied in his thrumming, controlled voice. "Would you consider this our second or third meeting, Cawdor?"

Ryan didn't rise to the bait. His stomach muscles fluttered in adrenaline-inspired spasms. He tried to meet the man's crimson gaze, unblinking and unflinching. "What do you want?"

Akhnaton leaned back in his camp chair, looking him up and down appraisingly. "No need to be afraid, Cawdor. If I wanted you dead, vultures would be feasting on your liver by now."

"I'm not afraid of you, Hell Eyes."

A rueful smile touched the man's lips. "I haven't been called that in many, many years. And then, not to my face."

"I asked you a question—what do you want?"

Akhnaton gestured expansively. "I have everything I want. An empire. A dynasty."

"Except," Ryan said, "a queen to share it with."

"You're far more astute than I gave you credit for. Perhaps a brain does lurk inside that grubber's shell." Akhnaton paused and added, "You're right, Cawdor. I have no queen. You can help me to rectify that."

Ryan's carefully maintained neutral expression slipped for a moment. "How?"

"I want you to tell Krysty Wroth that you understand she and I are fated to be together and you are releasing her from whatever vows she may have made to you. In exchange for that, I will grant you and your companions safe conduct back to the redoubt and the gateway. I will give you anything you need."

Ryan stared at the bronze mask, his mind awash with conflicting emotions. He said nothing for a very long time. Finally, he surprised Akhnaton and, to an extent, himself. He laughed, loud and scornfully.

"My proposition amuses you?" Akhnaton's tone was cold and hard.

"Deeply. I thought you were some kind of super mind mutie. Why don't you just mentally force me to do your bidding?"

Akhnaton didn't answer.

"Could it be," Ryan continued sarcastically, "that Krysty would instantly sense that you had me in your power and tell you what I'm telling you now...to go fuck yourself?"

The shock was so unexpected, so terrible that Ryan nearly collapsed. Time, space, the universe darkened and turned. His surroundings shattered into a kaleidoscope of flying fragments. He drifted among them, and the sudden terror of it dragged a scream up his throat. He clamped his jaws shut on it. The swirling fragments coalesced into the same image, infinitely repeated—a grinning, malevolent skull, the fires of hell erupting from the eye sockets.

Ryan had engaged in hundreds of battles in his life, but never one where a powerful will tried to beat down his spirit. But the image of Krysty and Dean were his anchors in reality. Ryan forced himself to stare at the hundreds of thousands of fiendish, grinning skulls. His love for Krysty and his son was a chain that a psychic assault couldn't break. He willed the skulls to fade, demanding that the world steady around him.

Quite suddenly, he was in the pavilion again, standing before Akhnaton. His heart trip-hammered in his chest, his head ached and his body was filmed with cold sweat. But he smiled, a contemptuous twist of his mouth.

In a low voice, Akhnaton said, "You stinking scavenger. You dung beetle of a man. I could kill you where you stand, give you a cerebral hemorrhage, cause your aorta to burst."

Breath rasping between his bared teeth, hands quivering, Ryan demanded, "Why don't you do it, then?"

Akhnaton didn't answer.

"You won't do it because Krysty will know. And if she doesn't hate you now, she will when she finds out."

"Listen to me, Cawdor. I was created to impose order on chaos. All of man's old social arrangements were destroyed. Lawlessness, terror, anarchy run unchecked. Only my vision and my resolve can prevail to restore a measure of peace and harmony on the world."

"By imposing a new form of terror," Ryan retorted.

"Don't goad me. I don't really expect you, a wandering, landless killer, to understand a fraction of my dream, a dynasty dedicated to virtue, as my namesake was dedicated to peace and justice. It is the only rational means to bring order out of chaos."

"I've heard similar speeches before," the one-eyed man scoffed. "Distill it all down and it's nothing more than a cheap justification for tyranny."

"You're a fool. A venal, dirt-grubbing scavenger."

"And you're just another fucking mutie with an attitude."

Ryan shot out his left leg in a sweeping kick that caught the underside of the table and heaved it upward into Akhnaton's face. He and the camp chair tipped over amid a heavy thud and a bellow of outraged surprise.

The one-eyed man was atop him in a shaved slice of a second, his warrior reflexes and fury driving him forward, knees slamming solidly into the man's flat stomach.

He pistoned both fists into the bronzed face beneath him in a flurry of jabs and left and right hooks. Akhnaton's head rocked back and forth under the steady tattoo, blood springing from his nostrils, flying from split lips.

"Come on, Pharaoh," Ryan snarled. He hit him on the chin, bouncing the back of his head against the ground. "Give me a cerebral hemorrhage."

A fierce downward jab opened a gash above Akhnaton's eyebrow.

Akhnaton tried to exchange punches with Ryan,

but his flailing fists missed their weaving target, or rebounded from his forearms. He bucked beneath him, hands darting for the one-eyed man's throat.

Ryan caught the wrists, noting fearfully it was like grabbing two bars of tempered steel. They tumbled over the ground, locked in each other's arms, tearing at each other like raging beasts. They grappled, and Akhnaton's fingers slipped on his opponent's sweat-slick arms, his grasp so powerful Ryan's skin peeled away in strips as if it were scalded.

Ryan realized that although Akhnaton's strength was immense, his combat acumen and skills weren't even up to the levels possessed by Dean. He had never fought hand-to-hand for survival before, and Ryan took vicious advantage of him. He kicked him, he clawed him, he head-butted him, he bit him, he tried to gouge out his crimson eyes.

But Ryan knew that because of his adversary's superior strength he couldn't kill him, so he single-mindedly inflicted as much pain and humiliation on Akhnaton as he could.

Then a bronze hand closed around his throat. Ryan tried first to poke his fingers into Akhnaton's eyes, but he straightened his arm and his hands couldn't reach him. He came up to his knees with Ryan struggling to pry those steely fingers apart. He kicked at him desperately, but his apronlike garment impeded his movements.

Akhnaton's hand mercilessly crushed tendons, muscles and ligaments against his vertebrae. Ryan was a strong man, far stronger than average, but he felt like a kitten, helpless in the hands of a sadist. Blood thundered in his ears.

Akhnaton flung him aside as if he were a dummy stuffed with straw. He landed flat on his right side, the impact knocking what little breath he had out through his nostrils and mouth. He lay where he had been tossed, his face against the ground, trying to cough, trying to breathe, trying to move.

Through the blurry vision of his eye, he saw Akhnaton stagger to his feet. Blood streamed from a score of wounds all over his body, his face a battered mask. He touched his lacerated lip, frowned at the crimson wetness shining on his fingertips and said unsteadily, "I underestimated you, Cawdor. You held your own in a face-to-face with me. I'll be damned. You actually hurt me."

Akhnaton's voice held no anger, only bewilderment.

"Good," Ryan said hoarsely. His throat felt raw, and his head throbbed.

Akhnaton smiled wryly. "No matter. I've lived so long with pain, I no longer really feel it."

Ryan got his hands under him and pushed. The pavilion swayed around him. Gradually the thunder in his ears faded to a dim mutter. He stumbled erect.

"Why didn't you use your psi-powers on me?" he croaked. "Give me a hemorrhage or burst my heart, like you said you could do?"

"You were ready for me to try that," Akhnaton answered calmly. "Your strength of will is greater than I initially figured. If a mind is strong enough, consciously resisting me, I can't do much more than inflict a headache."

Ryan massaged his throat. "So you're not quite up to the superhuman specs of Mission Invictus."

"Actually," he retorted matter-of-factly, "I am.

My bones are denser, my circulatory system is far more efficient than yours. I probably have three times your strength, as you found out. I have control over my body's autonomic functions and reflexes. I've already stopped the bleeding and nipped any chance of infection. I'll be fully healed by tomorrow. You won't be able to say the same."

Ryan stared at him, noting with despair that blood no longer flowed from the man's many wounds. "What now? Public execution for daring to lay hands on Pharaoh?"

Akhnaton shook his head derisively. "That's the act of a coward, Cawdor. No, you've made this a personal situation between us when it could have been a simple exchange. Torture, I think, is more appropriate."

Ryan chuckled dryly. "Torture isn't the act of a coward?"

Akhnaton grinned, exposing blood-filmed teeth. "Not the way I'll torture you. Hear my words and believe what I say—Krysty will be my queen. I'll just have to persuade her a little less subtly than I intended. In two days, the capstone of my pyramid will be placed. Then there will be a ceremony, culminating in our marriage."

Ryan didn't stir, didn't change expression.

"And she'll agree to it," Akhnaton continued. "By the time the ceremony is over, the only thing she'll care about is how soon and how many royal heirs I can plant in her belly. I'll enjoy the seeding, Cawdor. And so will she. I'll make sure of it."

Ryan struggled to keep his homicidal fury leashed. His mind seethed.

"Get back to your barracks, Cawdor," Akhnaton

commanded. "You'll be hurting tomorrow, but consider yourself the most fortunate dung beetle who ever lived. You went toe-to-toe with a god and lived to regret it."

Chapter Nineteen

Krysty saw the whole world spread out below her, like a tapestry of horror. She passed like a phantom wind over gloomy wastes, gazing down on the legacy of the nukecaust.

Where there had once been lush and fertile fields, the desert swept in, a sea of sand lapping at the spires of half-buried skyscrapers. Instead of cities and towns, only vast, ugly craters pockmarked the ground, seething with poison.

Ungainly caricatures of human beings lurched across the wastelands, forlorn monstrosities birthed and molded by outraged nature. She tried to cringe, praying they wouldn't see her.

She soared over toxic swamps, percolating with a foul and fetid soup, and she watched people desperately trying to snatch the most meager of existences from their half-dead surroundings.

She saw babies dragged cold and lifeless from rad-damaged wombs and she wanted to weep, but phantoms couldn't shed tears.

Flying up and arcing down again over bitter seas, she plunged through a maelstrom of buffeting memory, reliving in a heartbeat all of her own suffering at the hands and bestial imaginations of the depraved men who sought to rule Deathlands.

She didn't hate them now. She pitied them so

deeply it was almost a despair. Deathlands had made them, turned their ambitions into ugly cravings to control the chaos by any means necessary.

She was flung headlong on the swirling gales, the clean, fresh wind of hope filling her lungs with an intoxicating purity. She raced upward toward the sun, exulting in its life-giving heat, its eternal power.

The brilliant, fiery surface greeted her joyfully, miles-long tongues of flame lapping toward her in a burning yet arousing embrace.

She knew the sun would change the world, transform its horror into beauty, saturate it with *sekhem* and return it to health. She thought, Neither from nor toward…at the still point, the dance of life began anew.

But the sun wanted—needed—her help. It couldn't do it alone.

The sun caressed her, showered her with hot, fierce kisses. Love and desire swelled within her, building, rising, cresting.

The sun whispered, ''You belong to me. You have always belonged to me. Long have I awaited you. You are the mother of a dynasty that will last ten thousand years.''

She spread herself wide, inviting the sun to enter her, to fill her—

Krysty awoke with the echoes of her own cry ringing in her ears. She sat up, shuddering, feeling her hair knotting and twisting in wild convulsions. Her body was damp with sweat, damp with more than sweat. She whispered hoarsely, ''Your dew is in all my limbs.''

She flung aside the sheet and swung her legs out of bed, her knees weak and wobbling. In the dim light of the brass lamp suspended from the ceiling, she saw her sleeping gown was in disarray and saw the flush rising from her breasts up to her throat. Her heart beat fast and frantic, then slowed to steady rhythm.

She groaned, not with pleasure, but with shame and fear. Squeezing her eyes shut, she said aloud, "What's happening to me? Gaia, give me the strength."

AKHNATON OPENED HIS EYES, drawing in a shuddery breath. He murmured, "My dew is in all your limbs." He lay back on the couch in his private chamber, waiting for his wild pulse beat to steady and the throbbing in his temples to abate.

Perspiration gleamed on his near naked body, touching and stinging the wounds inflicted only hours before by Cawdor. The pain was sharp, almost exquisite, and allowed him to pull his mind back. He deliberately averted his gaze from the bulge stretching the fabric of his loincloth.

Penetrating Krysty Wroth's sleeping consciousness and directing it in the channels he wanted it to go had been more strenuous than he had anticipated. Though her natural empathic powers provided him with egress, her loyalty and love for Cawdor and the rest of her people formed a very strong barrier. Rather than try to batter it down, he had searched for ways around it.

The primal force of her sexuality was one route, but even that led only so far. It was deeply entangled with the higher emotions, not a separate thing easily isolated and manipulated as it had been with the others—O'Brien and Harrier.

O'Brien's intellect was so regimented that most of her emotions had been compartmentalized, locked away in a drawer in the dark recesses of her mind. It hadn't been difficult to unlock and use the contents of that drawer. In fact, she had been pathetically grateful to him for opening it.

His eyes grew wet when he thought of O'Brien. She had loved him madly, unconditionally. He had loved her as his mother, his mate, but never as his queen. He would have made her so if only she had lived.

Harrier had been quite different. Her emotions lurked very close to the surface and were rather shallow, at least compared to O'Brien's. She had loved him, too, though she really hadn't had much of a choice.

Akhnaton sat up and walked across the room to the window. He transmitted a tentative probe, seeking out Nefron's mind. Without much surprise, she detected his presence and deflected it. He smiled slightly. She possessed none of her mother's compliance of spirit.

He looked to the west and saw his pyramid thrusting up toward the deep, blue-black sky, gleaming white and ghostly in the starlight. It lacked only a few more casing blocks and the capstone. Then it would stand whole, a beacon of hope lighting a path of his glory over the barren face of the world.

Once it was complete, so would he be, able to shape and forge the planet into a paradise. He would know what it was like to be Osiris, the father of a new civilization.

And he would know again, at long last, what it was like to love.

Chapter Twenty

After Mildred returned to the hall of women after the indoctrination session, Grandmother sent her off to another part of the palace, to report to Mimses. The rambling building was divided into quarters, and one quarter was the domain of Pharaoh's chief counselor. As she padded along the corridors, she kept an eye out for either Kela or Nefron.

When the corridor branched to the right and to the left, she impulsively turned left, in the opposite direction of where Grandmother had instructed her to go.

Rich tapestries hung on the polished paneled walls, the lofty ceiling adorned with ornate and intricate carvings and silver-chased scrollwork. The concept she was walking through an old movie set was almost as hard to accept as the idea she had been transported back to ancient Egypt.

As she turned a corner, she nearly trod on Nefron's toes. The girl almost dropped the bowl of fruit in her hands and she regarded Mildred with wide, fearful eyes.

"What are you doing here?" she demanded in an accusatory whisper.

"I work here, thanks in part to you."

Nefron shook her head vehemently, her glossy black hair gleaming in the lights. "You are in Pharaoh's quarter. You have been assigned to Mimses. Go.''

Nefron made a move to step around her, but Mildred restrained her with a firm hand. ''You can spare a sec for Scheherazade. A girl came to me this morning. She told me you had sent her and that Jak Lauren was safe.''

''Kela, my maid. She spoke the truth. She also visited your friends in the cell blocks.''

''What's being done about Krysty?''

''I am on my way to her now,'' Nefron answered hesitantly. ''Pharaoh wishes to see her this morning.''

''What's the plan for getting us out of here?''

Nefron glanced up and down the corridor. ''I'll arrange transportation and provisions.''

''And our weapons?''

''I'll find them. Do not fear.''

''When and where?''

''Not here. You must trust me, Mildred. Be patient. Please.''

Nefron's dark eyes widened in a silent plea. Mildred felt compelled to step aside, and the woman swept past her. As she did so, she whispered, ''Go back the way you came and report to Mimses. *Now*.''

Mildred had retraced half of her steps before she realized she had done it.

She found Mimses's hall again without too much difficulty, wondering again at the absence of sentries posting along the corridors. Unlike the afternoon before, the black man was dressed in a flowing blue robe, an outfit she assumed was his robe of office.

He stood at the balustrade of the terrace and, when she entered, he beckoned for her to join him there.

"Did you spend a pleasant evening?" he asked, not looking at her.

"No," she answered.

"Good. If you had, Grandmother would be severely punished. As it is, if the decision was up to me, I'd have you and your scavenger friends staked out in the desert atop a bed of cactus."

An obscenely witty remark popped into her head, but she kept it from passing her lips.

Mimses turned, his eyes drifting up and down her body. "Do you know how Aten operates?"

"No."

"I'll spell it out for you, brown sugar. It's divided into classes, but we don't observe strict distinctions. We're not numerous enough for that. There's only a handful of what you might call royal insiders. I'm at the top of the heap since Osorkon lost his brain and took off."

The man's lips moved in his characteristically vulpine smile. "Life in Aten is easy. The system is smooth, except for a little spot of bother a year or so ago. Everybody has obligations and duties to discharge to the kingdom. All they have to do is discharge them and they earn privileges. You know what the first privilege you'll earn will be?"

She shook her head.

Mimses grabbed her by the upper arms and pulled her hard against him. She splayed out her hands on his chest, first trying to push him away, then relaxing into his arms. He closed a hand over her left breast, fingers kneading it through the thin leather covering. Into her ear, he crooned, "You get to let me fuck you."

She was careful to keep her face an expressionless, bland mask. Mimses snorted out a laugh at her lack of response and released her, leaning back on the terrace railing.

"But not for a while yet, brown sugar. You've got to prove you're worthy. Now, get to the kitchen. It's past time for my breakfast."

She turned, and he gave her a swat on the rear to inspire her to pick up her pace. She said not a word. Mildred wasn't moved by the threat of sexual victimization. She was too angry, too consumed by the desire to murder the man with her bare hands.

She was also too pleased with herself to speak, for fear of betraying her small triumph. She kept her hand closed tight around the metal ankh she had slipped from the delicate chain on Mimses's neck.

DOC'S FIRST DAY of servitude was, by and large, a bore. He had expected to feel the bite of an overseer's whip on his back or shackles to be welded to his ankles and all sorts of humiliating abuse. His long tenure as slave and court jester in Jordan Teague's vulgar little empire of Mocsin was still fresh in his memory and gave him an occasional nightmare.

Assigned to a maintenance detail, he followed a crew of four into a covered shed at the far side of the compound. Within were a number of the solar-powered chariots in various states of disrepair. His job was to help repair them, and so he did.

The first chariot he turned his attention upon had a burned-out wheel bearing, and under the helpful directions of his fellow workers, he rebuilt it by melting down the original in a small smelter and recasting it in a mold.

During the morning hours, he worked quickly and efficiently with a minimum of conversation. Only one man tried to engage him in small talk, an old gnarled fellow who looked to be his age or a trifle older. His name was Nasaris. His thin white hair was arranged in several looping braids over his brown scalp.

His smile was friendly. "Looks like we're the only snow-tops here."

Doc nodded a silent, smiling affirmative.

Nasaris touched one of his braids. "You know, for safety's sake, you ought to do your hair like mine. You don't want to get it tangled up in an axle or something and have yourself snatched bald. Almost happened to me once."

One of the other men overheard the comment and laughed. "Funny as hell, too."

"That's 'cause it didn't happen to you, Zophren!" Nasaris snapped. "I'm trying to give our new pal here a little safety tip—don't need to have you butting in."

Nasaris returned his attention to him. "I'll be glad to do it for you."

Doc thought it over for a moment, not particularly relishing having the old man style his hair for him, but also knowing he needed an ally and a source of information. He agreed.

During the noon meal break, he submitted to Nasaris's tonsorial ministrations, allowing the man to twist and plait and loop his hair. He felt a sharp sense of the ridiculous, but he was able to engage the fellow in conversation, in much the same way he used to pump his barber for local gossip.

Nasaris was garrulous, if not necessarily precise in everything he said. As he had halfway expected to hear, Nasaris was one of the first citizens of Aten, one of the first acolytes of Pharaoh Akhnaton. He yammered about the difficulty of excavating the city, telling tedious stories of heat, endless broken tools and days of thirst and hunger.

More to interrupt the flow of chatter than for any other reason, Doc said, "Shouldn't you be retired by now, on a pension from Pharaoh for all of your contributions?"

Nasaris fell silently, his hands and fingers stopping in midtwirl of a strand of Doc's hair. In a quiet, strained voice, he said, "There was a problem a while back. I made something I shouldn't have for Pharaoh's daughter. This is my punishment."

His voice brightened as he continued. "But what the hell. It's better than being dead, and at least I have something to do with my time."

"What did you make?" Doc asked.

Nasaris cleared his throat self-consciously. "Just a little piece of jewelry. See, I was one of Pharaoh's chief craftsmen. When Nefron asked me to make some little doodads for her and some of her friends, I didn't ask questions. I should have."

"What happened?"

Nasaris sighed. "I'd rather not say."

As his fingers busied themselves with Doc's hair again, the old man asked very quietly, "Did Nefron give one of these little doodads to Osorkon?"

The old man's fingers twitched, pulling Doc's hair painfully. He stepped away, and Doc, rubbing his smarting scalp, turned to look at him. The fellow's expression was commingled fear, guilt and grief.

"I've said too much. I'm old. My head gets mixed up. Forget what I told you." With that, he scuttled out of the shed.

Doc followed him, but Nasaris had decided to observe a board game between two of the other men. When the noon meal break was over, Doc decided he was tired. He hadn't slept very soundly the night before, so he hung around the shed doing as little work as was humanly possible. His deportment was an education in laziness.

The other three men labored on refitting a chariot's drive shaft and paid him no attention, so he went for a little stroll around the compound. No one hailed him as he passed among the workers in the yard stirring a puttylike substance in metal-walled cubes.

He found a back entrance into the palace and after walking down a hallway, he followed his nose to a huge, well-equipped and very hot kitchen.

Squinting through the steam and smoke rising from open grills and sinks full of hot water, he saw Mildred arranging food on a tray. She looked up as he sauntered over to her and she burst out laughing.

Doc had almost forgotten his looped, braided hair. He tried to glare at her, then gave it up and laughed, too. "How goes your career as a royal scullery maid?"

"I've had worse jobs," she told him with a smile. "When I was attending university I worked in a fast-food restaurant. That was more like slavery than this place."

She looked around furtively, then took him by the

elbow and guided him over to a corner where they were screened from casual view by steam and smoke. She slid her fingers into her cleavage. "I want to show you something."

Doc quickly looked away. "Please, Dr. Wyeth. I am fully aware of the old adage 'When in Rome, do as the Romans do,' but I'm afraid—"

"Oh, muzzle it, Doc," Mildred broke in exasperatedly. She held out her hand. "Look."

Squinting through the vapors, he saw a small metal object, nearly the size of her palm, nestled in her open hand. "An ankh amulet, like the one Danielson wore."

"I filched it from Mimses."

"Who?"

"He used to be called Stockbridge. He's Pharaoh's chief counselor."

"Ah. And you decided to lift his jewelry as a prank?"

Mildred grimaced. "Don't be deliberately obtuse, Doc. You're hard enough to stomach when you're unintentionally obtuse. It's more than jewelry. It's a talisman."

Doc's eyebrows crawled toward his hairline. "We have fallen on sorry times indeed when our resident adherent to hard science resorts to the bead-and-rattle explanation."

Mildred glared at him angrily. "Remember what Danielson said about Akhnaton stumbling on ancient principles of energy transference and manipulation? He traced a relationship between the body's electromagnetic field and certain Egyptian glyphs. The ankh he wore protected him from the Incarnates' weapons, and he indicated it was also a psychic shield."

Doc took the metal object from her hand and eyed it skeptically. "Yes, I recall him saying something along those lines. I do not recall that it correlated with the science I was taught...or practiced."

"Your science is out-of-date," Mildred retorted. "Every substance, organic and inorganic, is surrounded by an energy field, an aura. Each field's intensity and quality is determined by the structure of its component molecules."

"And?"

"And the human nervous system, which is itself a conductor of electrical energy, can be influenced by the proximity of other substances that have strong fields. The amount of influence depends upon the frequency of the nerve and the pulsating frequency of the object. If the frequencies are a match, the strength of the nerve impulses can be increased, through the principle known as electronic cadence. If the fields are out of sync, the effect can be deleterious."

Doc no longer looked so doubtful.

"We've already seen that the amulet worked to protect Danielson," Mildred continued. "This is basic biochemistry, actually. Silver, copper and gold resonate with the body's energy field. Remember those crystal-and-gold gadgets in Ti-Ra'-Wa?"

Doc nodded. The Amerindian inhabitants of that hidden Wyoming settlement had employed an ancient understanding of the relationship between piezoelectric quartz crystals, metals and the energy generated by the mind to communicate telepathically with each other and higher animal forms.

"Well, obviously, if the ankhs are made of certain metals and of certain designs, they can be used as a means of containing the life-force, what Danielson called the *sekhem*. He also said the ankh blocked Akhnaton's power so he couldn't be read."

Doc smiled. "I see. If we wear the same amulets, then we would not only be immune to the metauh rods, but shield our minds from Akhnaton."

"And possibly Nefron, his daughter. She's behind the so-called escape plan. She told me she sent a girl named Kela to talk to you."

"Yes, this morning. You suspect this—Nefron, is it?—possesses a marked degree of psychic ability?"

Mildred shrugged. "Stands to reason, doesn't it? She is her father's daughter, even if he doesn't want to recognize her as blood of his blood. Anyhow, she's made a lot of promises without mentioning any specifics. She keeps asking me to trust her. I don't."

"A wise precaution, under the circumstances," Doc replied. "Oddly, my hairstylist was an elderly slyboots named Nasaris. He claimed he fell out of Pharaoh's favor because he made something he shouldn't have for Nefron. I received the distinct impression she had used him in some fashion. Perhaps he was the craftsman Danielson mentioned who made his ankh."

"Perhaps. And if that's so, there may be a pot of intrigue boiling and Nefron wants to add us to the mix."

"If we don't care to rely on her promises, then I hope you have something of a plan in mind."

Mildred pinched the air between thumb and forefinger. "A germ of one. If you can, get the ankh to

Ryan and J.B. and tell them what we've discussed. You seem to have the run of the compound."

"So far." Doc slid the amulet into a fold of his breechclout. "I have yet to test my boundaries."

Mildred smiled at him fondly and patted his cheek. "Keep testing them. But don't end up on the business end of one of those magic frog giggers."

Chapter Twenty-One

Nefron fetched Krysty at midmorning, presenting her with a bowl of fresh fruit, which she didn't sample or even glance toward. The girl helped her to get dressed and apply her cosmetics.

Sitting at a dressing table and brushing out her hair, Nefron asked, "Did you sleep well?"

Krysty didn't answer. Her hair undulated and rippled under the soft, steady pressure of the brush.

Leaning down, Nefron whispered, "I've managed to contact all of your friends."

Krysty looked at her blankly. "What?"

"Your friends...Mildred, Doc, J.B., Jak—and Ryan."

Krysty's expression turned instantly into a mask of irritation. "Why whisper about them? Pharaoh is aware they are here."

Nefron resumed brushing her hair. Then Krysty asked a question in an oddly listless tone. "You are Akhnaton's daughter, aren't you?"

The brush halted in midstroke, and Krysty heard a sharp intake of breath from the young woman.

"I am. Your friend Mildred knew that, so I assumed you did, as well."

"You are the heir to the throne of Aten?"

"No," Nefron answered quietly. "My father decreed that I was not worthy to continue the dynasty. He desires a son, a prince, not a princess.''

"How do you feel about that decision?" Krysty asked.

"My feelings on the subject are not open for discussion." Nefron's voice carried a sharp edge. She added, "I do as Pharaoh commands."

There was silence until Nefron was finished brushing Krysty's hair. Wordlessly Nefron held a hand mirror before her. Krysty felt a shock at the unfamiliar features staring back at her. Every inch of her face was as carefully and sharply painted as an enameled doll's, her big eyes surrounded by fish-shaped black outlines.

"Well—" Krysty let out a pent-up breath "—thank you."

"We must go now. Pharaoh awaits."

Krysty and Nefron went out and down the corridors to Akhnaton's study. He wasn't there, so while Nefron busied herself with pouring goblets of the dandelion wine, Krysty scanned the spines of the heavily laden bookshelves. The collection of predark books in the study seemed to number in the thousands. Krysty drew a leather-bound volume from the shelf at random. The words *Alexander the Great* were embossed on the leather cover. Although she hadn't had the benefit of an extensive education, she was far better read than most people eking out uncertain existences in Deathlands and she recognized the name.

She flipped through the pages, scanning the life story of one of the ancient world's most famous conquerors. "From an early age, Alexander was not as other men," she read. "His abilities and powers of persuasion confounded all of his teachers, Aristotle among them.''

Krysty found herself frowning and she read the passage again. Powers of persuasion.

''Nefron, what mischief have you been plotting now?''

Akhnaton stood in the doorway, dressed much the same way as he had been the day before. His browned fists planted on his hips, he favored Nefron with an unblinking scarlet stare. ''Answer me.''

Nefron's slender shoulders stiffened at the question. ''What do you mean, Lord Pharaoh?''

''The day watch reported that you were seen leaving the city walls on more than one occasion yesterday. Since you should be preparing for the ceremony rather than taking the air, I find it rather curious.''

''There is nothing curious about it, Lord Pharaoh. I was indeed preparing for the ceremony. I dispatched my maid Kela to see if a new bed of flowers had bloomed.''

''Such fripperies are not within your realm of responsibility,'' Akhnaton rumbled. ''Speak the truth, girl.''

''I am, my lord. I swear it.''

Akhnaton barked out a scornful laugh. ''If so, it would be the first time since your birth. You think because I cannot get a deep read on you, I do not know if you're lying. I do know, darlingest daughter. I do.''

Krysty sensed Akhnaton's angry suspicion, and Nefron's fear came over her in a wave. The girl virtually cringed from her father's gaze. Krysty moved forward impulsively, gliding between the two. "There is no need for this."

For a moment, lines of anger furrowed the man's high brow. Then, with an obviously conscious effort, he smoothed them away. He nodded deferentially to Krysty. "You are right. I slept badly and am out of sorts this morning. Nefron, leave us. I will summon you if I need you."

The red glint of anger in the girl's eyes was masked by the downward sweep of her long lashes as she hurried out of the study.

After she was gone, Krysty said, "She is quite good to me, Pharaoh. She has helped me in many ways to make my stay comfortable."

"She was only following my express command. She has always followed her own agenda."

"Then why do you keep her around if you mistrust her?" Krysty asked.

Akhnaton frowned. "I have my reasons."

He dropped his eyes to the title of the book in her hands, and his frown turned into a rueful smile. "Is Alexander a subject of interest for you?"

She laid it down rather guiltily on his desk. "No, not really."

Akhnaton went to the sideboard and fetched her a goblet of the wine Nefron had poured. "In 332 B.C., Alexander the Great invaded Egypt and assumed the role of pharaoh. He didn't stay long, but his general and successor, Ptolemy, established a long dynasty, which included Cleopatra."

He handed her the drinking cup, and for the first time, Krysty saw the marks on his arms and face, the slightly reddened lines of almost healed wounds.

"She was queen in every sense of the word,"

Akhnaton continued. "And you look like a queen, as well...though a bit tired."

"I didn't sleep well last night...like you," she answered softly.

A sly smile touched Akhnaton's lips. "Bad dreams?"

Krysty sipped the sweet liquid. "I haven't decided yet. Time will tell."

"Perhaps you've made a decision regarding what we discussed yesterday."

Tilting her head back slightly, she looked him squarely in the eye. "It's a lot to absorb in such a short time. I need more proof of our intertwined destinies than a reproduction of an ancient bust dug out of the ground half a world away."

He angled an eyebrow at her. "Proof? Such as?"

"Proof of your assertion that during the capstone ceremony we'll both be imbued with the powers of the gods." She spoke with a teasing, slightly sarcastic drawl.

Akhnaton grinned boyishly, his teeth flashing whitely against his bronzed face. "I'll admit to overstating on that, simply for dramatic effect. However, the principle is sound and the results will be much the same."

"How?"

He regarded her keenly, contemplatively for a moment, then plucked the goblet from her fingers. "Come with me and I will show you how."

They left the study, walked side by side down the corridor, through an arched doorway into another corridor whose walls were inlaid with gold leaf and silver chasing. Brass centers swung from the ceiling, filling the passage with perfumed incense.

"This part of the palace is forbidden to all," he said. "You are the only human being other than myself who has been here."

They turned down a smaller, narrower hallway that ended at a brass door. Over the arch, etched into a stone tablet, was a glyph resembling an upside-down trident with jagged tines. Akhnaton turned the handle of the door and pushed it open.

"It's not locked?" Krysty inquired curiously.

Akhnaton pointed to the symbol above the door. "That is my cartouche. Any of my subjects who would dare trespass here would have to be mad or suicidal. Or both. Regardless of the cause, they would die."

The door led onto a stair that plunged down at a forty-five degree angle into pitch blackness. Krysty hesitated. "I can't see a thing."

Akhnaton held her hand tightly. "I'll see for both of us."

He led her down. The stairway wasn't as long as she had imagined. At the foot of the steps, he tugged a dangling cord, and a light fixture blazed into dazzling life overhead.

Shielding her eyes, Krysty said, "Electric lights?"

"Solar batteries," he replied, a tinge of pride coloring his tone. "My own application."

When her eyes adjusted to the glare, Krysty took a few steps forward, then stopped and stared. "Gaia," she breathed.

Resting on the floor, its base occupying almost every centimeter of it, loomed a miniature replica of the pyramid. The point still towered a dozen feet above the floor, and its base was at least thrice that.

The surface was incised with gold-painted hieroglyphic characters, and short inscriptions covered all four sides. It glittered and sparkled under the light, as if it were dusted with powdered diamonds.

"The capstone," Akhnaton announced. "A pyramidion I crafted myself, with my own hands, following descriptions I found in the decoded Scrolls of Amenemhat."

Krysty walked around the structure, noticing that its stone facade was shot through with gleaming specks of crystal. Reaching out to touch it, she felt a distinct tingling in her index finger. She murmured, "Piezoelectric properties."

Akhnaton glanced at her in pleased, respectful surprise. "You are absolutely correct. The secret of so-called pyramid power. I have found three distinct energy forms generated by pyramids. The first is piezoelectric, the second electrostatic and I refer to the third as bioaural. You impress me with your knowledge."

Krysty repressed a smile. She didn't mention how her training in manipulating earth energies had touched on the energy forces locked within crystalline minerals, or even her experiences with the telepathy-inducing devices used by the Lakota of Ti-Ra'-Wa.

"Certain types of crystal produce electromotive force," Akhnaton went on. "The King's Chamber in the pyramid is lined with tons of microscopic quartz and potassium-tartrate crystal particles. When this capstone is in place, the King's Chamber will be converted into a perpetual energy generator."

"What kind of energy are you talking about?" Krysty asked.

"*Sekhem*, the basic life-force of the universe." Akhnaton's voice was somber, portentous. "Do you know what this means?"

"No," Krysty replied, though a notion was beginning to occur to her.

"A normal human being inside the King's Chamber would be affected by the generated induction field. His brain-wave frequency would be disrupted, and his latent psionic talents may be triggered. He would no doubt dismiss these effects as hallucinations."

Akhnaton stepped closer to her, standing behind her. "You and I already possess enhanced and active psi-abilities. The *sekhem* would interact with our abilities, magnifying them, amplifying them."

Krysty felt a cold chill creep up her spine. "You're already one of the most powerful men I've ever met. Why do you want more?"

"There are many powerful men," Akhnaton replied. "The world has no need of more of them. What it needs is a savior, a god...and a goddess."

He touched her arms, turning her carefully to face him. "Can you conceive of the miracles we might work? Can you imagine what glories our offspring will be capable of? We will establish a new golden age for the earth, a place of beauty, free of fear, of want, of pain. Think of it—no more pain. We will be worshiped, and our memories will be worshiped for thousands of years. In that sense, our immortality is assured."

His hands tightened on her arms, and he bent his crimson, yearning gaze on her face. "Help me. For the love of humanity, help me build this dynasty.

Let us complete the dream we held in our earlier incarnations, all those millennia ago.''

His words echoed, like the brazen toll of a bell. She felt her soul being drawn out by his eyes, pulling into him, joining, intermingling, entwining with his own spirit. There was a sensation of all sanity and stability crumbling beneath her.

''Help me, Krysty. Love me as I love you. Help me.''

The roots of her prehensile hair prickled at her scalp. She could no longer see Akhnaton. It was as if the walls, the ceiling, the pyramidion had withdrawn from her. All she could see was a pair of eyes, flaming redly in the black gulfs of space.

From somewhere in the shadows, a voice whispered, ''I will.''

And she knew the voice had been her own.

Chapter Twenty-Two

Nefron strode swiftly but silently into a dim hallway, the last stretch of a labyrinth that twisted and turned within the palace walls. She came to a small inner chamber lit by a single flickering taper. A dark man in a blue robe lounged on a settee.

"Well, sweetie," Mimses said. "Your dupes are all in place. Strange tools, even for you."

Nefron leaned against the wall and smiled crookedly. "I imagine the newcomers believe me to be their tool."

"Yeah," Mimses grunted. "You moved a little too impulsively, don't you think? You should've consulted me."

"No time," Nefron retorted. "A profitable opportunity presented itself and I seized it, just like you taught me."

"Using my Incarnates was a good plan," he replied sourly.

She grinned mockingly. "Except the newcomers killed the only ones you could trust."

"And they'll pay for it."

"Not for a while yet. Pharaoh is suspicious."

Mimses's eyes widened at her words. "How do you know?"

"One of the wall sentries saw me outside of the

city yesterday, when Kela and I were hiding the albino.''

Mimses dry-washed his face with his hands. "Not good. Not good. If Pharaoh finds him—"

"They won't. Kela has moved him twice already. I'm not even sure where he is right now, just in case Pharaoh tried to probe me."

"What's the albino like?"

"Young and strong. He killed your Serapis in Baltic Alley, though he was debilitated by a metauh rod. We've kept him drugged since then, and I squeezed his mind while he slept."

Mimses dropped his hands and gazed at her skeptically. "Squeezed his mind how?"

"I stimulated his libido. I embedded certain perceptions about Kela and me into his consciousness. That, combined with the potion and Kela's attention to him, will keep him tractable until we need him."

"You hope."

"He's young, like I said," Nefron responded defensively. "Full of hormones, and his sex drive is very close to the surface, very easy to manipulate."

"As long as he's satisfied with Kela and will stay put for another couple of days."

Nefron sighed wearily. "If his attention wanders, I'll provide him with another distraction."

Mimses eyed her dourly. "You?"

She shrugged carelessly. "If need be. If I gauged his reaction to me correctly, the very thought of me gets him hard."

Mimses smirked. "Kind of like how that mutie whore affects Pharaoh. How goes it with her?"

"Her psychic defenses are strong but undisciplined. I encountered considerable resistance yesterday when I supplanted the image of the one-eyed man with that of Pharaoh. It is difficult to, on the one hand, verbally try to convince her Pharaoh is a monster, and on the other, mentally nudge her into his arms.''

''A little too complicated for my tastes.''

''Not really. Krysty is so busy trying to screen out Pharaoh's influence, she's completely unaware that I'm slipping in the back door and chipping away at her barriers.''

''Where is she now?''

''With Pharaoh. She seemed sluggish this morning, so I figure Pharaoh gave her mind a squeeze while she slept. Combined with the spiked wine I poured for her and Pharaoh's proximity, she should be a prime candidate for Spellbound City before the day is through.''

''Sort of like your mother,'' Mimses commented dryly.

Nefron pushed herself away from the wall, thrusting her head forward angrily. ''He seduced and tricked her and killed her.''

''He didn't kill her,'' Mimses stated. ''And it didn't take a whole hell of a lot of seducing.''

Nefron's lips peeled back from her teeth in a silent snarl. ''She wasn't in her right mind—you know that.''

''Oh, she was in her right mind,'' Mimses said with a smirk. ''It was her reproduction system that wasn't right. Pharaoh fixed her so she could give birth to you, but it was a one-time-only deal. The second time he played around with her insides, she wasn't so lucky.''

"He did operate on her, performed surgery against her will. That's the same as killing her."

"Nefron, sweetie," Mimses said, striving for a tone of condolence, "poor old Connie didn't have much will left to her."

"And who's fault was that?"

"I've managed to keep your dear old dad pretty much out of my head for the past few years."

"Aren't you lucky?" she said with a sneer.

Mimses chuckled. "Not as lucky as I'm going to be. The machinery is all in place in the King's Chamber. The newcomers won't cause you any trouble, since you're their only hope of getting out of here. They'll do what you say. If it's revenge you're after, you'll get it. So relax."

Nefron's tense, haughty expression slowly softened. "You're right. What about the Incarnates?"

"What's left of them, you mean?" Mimses replied in irritation. "They're primed and ready to play their parts. Are you sure you can count on the kid, the albino?"

"I'll be able to persuade him to push the deadfall lever. Since he's never been anywhere near Pharaoh, he will not be able to sense his intentions."

Mimses laughed and clapped his hands. "It's foolproof. Once that mutant whoreson and his mutie bitch are out of the way, I'll declare you queen. The newcomers will make perfect patsies."

Nefron didn't join in with the laughter. Her eyes narrowed, focusing on the open collar of Mimses's robe. "Where's your amulet?"

Mimses laughter clogged in his throat. He made a slapping grab for his throat, his upper chest.

"Shit," he hissed, his eyes showing fear. "I don't know what could have— I always wear it!"

"You'll have to be around Pharaoh a lot these next couple of days," Nefron said grimly. "You'd better find another one very quickly, or this fool-proof plan you're so proud of will be a foolproof way to get all of us executed."

LIKE AKHNATON HAD SAID, Ryan awoke feeling as if every muscle had been worked over by a meat tenderizer. He'd had no trouble getting back into the dormitory the night before and hadn't spoken to J.B. He collapsed onto his pallet and lay awake for a very long time, his body aching, his soul in agony. He managed to fall asleep after several hours and awakened when the dawn-to-noon labor shift shuffled out for breakfast. He tried to go back to sleep, but only dozed fitfully.

When he finally decided to get up, he saw J.B. staring at him disconcertedly. "What?" he asked irritably, his voice hoarse and thick.

"You've got bruises on your neck," his friend said mildly.

Ryan fingered the sore, tender flesh of his throat. "Not too far off the mark. It's the royal handprint of Pharaoh Akhnaton."

Tersely, without spicing it up, he told the Armorer of his violent encounter with Akhnaton.

His face a mask of astonishment, J.B. demanded, "Dark night! Why didn't he chill you?"

"He could have...or ordered some flunkies to do it. He said he'd rather punish me, hold Krysty over my head to control and torture me."

J.B. scowled. "Bastard coldheart."

"Yeah," Ryan grunted. "Let's see if there's anything to eat in this dump."

There was. A wheeled cart held savory biscuits, tea and a watered-down sort of fruit beverage. To their mild surprise, they had more or less free run of the dormitory and found a rec room where men played various board games. Curiously, their dorm mates were disinterested in them, treating them indifferently. After inviting them to join in a particularly boring-looking game and being promptly refused, J.B. and Ryan were pretty much left to themselves.

They found a shower room, which they took eager advantage of. Water flowed from amphorsae and ran down carefully chiseled channels and drains in the floor, dripping into purification tanks just below, and recirculated to supply tanks. So rare was the commodity, water had to be carefully conserved, no more permitted to evaporate than was unavoidable.

Adjacent to the shower room was a workshop equipped with a number of hand tools and even a band saw, drill press and a punch. Fasa was there at a bench, sharpening a number of chisels on a whetstone. He looked up when they entered and smiled. "Want to help me get the tools ready for the day?"

"Is it part of our responsibility?" J.B. asked.

Fasa's face acquired a faintly troubled look. "No, not exactly. Just thought you might care to make our shift go smoother. We can't use another shift's tools, you know."

Ryan shrugged and sat next to the man on the bench. He ran an oiled rag over the chisels to no real purpose except to appear helpful.

"Tell me about the capstone ceremony," Ryan suggested, hoping to sound ingenuous.

Fasa launched into a long, fancifully worded dissertation about how the capstone was a crystalline pyramidion built by Pharaoh's own hands, following ancient texts. Once in place, it would draw down the power of Osiris and fill Akhnaton with the supernal power of a god.

"Where's the capstone now?" J.B. asked.

Fasa regarded him solemnly. "Why do you want to know?"

"Won't we be the ones to put it into place?"

"No," Fasa retorted. "You have yet to be purified. You won't be allowed to touch it."

"Oh," Ryan said. "You can at least tell us where it is."

"I can't. Its location is a secret, known only to Pharaoh."

J.B. poked around in the contents of a wooden bin at the end of the table. He picked up a thin wafer of gray metal. "Some kind of alloy...lead and copper, mebbe."

"It is used in the manufacture of the metauh rods," Fasa said.

"This stuff?" J.B. said doubtfully. "Doesn't seem like it would be a very good conductor."

"That and other materials are used on the rods' handles to protect the Incarnates from their own mena energy." He glanced from J.B. to Ryan suspiciously. "You are a rather inquisitive pair."

"Why shouldn't we be?" Ryan responded smoothly. "If our futures lie in Aten and service to Pharaoh, we need to learn as much as possible."

The answer seemed to satisfy Fasa. He returned

his attention to sharpening the chisels, and J.B. and Ryan wandered away from the workroom.

"Did you understand any of that mumbo jumbo horseshit about the capstone?" J.B. asked.

Ryan shook his head impatiently. "Not nearly enough. We're getting nowhere fast."

A tall, scrawny, faintly ridiculous figure suddenly stepped from a side corridor. It required a second for them to recognize the lean figure wearing a kilt as Doc.

J.B. laughed. "What are you doing running around in that hairdo with your skinny shanks showing, Doc?"

Doc's lips tightened in disapproval. "I assure you that you present quite as ludicrous a picture as I, John Barrymore." In a low voice, he added, "I have felicitous news, but I cannot tarry overlong. So far, no one has prevented me from going where I will, however I do not care to—"

"Have you seen Mildred?" J.B. interrupted.

"Yes, yesterday. She is working on Mimses's staff."

"Mimses?"

"A counselor. His real name is Stockbridge."

"What about Krysty?" Ryan asked.

"I have not seen her, but I am sure she is being well treated."

"Any word from this Kela about efforts to get us out of here?" J.B. inquired.

"Not directly, though Dr. Wyeth informed me that Akhnaton's daughter, Nefron, is the guiding force behind the plan. Or plot. She seems to be in touch with Dr. Wyeth, and that is the reason I am here."

Doc dug around his loincloth and brought out an ankh, a smaller duplicate of the one Danielson had around his neck. "The doctor lifted this from Mimses. She theorizes it may be our key to getting out of here."

J.B. took it from his hand and inspected it closely. "It looks sort of like that alloy in the workroom. Why does Mildred think it's important?"

Doc quickly related their discussion of the day before, concluding, "The doctor feels that the ankh may dissipate or block psychic influence directed toward us by our hosts."

"I suppose I can make a couple with the odds and ends in the workroom," J.B. said musingly. "I'll use this one as the template...I just don't know if the metal is the same."

Ryan shook his head. "It's straw-grasping, but it's the only straw we have. Krysty may be under psychic influence. We'll need to make enough of those things for all of us."

"Has it occurred to anybody that we could already be under the influence of Hell Eyes and not know it?" J.B. inquired.

"An unnerving notion, indeed," Doc replied.

"He said something to me last night...if a strong mind consciously resists him, he can't do much," Ryan said.

Doc's blue eyes went wide. "You met Akhnaton? What kind of man is he?"

"Hey! Newcomers!" Shukeli's braying voice bawled from the door to the barracks room. "Get ready to go on shift! You! Old one! Go back to your station! You're impeding progress!"

The three of them exchanged grim glances and did as they were told. J.B. carefully slipped the ankh into an inner pocket of his apron.

Chapter Twenty-Three

It had taken most of the shift to lay down the casing blocks that would serve as the foundation and support pedestal for the pyramid's capstone. They were told that the following day, the morning shift would raise the roller rails in order to convey the pyramidion to the apex of the monument.

Ryan had given up on the idea of sowing the seeds of discontent among his fellow laborers. First, there was little time to get the idea percolating. Second, most of them still retained vivid memories of the aborted uprising of nearly two years before.

And third, if they were indeed in bondage, they didn't find it particularly difficult to bear.

When their shift was over and the workers were back in the dormitory, J.B. and Ryan went to the shower room. Doc was waiting for them there, a tool belt girding his bony waist. He pretended to be examining one of the water spouts, tapping on it with a small hammer.

Ryan and J.B. stood under the adjacent spout and showered, the sound of running water and the murmurs of the other men muffling their conversation. To their questions about Krysty, Jak and Mildred, Doc responded with doleful negatives.

J.B. gritted his teeth. "This is ridiculous. There's nothing to stop us from just strolling out of here."

"Stroll out to where?" Ryan snapped in a tone harsher than he intended. "The only place to go is Fort Fubar. And if we don't stay there and strike out on our own away from the redoubt, how can we carry enough food and water? We won't have our blasters and we won't have Krysty, Mildred and Jak."

"We know where Mildred is," the Armorer muttered. "And we've got a good idea of where Krysty is being held."

"It is my suspicion that Nefron plans to stage our escape during the pyramid ceremony," Doc said quietly. "From what I've heard, all of Aten will be caught up in the festivities."

J.B. dried himself with a ragged scrap of cloth serving as a towel. "I still don't understand this whole deal about the pyramid."

"Not even historians or Egyptologists really understood it," Doc replied. "In my day, there was a great deal of speculation regarding the Great Pyramid of Cheops. How old it was, what secrets it contained and, most important, how it was built."

"We know now how it was probably built," Ryan said wryly.

Doc smiled. "There was a lot more to the pyramids than most scientists wanted to admit. A correlation was found between some of the pyramid measurements and the circumference of the world and the value of pi."

Ryan and J.B. exchanged puzzled glances.

"That's all speculation, however," Doc continued. "What is known is that in order to get the great pyramids built, Egyptian society was made repressive to increase the efficiency of the human laborers.

The historical Akhnaton was obsessed with gaining spiritual knowledge through a mystic power created by the pyramids. Evidently, his red-eyed namesake shares the same esoteric objective.''

"The main difference," Ryan said grimly, "is that the first Akhnaton didn't hold Krysty as a hostage.''

Doc nodded sagely. "In which case, we need to assure ourselves she is acting under some sort of psychic duress.''

Ryan fixed him with a cold, blue-eyed glare. "You think she's not?''

"There's only one way to find out for certain. Get an ankh to her.''

J.B. nodded, patting the pocket of his apron. "I'll see what I can do about that tonight.''

Doc smiled wanly. "Good. I shall try to contact you tomorrow.''

Ryan watched him leave, saying to J.B., "Let's go to the workroom and get started. We'll brazen it out.''

Most of their workers were having their evening meal, so the room was deserted. While Ryan stood watch by the door, J.B. hunted through the metal scraps in the bin, comparing them with the composition of the ankh. He found several wafers that seemed similar and he traced the outline of the amulet with a piece of soapstone.

With much under-the-breath cursing, J.B. got the band saw working. He had to keep pumping a foot pedal so it would spin at a high speed and continuously apply oil to the metal wafer to dim the screech of the saw blade.

He managed to cut a fairly close approximation

of the ankh, then moved over to the drill press to punch a hole through it. With a hammer and grindstone, he smoothed down the rough edges and spurs, then tossed it to Ryan for inspection.

The one-eyed man stowed it in his apron, saying, "It'll have to do. Make another one."

J.B. repeated the process, laboriously forming a second ankh in less time than it took to make the first. He was busy outlining the third amulet when Ryan hissed, "Somebody's coming."

J.B. turned over the metal wafer a second before Fasa sauntered in. He regarded them both with surprise, then suspicion. "Why are you here?"

"No reason," J.B. replied.

Ryan winced.

Fasa swept his gaze over the drill press and band saw and announced, "You're not supposed to be using the tools without authorization or supervision. What have you been making?"

J.B. caught Ryan's eye. "Should I tell him?"

Sidling up behind the man, he replied, "Why not?"

J.B. turned over the piece of metal on the table, exposing the template ankh. Fasa's eyes widened, then bugged. "A forbidden thing. You're making a forbidden thing! Pharaoh will punish you!"

"Why?" J.B. demanded. "It's just jewelry, right?"

As if explaining a complex math problem to a child, Fasa said patiently, "It's not so much the symbol itself as the metal fashioned into that shape. It interferes with Pharaoh's power."

"Yeah," Ryan said quietly. "So we've heard. That's why we're making them."

He hit him hard, a short jab to the kidney. Fasa uttered a gargling cry, rising up on his toes and falling forward into J.B.'s arms. The Armorer wrestled him to the floor, squatted on his chest and covered his mouth with a hand.

"We don't want to chill you," J.B. said quietly, "but we will if you force us. All we want is to get out of here."

Fasa mumbled something through J.B.'s clamped fingers. The Armorer moved his hand away, ready to throttle him if the man spoke in anything other than a whisper.

"Why?" Fasa asked, voice tight with pain and confusion.

"Why do we want to leave?"

"Yes."

"My friends and me don't like living as property or as work animals."

"But you're well treated here!"

J.B. shook his head in disgust. "I'm not going to waste my time explaining things about freedom and liberty to you. All you need to know is this—if you betray us, you'll die."

While J.B. spoke, Ryan found a coil of rope and a handful of oily rags.

"Your choice, Fasa," the Armorer continued. "We'll tie you up and hide you, or kill you and hide you. Which one will it be?"

Fasa considered his options for only a heartbeat before replying, "Tie me up and hide me."

Securely binding and gagging the man was the work of only a few minutes. Hiding him presented another problem. An upright tool chest was affixed to the wall in a far corner. J.B. removed the hand tools, and Ryan dragged Fasa over to it, pushing him face first against the wood backing. The locker was tall but not particularly deep, and the fit was tight. The man's bound wrists were jammed fast against his hips when Ryan shut and locked the door. He immediately regretted not chilling him, but he knew it was a bit easier to conceal a live body for a couple of days than a dead one. If luck was with them, Fasa would suffocate before he managed to work the gag out of his mouth and call for help.

"Let's get back at it," J.B. said. "Next time somebody comes in, we'd better think about chilling them."

"Yeah," Ryan agreed. "It'd be simpler all the way around."

IN THE HOURS after sunset, the great, endless vista of the dark, star-sprinkled sky spread out above the city of Aten. The walls were made of dressed concrete, and vigilant sentries paced their length.

But no eye saw two black-cloaked figures emerging from a small postern gate that was always locked, but never guarded. The two moved across open ground swiftly, keeping to the shadows.

Mimses and Nefron walked through the sand, their concealing cloaks fluttering in the blessedly cool breeze. They strode silently until they reached the bottom of the stair at the base of the pyramid. It loomed above them, strangely beautiful in the starlight.

"You know where the entrance is?" Mimses asked doubtfully.

Nefron nodded. "Of course. I studied the blueprints. Follow me."

She went determinedly up the steps at a half trot. Mimses hiked up the hem of his cloak and followed at a considerably slower pace and without a fraction of her nimbleness of foot.

Halfway up the side of the pyramid, Nefron stopped and watched Mimses's panting ascent with a condescending half smile on her lips. She wasn't even slightly out of breath. Mimses reached her, swaying slightly on weak legs. "Now what?" he demanded between rasping gulps for air.

"The keystone sequence." Nefron stretched out her right arm and hammered twice with the heel of her hand against the corner of the closest casing stone. With a grating rumble, the square of stone sank inward, seemingly to sink beneath the surface of the pyramid.

Mimses scowled his astonishment. "How does that work?"

"Pressure-sensitive actuators connected to a hydraulic sleeve pivot," she replied breezily. "Predark engineering, nothing magic about it."

She stepped into a black abyss. After a hesitant moment, Mimses followed her into the darkness. He had to squeeze his bulk between the rope-wrapped drum of a winch-and-pulley device. Far away glimmered a pinpoint of light. He followed the cloaked girl as she went forward into the shadows, which slowly receded before them until they stood in the King's Chamber.

It was a vast, hollow pyramid within the pyramid, made of pink-hued granite. Workmen had set up flaming braziers at intervals of ten feet along either side of the room. Arrangements of fragrant white flowers stood between each brazier. The air was heavy with the scent of gardenias and incense.

At the apex of the pyramid, suspended by a web of wires, hung a copper sigil of an enormous, lidless eye. It stared down with a fathomless gaze upon the varnished sarcophagus. Light glittered from quartz inlays, gleamed on the gold-leaf face fashioned into an exaggeratedly noble likeness of Akhnaton.

High on the ceiling, two shaft openings aligned with mathematical precision allowed the diffused light of two carefully selected stars to reflect from the polished surface of the sarcophagus.

Nefron shivered. "It frightens me to be in here."

Mimses looked upward. "Yeah. Millions of tons of stone, held together by a small deadfall. Just waiting for someone to pull the right lever in the right way at the right time."

She shook her head. "That doesn't bother me. It's the thought that Pharaoh's scheme to increase his power might really work."

Mimses eyed the sarcophagus, then the copper sigil. "He explained it to me once. Didn't make a whole hell of a lot of sense."

Nefron shrugged out of her cloak, folding it over one arm. "It's simple, really. The crystal in the pyramid acts as energy condensers. They hold enough bioaural energy to trigger a series of synapses in Pharaoh's brain and relay the energy to his pineal gland. The process will take about an hour. If Krysty is with him, we'll have to deal with two insufferable chrysalides evolving into arrogant butterflies."

Mimses watched her, hearing the subtle undertone of hatred in her voice. "What happens if you undergo the process instead?" he asked.

Nefron snapped her head around, eyes narrowed. "Why do you ask that?"

"Just curious. You inherited some of your father's powers. Mebbe you could enhance them this way."

"Perhaps," she admitted. "I'd rather have him dead."

Mimses didn't reply as she paced with feline grace around the chamber. Acting as the consort of a queen, of a young goddess, might have been an exciting prospect if any woman other than Nefron was the candidate. She was certainly beautiful, but she was too bright and too sleek for his tastes, with her small, hard breasts and the rondure of her slim hips. He preferred the other court women, languid and fluttery though they were. The image of the new woman, Mildred, flashed into his mind.

The hollow chamber echoed with Nefron's weary sigh. "Still think she's the cure for your problem, Mimses?"

His shoulders jerked in surprised reaction to her words. "What are you talking about—?"

A rush of shame and humiliation brought heat to his face, drawing perspiration from his pores. He bared his teeth in a grimace. "You little bitch. You read my thoughts."

Nefron laughed, a cruel, tinkling sound. "You transmitted them, your lust for that woman is so strong. You should be wearing an ankh shield, like I told you."

Mimses turned his grimace into a frown. "Drop it. Are you sure nothing can accidentally trigger the deadfall?"

"No. But I'll have to warn Jak to be very careful

when he's in the relieving chamber not to dislodge the release mechanism.''

''Just make sure you're away from here before the ceremony begins.''

''I will.''

''What about the kid?''

She shrugged and gestured to the ceiling. ''Even if he gets stuck in the relieving chamber, he can crawl out through one of the shafts. We'll have our assassin.''

Mimses dabbed at a film of sweat on his upper lip. ''You sure he's under your control?''

''All he has to do is trip the keystone lever. He's under my control for that little task.''

''As long as Pharaoh doesn't hear anything in time for him to escape.''

''There's no way. The only thing he'll hear are the blocks falling down. The only way to escape is through the Grand Gallery, and that will be jammed with his counselors. Only the few people right by the mouth of the corridor will be able to reach safety.''

Mimses nodded. ''Mebbe we should put another of the newcomers up there in the relieving chamber, just in case your boy doesn't make it. How about the woman?''

Nefron regarded him with a sly, speculative look. ''Not until you're done with her, of course.''

Mimses opened his mouth to voice an angry denial, then he looked into the girl's dark eyes, glinting with a flicker of deep red, and realized he could hide nothing from her that she wanted to discover.

He forced an uneasy chuckle. ''Of course.''

Nefron's sly look suddenly vanished, replaced by

a slit-eyed, searching examination. "You're a fool," she said. "A lust-besotted fool."

Mimses clenched his fists. "What are you talking about?"

Nefron inhaled a sharp, fearful breath. "I see it in your mind."

"See what?"

"The woman, Mildred, took your shield. She lifted your ankh while you were busy pawing her and licking your lips. She knows."

"How?" Mimses demanded in a ragged voice. "How?"

Nefron shook her glossy black head. "That's not important. But she *knows!*"

Chapter Twenty-Four

Danielson was a yakker, not a communicator, and as the third day of Dean's stay in Fort Fubar crawled to a close, he seriously contemplated filling either the man's mouth or his own ears with sand.

It wasn't so much that he resented the old man, but was too angry at his father for leaving him again to even try to make the best of the situation. Still, he remembered a saying he had learned while at the Brody School, something to the effect that he also serves who only stands and waits. It was a very cold comfort.

Only a short time had passed since his father had rescued him from the gladitorial games staged by Vinge Connrad in Nevada, and he was insecure about being abandoned—though he wouldn't have admitted that fear to anyone, not even to Doc or Jak.

Dean spent most of his waking hours in Fort Fubar trying to avoid sunstroke or gazing out on the empty horizon in the direction his father and his friends had traveled. Nothing ever stirred on the wasteland but the wavery, watery heat shimmer.

One morning, before the heat of the day became unbearable and under the helpful eye of Danielson, he practiced maneuvering the chariot around the perimeter. Dean had expected his host to object to his experimentation with the vehicle, but all the old man had said was, "Don't appear like Pharaoh is going to send anybody out to claim it. You might as well try it out."

Dean didn't examine Danielson's words too closely until that night, lying on his sleeping bag with the old man's snores ringing in his ears. The only reason Pharaoh hadn't dispatched sec men to retrieve the chariot was that he already had what he wanted, and the wag was an acceptable loss. Dean slept very poorly that night.

The food eaten by the man and boy was strictly rationed, but there was plenty of water in the stream, though it had to be boiled and strained through a cloth before it was drinkable. Danielson and Dean took turns performing this procedure.

Sometimes when Danielson began one of his seemingly endless and pointless narratives, Dean would try to listen and construct and fit it into some kind of coherent chronology. So much of what Danielson said concerning his life was contradictory and came in no particular order. He thought he had learned how to tune out the man's disconnected ramblings.

On the fourth sunset in Fort Fubar, while Dean was gazing at the horizon, the Steyr in his hands, the wry realization came to him that he actually had absorbed a lot more than he would have guessed.

Danielson was born in what used to be called Indiana to a Farer family. He had joined up with the Trader's group when he was in his early thirties, so he looked older than he truly was. Ryan and J.B. had only been with Trader a short while before he was cut loose.

Danielson had lived peaceably in Aten for a long

time under the name of Osorkon. He shared counselor responsibilities with a man he referred to alternately as Mimses and Mel.

The names of his three wives were Pyatha, Flaresh and Iocol. He had three children, but all were dead now but his oldest daughter, Kela.

Something had happened in Aten, and Danielson had abandoned both Pharaoh's service and his own daughter to return to this pesthole.

As the sun slowly sank out of sight, Danielson called to him from the doorway of the storage building, "Time to eat, boy."

Dean pulled his gaze away from the color-splashed horizon and shifted the strap of the rifle on his shoulder. The Steyr was heavy, and constantly carrying it had worn a raw, tender abrasion on the skin of his right shoulder.

Inside the ramshackle building, Danielson stirred another of his stews simmering in a pot over a small fire. Without looking up, he said, "Tomorrow is the fourth day."

Dean didn't respond. He sat down cross-legged on the sandy floor and waited for Danielson to ladle the stew into a plate. The old man passed it to him, saying calmly, "If your pa isn't back by sundown, I think you'd better figure on rolling on to Pharaoh's tomb—the redoubt—by first light the day after."

Dean spooned some of the tepid, very nearly tasteless sludge into his mouth and fixed his eyes on a distant, invisible point, somewhere over Danielson's head.

The old man coughed a little self-consciously. "Can't deny it's been a pleasure having you here, son. Almost like having my own boy back with me. He was about your age when he—''

He coughed again and ate a mouthful of stew. Dean shifted his gaze and saw tears shining in the man's melancholy gray eyes. He couldn't help but feel a pang of sympathy.

Exhaling noisily, Danielson said, ''Guess I didn't know how lonesome I was. When you move out, I reckon I'll go with you.''

Dean shook his head. ''If my dad doesn't show by noon tomorrow, I'm off to this Aten place, not to some Pharaoh's tomb or redoubt.''

Danielson blinked at him. ''That's not a sound notion, son. If your pa hasn't come back, then it means he can't come back—''

''I'll *bring* him back,'' Dean declared fiercely. ''And the rest of them, too. I'm not going off and leaving them, not knowing what's happened to them.''

Tugging nervously at an earlobe, Danielson said quietly, ''I don't think your pa would like that, you ending up in the same kind of mess he's in. If you ask me—''

''I'm not,'' Dean snapped.

''—you'll be taking a hell of a big risk. I'm afraid I can't allow it.''

Dean dropped his plate and put his hand on the stock of the Steyr. ''You going to try and stop me?'' he challenged.

Man and boy locked gazes for a long moment. Danielson was the first to look away. ''No,'' he answered sadly. ''Even if I could hog-tie you without getting myself gut-shot, I couldn't keep you tied up all the time. I won't try to stop you.''

Resting his plate on his lap, Danielson slipped the thong and ankh amulet from around his neck. He tossed it to Dean, who caught it one-handed, eyeing it skeptically. "What good will this do me?"

Danielson began to eat again. "Mebbe none, mebbe all the good in the world. Never can tell. Now, eat up. I know it tastes like parboiled shit, but if you're determined to walk into the lion's den, you'll need every ounce of your strength."

JAK SETTLED into his twilight world without too much difficulty or too many questions. Everything was comfortably blurred, all hard edges softened and blunted. It smelled sweet and tasted like honey, though sometimes there was a sharp bitterness at the back of his palate. During these times, one part of his mind would occasionally come alive with fleeting, alarmed thoughts. But then Kela would offer him food or drink or herself, and the thoughts would be muddled and warmed by pleasure.

He had been told to always remain inside the small house and never to venture outside. He was never left alone except when he slept, which seemed to be often. When he mentioned this curious lethargy to Kela, she maintained sweetly it was all part of the healing process.

However, it seemed a little strange that his sexual energy wasn't adversely affected. In fact, it seemed enhanced. When he was awake, it was as if he were swimming under dreamy water. All he really remembered was lying atop Kela, thrusting into her, or she was atop him, thrusting down herself. The girl was smooth and warm and avid, and he loved her, really loved her. He thought.

Nefron appeared very infrequently, usually—though he could never be sure—at night. He looked upon her hungrily whenever she arrived. He loved her, really loved her, too. She would smile at him fondly, murmur to him, stroke his head. Desire rose in him like a column of fire. After she had departed, Kela would douse the fire with a fierce heat of her own.

The twilight routine seemed to go on for days, for weeks, but he was distantly aware that his sense of time was distorted.

One time when he awoke from a slumber, he realized with a start that he hadn't asked about Ryan, J.B., Krysty, Doc or Mildred for what felt like a very long time.

Naked, he arose from the pallet, guiltily forcing himself to remember their faces, straining his memory to count how many days and nights had passed. He couldn't. As far as he knew, as little as two days or as many as two months had passed since he had put himself in the care of Kela and Nefron.

He checked to make sure his weapons were where they were supposed to be. He clicked through the cylinder of the Colt Python, testing the smoothness of the action. He heard the soft scuff of feet behind him and caught a whiff of a familiar perfume. He didn't turn.

"You should have let me know you were awake," Nefron said softly.

"Where Kela?"

"Out to get food. She'll be back soon."

Jak didn't want to look at her. He found himself actually a little afraid to look at her. Already his body was responding to her presence. "When I leave?"

She laughed musically. "Growing bored with us, Jak?"

Sullenly, Jak demanded again, "When going?"

A note of anger entered Nefron's voice. "Why are you so anxious all of a sudden?"

He didn't respond to the question. Stubbornly, he said, "Need to see friends. Need to get out. Need talk to Ryan."

"It is impossible. He is in the men's workers barracks. I cannot get in there unnoticed."

Putting down his blaster, Jak massaged his eyes with the heels of his slightly trembling hands. "Need to get out," he said hoarsely.

"Every one of your friends is fine," Nefron said comfortingly. "Thanks to me. You must trust me."

"What about Krysty?" Jak asked.

"She is in high favor with Pharaoh."

Jak frowned, saying uneasily, "Tricking him until we escape."

"She is charmed by him, as well."

"No way. Not believe."

Sadly, Nefron replied, "You must come to terms with the possibility that your friend Krysty might not be able to help herself. Pharaoh possesses powers beyond your comprehension. It is a crafty, subtle power. He can enter a mind and deftly change what he finds there, and the victim of the tampering may never know what has happened until it is too late."

"Why wait to leave?" Jak asked.

"Akhnaton's pyramid is very close to completion. You and your friends can escape during the confusion surrounding the ceremony. If we plan it right, you can be many miles from here before your friends are missed.''

"Where go?"

"The gateway."

"You know about gateway?"

"Oh, yes. In Pharaoh's tomb."

"When pyramid ceremony?"

"Tomorrow. Sunset. I will arrange transportation and return your weapons to you." She paused. There was a rustling sound, and she whispered, "Look at me, Jak."

Taking a deep breath, he turned, jaw muscles bunched with determination. Nefron's eyes seemed to hit him with a dizzying force in the center of his chest, in the center of who he was. His breath caught in his throat as he drank in her nude beauty. He felt himself hardening, rising.

"I am baring myself to you Jak, because I need you. I need you to do something for me...for Kela...for your friends."

His tongue seemed frozen in his mouth, but he managed to ask, "What?"

"Pharaoh and his counselors will be at the dedication ceremony in the pyramid. The King's Chamber has been designed so that most of the weight of the stone is deflected by the relieving chambers above it. There is a mechanism built into one chamber that will cause the floors to collapse, one by one. The device is built to allow enough time to climb down to an escape shaft. I'll be waiting for you there with your friends. In the confusion, we will escape the city. Everyone will be trying to dig out Pharaoh and the people trapped inside the pyramid."

"You need me do this." Jak wasn't asking a question.

Tears welled up Nefron's eyes. Brimming, they flashed like wet black jewels. "If there was any other way to prevent Pharaoh from imprisoning us here, I would take it. What you have to understand is that Pharaoh is a monster, a mutant who cares for no one but himself. If you don't value your own freedom, then at least value that of your friends. You must do this thing."

"Who with Pharaoh in there?"

"Toadies who are as bad as he is. Nobody you need worry about, Jak."

Jak was silent for several moments as he mulled over Nefron's words. Finally, he asked, "Why me?"

Nefron's gaze was misted by tears, by love. "Because only you can do it. You're the only man in this whole corrupt city who isn't under Pharaoh's influence. You're strong and fast and agile."

She paused, eyeing him keenly. "Just give me another day...and we're free. I'll escape with you."

"Kela, too?"

Nefron smiled. "Kela, too. You won't let us down, will you? You won't back out on us after all I and Kela have done for you?"

She gazed unblinkingly into his ruby eyes. A fire seemed to dance in the depths of her own.

Jak stared back. "No. Not let you and Kela down."

It was the last thing he said before she came into his arms, kissing him passionately, inserting her tongue into his mouth, pressing her body tightly against his so he could feel and respond to the erotic, urgent heat of it. His whole being felt stunned, as if he had been flattened by a concussion gren.

They flowed together down to the floor. Nefron whispered into his ear, "Don't think. Just feel."

"Yeah," he said, and he did as he was told.

Chapter Twenty-Five

As Doc had promised, he met J.B. and Ryan in the dormitory the next morning. Surrounded by a milling crowd of men lining up for breakfast and the toilets, no one gave the three men more than a passing glance.

It was the work of only a few seconds to pass three of the ankhs, including the template original, to Doc. Though he quickly slipped them into his loincloth, he seemed inclined to linger.

"The streets are filling up," he said. "The festivities are under way."

"We know," Ryan said flatly. "We busted our humps yesterday cleaning up the top of the pyramid."

"Yeah," J.B. added. "We also found this stuff when we woke up." He pointed to a stack of clean linen tunics just outside of the shower room. "I guess we're to look our best today."

"I wish a pair of proper pants was in there," Doc said wistfully.

"We've got other things to worry about than pants," Ryan retorted. "Has anybody heard anything from Nefron?"

"No, but I have not spoken to Dr. Wyeth yet. I shall be going to her workstation straightaway. I am sure she has heard something by now."

Doc left the dormitory, the weight of the metal ankhs causing his loincloth to sag in an embarrassing place. He even jingled faintly when he walked.

No one called to him as he crossed the compound to the rear of the palace. Though it was full of people, striding purposefully to and fro, they were too caught up in the joy of being ruled by a god and goddess.

Doc understood that the pyramid had cast a truly entrancing spell over the population of Aten. The belief in Pharaoh's crazy vision to become a god was palpable.

The kitchen was as busy as the rest of Aten, filled with the clack and clatter of pots and the odors of several feasts being prepared at once. Doc found Mildred in a side room, looking hot and harried as she peeled fruit. He wasted no time on preambles. Handing her two of the ankhs, he said simply, "Let us hope they work."

Mildred slid them inside her breast coverings. "They'll work against Akhnaton, I'm pretty sure. I hope they're as effective against Nefron."

Doc stared in surprise. "You haven't heard from her?"

"Not a word from her or her maid, Kela."

"Still, she may be making the final preparations for our flight. No need to become paranoid at this late date that she is psychically influencing us."

Mildred wiped perspiration from her forehead with the back of her hand. "She's Pharaoh's daughter. Even if he doesn't claim her, it stands to reason she would have inherited some of his abilities."

"She's been helping us," Doc retorted. "And regardless, she is our best shot of escaping."

"So you think we should continue to rely on her?" Mildred asked.

"We do not have much choice," Doc answered grimly.

She sighed, eyeing an apple. "I'll try to get one of the amulets to Krysty as soon as possible."

"Hopefully," Doc commented dryly, "before she exchanges *I do's* with Pharaoh."

KRYSTY KNEW DIMLY something wasn't right. Not wrong, exactly, just not right. She knew it wasn't normal to be in a perpetual state between wakefulness and sleeping, but that was how she felt.

It was as if she wavered backward through time, as though she were irresistibly pulled toward eternity. She had flashes of images, of emotions. There was a scar-faced man. A child. Though she knew she loved them, she had difficulty remembering what they looked like. It all seemed so long ago, swept away by the ghostly currents of a river of memory.

Krysty tried to return her attention to her bath. It was her wedding day, and she wanted it to be perfect because her god wanted her to want it. The sunken bath was filled with steaming water and a mixture of scented oils. The mirror was fogged, and she sponged it dry and looked for a long moment at her face.

She wasn't sure if it was the face of Krysty Wroth or Nefertiti the queen. Memories came and went in a panoramic kaleidoscope. The scar-faced, one-eyed man was always there, but each time she tried to focus on him, he blurred, melted, transmogrifying into the hard, bronzed lines of her husband-to-be, beckoning to her, aching for her, all of him poised, erect and ready.

Krysty slid into her bath and tried to relax in the soothing heat of the perfumed water, letting the warmth ooze through her muscles, letting her thoughts drift free.

Once more the image of her lover, her husband-to-be, floated through her mind. Waves of desire radiated from him, an insatiable hunger, not a lust for her, but an obsession to propagate, to spawn and spread his hell-eyed seed over the ravaged face of the earth.

She glimpsed fortress cities, duplicates of Aten, on every continent, the subdued populations bowing in homage to the dynasty of red-haired god-kings. And she felt hatred—not springing from her, but from the heart of her beloved, hating the humans his offspring held in fearful thrall, hating humankind, desperate to shackle them to live and die in the service of his dynasty, his empire.

And hating, then loving, then hating again, he beckoned to her, his Krysty, his Nefertiti, his Connaught, his mother and lover and tool and breeder—

Krysty sat upright in the water, blinking against the dark, disturbing visions crowding into her mind. Her hair knotted tightly at her nape, like the fist of a frightened child. She wanted to weep, to run, to hide herself away. She didn't know why. Very vaguely, very distantly, she knew she had peered at a fragment of Akhnaton's soul he had tried to keep concealed.

Pushing the restless, uneasy thoughts far back into a recess of her mind, she concentrated on finishing her bath. She arose finally, dried and perfumed herself, wondering absently where Nefron might be.

She strolled out into the bedchamber, wrapped in a soft robe of blue wool. She had lingered in her bath overlong, and it was near midmorning. Leaning listlessly against the table, she dwelled on the future and what it might bring to her, as the consort of a god.

A quick three-rap rhythm sounded from the door, a signal that she almost recognized from another time, another life. Wearily, she called, "Enter."

One of the double doors opened just enough to admit a scantily clad black woman carrying a tray of sliced and artfully arranged fruit. Krysty had seen the woman before, but dressed in faded khakis, not dressed like a—

"Mildred?" Krysty asked, a faint line of consternation creasing her brow.

Placing the tray on the table, Mildred put a finger to her lips. "I've brought you breakfast."

"Where's Nefron? This is her job. She's supposed to help me dress."

Mildred shook her head at Krysty's troubled, slightly petulant tone. She pressed a large apple into her hands. "Eat this first. It's a gift from Ryan."

"Ryan? The one-eyed man."

Mildred stared hard into her face, examining every inch of it. With an index finger, she drew an invisible line before Krysty's eyes.

"What are you doing?" Krysty asked irritably.

"Eat the apple." Mildred's voice was flat, devoid of emotions.

"Why?"

"Just do it." Mildred turned to leave. Then, on

impulse, she turned and hugged her quickly. Before she left the chamber, Krysty was sure she had seen moisture in the woman's eyes.

Krysty looked at the apple in her hand, then bit into it thoughtfully. As she nibbled around the stem, her teeth struck a hard, unyielding object. Muttering peevishly, Krysty worked out the metal ankh cunningly concealed within the fruit.

Frowning, she studied it as it lay in her palm. There was something about its shape that seemed familiar. She closed her fingers around it.

An uncanny chill shook her. Her pulse and heartbeat rose, deafening her. Her fist trembled around the cool, slick metal. Within her was a maelstrom of spinning energies combining hate, fear and triumph.

Krysty Wroth's self, the center of consciousness that defined her identity, was sucked into this mental whirlpool. She forgot who Akhnaton wanted her to be and remembered who she was.

She took a deep breath and glanced around her chambers. They looked the same as in the previous moment, but they were undeniably, subtly different now. The walls exuded the same cold atmosphere as a prison cell and, for a moment, she couldn't understand why.

Then, like a crashing of a surf, she remembered what Danielson had said. *The shape of the amulet is a closed double-helix energy pattern. It protects my bioaural field from the resonating mena energies.*

She clenched her teeth so hard, they squeaked and her jaw muscles ached. She knew instantly what had been done to her, and she knew who had done it.

"You bitch," she hissed. "You double-dealing, vicious little bitch."

She also knew that Akhnaton had simply followed the path his daughter had blazed. He was equally responsible. Krysty remembered what she had vowed to Ryan four days and a thousand years ago: *He got into my head and played with me, like I was a sex puppet. Whether he's a pharaoh, god or mutant, and whether he wants me to bear his children or warm his bed, I'll provide him with a surprise that will give him nightmares for the rest of his life.*

She still meant every word of it.

MILDRED RECOGNIZED a hypnagogic state of consciousness, and Krysty was deep in the throes of one. The inability of her eyes to respond and track her finger had been the tip-off. If the state had been induced by drugs, then the ankh would probably do little to ameliorate it.

She hadn't gone more than twenty yards down the corridor when she sensed rather than heard a stealthy someone falling into step behind her. Pivoting sharply on her heel, she saw the Set-headed Incarnate looming there, a metauh rod held across his left breast. Fright leaped through her, dried the saliva in her mouth, set her heart to racing.

"Just keep going," he said tonelessly.

"To where?"

"To where I tell you."

Mildred did as he ordered, walking through what seemed like acres of shadowy, pillared halls. She knew she was back in the quarters of Mimses, and that he had sent one of his Incarnates to fetch her.

They went down a curving staircase with Set

nearly treading on her heels. The stair ended facing an open doorway. She hesitated, peering into it, trying to see or hear what lay beyond it.

With the serpentine quickness of his namesake, Set clapped his hand over Mildred's mouth and passed his other arm around her waist. He jerked her off her feet and carried her swiftly through the door. Mildred flailed at him with her fists, but the big man seemed impervious to her blows.

The room was lit only by a single, sputtering taper, and Mildred saw bleak, bare walls and a wooden bench in a corner. She also saw a metal ring bolted in the wall, well above the level of her head. From it dangled leather cuffs. Set yanked up her wrists, slid the cuffs around them, tightened the straps and released her. She hung with her arms above her head, only the balls of her feet touching the floor.

Hearing a footfall from a corner, she turned her head, looking over a shoulder. Mimses was swathed in a gaudy crimson-and-yellow robe, the big sleeves decorated with gleaming silver and gold braids. He smiled at her, vulpine lips spreading in an oily smirk of mock sympathy. Mildred felt his eyes running up and down her near naked body.

"You son of a bitch," she said calmly.

"Call me what you want, brown sugar. It'll only shorten your life."

Mimses stepped close to her, lightly stroking her bare back. The smirk was fixed on his face, but he saw the disgust flickering in her eyes and his lips compressed in anger.

"You stole from me." His tone was strident.

Mildred didn't reply.

Growling deep in his throat, Mimses raked his fingers over her body, clawing away her clothing. When her breastplates were stripped away, the ankh clinked to the stone floor. Mimses stooped to pick it up, holding it between thumb and forefinger.

"Danielson told you about the power of this," he said. "I should've guessed. Life in Aten has softened me. What did you do with it? Did you make copies?"

"Copies?" Mildred echoed. "Why would I do that?"

Mimses didn't answer, but Nefron did, in a cold voice from the doorway. "She's lying."

Shock and despair enfolded Mildred. Tears suddenly burned against her eyes, but she blinked them back angrily. Nefron stepped up beside her. Mildred didn't meet her gaze, and trying to keep her voice steady, she said, "I had my suspicions about you. I wish I'd acted on them."

Nefron's reply was a breathy, amused whisper. "You are more intelligent than I gave you credit for. You figured out the workings of the ankhs, how they set up a damping field that Pharaoh's power cannot penetrate."

"Or yours," Mildred said.

"Or mine."

"What's your agenda, Nefron? Why are you using us as pawns?"

Nefron shrugged. "In Aten, everyone is a pawn to one degree or another. The answer to your question is simple—I want the throne and I want that red-eyed monster dead."

"And you can't have one without the other."

Nefron chuckled. "See, Mimses? I told you she

was brighter than the usual women you take a fancy to.''

She tugged playfully on one of Mildred's braided plaits. "Because of some insane reaction to my mother's death, Pharaoh decided I was not his true heir. He stripped me of my rank and status. I am only the servant of the bitch he has chosen as his breeder. He expects her to bear him a litter of squalling gods and goddesses. I will not allow that to happen.''

"You want this sick little fantasyland all to yourself.''

"Fantasyland?'' All the humor vanished from Nefron's voice. "What do you mean?''

Mildred forced a dry chuckle. "I mean this isn't a kingdom. You're tromping around in an old movie set, playing 'let's pretend' to the point of imbecility. Akhnaton isn't a pharaoh—you aren't a princess. He's the product of an experiment in controlled eugenics, and you're his progeny. He's mutant, and so are you. Not royalty, not divine, just a couple of genetically twisted monstrosities with delusions.''

While she spoke, Nefron's face twisted into something ugly and hard. Her grip on Mildred's braid tightened, and she jerked Mildred's head back painfully. "The only thing separating fantasy from reality is a matter of perception," she snapped. "Since I am in charge, it is my perception of reality that matters.''

"Get to the goddamn point," Mimses said impatiently.

Nefron glanced his way with bright, venomous eyes. He hastily glanced away. Returning her gaze to Mildred, she asked, "Did you tell your friends

about the power of the ankhs? Did you make more
of them? You were found in Pharaoh's quarters. Did
you give one to Krysty? Answer me.''

Mildred didn't answer or even act as if she had
heard the questions. She focused her vision on the
wall only a few inches away from her face.

The room suddenly reverberated with a snapping
crack. It took all of Mildred's self-control not to
scream as streaks of agony blazed across her back.
Twisting her head back and around, she saw Mimses
holding a whip in his right hand. The lash consisted
of three pliant, knotted leather cords.

"Answer her," he said. The cold, lustful light
gleaming in his eyes showed that he really didn't
want her to cooperate.

"What difference does it make?" Mildred demanded between clenched teeth.

"The difference between life and death," Nefron
declared.

"Yours or mine?"

"Both. Our fates are intertwined at this moment."
She glared hard and unblinkingly at Mildred. As she
did so, she said, "I cannot get a read on her. She is
resisting me, and I cannot waste any more time here.
I have got to attend to Krysty. Mimses, make this
bitch talk or make her die.''

Chapter Twenty-Six

Jak was hot, thirsty, tired and cramped, a far cry from how he had felt in the hour before dawn when he had followed Nefron out of the small house on the outskirts of Aten.

She had led him along a mazelike path, circling around the city walls to the very base of the pyramid. Its massive proportions hadn't impressed him overmuch. He had eyes only for Nefron. The memory of her body was still fresh in his hands, the taste of her on his lips, and the erotic scent of her skin, her sex still sweetened the air he breathed.

She told him where to climb, how to get there, what to do and when to do it. She held him by the sides of the head and kissed him deeply and passionately.

Senses reeling, Jak began the long climb up the side of the monument, not feeling the weight of his holstered blaster or the water skin slung over a shoulder.

He found the mouth of the ventilation shaft leading to the relieving chamber with no trouble, just where Nefron had indicated it would be. But, even as thin as he was, he had difficulty squeezing into it. He put his back against one wall and braced his feet against the other and crept down at a snail's pace into darkness.

The rough-hewn surface of the stone scraped his back, snagged at folds in his shirt, and when the friction between flesh and rock increased, he began to sweat profusely. The painfully slow sliding of his boot treads and the inch-by-inch movements of his back had to be synchronized perfectly, or he would lose his precarious balance and pitch straight down into the King's Chamber.

The pressure he maintained with his upper body and legs strained even his steel-cable sinews and muscles, and his knees shook uncontrollably, knocking together from time to time.

Looking down between his legs, he saw a very dim yellow pinpoint of light, like a single star shining in the black gulf of space. He was seeing into the King's Chamber—Nefron had told him it was illuminated by several braziers.

Then, with a frightening suddenness, the narrow shaft he had been creeping down suddenly opened up. He nearly fell, but his rear end struck a shelf of stone projecting from the shaft wall. Though he couldn't see it, he knew a long finger of rock jutted out from the opposite side. As he eased his weight down on the shelf, he was very careful to place his feet properly, so as not to kick and dislodge the keystone lever.

For some time he sat on the stone slab, gasping for air, his back wet with sweat and a little blood from abrasions picked up during his ascent. Every muscle in his body seemed to be alive with pain, and he vigorously rubbed his calves so they wouldn't cramp.

He took a long drink from his water skin, and when he tilted his head back, he saw a dim circle of light far, far above. The sun was making its ascent into the sky. By the time it began its descent, the shaft would be flooded with sunlight and would throw the keystone lever into sharp relief.

Jak touched his blaster in its holster. The heavy butt would make a serviceable substitute for a hammer.

MILDRED WAITED for the next lash of the whip, tensed herself to hear it sing and crack through the air before it flayed the flesh from her body. She heard nothing but the heavy breathing of Mimses and the rustle of cloth.

Then she felt Mimses pressing his naked body against hers, his flabby belly on her hips, his reeking breath washing over her face. He caressed her breasts with one hand.

"Tell me, brown sugar," he husked out. "Tell me quick or I'll kiss your pretty flanks with this." He flicked out the whip so she could see it.

Mildred refused to answer.

Mimses chuckled and pushed himself away from her. She hazarded a quick backward glance, expecting to see him in a state of sexual arousal. Beneath his sagging stomach, his shriveled penis hung flaccid and limp. She groaned inwardly, and her stomach did a leap-frog of nausea.

She knew it made no difference whether she told him what he wanted to know. Mimses was impotent, and his exercise in sadism was either an alternative to the sex act itself or a preliminary to it, assuming he could get himself excited enough to perform.

The knotted thongs whistled through the air and curled around her loins. Mildred endured the humiliation and the pain without making an outcry. She strained against the cuffs imprisoning her wrists.

With each crackling snap, the lash left streaks of fire across Mildred's flesh. She kept her teeth sunk into her lower lip and continued to pull and twist at the cuffs as though she were writhing in hellish agony. Her skin dampened with perspiration. As the whip continued to flick out and stroke her, she realized she was able to slide her right wrist around within its restraint.

She allowed a low whimper to escape her lips. "Stop! Mercy. I'll tell you!"

Mimses panted, took a lungful of air and said hoarsely, "So soon? I could keep this up all night."

Mildred sagged in the cuffs, trembling violently. "I'll tell you, I'll tell you," she repeated brokenly.

Mimses came to her side, his body foul with the stink of exertion. He leaned in close, and Mildred felt a slight pressure against her thigh. Through slitted eyes, she saw his half-erect penis brushing her skin.

"And speaking of keeping it up," he said with a grin, "I'm not so sure I want to stop our game just now."

Mildred threw her body backward, bracing her feet against the wall, wrenching and yanking with all her strength. Her shoulder socket twinged, the skin on her wrist tore and her right elbow drove into Mimses's throat with a sound like an ax chopping into wood.

The man stumbled backward, one arm windmilling as he tried to keep his footing, clutching desperately at his throat with his other hand. The whip clacked to the floor.

Mildred didn't wait to see if he fell or not. Her fingers clawed frantically at the buckles and straps of the cuff encircling her left wrist. Behind her, she heard liquid, slurping gasps.

Her wrist free, Mildred whirled. Crimsons strings dripping from his open mouth, Mimses groped clumsily for the handle of the whip. She sprang forward, kicking out with her right leg. The sole of her foot slammed against the side of the man's head, knocking him sideways. He fetched up in a half-prone position against the bench in the corner.

Mildred snatched up the whip and looped the thongs around Mimses's neck, planting a knee between his shoulder blades. She heaved back with all her weight and the strength in her arms.

Hot tears spilled down her cheeks, and she heard herself chanting, "Die, you goddamn pervert, die, you diseased son of a bitch, die—"

Nearly a minute passed before she realized Mimses had accommodated her. He hung limply in the garroting embrace of the leather thongs, tongue protruding, glassy eyes bulging, limbs slack and motionless. Only his left foot moved, in a postmortem twitch. His bladder and bowels had let go, filling with the room with a stench.

Mildred let go of the whip, and Mimses dropped forward on his face with a mushy thud. Shuddering and shaking, she swallowed down the acidic bile that rose in a burning column up her throat. Her tear-blinded eyes glared with unregenerate, unforgiving hatred at the corpse lying at her feet.

In Deathlands, torture and torment were daily happenings, but she had never grown accustomed to it or accepted it. She never would.

Mildred eyed her torn clothing with loathing, then picked up the robe Mimses had discarded, slipping it over her head, ignoring the flare of pain ignited by the contact of the fabric with the raw abrasions on her back. The ankh rested in an inner breast pocket.

She forced herself to uncoil the whip from around Mimses's throat, stowing it in a voluminous bell sleeve. It wasn't much of a weapon, but under the circumstances, she had no intention of being choosy.

BY NOON, all of Aten roared with lusty life. Trumpets blared, the throng cheered, shouted and danced and children scattered flower petals in the plaza. The flowing wine was benign, the food sumptuous and savory.

Even in her chambers, Krysty heard the joyous clamor. She listened to it with a face as immobile as if it had been carved of stone. Dressed in a flowing white gown with gold-threaded darts, cut low in the front and high in the leg, she stood and listened and waited. A heavy collar of beaten gold, worked with ivory inlays, encircled the base of her neck, most of the weight distributed on her upper shoulders. She hadn't moved since she put it on. She kept her eyes on the double doors.

And waited.

Finally, the right-hand door opened. Nefron stepped in, saw Krysty and froze for an instant in midstride. Her smile faltered, then came back, toothy and dazzling.

Hurrying forward, she said, "You look beautiful, Krysty. A true queen. A goddess. But you should have waited for me to help you dress."

Krysty nodded.

Nefron walked around her, examining her ensemble with an approving eye. "Yes, like a goddess. The people will love you like Pharaoh and I love you. You are not nervous, are you?"

"Should I be?"

Nefron smiled wanly. "A little apprehension is understandable. By sunset, all the anxiety will be over."

"Yes," Krysty said softly. "All over."

She drew back with her right arm and punched Nefron on the point of her chin. The girl spun almost completely around, stumbled, tried to catch herself on the table and dragged it down with her to the floor.

Krysty walked gracefully to her, hand stabbing down and grasping her by the hair. She jerked Nefron erect. The girl opened her mouth to scream in pain, but Krysty drove it back into her throat with a fist to the jaw, splitting her lip.

Fear showed in Nefron's eyes for a split second, then it was washed away by anger and hatred. She began to struggle, to pry at the fingers entangled in her glossy black locks.

Krysty's backhand took Nefron high on a contoured cheekbone, just under her mascaraed right eye. She released her grip on her hair at the same time, and the girl staggered backward, tripped over the fallen table and went down with her long legs sprawled awkwardly.

Krysty watched her dazedly grope around on the floor, blood streaking her chin in a thin red line. Her eyes were unfocused, but when they fixed on Krysty, the hot sheen of fury and arrogance blazed in them.

"The only reason I don't break your neck," Krysty said unemotionally, "is that you can be of use to me."

Nefron hiked herself up to a sitting position and spit blood on the polished floor.

"But if you refuse to be of use to me," the Titian-haired woman continued, "then I'll chill you here and now. On the spot. Gladly."

Nefron bared red-filmed teeth in a ferocious grin. "Mildred got an ankh to you after all."

Krysty tapped the collar at her throat with a finger. "And here it will stay. I know what you and your father have been doing to me for the last few days. I don't think I need to let you know how little I care for it."

"May I get up?"

"No."

"Are you not interested in why we did this to you?"

Krysty's eyes glowed brilliantly with an almost insane fury. But when she spoke, her voice was pitched low and steady. "I know why. Hatred. I picked up that much and sensed the rot in your souls. You use love as a control mechanism, to further the hatred that motivates you."

"Pharaoh truly loves you, Krysty," Nefron said quietly.

A flicker of uncertainty dimmed the blaze of rage in her eyes for a microsecond, but it passed. "He loved the idea of me, the concept of me. His lover, his mother, his whimpering, willing sex slave all in one package. Both you and Akhnaton have set yourselves above humanity and you toy with our most primal impulses to keep us under your control. You stimulate certain parts of the brain in certain ways and flood the nervous system with endorphins. The critical, reasoning parts of the brain move slowly. Erotic thoughts and a fixation on physical pleasures dominate.''

Nefron said nothing, voiced no denials or questions.

''Your father learned how to do this during his upbringing,'' Krysty continued. ''It was easier than outright mind-control because he can arrange for the endorphins to be subject to a feedback loop. If anybody gets out of line and starts entertaining independent thought, he forces the release of more endorphins.''

Krysty's lips curved in a sneering half smile. ''He was bred to be a superhuman, to summon the future, and he wasted all his powers on seeking the worship of puppets. He can't love his puppets—he can only love pulling their strings.''

Nefron chuckled humorlessly. Krysty noted that blood had ceased flowing from her lip and the laceration had closed up. ''I won't presume to debate you, since your guesses are more on target than off. However, if you value the lives of your friends, you'll at least pretend the strings are still attached to you and go through with the marriage ceremony.''

Krysty regarded her silently for a moment. ''Tell me why I should.''

''Will you let me get up?''

Krysty inclined her head in a short nod. ''You make a move I don't care for or even say something that rubs me the wrong way, and you'll die.''

Carefully, with deliberate, slow caution, Nefron

climbed to her feet, smoothing her tunic. Clearly, coldly, she declared, "Mildred is imprisoned. Only I know where she is, only I can save her life. And to employ your quaint puppet analogy, Jak dances to every one of my string tugs. As for the others, I can arrange to have their lives snuffed out in the blink of an eye. Even if you kill me, they will still die. All of them."

"And if I play along with this sick marriage farce, then what?"

"The only death will be Pharaoh's. I don't care about you or your people. After that's done, you can all go on your way."

"Why should I believe anything you say?"

"You shouldn't, but your options are severely limited. I admit to using you so my father would be occupied with gaining control over you and not sense what I have planned. But I never meant you harm. There was nothing personal in what I did."

Krysty lurched forward, fists clenched. Nefron stood her ground, head canted at a fearless, arrogant angle. "Kill me and you kill your friends. At this point, Pharaoh would not accept your refusal to wed him. He would force you, in shackles, to do so. Do it my way and you will be a widow within minutes of exchanging vows. You and your friends will be alive and free."

Some of the reckless anger went out of Krysty's posture. She shivered with the effort resisting the urge to call on the power of Gaia and rip Nefron's beautiful head from her shoulders. From between clenched teeth, she bit out three words. "I'll do it."

Chapter Twenty-Seven

Mildred ran like a panicked deer, heedless of obstacles as she shouldered her way through the bustle of people in the compound. She had only one objective in mind—to reach the laborers' dormitory as quickly as possible before the body of Mimses was discovered.

She knew she looked ridiculous in his billowing, luridly colored robe, but bright hues were everywhere, from fluttering banners, bunting to body paint.

She squeezed her way through the revelers, and her toes caught on the dragging hem of the robe. She stumbled, nearly falling headlong to the ground. When a leanly muscled arm encircled her waist and kept her upright, she tried to struggle free, then saw the arm was attached to Doc Tanner.

With a half sigh, half sob of relief, she caught the startled man in an embrace. Hands on her shoulders, Doc gently pushed her back. When he saw the terror in her eyes, he didn't employ his usual bantering tone or address her formally.

"Mildred, what are you doing here? Are you all right?"

She shook her head, beads clattering and rattling. Grabbing him by the forearm, she dragged him bodily through the press of the crowd. "Show me where John and Ryan are. Things have gone sour."

Doc tried to keep pace with her. "It is too dangerous for all of us to be together in one place. It might jeopardize the escape plan."

"There is no escape plan," she blurted.

Doc's eyebrows lifted, but he didn't interrogate her. He took the lead and guided her into the dormitory. Though usually off-limits to women, there were plenty of females in attendance now, in various states of undress and sexual positions. He stepped over a man wildly humping between the outflung legs of a woman and checked the shower room. It was crowded with naked, coupling men and women.

Peering into the workroom, he saw it was virtually deserted except for Ryan and J.B. standing near a locker on the far wall. They were attired in clean tunics, and when they caught sight of him, their faces registered surprise and they gestured. Doc ducked back into the foyer, beckoned to Mildred and the two of them rushed in. She allowed J.B. to kiss her, then began talking rapidly and without pause.

Snarling, Ryan slammed a fist against the locker door. A muffled murmur from behind it made Doc and Mildred narrow their eyes. "That lying slut. I figured she was conning us."

"What are we going to do now?" J.B. demanded. "We still don't know where Jak is—or Krysty."

"I found Krysty and slipped her an ankh," Mildred said. "We can only hope it works and she'll make some moves of her own. What about you two?"

J.B. and Ryan indicated their upper chests. "We're wearing them," Ryan replied. "If Krysty doesn't move, then our only chance of snatching her is at the pyramid this evening.''

"We've got to hole up somewhere until then," J.B. said. "And do something about—" he jerked his head toward the locker "— him."

"Who is 'him'?" Mildred asked.

"One of Pharaoh's drones," Ryan explained. "He came on us while we were making the amulets. He's been in the locker since last night."

"I suggest you leave him where he is," Doc said. "Once the body of Mimses is found, another squealer won't make much difference to our overall situation."

Ryan nodded grimly. "Let's split up, lose ourselves in the crowd. If anyone comes looking for us, they'll have a hell of a time finding us."

Doc frowned slightly. "Where and when should we meet you?"

"This evening, at the southwest corner of the pyramid. If anything goes wrong and I'm not there, you'll have to find your way back to Fort Fubar…and to Dean."

Mildred gazed at him worriedly. "What's your plan?"

Ryan shook his head, face contorted as if he tasted something sour. "I'm hoping one will occur to me…eventually."

THE SUN WAS HOT on his face despite the shade provided by the brittle bush he lay beneath. Sand fleas hopped along his exposed hands and face, biting him. Dean didn't slap them away. He was watching the towering walls of the city of Aten, less than half a mile away. It lay bathed in golden glory of the midafteroon sun.

Beyond, seeming to block half the sky and the horizon, a massive monument reared from the sands. On the very top of it, supported by a wooden framework, a smaller version of the pyramid glistened and sparkled in the brilliant light, as if it were coated with diamonds.

Dean had never seen anything like it as he peered through the telescopic sight of the Steyr. The gates of the city hung open, and people milled to and fro, seeming to leap, caper and dance. Faintly, he heard the shrill piping of flutes, the blare of horns and ceaseless, distant roar of many raised voices.

He had departed Fort Fubar at noon, like he had vowed. The chariot clicked and carried him away from the forlorn collection of buildings and the forlorn figure of Danielson, standing in the street and watching him go.

He felt bad about leaving the old man, but not bad enough to go back on the promise he had made to himself—to find either his father or his fate.

He had draped himself in a bed-sheet burnoose and carried plenty of water, then followed the tracks cut by the chariot that had conveyed Ryan and his friends away four dawns earlier.

The wag maintained a steady twenty-five miles per hour, even over some treacherous sand drifts. It wasn't quite two o'clock when the desert turned into a road and he sighted the lofty ramparts of Aten. Parking the chariot in inadequate cover in a patch of weeds, he had walked the rest of the way, the rifle beneath the burnoose.

Dean had been checking out the zone for the past

ten minutes. He had no idea what was going on in the city, but the activity seemed celebratory, like a big wild party.

He figured to devote another few minutes to screwing up his nerve, then he would stroll right in and crash it.

AKHNATON STOOD on a balcony, staring down into the feasting hall. Hanging draperies obscured him from any eye looking up from below, but he could see clearly through the gauzy material.

His court staff lay sprawled on nests of cushions and pillows, forming a semicircle around platters of delicately spiced mutton, chilled goblets of wine, mounds of fruit and pastries.

Sinuous serving girls slid among the men, allowing themselves to be caressed, fondled and groped. Their tawny, oiled bodies were naked except for a few jeweled bangles.

His eyes scanned the slack, drunken faces. He didn't expend any energy on probing their minds. Their feelings were displayed for even the most unperceptive of creatures to recognize.

He had awakened at dawn and dressed himself in ceremonial robes dyed with thirty contrasting colors. The heavy golden collar of state rested on his broad shoulders. He wouldn't don the king-cobra headdress until it was time for the processional march to the pyramid.

The bioaural field in the balcony shifted ever so slightly. Without turning, he asked, "Is my bride prepared?"

"Yes, Pharaoh," Nefron answered meekly. "You have chosen well. She is every inch a goddess."

"Come here," Akhnaton said.

Nefron soft-footed to his side. He nodded to the feasting hall. "Look there. Whom do you see?"

"Your counselors and retainers, my lord," she responded crisply.

"Whom do you *not* see?"

Nefron hesitated a long moment before answering. "I do not understand."

"I think you do. You do not see Mimses. Do you know where he is?"

"No, my lord Pharaoh, I do not."

Like a pair of striking asps, Akhnaton's hands darted out, clasped the sides of Nefron's head and turned it up and toward him. He stared unblinkingly into her eyes. She didn't struggle or glance away. She returned his stare, and a reflection of his crimson orbs glinted in her dark eyes.

He released her as swiftly as he had grabbed her. "I had hoped to take you by surprise, before you had the chance to erect your defenses. I should have known that you never let your defenses down."

Nefron didn't respond.

"One of Mimses's Incarnates came to me not an hour ago," Akhnaton said conversationally. "He reported he had found the sack of suet dead by strangulation. He mentioned the female newcomer. Your name figured prominently, as well."

Nefron still refused to speak.

Akhnaton sighed. "I will not miss Mimses. Nor will I divert my attention to finding either the woman...or your other conspirators in whatever intrigue you have schemed. I will say only this and I urge you to believe it—if anything happens to disrupt today's ceremony, before, after or during, I will hold you responsible, even if you are not. You will die a particularly undignified death.''

Nefron finally spoke, a contemptuous edge to her voice. ''Like mother like daughter.''

Akhnaton's face twisted into an ugly scowl of sudden rage, then quickly composed itself into a mocking smile. Softly, intimately, he said, ''You know me so well, daughter. Now, get out of my sight.''

THEY WERE SOME of the grimmest, most bleak and hopeless hours Ryan Cawdor had ever known.

He mingled with the crowd flowing and eddying in the compound. His jaw muscles ached with the strain of keeping a half-witted, vacant grin frozen on his face. He allowed wine to be poured on him, garlands of flowers hung around his neck and drunken women to plant slobbery kisses on his lips. He kept moving, constantly shifting, sometimes joining in with a snatch of ludicrous song, moving his lips to the lyrics he didn't know.

Always he kept watch for an animal-headed Incarnate. He assumed the worst, that Mimses's body had been discovered or that Fasa had been released from his cramped confinement. Regardless of the riotously festive mood in the city, the newcomers would be sought out.

As the afternoon staggered toward sunset, Ryan found it more and more difficult to keep the fire of hope and courage burning inside of him. He had believed he had lost Krysty before, but to death, the inevitable dark embrace no one could truly escape. The possibility that she was enraptured, seduced by the charismatic Hell Eyes, was almost too agonizing for him to consider.

Ryan had called him a mutie with an attitude, but that was so far from the truth it wasn't even a lie. He realized he couldn't truly comprehend exactly what he was. He wondered if the last Neanderthal had felt the same way when he snarled at the smooth, intelligent countenance of the first Cro-Magnon, understanding on a deep, visceral level he had met not only his superior but the symbol of his extinction.

Ryan tried to dispel the notion. A superhuman Hell Eyes might conceivably be, but he was still driven by ordinary human emotions, still weakened by human frailties.

He joined a clot of people near the open gate and relaxed into them, allowing himself to carried by the current out of the compound. Already a considerable number of Aten's citizenry clustered around the base of the pyramid. He looked up toward its apex and saw the capstone resting on a platform made of wooden timbers. The sun shone from its crystal-shot surface in a thousand dancing, sparkling pinpoints.

From what he had overhead in the crowd of celebrants, the pyramidion had been rolled into place right at sunset, by a select crew of laborers—evidently purified, as Fasa had said. When the time came, men with huge mallets would knock the supporting timbers out from under it, and the capstone would settle atop the monument and imbue Pharaoh and his bride with the power of the gods.

The crowd was large and noisy around the monument, and a band of musicians strolled among them, the stuttering whine of flutes and the bleat of horns lifted above the beat of drums.

Ryan stayed deep within the jostling, singing and laughing throng, refusing to acknowledge his growing claustrophobia. He had spent too many years in the wild, unpopulated places of Deathlands to be comfortable in crowds. He kept consulting the position of the sun, willing it savagely to sink. Like he expected, it ignored him.

He continued to shuffle around, past and with the people. He ceased to think about much of anything except to keep his feet from being trod upon.

Suddenly, the music stopped and the tempo of the crowd's voice quieted. Ryan dully looked up and saw a pastel mixture of oranges, yellows and muted reds spreading across the sky. Silence seemed to descend on the crowd as if a giant bell jar had dropped over it. The wind hissed eerily through the sand.

A new sound began, a steady squeak underscored by a dry, castanetlike clicking. Ryan concentrated on the rhythmic noise, tracked it to a spot high above, somewhere on the pyramid itself.

On the railed track overhead, a shape rolled into view, a silk-veiled and flower-drenched palaquin. It was slowly pulled up to the pyramid by men working at the winch and pulley from a concealed recess on the side of it.

Ryan pushed his way through the motionless, silent, upstaring people to get a better view. An opening gaped in the casing stones beside the long stairway, at a little above the midpoint of the monument. From the opening, taut ropes stretched up to eyebolts on the underside of the wheeled palaquin.

Ryan's gaze followed the lines and he squinted at the colorful cart.

Though the interior was obscured by fluttering pennants, he was able to see two figures standing there. Bright scarlet tresses floated in the wind like flames.

Ryan elbowed and pushed people out of his path as he headed for the stair.

Chapter Twenty-Eight

A silent scream of frustrated fury welled in Krysty's throat. She choked it back, beat it down, not allowing the ferocity of her emotions to be mirrored in her dreamy, slightly aloof eyes.

Standing beside Akhnaton in the flower-and-silk-bedecked palaquin, she kept her eyes fixed on the glittering capstone of the pyramid, not on the people milling around below. She was aware of the man's crimson gaze upon her, but she refused to meet it.

Akhnaton heaved a gusty, weary sigh. "My beloved, you are shielded from me."

Krysty groped for a reply, then decided she had no more tolerance for dissembling. "How do you know?"

"I reached out for your feelings. I touched only a cold void. Like a squall of static."

Slowly, Krysty swiveled her head. Akhnaton's expression was unreadable. "Now what? Will you cancel the ceremony?"

A hard smile touched his lips. "And disappoint my subjects? They are anxious to be ruled by a god and goddess and will be inconsolable if they are not. Therefore, their wishes shall be granted."

"Against my will?"

Akhnaton shrugged. "Will is malleable, putty and

clay to be shaped and molded by the master craftsman.''

"You won't be molding me again," Krysty replied grimly.

Akhnaton's smile broadened. "I should remind you that by wearing an ankh on your person, you will not benefit from the energies pouring into the King's Chamber. You will remain a mortal, wed to a god."

"Like Connie Harrier?"

"Exactly. And you may share her fate."

The palaquin lurched slightly on the tracks. Akhnaton reached out to steady her, but she slapped his hand away. "Or mebbe I'll share the fate of your first predestined mate, Epsilon," she said coldly. "You arranged for the accident that killed her. Even at such an early age, you couldn't stand the thought of dividing the world with an equal. Even as an infant, you were a jealous god."

"I want you to be a goddess, ruling at my side." Akhnaton's voice was pitched low.

"You want me to be a thing at your side, a goddess under your mastery. You instinctively knew you couldn't control Epsilon because she was bred to be your equal. Who knows, she might have matured to be your superior. That notion terrified you, didn't it?"

"The world must be brought under control," he said calmly. "And that cannot happen unless the people on it are brought to heel. Ancient Egypt was one of the most orderly civilizations in the history of humankind. People respond best when they work to earn the approbation of a superior, a pharaoh, a god. I'm only applying that old system to the present day. You and I will build a utopia."

Krysty snorted. "You'll build another tyrannical fiefdom, no different than all the other petty little kingdoms ruled by petty little dictators. I won't help you build another."

Akhnaton sighed again. He lifted a hand as if to stroke her face. His fingers closed around her throat, pressing the golden collar cruelly into the soft flesh of her throat. Krysty didn't struggle. She stared fearlessly into his hell-hued eyes.

"It's too late for you to think you have a choice," he rasped. "Too late to rebel, too late to find a spine. You'll cooperate with the ceremony. You'll join me in the sarcophagus as I undergo the transformation, the ascension. You will submit to me as I fill you with my sperm. You will carry the seeds of my dynasty."

Akhnaton released her as swiftly as he had grabbed her. She swayed, catching herself on the edge of the cart. He stared at the pyramidion and said tonelessly, "I hoped to love you, Krysty. I wanted to love you. If I cannot have that, then I'll accept your obedience as a substitute."

Krysty said nothing. She followed his gaze to the sparkling capstone, but focused her vision through it, beyond it. It was difficult to call on the power of the Earth Mother without a short period of meditation. She wasn't sure if she could do it, but it was the only alternative left to her.

RYAN BOUNDED UP THE SIDE of the pyramid like a cat. The crowd below him paid no attention. They stood silent and spellbound, struck dumb by the spectacle of the palaquin reaching the apex of Pharaoh's monument.

Ryan sluiced sweat away from his forehead before it flowed into his eye and blinded him. Air whistled in his throat, and his lungs labored. Leg muscles strained and twinged with the effort of propelling him at a reckless speed up the steep stairs.

He had no plan except to do what he could do to disrupt the ceremony of Hell Eyes. He refused to speculate on Krysty's possible willing participation in it.

By the time he reached the opening in the face of the pyramid, Ryan's legs were weak and rubbery and his heart pounded heavily. The steady creaking from the winch and pulley had ceased. In spite of the silence, the atmosphere around the pyramid was electric with expectancy. In the dimming light of the setting sun, Aten seemed to wait breathlessly.

Ryan didn't wait, despite wanting to sit down to find his second wind. He stepped over to the recessed opening, feet on the stone lip, and pulled himself inside, holding on to a taut rope for support. The drum of the winch occupied most of the space, and he squirmed around it. A sharp edge caught a fold of his tunic and it ripped.

"Hey, you!" a surprised voice called from the dimness. "What are you doing here?"

"I'm lost," Ryan called back.

"What?"

Two figures emerged from the shadows, dressed in the animal helmets of the Incarnates and carrying the metauh staves. One wore the likeness of Thoth, the other of Set. Due to their size and strength, they had been given the honor of winching Pharaoh and his bride to the place of marriage.

Ryan's hands explored swiftly the area around the drum and winch, searching for anything he could use, or even improvise, as a weapon. All he found was a crank handle propped against the wall. It was of heavy cold-rolled iron, with one end bearing thick flanges.

Snatching it up, he hefted it experimentally and sprang out of the alcove in blind desperation. All of his strength and weight went into the arm that swung the handle. It crashed against the side of Thoth's jaw, and the big man rolled lifeless to the floor, face shattered, cervical vertebrae fractured.

Set cursed, and the prongs of the metauh rod stabbed toward Ryan, light dancing in a strobing flicker from them. Ryan felt like a bucket of water drawn from a polar sea had been dashed into his face. A shocking cold penetrated to his bones. He kept lunging, and a sweeping backhand swept the metal rod from Set's fist and caught him squarely across the belly.

The Incarnate bent double and staggered, fetching up against the wall. He bounced away from it and directly into an overhead blow with the handle that cleft his helmet and the cranium beneath. He fell face first to the floor, staining the stone with blood and brain matter.

Tremors shook Ryan's body, but they passed quickly. Fingering the ankh beneath his tunic, he felt it tingle to his touch. He whirled toward a square doorway at the end of the short hallway. Yellow light streamed from it. Pausing at its edge, he looked out. Wonder rose in him.

The chamber was shaped like a pyramid and much larger than looked possible from the outside. A dim glow shone down from the pointed roof, two faint columns of light beaming from twin openings. The light gleamed from an elaborately carved sarcophagus resting in the exact center of the floor.

Between the slanting shafts of light stood three people—a shaved-headed man dressed in an elaborately embroidered robe reading aloud from a scroll, Akhnaton and Krysty.

The bald man Ryan took to be a priest or mummer of some kind, since he mumbled and bobbed his head over the square of papyrus. He looked at Krysty's pale face and felt prickles of pain all through his heart and mind. Dressed and made up as she was, she looked heartachingly beautiful, but her green eyes were dull and vacant, and her lips moved silently, as if she were mouthing the words read aloud by the priest. Like, he thought despairingly, a puppet.

Akhnaton towered over her, as grim and as impassive as a statue wrought of brass. He slipped an arm around her waist and rested a hand possessively on her hip.

Fury erupted within Ryan. He became the fury, filled with the mad need to claw, to bite, to kill. His surroundings receded and faded, and he saw only Krysty with Akhnaton's hand on her body.

Ryan bounded forward across the chamber, vaulting the sarcophagus, swinging the winch handle over his head like a battle-ax. The iron bar crunched against the back of the priest's bald head. His mumblings terminated in a gurgling cry before he rolled to the floor.

For a split second, the scene held frozen and motionless. During this interval, Ryan realized that the rage in his eyes had a sudden, answering reflection in those of Krysty's. Roaring, he leaped at Akhnaton.

Akhnaton thrust Krysty aside and lunged to meet Ryan's charge. His hand locked around Ryan's right wrist, and as his free hand went for his throat, Ryan clasped it. They strained against each other for a long moment.

Akhnaton's breath was hot on his face. The muscles of both men bulged. From far away, on the very fringes of his awareness, Ryan heard a thready, breathy whisper. "Mother of the Earth, give your daughter the power, the power, the power…"

Akhnaton's knee flashed up, splitting and ripping through the thin material of his robe. It pounded into Ryan's lower belly like a sledgehammer, and he folded over in the direction of the pain. Bile boiled up his throat.

The hand of Akhnaton wrenched brutally at his right arm, snapping his entire body up and over in a half cartwheel. Agony ripped up and down his arm, a deep, boring pain that settled and exploded in his shoulder socket. The winch handle clanged loudly on the floor.

Ryan's back slapped against the polished veneer of the sarcophagus, the bone-jarring impact slamming air out through his mouth and nostrils. Blinking against the swirling pain-haze, he saw Akhnaton saunter toward him, carrying himself with the self-assured manner of a tiger approaching its wounded prey.

"I allowed you to live after our encounter two

nights ago,'' he said. ''I don't extend the same mercy to the same fool twice in one lifetime.''

Then Krysty's arm encircled Akhnaton's neck from behind and jerked him off his feet.

JAK AWAKENED with a start. His impression was that he had been sleeping a long time and that he had been dreaming. In his dream, he had come to the frightening realization something was terribly wrong.

To loosen his stiff neck tendons, Jak rolled his head. Through the open mouth of the shaft, the light of the setting sun colored his restricted view of the sky. He heard a dim murmur of sound from far below, but it was too faint to identify.

He thought of his love, of Nefron, of what she wanted him to do, and flickers of raw emotion passed through his mind. As he eyed the projecting knob of the deadfall lever, revulsion filled him. Chilling an enemy in a face-to-face was one thing, but crushing him through traps and treachery was the act of a cowardly mercenary, like the coldhearts who had murdered his wife and baby.

Jak desperately sought the image of Nefron and the feelings of love she had expressed for him. He found the image, but no feelings of love—only anger overlaid with sexual energies and lust. Not lust for him, but for power.

His revulsion deepened, and he tried to talk his gut out of it. He couldn't. His heart lurched and his breathing was suddenly heavy. Jak knew on a profound, intuitive level that he had been tricked, hoaxed, conned and used.

He didn't know why he felt this way so intensely,

but he wasn't going to analyze the reasons. The taste of his own shame was so bitter he almost vomited.

Bitter.

He replayed in his memory the many, almost countless cups of astringent liquid both Kela and Nefron had cajoled him to drink.

Jak climbed unsteadily to his feet, teetering for the moment on the edge of the rock shelf. Whether Pharaoh was indeed the monster Nefron had described, he knew that his actions could be no more loathsome than her own.

He sprang up, bracing himself with sweaty palms against the shaft walls, feet scrabbling to secure a hold. Inches at a time, he began worming his body up the vertical passage, pushing with his hands and heels. Climbing up would be far more laborious than climbing down.

A ghostly wail full of soul-deep pain wafted up from below. He froze for a second, nape hairs tingling in fright. His boot soles suddenly slipped, and he plummeted downward, shoulders and back scalding with friction-induced heat. His right leg flailed wildly, kicking out for some kind of purchase or support.

His foot found it, and when Jak pushed himself up, a gunshot-loud *crack* echoed within the shaft. He froze for only a microsecond, listening. Immediately following the fading echoes of the sound, he heard a rumble.

"Shit," he said aloud.

Frantically, he began to climb again, clawing and dragging his way up the shaft.

Chapter Twenty-Nine

Akhnaton was at least a hundred pounds heavier than Krysty, yet she sent him reeling half the length of the King's Chamber with one arm. The bronzed giant staggered and stumbled, losing his headdress but managing to regain his balance.

He gaped at Krysty, his face sagging in an expression of astonishment that was almost comical. Then, snarling, his upper lip curled back over his teeth. He straightened to his full six-foot-plus height, raising his fists over his head in rage.

"You bitch! You mutie whore! You dare to profane me with your soiled touch?"

Akhnaton was on her in a roaring rush, swinging keglike fists in a flurry of punches. Krysty managed to duck and backpedal out of the reach of his arms.

Ryan resisted the urge to interfere. He recognized that strange, dreamy half smirk on Krysty's lips. She was in the grip of Gaia now and far more dangerous than Akhnaton had ever dreamed she could be.

Akhnaton came at her again, sweeping both arms at her head. Krysty ducked the first punch and stepped inside the second. She put her right fist into his belly and swung her left in an uppercut that rocked him back on his heels.

Though Akhnaton had no knowledge of the finer points of hand-to-hand combat, Ryan knew he would depend on his strength to absorb punishment to carry him through a fight. Krysty's problem lay in avoiding his punches and landing enough of her own to wear him down. He prayed she had the stamina before the power of the Earth Mother left her.

Akhnaton launched himself at her, one of his fists grazing her shoulder. She shot her right into his face in a short jab. Akhnaton's head snapped back, and blood sprang from his lips. Snarling, he came boring in, head tucked against his shoulder, swinging wildly.

Krysty weaved gracefully, spun and back-stepped, letting his blows go above her head or pass over her shoulders. Even in her altered state of consciousness, she remembered Ryan's training. She suddenly dropped, one leg stretching out and sweeping Akhnaton's legs out from under him. He went over sideways, bellowing a curse.

She kicked at his head, but he closed a hand around her ankle and another around her waist, fingers sinking deep. She made no outcry, not even when he rose and lifted her bodily over his head. Cloth ripped, and Krysty was hurled to the floor. Half of her gown came away in Akhnaton's fist, leaving most of her legs bare.

Krysty struggled up to a sitting position, snapping at air. Akhnaton clutched her by the hair and violently hauled her to her feet. She didn't resist his pull, but went with it, kicking herself off the ground and driving the crown of her head into his face. Cartilage crunched loudly. She raked her nails over his chest, ripping rents in his robe and the flesh beneath. They caromed away from each other, and Akhnaton fell, blood spurting from his nostrils.

The red-haired woman was over him before he gained even a crouching position. She caught him in the head with a side-kick and threw a down-plunging straight-arm punch that opened a cut over his right eye and slammed him back to the floor. Akhnaton snatched at her legs and tried to drag her down. She hammered overhead blows on the back of his head, neck and shoulders. He pulled up suddenly on her leg, dumping her onto her back.

Akhnaton swarmed all over her, snarling and striking and trying to achieve a stranglehold. They wrestled and grappled, and cloth tore. Ryan started to rush in, but Krysty forced the man's head back with the heel of one hand against his chin and chopped him across the windpipe with the edge of the other. Akhnaton gagged for air long enough for Krysty to heave him to one side. She scrambled to her feet.

She was gasping, face wet with sweat, and Ryan noticed a definite wobble in her knees. Most of the time when she called on the power of Gaia to increase her strength, it was for a limited duration. He couldn't recall an incident where she had faced an adversary whose natural strength matched or even exceeded that given to her by the Earth Mother.

Akhnaton lumbered to his feet. His robe was ripped in many places. One eye was but a slit in his face. His lips were blood-oozing pulp. His nose was streaming scarlet, but he smiled with red-stained teeth. With a shock, Ryan realized he had an erection and it strained against the rags of his clothes.

He beckoned to Krysty with a hand. "Beloved," he crooned, "you are truly a revelation. What mighty offspring we will create. Come to me."

Krysty went to him in an eye-blurring lunge, pumping first her left, then her right fist into his face. She kicked him in the stomach.

Akhnaton took her blows without a sound, stepping close to her. He hooked his right into her body. His fist, starting from his hip, smashed directly into her midriff. The force of the punch lifted Krysty from her feet, and for a second she hung suspended, folded over Akhnaton's fist and forearm.

As she slid limply to the floor, Ryan dived toward the hell-eyed man, fingers spread to rip the crimson orbs from his head. Akhnaton leaned away from him and linked his hands, as if he were swinging a club. He swung both fists into the center of Ryan's chest, directly over the heart.

Bubbles of pain burst with explosions of agonizing color. The impact slammed him backward and dropped him to within a foot of the sarcophagus. The back of his head struck the stone sharply. Only the fierce pain in his dislocated shoulder and chest kept him from losing consciousness. It was an effort to breathe, to think, to blink. Even the blood seemed to cease flowing through his body.

He watched as Akhnaton lurched toward Krysty, who huddled in a gasping ball on the floor. Gripping her by the hair, he pulled her to her knees and slowly forced her head back. Her eyes were glassy, fogged with exhaustion and pain. With his free hand, he stripped away what was left of his robe, and his erection sprang out, thick and throbbing. His burning eyes seethed with a volcanic fury and he grinned in unholy glee.

"You'll still have me," he said harshly. "You'll still give birth to my dynasty. Now more than ever,

I want you. If I can't have you as my bride, I'll take you as my slave.''

Then Krysty's hand flashed up, slashing swiftly and savagely like a scythe or the claws of an enraged lioness. Blood spewed in liquid tendrils from the shredded flesh between Akhnaton's legs. He stood frozen to the spot by shock, by the sudden, overwhelming pain.

Only when Krysty tossed aside his bloody testicles did he scream, a full-throated shriek of outraged agony that seemed to collect at the point of the ceiling and stay there, the echoes chasing each other back and forth.

Akhnaton flung his head back and howled. Grasping at his crotch, scarlet squirting from between his fingers, he sank to his knees, roaring and screaming at the top of his lungs.

Krysty scrambled out of his reach and rolled to her feet. She tangled the fingers of her right hand in the hair and scalp at the back of his head. She yanked his head back, his face turned to the ceiling. Locking her wrist, extending and stiffening the first two fingers of her right hand, Krysty drove them through Akhnaton's eyeballs, up to the knuckles.

His eyes burst, and her fingers punched through the delicate bone of his sinus cavities, cramming splinters into his brain. Akhnaton ceased his howling. Krysty jerked her hand back, blood and gelatinous matter trailing from her fingertips. He toppled over backward, legs still tucked beneath him. Blood continued to jet from the ruined swatch of flesh at his groin.

Krysty swayed over him, drawing a trembling hand across her face, wiping the man's blood from it. Her breathing sounded like steam escaping from a faulty valve. She shambled around to face Ryan, took a faltering step, then fell to one knee.

Still dazed and fighting to control the pain that threatened to consume him, Ryan got to his feet. He heard a new sound, a grating, crunching rumble that swallowed up the echoes of Akhnaton's scream. He looked up. The ceiling blocks quivered, and a fine rain of power sifted down from between the cracks. The uppermost stones seemed to bulge outward.

Ryan wrestled Krysty to her feet, shouting, "We've got to go!"

She looked at him, her eyes fathomless in her blood-streaked face. For a moment, she stared at him without recognition.

He shook her. "Krysty! Get it together!"

She moved then, sprinting with him toward the alcove. With a thunderous roar, a torrent of stone blocks poured down from above. Great slabs of rock fell and crashed. The floor quaked beneath their feet.

Ryan grasped Krysty by the wrist and pulled her past the winch and pulley and out of the opening. They reached the stairs, and Krysty took the lead, leaping down the steps four at a time. Ryan followed her closely, not daring to look behind him. One misstep would be fatal.

Fragments of flying rock pattered down all around them. Millions of tons of thundering stone collapsed behind them, and they barely kept a few yards ahead of it. The pyramid imploded, and the sound was like doomsday.

Below, the crowd lifted faces pale and wet with terror to see their pharaoh's mighty monument falling in on itself. They scattered, squealing in fright as titanic stone cubes went bounding and skipping down the shivering face of the pyramid.

Giant black cracks zigzagged through the smooth white face of the pyramid. Great clefts were riven deep as the structure split asunder.

The stairs jumped and trembled under Ryan and Krysty's feet. Almost without thinking, they dived from it. The two people hit the ground hard and kept rolling, not just to absorb the impact and minimize their chances of breaking bones but to put as much distance between them and the avalanche of stone blocks. Ryan grunted as flares of pain ignited in his shoulder, but he rolled frantically.

In the dim light, veiled by swirling clouds of dust, the pyramid seemed to come apart in some weird slow motion, like on a vid loop. Fragments of casing stone floated in the vapors, turning slowly like revolving planets. They tumbled and toppled and crashed.

Ryan and Krysty clung to each other and watched in blank shock at the scene of havoc and destruction. She said something, but her voice was lost in the fury of the stony, thunderous tempest that roared about them.

Then, mercifully, the cataclysmic sounds began to fade, replaced by the clink and crunch of settling stone. A pillar of whirling dust and rock particles rose toward the sky, like a shadowy grave marker.

Driven by the terror and awe of the moment, Ryan crushed Krysty in his arms and kissed her passionately. Voices came to them, tones of terror, confusion and anger.

"They destroyed Pharaoh's monument!"

"Where is Pharaoh? Tell us!"

Most of the crowd was creeping back, but they were no longer joyful or in a celebratory humor. A woman pointed at Krysty and screeched, "Pharaoh's bride! She betrayed Pharaoh!"

Ryan and Krysty climbed to their feet. She was very weak now that the Gaia energy had left her. Still, she was able to exchange grim smiles with Ryan. A segment of the crowd surged forward. He tensed himself to fight and die. His ankh was no protection against an enraged mob.

A man jumped at him, and Ryan recognized him as fat Shukeli. The truncheon in his fist swept down, straight at his head. Ryan recoiled.

The man's bloated body twisted convulsively aside. He fell past Ryan, onto the ground. A red-rimmed hole spurted blood from the center of his back. Only then did Ryan hear the familiar twig-snapping report of his Steyr.

The crowd suddenly parted. Dean shouldered his way through, grimacing fiercely, the Steyr in one hand, his Browning Hi-Power in the other. Ryan swiped a hand over his eye, not knowing if the image of his son was indeed real or a pain- and stress-induced hallucination. Dean stepped up beside him and told him simply, "You said we'd be together again."

Ryan's knees sagged in relief, and he took the Browning from Dean's hand. They covered the angry throng with the barrels of the blasters. "Where is everybody else?" Dean asked.

"Right here," J.B. said.

The Armorer, Mildred and Doc bracketed Ryan and Krysty. Dean glanced at Doc strangely, but said nothing.

"They only got two blasters between them!" a man's voice snarled. "We can take them in a rush!"

The sound of the Colt Python was a deep-throated boom, only slightly less loud than the collapse of the pyramid a few moments before. Jak limped up, his blaster pointed at the crowd. "That you do," he stated. "But you die first."

Jak was gray with dust. The only color about him was the trickle of blood from small lacerations on his face and the brilliant blaze of his ruby eyes. He held his revolver in a two-fisted grip.

Ryan knew that even with three blasters in the hands of experts, they couldn't hope to fight their way through the incensed citizenry of Aten. The crowd shifted forward, then suddenly receded, drawing back like a wave of flesh.

"Let me pass, damn you! Let me pass!" a woman cried imperiously.

Nefron shouldered her way out of the throng. Jak centered the sights of the Colt on her face, but she swept him with a cold glare before turning away to face the mob.

She addressed the crowd in a razor-edged, matter-of-fact voice. "People of Aten, hear me and listen well. I stand here as your queen. The only child of Pharaoh, the true and rightful heir to the throne. You know this to be true."

The people gaped at her dumbly, numbly.

Nefron's eyes suddenly blazed, and a crimson glow swallowed her dark irises. The crowd murmured in horror, clenching their hands.

"I am the law in Aten." The echoes of her words hung in the air, vibrating against the ear.

"You are the law," a few voices mumbled.

"You will obey me. I struggled against and swallowed the injustices of my father, but no longer. I am the law. I shall rule. I am your queen."

She gestured behind her. "The newcomers are under my protection. Harm them, and I will view it as an act of treason against the throne. Do you hear me? I am your queen."

Slowly, the shocked men and women lowered themselves to their knees, bowing their heads in reverence, in awe and obedience to the hell-eyed woman standing before them.

"I am your queen!"

From dozens of throats came the repetitive murmur, "You are the queen."

Nefron turned to face Ryan and his companions. Jak flinched at the sight of the bloodred eyes. She was still beautiful, but remote and somehow removed from any humanity he could understand.

"You have done me a service," she stated. "You may stay or you may go."

None of them responded to her words. Krysty stared at her, green eyes seething with hatred. "You are your father's daughter," she said quietly. "You have his power."

Nefron smiled coldly. "And more."

She turned away from them as Kela stepped from the kneeling crowd. Nefron embraced her and kissed her tenderly on the lips. Without looking their way, she demanded, "What is your wish? To stay or to go?"

"To go," Ryan said hoarsely.

With a negligent wave of her hand, Nefron announced, "So be it. Your possessions will be returned to you. I will give you the use of a chariot and ask only one favor in return.''

''Haven't we done enough?'' Mildred muttered.

Nefron ignored the comment. ''Will you grant it?''

''What?'' J.B. asked.

''Ask my father to return to Aten,'' Kela breathed. ''A place of honor awaits him.''

The two women strode into the crowd, Kela following a few steps behind the swaggering Nefron. The people rose and fell into line behind them as they shuffled back toward the walls of the city.

The seven companions watched them go. Ryan briefly considered the wisdom of shooting Nefron through the back of the head. He realized bleakly he didn't want revenge. He simply wanted to leave Aten as soon as possible and try to forget it—though he knew he never would.

Doc, watching the crowd following Nefron, quoted softly, '''*La belle Dame sans Merci* hath thee in thrall.'''

Chapter Thirty

The next afternoon, when they spied the gray half dome of the installation rearing out of the Barrens, none of them felt like cheering. Though their clothes, blasters and other belongings were now back in their possession, all but Dean still felt slightly out of sync with reality, vaguely dissociated not only from their surroundings but from themselves.

They had stopped early that morning in Fort Fubar to convey Kela's message to Danielson and gone on their way. Ryan was too numbed and exhausted to even thank the man for looking after his son.

Despite Dean's questions, none of the companions were inclined to talk about what they had gone through in Aten. Jak in particular was stiff-lipped and more taciturn than usual. Ryan was in pain. His shoulder had been reset by Mildred and J.B., and medication she had taken from the installation's laboratory had made it tolerable. Still, he looked haggard and haunted and he spoke only when spoken to—and then only the bare minimum of words.

They disembarked from the chariot, and the massive vanadium-steel sec door opened to the code Dean punched in. They trooped inside, making directly for the mat-trans chamber. None of them dared voice their secret fear, that they were the victims of a cruel practical joke on Nefron's part, the controls were still frozen, trapping them in the Barrens with no place to go but back to Aten.

Ryan brought up the rear, lingering to close the door behind them. Krysty hung back, too, waiting for him. He didn't meet her gaze.

"Let's get to the gateway. Sooner we find out which way the stick floats, the sooner we can plan for the future."

Krysty didn't move. She blocked his path and said, "That's what I want to talk about. *Our* future and how the recent past may affect it."

"What?" he asked flatly, his eye questioning her.

"I know what's troubling you, lover."

He shrugged, making a move to step around her. "You weren't responsible. Let's go."

She caught his arm, fingers biting into it. "You say that, but you don't know how sure you are of it." She laughed bitterly. "I was under Akhnaton's will, I can't deny it. But I love you, Ryan. I will *always* love you. My love warred with Akhnaton's will even as he tried to make me his own."

Her hands stroked both sides of his face. "You aren't physically hurt too badly, but your spirit is wounded. Your pride bleeds because you think you were unable to protect me."

Ryan said nothing.

"Don't you see?" Krysty asked desperately. "You did protect me. It was your love for me and my love for you that broke his power, broke Nefron's power. It was your strength that gave me the resolve to battle him. We defeated him together."

Ryan released his breath slowly, then he pulled Krysty to him. He didn't kiss her; he simply held her tightly. She whispered, "Living is struggling. The unavoidable thing. But love makes it worthwhile."

"Yeah," he replied very quietly. "You taught me that."

He relaxed his arms around her. Krysty's eyes shone like wet emeralds, but her mouth smiled. He took her hand, and they walked along the passage. Even if the gateway functioned, it could whisk them into another nightmare, but there was little point in contemplating that possibility.

Sometimes, Ryan thought, it was better to travel hopefully than to arrive.

James Axler

OUTLANDERS™

OMEGA PATH

A dark and unfathomable power governs post-nuclear America. As a former warrior of the secretive regime, Kane races to expose the blueprint of a power that's immeasurably evil, with the aid of fellow outcasts Brigid Baptiste and Grant. In a pre-apocalyptic New York City, hope lies in their ability to reach one young man who can perhaps alter the future....

Nothing is as it seems. Not even the invincible past....

Available February 1998,
wherever Gold Eagle books are sold.

Taking Fiction to Another Dimension!